THE THEFT OF

Out of the bottle on the table, there came a blood-chilling roar. The sound shocked Tralane into action. He tore violently through the Sorcerer King's possessions in his frantic need for haste. Then the amulet, the key to his escape, was in his fingers. Wyden's Eye was cool to the touch and sent strange pulsations through his arm. He turned to leave — and felt the blood drain from his face.

Rising from the bottle was a smoky apparition. It was a woman with fierce eyes, and teeth that were sharp between her full, cruel lips. As her body grew from the smoke belching out of the bottle, her voice cut through the air like a whistling sword, keen with hate.

"Now you will pay, mortal," she screamed, her eyes gleaming like cold steel. "Suffer! Anguish over your foolishness as I let the blood run from your human veins!"

Gerard Daniel Houarner

The Bard of SORCERY

A Del Rey Book

BALLANTINE BOOKS • NEW YORK

A Del Rey Book
Published by Ballantine Books

Copyright © 1986 by Gerard Daniel Houarner

Library of Congress Catalog Card Number: 86-91101

ISBN 0-345-31138-8

Printed in Canada

First Edition: May 1986

Cover Art by Romas

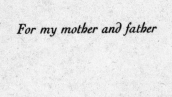

For my mother and father

Chapter 1

Tralane lay among the tall grasses of the Ousho Plains, staring up at the cloudless sky. The bright yellow sun lay low on the eastern horizon. From the newborn sun ran the breath of a breeze that made the plain's grass undulate like a sea of green. Tralane felt the coolness of the morning air on his naked chest as he gazed up at the clean blue slate that had so recently borne the passage of two moons—the Wanderer, and the smaller, swifter Star Speaker—savoring the freedom of the moment and indulging himself in the luxury of a lack of responsibilities. He had been running for almost two months, having left the company of his most recent acquaintances for dead on a hopelessly lost battlefield. He was content to remain where he was, resting and contemplating nothingness.

His confidence was shaken, however, when a shadow fell across him. His sense of security and peace of mind were irrevocably shattered by a rush of fear when a lance point pricked his throat.

"Who are you?" asked the armored figure astride the heavy, gray-and blue-scaled kruushka suddenly filling his view. The voice was even and emotionless, and there was a hollow ring to it. The warrior was completely covered with mail and plating, his face hidden behind his helmet's lowered visor. It was the armor of the warriors Tralane

1

had been watching and avoiding during his flight across the Ousho Plains, the armor of the warriors who had broken two battling armies further north.

"My name is Tralane," he answered, recovering from his initial shock and trying to sound amiable, "a bard and former archer in the service of King Peayn's army, until he so incompetently defended the pass through the Recho-choake Mountains and thus lost his petty kingdom." Tralane paused, watching how well his feigned ignorance of affairs in the north was being accepted. He assumed a casual air and was careful to modulate his voice to appear more self-confident than he felt. "And you, good sir?"

The armored figure was silent and still, considering Tralane's words. The bard found it difficult to remain comfortable lying on the ground with a weapon at his throat, but he did not dare move.

"I know of no king named Peayn," the mysterious warrior snapped suddenly. "But there was a fight in the north. What was the land he ruled?"

"Why, it was Gynnuland that Peayn ruled," Tralane asserted. "It was situated near Harthror, a country of oafs led by that usurious clown of a king, Uthreten. But Gynnuland is now a part of Harthror, if I know my kings well enough." And, if he knew the ways of battle well enough, Tralane was certain neither kings nor their domains remained intact.

The armored warriors had sliced through the opposing armies and slaughtered everyone before them. They had appeared suddenly and had seemed invulnerable to sword edge and arrow point. It was then that Tralane had decided he had enough of the north and had staged a one-man retreat to the south, to where he had supposed he might find safety and a modest income as storyteller in some small colony.

But all he had found were bands of armored warriors. He had tried to evade them, heading further east where their number seemed to diminish. But he had never gone more than two days without at least hearing their mounts' pounding hoofbeats in the earth. And now they—whoever they were and, even worse, whomever they served—had found him.

"All that mess lies many days' ride to the northwest," he said quickly, dismissing the lands of his birth as casually as he had left them, hoping to win favor in the warrior's eyes by his lack of allegiance. "Which reminds me, if you wouldn't mind telling me, what is the name of this land? Who rules? And what is the general disposition towards strangers?"

The armored figure did not answer. Tralane coughed and wondered at the strength of the warrior's arm. The lance had remained steady against his throat for all the time they had been talking. He wondered also over the enigma of the warrior's identity, his allegiances, his presence, and the presence of his comrades throughout the Ousho Plains. He had considered these mysteries ever since sighting the warriors at the battle, as it had been a simple way to pass the time. Up until now, he had not deemed these mysteries profitable or safe to solve.

Aside from the simple farming colonies from the northern kingdoms and the nomadic Tribe Nations, there were no other known inhabitants of the plain country below the Rechochoake Mountains, unless one considered the stories that had been cropping up in the taverns of Gynnuland over the six months prior to the final battle between that country and its archrival Harthror. The tales had too often been told by drunken traders and trappers and were entirely too fanciful for the locals to take seriously. Tralane, who had not forgotten the sights of his childhood in the care of a sorcerer, had listened more carefully, but had not been able to make any sense of tales of a new and mighty kingdom forming somewhere on the Ousho Plains. Rumors of a powerful new lord from the south, a sorcerer, had also been racing through King Peayn's court. But Tralane had dismissed these as an attempt by Harthror's spies to dissuade King Peayn from moving against their kingdom.

After all, nations did not suddenly spring into being overnight, especially in sparsely peopled territories, any more than great sorcerers were formed after only a few years of trial. Logic dictated that, as surely and truly as Mathi, the sorcerer-guardian who had raised Tralane and tried to make a magician of him, had lectured on the subject. And since no large migration of people had been observed heading south, nor had any stories circulated concerning a new and powerful wizard having broken from the tutelage of one of the wise and largely benign old sorcerers from the north, Tralane had not found it difficult to dismiss the stories and rumors with a laugh and a swig of strong liquor.

King Peayn and King Uthreten had probably followed the same dictates of logic; Tralane began to perspire when he started thinking too deeply of what had befallen them.

The kruushka suddenly shuddered and backed off, and the lance was withdrawn. Tralane sat up and waited a few moments for some command from the warrior. Testing the limits of the warrior's mercy, he donned his shirt and tied the thongs across his stomach and chest. Then he gathered the rest of his belongings—a shoulder pouch made from the same leather as his shirt, a bow and quiver of arrows, and a netting pack lumpy with water bags and the sun-dried, meaty remains of rodents. He had slept in his torn, blue pantaloons, tucked into the calf-length boots he had also disdained to remove.

"Where to now, warrior?" he asked as he stood. "To your captain, or do you plan to skewer me on the spot?" He was prepared to bolt into the cover of the surrounding grass if the answer leaned towards the latter.

"Follow," the armored figure ordered, ignoring Tralane's brazenness. The kruushka wheeled about slowly and began walking towards the rising sun. Tralane looked back for a moment to see the pale, fading image of the Wanderer hovering over the horizon. "Beware the moonless hours," went the old saying that rang through Tralane's mind, "when the sun and stars rule unchecked."

It was a piece of wisdom from Mathi the wizard, imparted after Tralane had tried to work a spell without considering the cosmic influences that would affect his magic. He had precociously opened the door to the House of the Dead, hoping to find some clue to his parents' identities. But there had been miscalculations and a demon unbound. The price of his experience was the scar on his right shoulder, and his abandonment of Mathi and his teachings. However, the occasional pain from the wound had helped to etch Mathi's words on that occasion in his memory, if not their meaning.

Tralane's resentment towards Mathi for the detached manner and aloof attention the wizard had treated him with during his childhood and for the wizard's steadfast refusal to reveal the identities of his true parents surged into his awareness following his brief recollection. His heart raced with anger, and a tremor took hold of his hand. He fought against the full surfacing from the pool of memory of this first and most painful injustice done to him. He needed calm nerves and a clear head to cope with the current situation. He breathed deeply and followed the trail the mounted warrior blazed through the grass. He hoped nothing too drastic would happen before he was once more under the moons' protection.

Relieved of the last meager task of guiding himself to safety and assured that he was in no immediate danger, Tralane occupied himself by watching his shadow diminish as the sun rose and reviling his predicament. He did not notice the camp until he had passed the first outlying tents and was startled when the grass cleared and a field of tents stretched before him.

The camp was alive and bustling with warriors and women setting up tents, leading kruushkas and the lighter, swifter thorts to pens, feeding the grunting, thick-skinned camutels and the milk-giving herrenas, and moving supply wagons into defensive formations around seige machines. The men were stout and strong-limbed, but they did not appear, by their preference for as little clothing as possible, to be the types to be completely covered in armor during battle or the reconnaisance of the Ousho Plains. There were children underfoot, the smaller ones running in packs through the lanes between tents, while the older children helped with the chores. Banners bearing fearsome portraits of heroes and monsters fluttered in the breeze. The smell of smoke from the first cooking fires fought the smell of animals for ascendance.

The uncommunicative warrior led Tralane to a shimmering green pavilion in the heart of the camp. Then he dismounted and stood, unnaturally rigid, by his mount and faced the tent. Attendants came out and took his lance and mount. Shortly after they left, Tralane hesitantly approached the figure from behind, ready to dart out of the way of any sudden blow. Tralane was a little awed by the warrior's discipline. Even the High Captains of the Karthasian Empire, who had occasionally visited King Peayn's court to pay homage to the Empire's mighty southern ally and secretly snigger at Gynnuland's primitive forces, had not displayed such self-control. There was something inhuman in the warrior's attitude. As he walked around the warrior and aligned himself with his escort in facing the pavilion, Tralane decided he disliked his discoverer.

A man in his middle years, with a long, gaunt face and eyes like circles of night, emerged from a flap in the smooth, almost seamless material of the pavilion. His white hair was thin and short, revealing a bald spot above his brow on which runes had been tatooed. He wore a black-trimmed and rune-decorated scarlet robe.

"Greetings, young one," the man said smoothly. "I believe your name is Tralane?"

Tralane smiled his most charming smile while trying not to squirm beneath the man's penetrating gaze. He wondered how his name had become known without anyone having asked the warrior. "Quite right, sir. And may I inquire as to your name?"

"Agathom." Then, in a tone that suggested that the words were meaningless, he continued, "Sorcerer King of Eiring-Cor."

"I am honored," Tralane said, dumping his net pack on the ground, "though I shame myself by admitting that

I, a bard and knowledgeable traveler, have never heard of you or your land."

"Ah yes, you are the bard my knight found earlier this morning. This is a piece of good fortune. I have but recently come to this part of the world and I have a desperate need for a guide."

Tralane maintained his smile in the face of the Sorcerer King's gentle avoidance of explaining his origins. He refrained from pressing the matter. Whatever and wherever Eiring-Cor was, Tralane had no doubts he would eventually hear about it from the more talkative members of the King's following. This time, he promised himself, he would listen with less disbelief to the rumors and tales he heard.

He silently appraised the Sorcerer King while pretending to consider Agathom's open-ended offer. At a superficial glance, Agathom appeared to be no different from many of the sorcerers Tralane had seen at the various courts he had served in. Nor did the mixture of artfully deceptive mannerisms designed to put others at ease and the hint of cruelty in the upturned corners of his mouth and lines of his face set him apart from the host of ambitiously scheming lords, princes, captains, and courtiers it had been Tralane's privilege to observe and occasionally suffer from. Yet something in the combination warned him that Agathom was even less worthy of trust than most other rulers. His experience with the art of sorcery made him sensitive to Agathom's awesome power, but as Mathi and the few great wizards of power who had occasionally visited Mathi's tower had shown him, great power in magic was earned by study and practice. There was little room for ambition and politics among men when one played with gods and demons for knowledge and power. That a sorcerer of Agathom's stature would place himself at the head of an army for mere physical gains—unless he misread the intentions of the host around him—was an incongruity which Tralane could not resolve. And there was nothing in the rumors he had heard in Gynnuland to help him, other than whispers of grave, world-ending danger that he had treated as the spice in a drunken storyteller's art.

"I would be honored if you would have me," Tralane said finally.

"Done! I'm glad our paths have crossed." Agathom raised one hand and a servant bounded out of the pavilion and scuttled to his side. "This one will take you to a suitable tent. Settle yourself and I will call for you later on in the day."

Tralane thanked him and followed the servant to a drab tent not far from the sorcerer's headquarters. On the way Tralane attempted to engage the servant in conversation, asking him about himself and the place of his birth. But the servant walked ahead with an ungainly gait, like a street-player's wooden puppet, immune to Tralane's friendly probing. The lack of response troubled him, since he had seldom met a servitor doomed to following orders and performing menial tasks who did not jump to the opportunity of gossiping about the master. Their brief and unrewarding time together only enhanced Agathom's aura of unnaturalness.

Tralane entered the tent, pausing to look back at the awkward creature shuffling back to his lord. A husky shout called his attention back to the quarters he was about to claim as his own.

"Hey!" yelled a large, half-naked white-haired man sprawled across a fur-covered floor. "Close that flap, before I wrap it around your head and throw you to the kruushkas."

Tralane accommodated the speaker, and threw his belongings on a pile of animal skins in a corner. His glance flitted over his new environment as he catalogued the wealth of the skins and furs strewn about, the exquisite craftsmanship—pre-Karthasian Empire by the looks of it—of the chest his host was leaning against, and the number of empty wine sacks flung into the corner of the tent. They were alone and there was no sign of anyone else sharing the tent, though there was enough space for four.

Tralane came over to the giant and twisted into a cross-legged sitting position next to him.

"You're the nearest thing I've seen to a human today," he said, peering with mock interest into his tent mate's face. "What's your name?"

The man groaned and rolled away from Tralane, ignoring his overtures of friendship and sinking back into a loud sleep. The bard insisted by poking a finger in the fellow's back, noting that, though the man's hair was bleached with age, his muscles were still thick and firm. Finally the giant dragged himself up to a sitting position, opened his bleary eyes and looked down on Tralane.

"You take your chances," the giant grumbled roughly. "Luckily for you, I'm too worn out to give you a poke in kind."

"Come now," Tralane reproached him, "it's the middle of the day. How can you sleep so late?"

"Oram is my name, and you would sleep late, too, if you'd been forced to march half the night."

The man's size, strength, and general disposition gave him potential as a valuable ally in the strange camp, as well as a convenient source of information. Tralane gave his next words a veneer of comradeship.

"So you've only just arrived in these parts? So have I." He paused. "Your Sorcerer King seems anxious to move, if he's marching through the country of the Tribe Nations at night."

Oram looked at him and shook his shaggy head.

"I don't understand what you're saying—it's too early. Who are you, and what are you doing here anyway?"

"Tralane, and this is where I'll be sleeping," he said, and patted the fur-covered earth, raising the ashes of burned grass that escaped through a crack between two skins. "I was discovered by one of the King's men, who brought me to this camp. He was a strange fellow. And that servant who brought me to this tent—have the gods given him a vision? He doesn't hear anyone but his master."

Oram grunted, then nodded. "Ah, the King's men," he

said wearily. "They're all dead, mere shadows of souls."
He slowly rose to his feet and lumbered behind the wooden
chest. He picked up a large wine sack and handed it to
Tralane, who took a long draught and immediately felt his
head spin.

"If you raise the visors on those armored men," Oram
continued, "all you'll see is the inside of the helmet." He
walked unsteadily to the tent's opening, surreptitiously
peeking through a crack as if to satisfy himself that no
one was near. "The Sorcerer King, whose name I've been
told to avoid for fear of calling down a curse on my head,
makes certain pacts with living men. They are granted a
brief span of power and, after they've died, they are bound
to his service." He looked out more boldly, squinted pain-
fully at the light, and returned to his makeshift bed. "Spirits of the dead form his personal guard. He calls them
Knights of Blackness." Oram's throat rumbled, and Tralane was not sure if the sound was meant to be laughter
or a sigh of relief at being able to sit down again. "That's
who brought you here, that's what you call a King's man.
They're nothing more than ghosts—less, because even
ghosts can dream of redemption, even ghosts can be
released from their ties to mortal pasts by the merciful
hand of a god, or the enticing lies of a demon. These are
helpless without his will to guide them, just as he is pow-
erless to move those suits of armor without the raw stuff
of life men call souls. Magic is a curious little art." He
sighed to himself.

Oram glanced at Tralane. He was warming to his subject as much as to the act of speaking. His sour expression
relaxed as he forgot about his lost sleep, and his more
affable nature surfaced. To Tralane's surprise, the giant
seemed on the border of joviality.

"He is in constant contact with these knights, so I'd
be thrifty with my words around them. As for the servant,
well, his mind is a blank. He is like a hand or a finger to
the Sorcerer King. I've heard that he once saw the Sorcerer King converse with certain unearthly beings, and
the sight of it made his mind wither and die. But then

these people blame everything on their King. Perhaps the man was just born simple. Here, give me a swig of that water."

Tralane handed him the bag, rasping, "I'd hardly call it water."

Then he stood, somewhat shakily, and poked his head through the tent's flap, following Oram's precautionary move.

"It's a large army out there," Tralane said, retreating back into the tent. "Where did it come from? The people are not familiar to me, and I've never heard of Eiring-Cor. Have new kingdoms formed down here? Is there a war?"

"Hasn't the King told you?"

"I haven't had the chance to learn much from the Sorcerer King."

Oram shook his head slowly. "And you won't get the chance. The only reason you still live is so he can learn the ways of this world."

Tralane's head jerked to face Oram, fixing on the giant's pale blue eyes. The Sorcerer King's power, while impressive, did not seem capable of carrying such an armed force across dimensions and worlds. Even the proposition of an other-worldly visitation by a single being was rare enough to have caused consternation among the northern wizards, even during the time of the Wizard Kings. The mystery of Agathom and his people sharpened Tralane's curiosity.

"This world?" Tralane queried nonchalantly, relaxing himself so that Oram received only a mildly quizzical look after the moment's surprise. "Now I'm the one who doesn't understand your words, my friend."

Sighing heavily, Oram threw the wineskin behind the chest and drew out a dried side of meat wrapped in cloth. He offered Tralane a chunk, but the bard declined and unpacked his own provisions.

"You've interrupted my sleep, and now you plague my morning meal with questions. I should have offered you a sword and a challenge instead of a drink and friendship."

Oram spoke roughly, but seemed to wait with some eagerness for encouragement to continue. He glanced knowingly at Tralane.

"I await your story," Tralane said implacably. He drowned the yeul meat, the tastiest of the rodents on the Ousho Plain, with water from the Plain's rivers, and looked with regret as Oram devoured his morning meal. He had become bored with his monotonous diet, yet he did not want to become too close to the man by sharing so casually his food as well as his tent and drink. He swallowed quickly, sacrificing pleasure for distance.

"Impudence. You'd better curb that habit when you're around the Sorcerer King. He has a notable lack of humor." Oram lifted the edge of a skin and spat out a bone. Then he smiled at Tralane, the last vestige of surliness crumbling before the prospect of taking his guest into his confidence.

"As for my story? My collection of skins and furs should tell you I'm a hunter by trade. I've been roaming these plains for ages. My family fled here—"

As he listened to Oram recount his history with the same zeal and relish he devoted to his meal, Tralane's attention began to waver. It was a tale whose structure Tralane was already familiar with, a tale that started with the Karthasian Empire's civil wars and the Wizard Kings' attempt to carve up the Empire from within and break the power of the Lower Kingdoms. Tralane heard Mathi's voice from out of the past, droning in his cool, cryptlike tower library chamber, telling, as Oram was doing, the history of a period that had destroyed so many families.

Oram's father had been a captain in the Empire's services, whose lord became another casualty in the Wizard Kings' games of succession. As Tralane had always assumed his lineage to be noble and tragic, he imagined the lord in Oram's story to be his own father. In those chaotic days, it would indeed have been wiser for the captain to flee with his wife, his fifteen-year-old son, and his two younger daughters, as Oram went on to claim.

But what of Tralane's supposed mother, the wife of the

assassinated lord, the lady of the Empire, Tralane's pregnant mother? He doubted if he had been born yet; he was certain he would have remembered something had he been an infant in the midst of the wars. But he could never remember anything about his mother or father. His earliest memories were only of Mathi and the cold, damp tower.

So this captain, who may very well have been Tralane's father's closest servant, abandoned his charges and left the Empire's territories. They were comfortable living in the foothills of the Rechochoake Mountains while Tralane's mother fled on her own or, perhaps, Tralane embellished, in the company of some handmaidens, a chaste man-at-arms—no, there were no such—or better yet, some warrior eunuchs. Surely, Tralane thought, there had been warrior eunuchs during the latter Karthasian Empire, or was that only a a story from his repertoire of tales?

Oram elaborated on the happiness of his youth at the edge of the Ousho Plains, learning to hunt, tracking the wild gersin and camutels, trading skins, tusks, and meats for the manufactured staples of civilized life that still managed to trickle down from the north despite the civil wars. Tralane pictured himself in the wizard's arms, shivering even then—did Mathi deliver him, watch his mother die?— as Oram broadened his personal history to include friendship with one of the Tribe nations, the Succacor.

While Tralane had grown up lonely, with nothing more than the preoccupied wizard, his occasional and equally detached visitors, and the hostile, whining voices of captive demons and spirits for company, Oram had enjoyed a wealth of family and friends. One sister married a Clan Lord, while the other married a merchant—Tralane wondered if he had ever had an older sister, or sisters, and whether they, like his supposed father, had been sacrificed to the hunger of the Wizard Kings. Oram recited a litany of beasts hunted, friends met, and trials of manhood passed, as Tralane half-listened, skimming through those same years of his own life.

He had suffered. Tralane had reminded himself of his

own suffering frequently enough over the years, and Oram's speech drove him once more into the maelstrom of his past. He was an orphan, to start with. No one loved him, no one had ever extended to him the same kindnesses that Oram had experienced.

There *had* been the Princess Amalkys, later, during his traveling days. A sweet young woman from—which kingdom had that been? Corru. How could such a tender young woman have come from such a terror of a father, he had asked himself whenever he recalled that incident. He was known to have slain his first two wives, and the daughters they had from him, simply because he felt cheated out of a male heir.

Amalkys had said she loved Tralane, who had been nothing more than a court bard in her father's castle. Tralane had not discouraged her displays of affection, for they had reflected well on his nature and had given him a measure of protection against her father's easily roused rages. But she had been far too innocent and could never understand Tralane's tormented soul.

No, she had not loved him, she had stayed behind in Corru when the time had come for him to flee her father's ire. The matter of his quite accidental friendship with the leaders of the rebellion against the King had proved too much for the old volcano to bear. His friends dead, Tralane had bid the Princess Amalkys farewell. Had she tried to run away with him? No, foolish woman, she had tried instead to defend Tralane in the face of her father's anger. Tralane was certain that true love would have dictated she go with him. But no, Princess Amalkys had been false, like all the others. And it was just as well she never came with him, because then he never would have had as much fun with the witch of Jobkol Hill. Tralane had never known what had become of the Princess Amalkys, or the witch of Jobkol Hill, for that matter.

But all that piece of history was irrelevant. They and the giant sitting in front of him at the moment spouting fond memories of a youthful golden age, knew nothing of suffering. And if they did not know suffering, they could not have known Tralane.

The years with Mathi had been uniform in their boredom. People did not understand, Tralane had discovered over the years of telling his story, that a lifetime of being watched over sternly, with every freedom curtailed, without love or kindly attention, and without company and playmates, was itself a wound that cut deeply into the soul, a wound that never ceased to be painful.

The wizard had, in the end, driven Tralane away with his coldness. And though Tralane at last tasted the richness of the world as he made his way from village to town, from one kingdom to the next, the pain had never left him. No, he was, he had long ago decided, forever the lost orphan, abandoned to the vagaries of powers greater than himself. Would he now be somewhere out on the Ousho Plains, he thought bitterly, listening to an overfed giant talk about an unbearably happy life, in the clutches of a mysterious sorcerer at the head of a huge host, if his noble heritage had ever been properly recognized, if indeed his parents had lived and raised him to be the prince and lord he felt himself secretly to be? No, he would have been in some palace, amusing himself with his servants, well-protected from Agathom's power by the best wizards and mercenaries his considerable fortunes could buy.

Oram had lapsed into reciting political history once more, and Tralane's attention was drawn to his words.

"The civil wars were over. The Emperor Tayth Halor had bound the princes and lords of the land to his banner. The Wizard Kings were broken, their ice palaces and sorcerous allies shattered by the cold steel and magical arts of the Empire's people. With his northern borders secure, Halor sent his armies through the middle kingdoms and won their allegiance. Then, as a final show of strength, his warriors came south to drive the Tribe Nations away from the lands claimed by rulers of men. The Nations were beaten back far out into the plains, and the Emperor earned the undying gratitude of the local petty kingdoms."

Tralane nodded, but he could have fleshed out Oram's history with certain tales he had heard and learned of how the gods had formed a pact with some ambitious men to strengthen their hold on the world by overthrowing the Empire. If he had been in the mood, he could even have thrown in the tale of Suthra and the raped goddess, Genjima. However, he preferred to interject an ending to Oram's story that agreed with the fantasies he had been entertaining about the contrast in their lives.

"So your father returned to the Empire," Tralane said, "taking his wife with him and leaving you here to enjoy your freedom. He was well received, since the Empire needed seasoned captains to guard its borders, regardless of their pasts. He's probably a garrison commander by now, or perhaps one of the Emperor's military advisors?"

Oram gave him an odd look, as if the bard were speaking in an unknown tongue.

"My parents were killed by Karthasian warriors. Our home was burned out, our small riches pillaged. Both my sisters are lost—I was never able to track down either of them."

Oram shifted his weight and continued, ignoring Tralane's uneasy silence. The shattering of Tralane's illusions brought him back to the uncomfortable realities of his early youth. He could not remember a single detail about his parents and had been told by Mathi that they had been slain in an incident similar to the one Oram had just described. On the one hand, Tralane had felt abandoned by his parents and sought solace from the unresponsive Mathi, and on the other, he had nursed a secret suspicion that his tutor had taken him from his true parents, who would some day come and rescue him.

Only frequent exposure to tales of death from that period during his travels had prepared Tralane to consider the verity of Mathi's brief but incisive words. Those who, like Mathi, sequestered themselves from the well-traveled paths of men to study magic and learn all the subtleties of the art, had no time for or interest in lies. They sought truths, the revelation of mysteries, the paths to transformation. Mathi claimed he rescued the infant Tralane from the ruins of his parents' home on his way to his retreat, and had thought the raising of the child would lead to a useful apprentice and assistant in his future work. The time Tralane had spent away from Mathi had given him a new, bitter perspective on his upbringing, and little reason to doubt his adoptive parent's version of his origin.

The bard continued to listen to Oram, though he was suddenly anxious to leave the giant and start exploring the camp. He wanted to run away from the memories and emotions evoked by Oram's history, memories that had haunted him in his nightmares and destroyed the fantastic edifices he preferred to construct over the basic frameworks of truth. But Tralane stayed, aware that Oram, for all his rambling, had not yet touched on the matter of Agathom's place in, or out, of this world. As this was the subject that had originally piqued his interest, Tralane hoped Oram would come back to it soon.

For the moment, Oram showed no inclination to address his current situation. His easy manner and good spirits seemed to evaporate after Tralane's outburst, and he spoke slowly, sadly, about the years that followed the massacre of his family.

Tralane listened with tepid interest as Oram traced the trails he took, trying to find survivors from the Succacor Tribe Nation for news of his sister, and his fruitless journey north to find his other sister, who reportedly had been evacuated to avoid contact with and retaliatory raids from the Tribe Nations. It was a solitary life Oram had led, avoiding towns and divorcing himself from the affairs of men, and it was the complement of Tralane's life at that time. For, if Tralane had the years figured correctly, it was about the time of the destruction of Oram's family that he had finally left Mathi.

He had been twelve, and the Emperor Tayth Halor was finishing his war against the encroachment of the Tribe Nations. Tralane watched the Emperor's army returning to the restored Karthasian Empire in the north, but he dared not join their march. The faces of the war-

riors seemed far too hard, the speech of the nobles terse
and ill-humored despite their triumphs. Perhaps the years
of war and betrayal had soured their temper, or perhaps
it was simply the character of northerners to be grim.
Whichever was true, Tralane found the south more to his
liking. The courts of the newly formed southern kingdoms, survivors of the Low Kingdoms disrupted by the
civil wars, were as open to tale-tellers and adventurers
then as they were now.

While Oram had been pursuing his solitary life, Tralane
plunged into the life of traveler and bard, drawing the
attention of courtiers and peasants alike with tales of gods
and heroes learned from Mathi and his books. He remembered his early days in the courts of the southern kingdoms, basking in the praise and favors lavished on him.
He had been there when Lord Yshaleth eliminated his
seven brothers. Tralane had been the court fool and had
promised to provide the brothers with a means to escape
the mad Lord. Had they really taken him, the court fool,
seriously? He shrugged the memory aside, as Oram continued.

Tralane knew of the boredom and melancholy that had
assailed Oram during his self-imposed exile. They were
the same feelings he had known with Mathi, the same
feelings which returned to him whenever he spent too
much time away from people. He understood Oram's pain,
loss, and hunger for the raw emotions and excitement
generated whenever people came together. Tralane's
uneasiness with his own past and the feelings that lay
beneath his fantasies shifted to his growing identification
with Oram.

He was relieved when Oram's story finally seemed
ready to land in the present. Tralane tore himself away
from his own thoughts and focused his attention on Oram.

"Thus was I living until recently, camped by the inland
sea the Tribe Nations call the Thesa," Oram was saying.
"I was hunting with a party of Geshayen when we came
across four of those grim knights. We hailed them and
held our weapons aloft as a sign of peace, thinking perhaps

they were part of some kingdom's exploratory expedition. But no sooner were we among them than we felt their steel and lances. We could not bring them down. Our arrows found chinks in their armor and our blows dented their helmets, but all our skill and strength was wasted on them. They could not be stopped. Three of us survived and broke off. Together we rode back to the Geshayen camp.

"We found the Clan Lord and told him what had happened. Before he could gather the family heads, a large band of knights appeared behind us and charged into the camp. They came on us like a sudden tempest wind, blowing through the camp before we could even see who they were. We were lost. The warning was for nothing."

Oram shrugged and tossed a bone aside. He was talking with new-found intensity.

"No doubt their sudden appearance was the Sorcerer King's doing. Behind the knights came the human foes, and from these the Geshayen took a heavy toll. But there were too many enemy swords and lances, far to many for the few hundred of us in the camp. Everything was burned or taken. My wagon and most of my load was destroyed. The earth was muddy with blood from slaughter.

"I knew then what my father had felt, when his life and home were taken away from him. I fought with a madness on me. I took a glancing blow on the head from a knight's lance, and when I awoke I was discovered and taken prisoner. My rage by then was dead. I had nothing left. The King saw I had knowledge he needed, so he spared me, made me his guide. What could I do but accept? The remaining Geshayen were killed after they were questioned and deemed useless by the King. Their bodies were fed to the kruushkas.

"I managed to salvage some of my goods, though I don't know why I bothered. I'll never trade them. All they do is remind me of the past, and I can't bring myself to part with that. It's all I have left."

Oram turned to Tralane and spoke to him directly. "This host is stronger, by virtue of the King and his unnat-

ural allies, than any that has seen the light of our sun.
I'm sure by now you've realized his intentions are not
friendly. I have been told by the camp followers, whom
I travel with, that this army comes from a world parallel
to ours, though it is not an exact duplicate in every detail.
The run of the land is similar; it has two moons and the
same beasts and plants, and the folk speak the Sky Speech
just as we do. Perhaps we both have twins who are following roughly the same road through life."

He stopped and seemed to ponder the thought of another
life for himself, catching up with himself on another world
where he had chosen another path. There was an instant
of hope, but it died as it was born, and Oram's gaze fell.

"However, different fates rule this other world, and so
the course of history has followed a slightly different path.
In that world the Sorceror King rose to supreme power.
He answered to no one, not even the gods. But the gods
have no love of men who would be greater than they, and
caused the Wandering Moon to start falling slowly to earth.
So the King led his army here, since it is easier for him
to flee than to fight the gods. He intends to conquer and
subdue this world. Then, with the power of this world's
sorcery in his control, he'll challenge the gods directly."

Tralane fixed his mind on Oram's revelations concerning Agathom and his background. He was fascinated by
the prospect of meeting his own double on an alternate
earth. He took the premise a step further: how many other
parallel worlds were there? How many Tralanes? The
works of magic he had studied had hinted at an infinity
of existences, but had not discussed any method of reaching them. Would it not make a fine adventure, he asked
himself with swelling pride and a sense of grandeur, to
seek his other selves out, to gather them all and form a
merry band of bards and archers? And if some were not
quite like him, if some were outright cutthroats, thieves,
or perhaps warrior heroes and kings...

Tralane chuckled, escaping into his dreams, forgetting
the man before him.

"I see nothing amusing in what I've told you," Oram

said, gnawing at the end of a bone, glaring at him through sullen eyes.

"Oh no, I wasn't laughing at you. I was thinking of something else," Tralane said lightly. Then he asked, "But what of these gods? Is their wrath going to follow the Sorcerer King?"

Oram finished his meal, replaced the cloth-wrapped side of meat behind the chest, stood up, and stretched. He picked up several furs which were loosely tied together by thongs, slipped them on and tightened the knots so they fitted snugly around his body. He scratched at the white hide britches he wore and smoothed them against his skin.

"I don't know," he said finally, sleepily. His eyes were dull, his mouth hung slightly open. His every word was an effort. The energy which had possessed him was gone. He had reached for something in his remembrances, striven for a hidden meaning and fallen short. He collapsed back into the present. "But perhaps our gods will be offended by his lust before he can gather the strength to topple them, and one of our moons will fall in answer to his greed."

"A fascinating, though unpleasant proposition." Tralane leaned back and blew out his breath in disgust. "I'm beginning to regret my ready acceptance of the Sorcerer King's hospitality."

"That, my friend, is your problem." The white-haired giant slung some furs over his shoulder and headed for the tent flap. "Give him what he wants, and he'll let you live. The price he asks is not too high."

"No. I just hope my funds don't run out."

Oram grunted. "I have some business to attend to among the camp followers. I leave you to your own thoughts and questions."

Tralane nodded and watched Oram stride out into the sunlight. Neither moon had risen. He wished Mathi had trained him in the arts of sky watching so that he might have known when Star Speaker or Wanderer would make their next appearance. Mathi had never been generous with his knowledge, even to his only apprentice and adopted son. Basic spells and the remnants of a discipline he had rebelled against, a wealth of legends drawn from books and Mathi's lectures, and the skills of archery and mannered speech were Tralane's only legacies. They would be of no help in his current situation; only the things he had learned in his travels would buy his continued existence.

Tralane shook his head and dismissed his useless recollections with a curse. He settled in a comfortable corner of the tent, gathered some furs over him, and began going over his knowledge of the world, like a farmer counting his coin before going to market.

Chapter 2

The King's puppetlike servant called for Tralane well after Oram had departed. He appeared at the tent opening, peered in and made several guttural noises. Startled, Tralane whirled around to face the source of the noise, saw the servant, and smiled.

"Your master calls, eh? Tell him I'll be right along."

Tralane threw the remaining furs off of his legs and stood, then straightened his soiled and slightly ragged clothes. If he had lingered a little while longer on the battlefield, he might have pieced together a decent suit of clothes from the soldiers who would no longer need any garments. But such were the rigors of war that he had not had time to rummage through a field of corpses. He had been fortunate to escape without a wound.

He found the servant waiting for him outside the tent. At the sight of the bard, Agathom's lackey limped toward the Sorcerer King's pavilion. Tralane followed him at a leisurely pace, preferring to bask along with the rest of the members of the host in the late afternoon sun and so steady his nerves, rather than rushing headlong into a conference on which his life in Agathom's camp might depend. He relaxed by taking in his surroundings.

Above, long wispy clouds stretched across the darkening sky. Star Speaker had finally risen and was hovering low on the edge of the world. Troop banners barely stirred as the hint of a breeze ran its cool fingers over the land, heralding the night which crept up behind it. Women, their skirts trailing in the dirt and their breasts bared, hurried about, preparing food and ignoring the men's taunts and openly playful invitations. The flocks of wenoths were being driven into the stockades, their gray hides blending into the dusk so that their short, high-pitched bleats sounded like the calling of ghosts. Shui skins were stretched between poles while, beneath them, young girls wrestled with the carcasses, separating meat from the bones.

Some of the men were playing games of chance with sticks notched with symbols, but most were concerned with fortifying their camp and cleaning their weapons and armor. Not far from Tralane's path, an herb healer accompanied by a wizard of mediocre strength was visiting a cluster of people injured during the course of the day. Tralane did not see any young children, an unusual trait for a host with so many women and in exile from its land of origin. He wondered what price the women had been forced to pay for their part in Agathom's scheme of existence.

Despite the martial atmosphere, the camp lacked the tension of an army preparing for war. Tralane could not but admire the host's confidence and well-disciplined organization. Like the servant and the knights, Agathom's people seemed to be an extension of his will, answerable only to him and thus protected from any external danger by his power over them. Like the nobility of courts ruled by mad lords, Agathom's people had in them arrogance founded on their King's strength and fear for the safety of their own positions, should they ever fail their master or outlive their worth.

The servant stopped just outside the entrance to the Sorcerer King's pavilion, next to a knight standing guard. Tralane gave them both a mock bow of thanks and entered.

"Greetings, Tralane," the Sorcerer King said without looking up from a large map spread out on a table at the other end of the enclosure. His short, limp hair had fallen

over his bald spot as he bent down to his work. "I hope
you rested well?"

"I used the time to my advantage." Tralane approached
the table, weaving his way through groupings of unlit
candles stuck into man-sized holders ornately carved into
stretched-out figures of demons. The air was thick with
many-colored smoke and unrecognizable scents. The tent's
roof shimmered with unearthly greens and reds. Tralane's
eyes watered and his stomach felt queasy from some of
the more pungent aromas. Tralane had the sensation of
having entered a new, alien environment. He tried to ignore
his discomfort, and suppressed a dizzying rush of anxiety.

When he reached Agathom's side, he peered intently
at the finely detailed chart before him, then gave the Sorcerer King's abode a quick study. He found nothing more
unusual than a collection of cabinets, chests, and a few
plush, wood-framed chairs. There was no tangible source
of danger which would explain the uneasiness which
gnawed at Tralane's will. His experiences with sorcery
had not prepared him for the intensely ambiguous atmosphere in which Agathom seemed so comfortable. It contradicted Mathi's practice of attempting to clarify visions
of the earthly and unearthly, to see mysteries in the light
of hidden truths and not fear.

Smoke rolled back and forth across the enclosed space
with tidal regularity, eddies curling around candleholders
and waves breaking against Tralane's body.

"I noticed your army is well provisioned," Tralane ventured in a thick voice. "You even brought your own herd
animals. How long have you been traveling?"

The Sorcerer King glanced up from the table and gave
Tralane a quizzical look. "How much has Oram told you?"

Confused by the directness of the question, Tralane
hesitated in answering.

"Never mind. I suppose the oaf told you all he knows
and thinks he knows about me. I've seen him questioning
my people." The King turned his attention back to the
map. "It will save me the time of explaining my purpose
to you."

Tralane felt as if he had somehow lost an advantage by his hesitation. He rubbed his moist palm across his sweating brow and gasped for more air.

"That is the most detailed map of the world I've ever seen," he said.

The Sorcerer King ignored his statement and moved around the table. "Tell me," he said curtly after a few moments had passed, "are there any major cities along this river?"

Tralane answered, and the Sorcerer King followed with another question. He continued into the night. As Tralane added details to the map, Agathom made notations and pressed for further information. Slowly but accurately, Tralane fielded the probes. He became a living book of knowledge, all other aspects of his personality having disintegrated. Under the Sorcerer King's influence, he was reduced to the sum of his objective observations of the lands he had passed through, without the feelings and memories, both sad and happy, which were attached to his adventures. Agathom showed him the true meaning of detachment, a state Tralane had always prided himself in having. Buried beneath the weight of strange sensations, a part of the bard was shocked into wakefulness and cried in horror at what it saw.

Finally, the Sorcerer King held up his hand. "That is enough for tonight. We will remain encamped until I've gained a working knowledge of these southern kingdoms and their politics, which you seem to know so well. But they won't pose as much of a problem as this Empire. You must tell me all you know of its great sorcerers, what they have done and when they seek to rest, so that I can divine the source of their strength. I will call for you tomorrow morning."

He dismissed Tralane with a wave of his hand and rolled up the map. Tralane nodded dumbly and walked out without so much as a backward glance to see what the Sorcerer King's next act might be.

Once outside, Tralane's head cleared as the sharp night air, with an edge of smoke from the cooking fires, cut through the webs of Agathom's lair. The raucous laughter of people shook him out of his stupor. A belligerent self-confidence filled the void left by his encounter. He had survived and returned to his own world. Feeling relieved and refreshed, Tralane gratefully put to rest his ordeal and started towards the nearest fire, ignoring the efforts of the Sorcerer King's servant to lead him back to his tent. He was careful to avoid paying any heed to the stoic Knights of Blackness who now ringed the Sorcerer King's pavilion.

As he approached the fire, he spotted Oram, who was surrounded by a jovial group of warriors and women laughing at the big man's talk. Tralane stopped for a moment, observing the crowd. Most were drunk, and Oram's wineskin was making its way through their number, leaving a wake of fortified merriment behind it. Here was a chance for Tralane to make himself popular in the camp and gain friends, influence and information. He might one day need the security of friends to mediate between him and the Sorcerer King, and he had to discover whom in the camp he could count on for a patron.

And in the crowd there was also the opportunity to relieve his mind of the weight that had gradually accumulated over the course of the day, and to assert himself over his surroundings. He strode forward.

He greeted Oram with a shout. "Hey, large one, we meet again!"

Oram squinted at Tralane, his face creasing into a relief map of rugged terrain. "Is that the newcomer? Yes, yes, that's the one I was telling you about. That's the whelp in my tent."

The people stared with bemused expectation at Tralane. He smiled at them benignly, then took a barrel lying on its side and rolled it into the middle of the gathering. He upended it, sat, and looked at Oram.

"I see you've found some company tonight," he said, pointing at the women on either side of Oram. "Will I be able to come in tonight to get some sleep?"

"Ah, dark Crecia and my lively little Fatome," the giant

cooed amorously, fondling both of them in his hefty arms. "Yes, they've been very comforting, haven't they, eh?"

Fatome laughed, her husky voice mingling with Oram's. But Crecia flashed her eyes across Tralane's figure, and her gaze warmed him.

"Well, I've had less pleasant company tonight. I've been giving old Agathom a lesson in geography and politics. He's a queer one, isn't he?"

An old woman, sober by her walk, parted from the suddenly stilled crowd. She came up to Tralane and whispered hoarsely, "Don't mention his name, fool, or do you *want* his wrath to fall down on all of us?"

"Eh? What did the old witch say?" Oram mumbled, clumsily rising to his feet with the help of Fatome. he staggered over to Tralane, leaned on him and said to the old woman, "Did you say not to mention Agathom's name? Why shouldn't my young friend say it? Let him shout it, scream it!" Oram started back towards his friends.

Tralane tried to hold him back, admonishing him to be still, but Oram broke free, spinning and stumbling over prostrate, drunken bodies. He turned his face to the sky, and the fire and moonlight cast eerily conflicting shadows across his visage, shading his skin and hair in unnatural colors. His eyes flickered as emotions clashed, battering at the core of his being. Whatever demonic passion possessed him seemed ready to burst out into the night. Tralane looked away, embarrassed at the spectacle Oram was making of himself and at the unexpected pity he felt for the giant. Instead, he watched the fire. The fuel consisted of broken boards, wheel spokes, clumps of brush and wood, and several dried-grass mats the Tribe Nations used to build their shelters. A part of Oram's past was burning before uncaring revelers.

For a moment, Tralane understood Oram's madness.

Several men managed to pull Oram down, wrestling with him good-naturedly before dragging him off to his former place between Fatome and Crecia, who gathered him in their soft, strong arms and legs, whispering soothing words to him. He was oblivious at first to their comforting, preferring to grunt Agathom's name over to himself savagely, as if by saying it the turmoil within him would be expelled. Fatome finally managed to distract him with her deft fingers. After a few brief moments of play, he laid his head quietly in her lap and stared off into the distance.

A hush had fallen over the gathering which no one dared to break; uncertain glances were exchanged among the warriors. Tralane saw some stirring to leave and felt the opportunity of breaking into their confidence rapidly vanishing. Just then the Wanderer broke over the horizon, illuminating the plain with a new source of soft white light. Around the fire, a third shadow sprang into life at everyone's feet.

"Good people," shouted Tralane, acting on a sudden impulse. "Stay, and hear. I have a story to tell." He leaped atop the barrel, glanced at Crecia, and continued. "Earlier today Oram gave me drink and the tale of his adventures, and so we became friends. Let me repay him and entertain you all with a legend I once won from a waif spirit when I was a sorcerer's apprentice."

His heart fluttered nervously as the people waited for him to fill the void. His first thought was to plunge into the tale of CuChani, who stole the light from the moon Star Speaker, then called Star Treader, and how that theft eventually brought the moon Wanderer to the world's skies. But he sensed a need for a tale closer to the lives and appetites of his audience, one that would reflect the pride, hopes, and fears of a people who had crossed the boundary between worlds. He chose a tale that had only recently become popular among the southern kingdoms. Then he laughed off his body's failings and fell easily into the style of speech he reserved for his storytelling.

"I have the tale of Suthra, and how the goddess Genjima was taken by a mortal, and it lies restless on my tongue. Will you give it a home in your hearts?"

His audience gave him their silent, nodding approval.

"I talk of a time of waning gods, of bold mortals, and ambitious wizards. I talk of a recent time, when the Wizard Kings made their pacts with Pichen-ma-thele and the rest of the gods, raised their ice palaces, and cast their shadow across the Karthasian Empire. It is a tale of this land and its gods, it is a tale of the people you will meet.

"The Wizard Kings came from a people bound by snow. They lived in the far north, where even the Karthasian Empire did not bother to force its will. They were hunters and raiders and they were a dwindling people. They prayed at the altar of Pichen-ma-thele, as have all the people in all the empires and kingdoms in this world.

"Perhaps it was the desperation in their voices, perhaps it was because of the lack of faith that accompanied the prayers of the people from other lands, but it was the pleas of the northern people that Pichen-ma-thele heard above all others. It was to them that he and the other gods granted an audience, and in them that the gods saw the instruments of their passion.

"For you see, in the days when there was only one moon in our skies, a thief among the gods stole the precious light from that moon, and brought darkness to the world. And though the light was restored, many gods died in the quest to find it. The people of the world lost their faith in the power and benevolence of the gods in the darkness, and it was a long time before the kingdoms and empires of the world could bring back order and inspire at least some reverence towards the immortal powers. So Pichen-ma-thele, father and ruler of all the gods, and all the children left to him planned and prepared for a time when once again they might be strong in the hearts of men and have a play in the games of mortals.

"So it came to the people of the north to restore the gods to their high place, just as the gods had restored the light to Star Treader and caused it to be renamed Star Speaker when the Wanderer came, attracted by the new brightness in the heavens. So the Wizard Kings were born, and so also was born the downfall of the gods.

"The Wizard Kings were great in power, but few in number. Their people were fearsome warriors, but all of the tribes put together did not equal a legion of Karthasian warriors. So they were sly, they were crafty. They nurtured the seeds of greed and corruption in the Karthasian Empire, seduced lords and princes with works of sorcery and promises of greatness. Pichen-ma-thele counseled the Wizard Kings and guided them in their subterfuge, for it was his wish that the strength of men be sapped by hatred and warfare, by betrayal, and by broken love. It was in the weakness of mortals that the gods see their path to a return to power, then as it is now.

"But the gods taught the Wizard Kings the craft of deceit too well. For it was a Wizard King who uncovered a secret and was stricken by a passion as powerful as the gods'.

"Suthra was the Wizard King's name. Tall and dark, he walked through the halls of the ice palaces and struck fear among his fellow Wizards. He was one who never ceased to cast his eyes for new realms to conquer, and one whose appetites were never satisfied. Mountains broke before his rages, and rivers dried when he lowered his withering gaze on them. He called no one friend, and no one loved him.

"It was Suthra who turned his attention away from the ploys being worked in the Karthasian Empire and spied instead on the gods who had granted him his power. He followed in spirit the trail of Pichen-ma-thele and found the place gods call home, where all prayers and curses come to rest, the place mortals call Daanthel. He passed among the gods without their taking notice and brazenly entered the dwelling of Pichen-ma-thele.

"There even Suthra knew fear, for though the power of Pichen-ma-thele had diminished, he was and is still a power a lone mortal would not wish to face. But Suthra did not waver in his purpose; Suthra did not cower in a corner like some mouse caught in the open field. He went gently through the house of Pichen-ma-thele and saw what even the other gods did not see.

"For it was Pichen-ma-thele's purpose not only to regain his influence over the affairs of men, but to make his hold over the gods and mortals unbreakable, to recast the creation of all life in a mold of his making. And to this end Pichen-ma-thele gave birth to a goddess, Gen-jima, whom Suthra saw crawl out from the god's stomach and take her place by his side. And when Suthra saw Gen-jima, he uncovered a burning need for her love.

"Suthra left then, for he was not so foolish as to challenge Pichen-ma-thele for the goddess. Suthra waited, practicing his intrigues in the courts of the Karthasian Empire along with his fellow Wizard Kings and listened to Pichen-ma-thele and planned. He made the journey to Daanthel once, twice, three times, and watched Gen-jima blossom into a goddess above all other gods and goddesses. And he listened to Pichen-ma-thele whisper to her how she would be the mother of a new race of gods, how the old gods would be banished, and the people of the world bound to Pichen-ma-thele, Gen-jima, and their children, through the work of the Wizard Kings.

"And Suthra saw how jealously he guarded Gen-jima from mortals and immortals, and this served only to stroke the fires of his desire even higher.

"The time came for Suthra to act. The Wizard Kings pleaded for an audience with Pichen-ma-thele, as their machinations were uncovered and they were faced with the wrath of the world. The god came and brought with him his children dressed for war, hoping a battle between mortals and immortals would weaken both and pave the way for his plan to become reality. And while the gods and the Wizard Kings planned the final battle, Suthra left the ice palaces and traveled the road to Daanthel, where he found at last Gen-jima alone.

"He appeared before her in all his flesh and terror, and Gen-jima, who had seen no one but Pichen-ma-thele in his gentlest mood, was frightened. He approached her, and Gen-jima, who did not know the power of godhood, though it coursed through her form, screamed for succor. Pichem-ma-thele had protected all too well. And Suthra was angry.

"The beauty of Gen-jima blinded him, the grace of her form melted his heart, the strength of his desire warped his reason. More than ever, he wanted only a word of love from the goddess. But she fled from him as if he were a demon, and so he became one. He became the demons Lust, Jealousy, and Pain. He wanted in the matter of flesh what had been denied to him in the matter of spirit, and he wanted to break Pichen-ma-thele's influence over her. Most of all, Suthra wanted Gen-jima, Pichen-ma-thele, all the gods, and all the mortals of the world to feel the agony of the love denied him. So Suthra took Gen-jima, and the goddess screamed.

"Her cry rang throughout Daanthel, and there was no one to hear her. But the echoes of her pain and outrage came down to the world of mortal men, and Pichen-ma-thele heard it. And in that cry he did not hear the pain of one he loved, but the doom of all he had striven for. He abandoned the battle between the Wizard Kings and the Karthasian Empire to return to Daanthel. There he found his goddess weeping on his bed and Suthra the Wizard King wandering in his house, wrath spent and spirit broken by the magnitude of his folly in destroying his only hope of finding love. Then Pichen-ma-thele released his own rage and, as armies battled and sorcerers dueled among the ice palaces below, the god cast both mortal and goddess to the earth. He buried them, still living, beneath a mountain and sentenced them both to the slow, frigid, creeping darkness of death.

"The Wizard Kings and the children of Pichen-ma-thel fell back before the might and number of mortal arms and magics. The power of the gods was broken, and they fled back to Daanthel to be worshipped and praised and bound to the will of mortals. And Pichen-ma-thele withdrew to his house, where he sits even now contemplating his next foray into the world of restless mortality.

"So goes the story of Suthra and Gen-jima..."

When Tralane had finished, the crowd cheered its approval. They seemed surprised at his taletelling style, which contrasted so sharply with his more traditional intonations, figures of speech and mannerisms, and Tralane once again found his talents appreciated. Coins were thrown to him, but he returned them all as a sign of friendship. His gesture brought on another round of happy exclamations and claps on the back, and he exchanged names with many people between gulps of Oram's heady brew. His laughter relaxed into easy camaraderie as he was accepted into their company and confidence, and he felt his spirits rise and his guarded manner evaporate. He had won something of greater value than the mere wealth of their coins; their trust had a hearty openness, despite their fear of the Sorcerer King, which he had rarely found in the lands he had traveled. His initial impression of Agathom's people was softened by their treatment of him, and he wondered if, in the past, he had always looked in the right places for such comradeship.

As the crowd began to break up, Tralane noticed Crecia's dark eyes lingering on him. He smiled and walked to her.

"You tell an interesting tale, Tralane," she purred as she put a hand on his forearm and led him away from Oram and Fatome.

"Ah, and what rumors has Oram been spreading about me?" he asked teasingly. He gave her a sidelong glance.

Crecia tossed her head from side to side, snapping her long hair back and forth, and laughed. "He's told me you're an arrogant, obnoxious, cold, and dangerous young man, and that you won't see too many more summers if you keep up the same attitude. But then, Oram's tongue was always loose."

Tralane noticed they were headed away from the main fires around which people had gathered. Where they walked only darkened tents rested. He did not resist. "And what about you?" he asked nonchalantly. "What is your story?"

"Oh no, I'm not about to tell you about my life. I'd be afraid of seeing you atop a barrel some day and hearing it repeated between rough jests and smirks."

Tralane turned his head away to hide his embarrassment over her acuity. "What do you do in this camp?" he asked awkwardly.

Crecia stopped in front of a tent. "Here's where I sleep. You'll have no need to ask stupid questions there."

Tralane hesitated for a moment, grasping for a quick retort that would allow him to regain mastery over the situation. But like his encounter with the Sorcerer King, he had acquiesced and followed instead of demanding and leading. Still, his game with Crecia promised delight, not danger and pain, and his surrender to her was only temporary. Fear was at rest, and pleasure was awakening. He smiled ironically as memories of other seductions he had instigated came to him, and he started to enter the tent.

Suddenly, a bright green light burst into existence behind him, jabbing lurid shadows across the face of Crecia. Both turned towards the source of the glow. Crecia gasped; Tralane twisted his face into a scowl and bit his lower lip. The Sorcerer King was standing by the fire they had just left. His left hand held a staff, his right a green-flaming torch. The golden runes on his scarlet robe and forehead blazed with fierce intensity. Everyone fled from him except for Oram. The giant lay sprawled at the Sorcerer King's feet, paralyzed with fear and drunkenness.

"You!" the Sorcerer King's voice boomed. "You have dared to speak my name, babble it like some insignificant thing. You have ignored my warnings and endangered me with the gods. You have challenged me by your refusal to obey. You will be punished."

Oram sat up, and Tralane could see, even at that distance, how the man trembled. Had he been able to stand, he would have dwarfed the King, but the hellish light made Agathom seem twice his natural height. Tralane shuddered at the illusion, hoping that was all it was.

Oram's mouth opened and closed; though Tralane could not hear any words, it was apparent the giant was pleading for his life.

"You are worthless." The Sorcerer King dismissed him. "Your knowledge is no longer useful. I have a new guide, the first of many I will have on my way north. Your time has passed."

Agathom raised his staff, one end pointing to the stars and the other aimed at Oram's chest. Green fire leaped from the staff, enveloped Oram, and burned away flesh, muscle, and bone in fiery strips until nothing was left. His screams could be heard even after his body had vanished; when even the sound of his voice had trailed away, the green fire that had outlined his form faded from sight. The light from Agathom's torch dimmed, its hellish rage appeased. The Sorcerer King left the scene and went back to his pavilion. One of his knights came to stand guard over the spot Oram had died, lance point threatening the sky. No one returned to the camp fire, and it started to sputter and die for lack of tending. There was not a man or woman to be seen in the vicinity.

Tralane was intimidated by the demonstration. He had often told tales of men performing such feats of sorcery and had read and heard of the ancient sorcerers of the Bright Empire and their power. He had seen wizards make fire leap and stream currents stop and he had even learned some spells and summonings during his tenure with Mathi. But he had never seen or heard of a mortal creature, not even the old Wizard Kings, using his power so gratuitously and without even showing signs of strain. He knew better than most the limitations of magic and that it was not a thing to be wasted on the execution of what amounted to a servant. A heavy price was demanded for the working of sorcery by mortals. The number of knights who stood guard, the startling demonstration of strength that had just occurred, and the awe with which his people regarded him all raised questions as to the extent of his power. The only answers Tralane could find did not please him.

"Get in," Crecia said softly, after a while. He looked at her and realized her eyes had been on him while Oram burned. He nodded and eased into her private world, letting other matters banish thoughts of gods and magic from his mind for the moment.

Chapter 3

"That was an impressive performance," Tralane whispered languidly, stretching his body and untwining his legs from hers.

"Are you talking about me or the Sorcerer King?" Crecia asked, turning over on her side to look at him.

"Why both, of course." Tralane was amused by his own wit. He reached over her to put out the candle that had burned during their love making, but he felt her fingers touch his side and stopped.

"Leave the light on. It's for Fatome. She hasn't come back yet and I don't want her to step on anything vital."

"Of course." Tralane sat up against a pole that supported the tent roof and threw off the heavy fur that covered him. It reminded him of Oram. "Fatome must still be mourning for her lost lover," he said carelessly.

"She always was a sensitive one—she really shouldn't be a camp follower. She always becomes attached to one man, and that makes the blow harder to take when that man finally dies or moves on. And on campaigns, it's usually the man who disappears first."

"Yes, I suppose so." Tralane found himself frowning, though he was not sure what was troubling him. He tried to change the subject.

"And you, how many lovers do you have?"

Crecia sighed and pulled her part of the blanket over the enticing mounds of her breasts. Her attention was fixed on some remote inner vision. "Quite a few, though I like to stay under the protection of one man. Of course, I don't become attached to him. I just take care of him a little more than the others, and he watches over me. Oram was my second man on this campaign. The other was a member of some tribe further south, by the Inland Sea, where we made our way into this world. He was the Sorcerer King's first guide."

"What happened to him?"

"He died before we found Oram. Not as spectacularly as your tentmate, perhaps, but it was just as certain."

He found Crecia's detachment unsettling, perhaps because he did not have the option to be equally detached. It was his life that was at stake, and the magnitude of the risk he was running was becoming alarmingly vivid.

"So he kills those who help him," he mused aloud, not letting Crecia see his fright.

"Only when he's done with them. He doesn't want to waste provisions on those who do not owe him allegiance."

"Then it's only a matter of time before my usefulness ends..."

"Brilliantly deduced, Tralane," she said with sarcasm. "I must say, you caught on quicker than Oram. I had to lay everything down for him, and even then he didn't care. Something must have touched his mind."

Tralane stood and began to dress. He did not bother explaining Oram to her, since he did not want to remember the man's story. He was vaguely annoyed that Oram had chosen him and not Crecia to confide his past to.

"What, exactly, happened to the first one, the tribal guide?" he asked curtly.

"I warned him a few nights after he came into the camp that his life was not safe with the Sorcerer King, so he left, just as you're doing now. The next morning a party of knights returned from patrol, and one of them was dragging the tribesman behind his kruushka, in the dust."

"I see." Tralane fumbled with the thongs of his shirt. He cast nervous glances at the tent entrance and cursed his luck. "Is there any escape? Or have I finally talked myself into my grave?"

Crecia sat up quickly and stared at Tralane as if he had granted her a new life. "Yes, if you would dare it."

He shrugged. "I have no choice. What's your plan?"

She spoke quickly and energetically. Tralane listened thoughtfully.

"The Sorcerer King has an amulet called Wyden's Eye. It is with this instrument that he has been able to cross from his world into yours. Steal it, and you and I can leave this place for other worlds. We'll be safe in a land that won't be too different from the ones we were born to, and the King will be trapped here, unable to follow us. The wrath of your gods will no doubt fall on him as it did where he came from, and there will be a great war as the gods defend themselves from his lust for dominance. But all that is beyond our power to stop. At least *we* will escape that fate."

Tralane studied her, trying to estimate the strength and direction of her motivations. "Wouldn't it be easier to assassinate him?" he asked, puzzled. "Death is the common fruit of such political ambitions. I'd save my world and, while a new leader is chosen among your people, I could escape your camp in the confusion."

Crecia shook her head vehemently. "First, it would take more than a well-placed dagger to destroy the King. He keeps himself surrounded with defensive spirits and forces. And even if you were to penetrate them and succeed, he would be avenged by creatures held in check by his will alone. I do not think you wish to become a martyr."

There was sharp humor in her eyes, for she saw that her words had cut off yet another of Tralane's hopes for escape.

"And then Wyden's Eye remains," she continued, "along with the King's army. Another sorcerer will gain control of the amulet, and someone else will lead the host against your world. The King's secrets will fall into another's hands, and the pattern will repeat itself. So even if you should survive the Sorcerer King's measures of protection, your lands will not be safe to travel through for some time."

"You have a large store of convincing arguments." Tralane said sourly.

He was not enthusiastic at the thought of deserting his world to the Sorcerer King. The rumors he had heard in Gynnuland had proven all too true, and Agathom's willingness to send his knights against warring southern kingdoms signaled his readiness to begin challenging those kingdoms, the Karthasian Empire, and even the gods for dominance in the world. Word no doubt had spread by now of the invulnerable, armored riders. There would be blood and fire, and Tralane had little confidence in any country's or band of nations' ability to resist Agathom's advance. He tried to take comfort in the fact that there was nothing he could do. If he could not save his race, the least he could do was save his skin.

"Taking everything into consideration," he said, with resignation, "your plan is the most promising. Besides, it fits well with a notion I had earlier today of meeting some of my other selves. And perhaps Agathom will be thwarted after all—"

Crecia pulled Tralane down to her with surprising strength and whispered angrily, "Must you keep repeating his name? You'll bring him down on us before my plans are even set in motion."

Tralane sat back down and let her continue explaining her plans. Crecia's fingers worked the edge of the blanket, and her face was as white and hard as the walls of the ancient Temple City from the days of the Bright Empire.

"The amulet is kept in a small blue case; it shouldn't be too difficult to find. Tonight the King will be entertained by one of several creatures he holds prisoner. If you're silent and do not call him back from his pleasures, you'll have time to search through his belongings. I'll meet you behind the pavilion with two fast thorts, and together we'll gain our freedom."

Having quelled any doubts over his course of action with the justification of his personal survival, Tralane set his thoughts to the task at hand.

"Any guards, human or otherwise?"

"No, he's thrifty with his sorcery."

"Oh? I would have thought otherwise after tonight's display."

She smiled at his suspiciousness. "That was the King's way of amusing himself. Killing Oram hardly taxed his powers, though it reminded his subjects of their proper position and evidently impressed you. Most of his strength is bound in keeping his demonic allies under control. What remains is for his pleasure, which he does not like to sacrifice to the tedious maintenance of defensive spells and traps. He relies on such demonstrations of power as you saw tonight, as well as the common knowledge of his personal spirits and demons who would rise to his defense if he were attacked, to keep himself safe. Of course, his knights are his eyes and ears throughout the camp; with them he can keep his followers in check before they even have the chance to conspire. But I've been careful, choosing only outsiders.

"Since you're not going to attack him directly, the Sorcerer King's demons will not be disturbed. And, as I told you, he will be distracted tonight, so his eyes and ears will see and hear only his pleasure."

Tralane was silent for a moment, thinking of the dangers she had surely faced in obtaining all her information. Her smooth skin and sensuous curves were not marred by any scars of punishment—she had paid a private price. Hardness glinted through the lush darkness of her eyes.

"You are a brave woman, Crecia."

"I know," she replied, laughing harshly. "Oh, but we'll have to curb our pride when we travel the roads together."

"I suppose so," he said without humor. "But why are you helping me? I thought you didn't want to become attached to your lovers. Besides, there must be someone else in this camp you can trust to carry out your plan."

Crecia spat in disgust and shook her head. "I told you,

he has his subjects well in hand, and he would see their fearful glances through his knights. I've never been able to find anyone willing to face him, anyway, and I've been searching for years. I am the daughter of a camp follower. I've known warriors and their ways since you were a cub. Do you know what it's like to be a tramp, a tool for men to use and throw away? Do you know what it is to be a slave? No, you're too young and, even with your travels and stock of tales, too inexperienced to know. Simply put, I hate my place in this army. I am lower than the servile wretches, the men who call themselves warriors and heroes and tremble in the presence of the Sorcerer King. You're the only one who can help me escape."

The hardness of her tone did not escape Tralane. When he added it to her previous display of detachment, he knew he would not figure far in her plans. She was using him as boldly as was the Sorcerer King, with the same cold calculation. He needed a shield to protect himself from her ambition, or he would find himself no better off than he was now.

"I assume you know how to use Wyden's Eye?"

"Naturally. It would be of no use to us if I didn't."

They exchanged looks, and for a while Crecia would not speak. Tralane could see her weighing her trust in him against her desire for freedom. He knew she had no choice.

"You must tell me some more of your tales, someday," she said in a sullen voice.

"I've heard, seen, and invented many of them. I would be only too glad to entertain you with some of the livelier ones."

She smirked, then bent down and drew a diagram of the amulet on the ground. She pointed to the places where he had to touch the massive center jewel, and in what sequence, to invoke its power. Her hair hid her face. After she had finished, Tralane erased the picture and started to leave.

"I'll see you later tonight, then," was Tralane's casual parting comment.

"I will be waiting," Crecia whispered, with passion lighting her eyes.

Tralane left, and found the camp deep in sleep. There were still a few fires burning, but they were widely scattered and kept up for the benefit of the sentries. He glanced up at the sky and saw clouds overtaking Wanderer. But Star Speaker was still bright overhead, and that suited him just as well. He felt secure with the knowledge that Pichen-ma-thele was watching over him during his moment of trial, then laughed at his belief. Even if the gods, by chance, were watching his progress, he doubted they would condone a piece of work that so resembled CuChani's theft of the light, for Wyden's Eye was to the Sorcerer King what the light of Star Speaker was to the rule of the gods. But then, since Agathom himself was a threat to that rule, the gods might well want him to succeed. Tralane shook his head and abandoned his metaphysical reflections. All he could do was hope that whatever fates were involved would favor him.

Tralane passed a solitary figure kneeling on the ground, still as a stone, and recognized Fatome. She was staring blankly at the knight who stood over Oram's unmarked grave. He felt as if he should comfort her, but he did not know how, and so passed on.

He reached his quarters without incident and gathered his belongings, all the while evaluating Oram's furs. He lined his netting with some, in the event he should find himself in cold lands, and left Oram's chest untouched. Then Tralane crept out and headed for a thort pen, where he led one of the creatures out, saddled it and guided the animal to a cluster of wagons near the Sorcerer King's pavilion. Making sure his pack, pouch, bow and arrows were all secured, Tralane tied his mount to the back of a wagon and started out towards his objective.

He reached the Sorcerer King's sanctuary after evading a patrol coming in from the camp perimeter. The warriors were silent as they passed the green pavilion, which glowed as if a large fire were burning from within. Their eyes were downcast, following the long, sharp spears of the knights' shadows which crossed their path. When the party had passed, Tralane quickly took in the dispersal of the knights stationed around the entrance. He took a deep breath, deciding on a bold approach, and walked slowly, silently past them. The knights, like a forest of dead trees in the path of a gentle breeze, did not stir.

Tralane entered the King's quarters and stood shakily by the flap, wondering what could distract Agathom to the point where he would lose awareness of his surroundings. He quickly decided he would rather not know.

The sights and smells that had overwhelmed him earlier assaulted his senses once again. The air vibrated with enchantments; the scrolls, parchments, and cabinets full of bottles, powders, and tubes all seemed to be warning him, forbidding him to go on. The subtle, murmurous voices filled his head with fear. He plunged into his search.

He scanned the objects the Sorcerer King had left out in the open, but the blue case was not among them. The only thing of interest which caught his attention was a long, thin bottle with gaseous, iridescent colors swirling within, standing on top of the table. Tralane thought he could hear the bottle sigh and moan and looked away, fearing it to be a trick to capture his mind.

After some hesitation, Tralane proceeded to open every large chest and cabinet he could find and rummage through their contents. He winced at every creak of a hinge and rustle of fabric against wood; he tried to assuage his anxiety by attributing it to his falling out of practice in the handling of magical implements. But the little noise he made did not bring the Sorcerer King back from whatever pleasures distracted him, and Tralane continued hunting for the amulet.

Then, as he opened a cabinet, a vial that had been placed on the edge of a shelf fell and broke. The tinkling sound seemed to shatter the air, and the voices that had been warning Tralane suddenly ceased to speak. The silence was heavy until, from out of the bottle on the table, there came a blood-chilling roar.

The sound shocked Tralane into action. He toppled the

cabinet and glanced over its scattered contents. When he did not find the amulet, he tore violently through the rest of the King's possessions, tossing aside and smashing everything that came before him in his frantic effort for haste.

He saw the blue case in his hand even as he was beginning to throw it away. Ripping away the cover, he found the amulet Crecia had described to him and clutched it hard in his fingers. Wyden's Eye was cool to the touch, and sent strange pulsations through his arm. Too frightened to feel relief, Tralane turned to leave and felt the blood drain from his face.

In front of him, rising out of the bottle he had noticed earlier, was a smoky apparition whose face was Agathom's. It stared at Tralane with hard, red eyes, and its mouth, which was becoming as solid as its eyes, moved as if shouting terrible curses. Next to this wraith, another creature was beginning to take form. It was a woman of some kind, with fierce, seductive eyes, and teeth that were sharp between her full, cruel lips. As her body grew from the smoke belching out of the bottle, Agathom emerged from some curtained alcove, and she sprang at the Sorcerer King and pinned his arms to his side. Her voice cut through the air like a whistling sword, keen with hate.

"Now you will pay, mortal," she screamed, eyes gleaming like cold steel in the sun. "I will have my vengeance for the vile service you forced upon me. Suffer! Anguish over your foolishness as I let the blood run from your human veins."

Tralane suppressed a cry of terror and edged his way around the two struggling figures. Agathom, pressed by the demon, could only watch as Tralane passed out of his pavilion.

Once outside, Tralane broke into a run, heading for the wagons where he had left his thort and provisions. Some of the knights were moving, but the Sorcerer King was too preoccupied to control his minions with any accuracy. Tralane had no difficulty in evading their clumsy attempts to stop him. He urged himself on, relieved to find his voice and reason intact—he would not end up like Agathom's crippled servant.

A woman shouting his name made him look back over his shoulder. Crecia was standing by the King's quarters, waving her hands over her head.

"Over here, in the back," she yelled, pointing to a cluster of tents where two thorts were waiting, fidgeting nervously.

At some future time, he hoped he would smile at Crecia's position with unburdened good humor. Had she truly wanted to leave the trade she had been born into, she would have stolen the Eye herself a long time ago. He thought righteously of his escape from Mathi and ignored the pleas for help she was sending after him. She had in her all the evils he knew so well—hardness, deceit, and passionate hatred for the past—and which he did not trust in himself, much less in her. She was not, he had carefully reasoned, a proper companion for him. She was also standing too close to what he felt would very soon become the center of violent activity. He waved back to her, warning her away, and continued running. His conscience was for the moment assuaged.

As he reached his thort, a sound like a great gust of wind, bringing with it a storm, gave him an unwanted shove. Tralane looked back as he mounted and saw the pavilion burst into flame, then partially collapse. Agathom, who once again seemed to be twice his normal size, had broken free of the demon's grasp and was forcing her back into the flames in which they both stood. The demon wailed, and blood trickled from her mouth like molten metal. The knights were fully animated and, just as he had thought, were surrounding Crecia. He shrugged apologetically and urged his thort to a run, thankful of his escape.

The pounding hooves of kruushkas and the leveled lances of the knights reminded him of his uncompleted escape. The camp was stirring, springing to life as warriors tumbled out of tents and wagons, swords in their hands. Amid the shouts and curses, Tralane ran the formula of motions Crecia had taught him over in his mind, and passed his hand over the amulet he had been desperately holding in his fist all the while.

There was no change, and a fear that Crecia had lied to him pierced him with the force of an arrow. But then the sounds of pursuit began to fade, and with every stride the camp lost a little more of its solid reality. He rode low and hugged the thort's bobbing neck.

"Agathom! Agathom! Agathom!" he shouted in a wild, jubilant voice. Then he laughed as he thought a demon would, or as CuChani had done in another age, and drove his mount into an unrelenting gallop until dawn broke over the new world's horizon.

Chapter 4

Tralane rode into the town the caravan leader had called Fargouet, grateful for the food and shelter it promised. He had already thanked the traders he had met a few days past with some lively songs and tales and felt no need to appease their guardian spirits with any more gratitude. The long, dreary days spent on the Ousho Plains, buffeted since his escape from Agathom by a raging storm and with nothing more than an ill-tempered thort for companionship, had washed away the shell of fine sentiments Tralane had cultivated over the course of his many pledges of service as a courtier. He had been reduced to little more than a core of cold, hungry desire for survival.

However, after the brief renewal of companionship and the enjoyment of physical comfort in the caravan camp, Tralane's single-minded pursuit of survival had been colored with other thoughts. The abandonment of his world to the Sorcerer King, and the ties broken by death or betrayal with Oram and, presumably, Crecia, were sources of discomfort even more irritating than storms and thorts. The boredom of leaving the caravan camp and returning into the wilderness had left fertile ground in which guilt and self-recrimination could grow. He was anxious to acquire the constant company and distractions of civilized society.

The town was veiled by sheets of rain and mist. Most of the windows were shuttered, and only an occasional figure hid in a doorway or struggled along the muddy street. The light that managed to escape through cracks was cheerless and uninviting. Tralane was well up along the main street before he found a lively-looking tavern that was both welcoming and suitable for distraction.

A stable boy appeared and hurriedly took the reins of his thort. Tralane dismounted, removed his pack, bow, and arrows from the saddle and ran to the shelter of the doorway. He hesitated before entering, listening to the voices and snatches of conversation drifting down into the street from the windows above. For a moment, he had an urge to stay outside and listen all night, piecing together involuted life histories from the overheard conversations, and letting his imagination introduce him to people far more interesting and complicated than the speakers themselves. It was a childhood habit that had entertained him during Mathi's infrequent visitations, and which had gained him renown and notoriety as a gossip in courts.

But his shivering body refused to allow him the luxury of fantasy. He entered the tavern, wiping his nose on his drenched shirt sleeve as he closed the door behind him.

He found himself in a wide hall with a low ceiling. The space was hazy with smoke and thick with aromas. Wind and string instruments played against one another as numerous musicians, some unprofessionally drunk or otherwise incapacitated, practiced their trade at tables across the room. The buzzing undercurrent of laughter and speech was occasionally broken by sharp-tongued serving maids putting to rest lewd suggestions and advances that sprinkled the talk like overripe spice, while gamesters and debaters rose above the din with shouts of disgust and curses. The atmosphere of revelry, with drunkards vying with entertainers for the attention of the general public, cheered Tralane. Already, the clouds of weariness and depression were parting, allowing good humor to prevail.

He stopped a passing servant with a grab and pull and inquired after the proprietor. He received an inarticulate reply and a wave toward the opposite end of the hall. Following the servant's vague instructions, Tralane maneuvered his way across the width of the hall until he reached a heavy-set man with enormous hands and forearms, whose massive solidity was the equal of Oram's giant proportions. The servants roaming the hall were well protected.

The owner was busy administering draughts of wine, ale, and liquors to anyone who held out a coin to him. Tralane fished through his pouch until he found a coin of similar weight, though with different markings, and held it out. It was immediately snatched from his hand and replaced by a mug of ale.

Before the man could move away, Tralane blurted out, "I'm looking for a room—"

"See my wife," growled the innkeeper, thrusting an elbow in the direction of a door further down the hall. He had not even glanced at the youth.

The bard nodded, picked up his belongings, and jostled his way toward the door. His ale was gone by the time he reached his destination, and he could only hope whatever bugs and creatures that survived the stomping of so many feet enjoyed what he had spilled on the floor. He knocked on the door and, when no one answered, he entered.

A woman sat on a stool, engrossed in the task of peeling vegetables, which she threw into a large cauldron hanging over a roaring hearth fire next to her. A few servants were sleeping on beds of dried grass, stuck between piles of produce, dried meats, and neatly stacked barrels. Tralane closed the door and walked up behind her.

"Greetings," he introduced himself. "I am a bard, in need of shelter. I'm willing to pay with coin or, if your prices are too high, with tales and entertainments." He was about to launch into a brief but concerted summary of the courts he had performed at, knowing that the mention of nobles and ladies usually cut off protestations before they were started. However, her startled expression and paled complexion stilled his tongue.

She glanced at the door with wide eyes, then whispered harshly, "Are you a fool to return here so soon?"

Tralane was at a loss to respond. At last, controlling his surprise, he replied, "I beg forgiveness, madame, but I can assure you I've never traveled in these parts before."

The woman stood, spilling the peelings that had gathered in her lap. Beneath the layers of sweat, dirt, and soiled garments, she was youthful and full-bodied. He found her deep-set brown eyes and sensual lips attractive.

She ran to the door, opened it a crack, and looked out. After a few moments, she turned and looked him over worriedly.

"You're out of uniform, and you look as if you've spent a month out in the middle of nowhere. That's why they didn't recognize you. Those clothes! Where have you been and what have you done that you had to wear such finery into rags? Gods, but it's lucky you didn't get a knife in the back out there!"

Tralane thought it wise to correct her mistake before an unfortunate scene occurred. The idea of being held responsible for mischief that was none of his doing struck him as unpalatable.

"My dear one, not only have I never been in these parts before now, but, until quite recently, it was utterly impossible for me to have even known you. I've never honored any army by wearing their uniform, since the services I rendered them did not require I do so. As for my clothes, they are those of a courtier-turned-bowman, and have seen better days. And by the way, who would be so anxious to plant a knife in my innocent back?"

"My husband, you idiot! Have you downed too much wine, or taken a blow on the head? Have you forgotten our pledge of love, my husband's jealousy, and your oath before the town chief never to see me again on pain of death?" Her eyes narrowed suspiciously. "Have you been raiding the caravans again? Is that why you joined the

Golden King's forces, to run the escorts and caravans into your traps?"

Tralane was silent, unable to express his stupefaction. The mention of Wyden's Eye and its power might make him the target of unscrupulous conspiracies, yet he could not remove the burden of another man's identity without explaining why it was impossible for him to be other than what he was. At the last, he found the needless complications that had arisen out of his simple search for shelter mildly amusing. But his laughter would not satisfy the woman. He sighed, crossed his hand over his eyes and looked down at his feet. He was twisting and turning the facts to form a suitable story when she left the door, pushed a panel on the far wall, and stood aside as a trap door opened from above and a ladder descended. The noise of the mechanism caused the servants to turn and mutter in their sleep.

"Up with you, quickly," she said, her shock and anger having regressed to annoyance with a favored but disobedient child. "You can hide upstairs in the loft until the place quiets down, and then you can explain the reasoning behind this new escapade of yours."

Accepting the lodgings that were at last being offered, Tralane climbed the ladder. The notion that the woman was mad suddenly occurred to him, and he felt sorry for her and the innkeeper. There could be no reasoning with her, and he felt foolish for having been taken in by her delusion and fighting against it. If she thought that he, a stranger, was her banished lover, then why not let the farce continue? He had evaded eyes made sharper by jealousy than the innkeeper's, and the danger of discovery only made the affair more attractive.

He was still climbing when his thoughts had run their course. The journey took longer than he had anticipated; when he finally reached his room, he found it to be nothing more than an attic with dried grass and dust spread liberally on the floor, a chamber pot in a corner, and a burning candle in a holder hanging from a roof beam. Beneath the candle sat an emaciated, bald-headed old man with veins tracing their way along his arms and legs like starving rivers in a pale desert. He wore a soiled breech cloth and sash and the remnants of a pair of sandals.

"Welcome, young man," he said, his voice dimmed and cracked with age. "There's plenty of room for two refugees."

Tralane dropped his pack, bow, and quiver in a corner of the room. He nodded sullenly at the old man, unhappy over sharing a room with a stranger. Then he heard the trap door slide shut below him, and he realized he was in a secret room above the tavern.

The old man laughed drily. "I am Gibron the Mage, weaver of potent spells and lasting charms."

Tralane stiffened defensively, the sight of Agathom wrestling with a demon bursting into his memory.

"And I am Tralane, bard and bowman currently without employment." His reply was not steady.

Gibron's eyes seemed to gleam and twinkle as he passed his gaze over Tralane. "A bard, eh? You have an aura about you that makes me think you've had some experience with magic. Were you a disciple once?"

"Yes, but my teacher was a poor one, and I left him to follow my own path."

"And your parents, did they have dealings with beings of power, or with death?"

Tralane shook his head and almost sneered. "I don't know; I never knew them. My teacher was also my guardian—it is his influence you sense. My own magics were never very effective or successful." He refrained from mentioning Wyden's Eye, afraid its power might tempt the old man. "But you said something about being a refugee?"

The mage cackled, as if he knew something Tralane did not. "Young ones are always so secretive with their elders. Well, no matter, I have no secrets. I am fleeing Sagamourin, the Golden King who rules half these southern lands and is extending his borders even further. I am his enemy now, because I would not help satisfy his imperial dreams. He is a sorcerer of the material. His passions are power and rule. My goals are merely spiritual, as I seek transcendence through transformation. His riches and knowledge would not help me escape the cycle of life and death that binds even the gods, and so I was not tempted to his cause. And those with power who do not serve the Golden King must die."

Tralane appreciated Gibron's honesty, since he himself was not always so ready to offer his problems up for public scrutiny. He also understood Gibron's refusal to serve. Like Mathi, Gibron was engaged on a private quest for the sorcery that could save the individual soul, shaped by a lifetime of experience into an identity, from being hurtled by death into the formless Sea, there to be crushed, torn apart, and used once again in the making of a new, fresh life. The comforts and pleasures of the flesh did not interest those who sought to escape the final price of having flesh.

"I managed to escape," the mage continued, "and after many days of traveling, deceiving the searching spells and spirits Sagamourin has sent after me, and surviving as best I could as far from the main roads as possible, I arrived here in Fargouet on the Golden King's most distant border. I'm now waiting for a guide, to be procured by the kind owner of this tavern—a man named Rimskiel—and with the guide's help I hope to journey across the plains and find some new, unknown lands. Perhaps I'll cross the seas and find some new continent. Whatever happens, I will be far removed from Sagamourin's ambitions, and free to pursue my goal."

The rise of a sorcerous power in Gibron's world seemed to parallel the events of Tralane's home. A stone had been cast into an infinite pool, sending ripples of disturbance across parallel worlds.

"I wish you well," Tralane said, breaking off his musings when he noticed the silence that had fallen over the attic. "As for myself, I've somehow managed to involve myself with that madwoman downstairs. I take it she's Rimskiel's wife. I pity the life he must have with such a frantic mate."

"You mean Marzen?" The mage shook his head with a smile. "Her mind is whole and sharp, like the edge of an assassin's blade. She and I have often talked since I came here. I would trust her with my life." He stopped, seemed surprised, and laughed. "I have done so."

"But there must be some mistake," Tralane protested. "She took me for her lover and sent me up here so I could hide from her husband."

"I am new to these parts, so I cannot swear if what she says is true. But I have heard her speak at some length of a rascal she calls Detrexan, and she seemed quite in her wits, if bitter, when on that subject. If I were you, I would not dismiss the situation as her madness."

"But I've never seen her before. It's quite impossible."

"Perhaps in another town—"

Once again, Tralane withheld the knowledge of Wyden's Eye. "No, no, it cannot be—I know, I'm sure."

Gibron studied Tralane closely, with penetrating intensity. The bard turned away, annoyed over displaying such unaccustomed agitation. The mage's suspicious attention was the antithesis of the reaction Tralane had usually received from Mathi, whom he had always considered easy to deceive. Gibron seemed as wise and powerful, and yet more humane than any practitioner of the arts he had ever met. Tralane shrank from the elder's gaze.

"It would seem the fates have much in store for you," Gibron said at last, closing his eyes and leaning back against a wall. Soon, his breathing fell into the steady, shallow rhythm of sleep.

Chapter 5

Though weary from traveling, Tralane had difficulty sleeping that night. The comforts and company he had received so far were not those he had anticipated. Secrets stirred in his mind, prompted by his spirit.

He had nightmares. He was pursued by demons—hideous creatures formed from beasts and men, drooling blood, with misplaced eyes and mouths leering at him and shouting curses after him as he ran. Their slavering jaws nipped at his heels; their claws clutched at strands of his hair. He fell to the soft, moist earth. His legs would not carry him. He lay quietly, drinking in the soft warmth. He was embraced by the rich, nurturing soil that molded itself so willingly to the contours of his body. He merged with the warm darkness and knew he had escaped. He looked behind him and saw the demons dancing madly over him. They tore off his limbs, smothered and crushed him beneath their weight. They ate his flesh and drank his blood. He shrieked, as the warmth fell away and their cold, hard touch lifted him into the sky. Then he woke.

He lay trembling in his corner of the attic, listening to his heart beating wildly, pounding against the silence. It was the third time he had been thus visited that night. His condescending smile and scoffing dismissals of the feelings of remorse and guilt did not steady his hands nor pump back the strength to his arms and legs. After a concerted effort, the sharp talons and angry eyes of demons gave way to mortal steel and jealous hearts. He sank into the present, into the moment. He welcomed Rimskiel's anger and the dangerously precarious position he was in, and applied himself to escaping it. The ghosts would vanish as easily as the physical threat, by the simple expedience of danger.

He had to move on, as quickly as possible. Whatever conflicts had been renewed by his arrival would just as suddenly be forgotten by his rapid departure. He would go someplace where a gifted bard and talented archer was appreciated, perhaps to the Golden King's court; he seemed by Gibron's account to be the destined ruler of the world. From there, Tralane would have the opportunity to plot out his future along the familiar lines of court politics. Once settled into a familiar pattern, he would have time to explore the possibilities Wyden's Eye offered to those with wit to see them.

He was enumerating the promises life had made to him when he had stolen the amulet when the noise of the trap door mechanism creaking into service snapped the thread of his thoughts. He tensed and waited for the shouts and angry voices of vengeful men to burst up the passage. But there was only the sound of a single pair of feet treading softly up the ladder.

Marzen appeared, holding a candle in her left hand and a sack in her right. She placed the sack and light on the floor and climbed up the rest of the way. She had washed and changed into a more comely dress. Tralane smiled appreciatively.

"Ah, you're not sleeping," she whispered. She glanced at Gibron's sleeping form, then continued. "It must be your sins that keep you awake. You should follow the old man's example. He doesn't let anything worry him."

"I was only thinking, Marzen. People do that late at night."

"Why? Because they're ashamed to do it in the daytime?" She gave him a facetious smirk and placed the bag in the middle of the attic. "Well, at least you remember my name. That's a good sign. There's food in the sack, which you'll have to share with the old man. And I brought some sheremain nuts. You see, I remember what you like."

Tralane opened the bag and inspected the contents. There was a loaf of bread, a ball of cheese, some smoked camulet strips, fruit, and a cluster of branches from which hung small, round nuts. He picked one, cracked it with a knife he also found in the bag, and sampled the meat. After a few chews, the room began to sway from side to side, and the walls seemed to move away from him. He found it too bitter and potent for his taste and spat the meat out.

"I'm afraid this is going to upset you, Marzen, but in all my eighteen winters, I've never tasted anything like this before." He dropped the branches and knife back into the bag. "Nor have I ever seen you before this night. I learned your name from Gibron, who also informed me you were not mad. But if he's right, why do you insist on calling me your lover? Mind you, it's not an unpleasant proposition, but I'd prefer a more straightforward approach."

Marzen sat close beside him. Her fresh scent made him conscious of his own odor and, as the effects of the sheremain nut quickly wore off, the cramped confines of the room they were in. Her body was hard with the years of her service in the inn, but her face was softened by wide, sensuous lips that were parted, as if ready to speak, and by the long, brown curls that fell to her shoulders. Her skin was smooth and her hands were calloused by hard work, so he could not tell her age with too much accuracy.

As he studied her, lines of anxiety arched across her forehead.

"Don't you remember anything?" she asked, leaning closer to him. "Please, don't jest, not now."

"All right," he acquiesced, curious to see why she was so adamant. "Tell me about myself."

She placed the candle in front of her and locked her fingers together on her lap. She smiled as if he were playing a game with her, but she could not look long into his eyes and glanced frequently at the flame. She drew in a deep breath and began.

"You said your name was Tralane? I know you as Detrexan, a thief and a warrior. You came to this town two years ago, running from King Garice's guards. You told me of how you had left your mountain village and the old hag who took care of you there in your youth, and went north to the cities among the rivers to learn the tricks of thieving. Your skills, or lack of them, forced you to travel constantly or face a hangman's noose. When the Golden King's host passed through here, you joined, hoping to avenge yourself on King Garice's forces, and have been with Sagamourin ever since. The Detrexan I know has an unnatural love of pleasure that has gotten him in trouble more than once, the latest being an ill-timed return to the town that banished him for being caught sleeping with an important man's wife. Did you desert? You'll be caught, if not by my husband, then by your own comrades-at-arms. Couldn't you have waited for a better time?"

The life he was supposed to have led did not strike Tralane as wholly improbable. He often fantasized himself in more daring and actively roguish adventures than those which he found himself undertaking in real life. But his hold on the past was firm—he knew where he had been and what he had done. He also knew the possibility existed of his having a twin on this new-found world. Yet the chance of his family line surviving so exactly in a world that differed in so many other ways made Tralane shiver. While vaguely parallel, this world was dissimilar enough in major facets to change the shape of humble lineages such as the one he assumed he had descended from. Even if his wildest dreams were true, and he was indeed some lost prince of the Karthasian Empire, he doubted he would be so lucky as to fall into a world in which his family had survived the vagaries of political life so exactly as to produce an identical twin.

Was it chance that had led him out of Agathom's camp, or had an unknown power guided him into his present situation? Crecia had shown him how to invoke the amulet's magic, but not how to direct it. Tralane's confidence wavered before the realization that, indeed, the door to many worlds had been opened to him; but he was blind to the choices. The demons of his past pursued him while something led him helplessly into the unknown.

"Detrexan?" Marzen probed.

"No." He moved sluggishly out of his ruminations. "Tralane. I am different. I'm not the one you love. If you must know, if you can understand, I come from another Earth." He saw her draw back fearfully. "No, no, I'm not a demon. I've been . . . guided here, I think, though by whom, and why, I don't know. I don't understand." He grinned suddenly and gave her a wink. He put an arm around her waist and brought her closer to him. "I'm talking too much and taking my words too seriously. I can't be so different from your Detrexan in love, can I? Why don't we see—"

She edged away from him, prying his hand from around her waist. "No, I'm not sure—I don't know." She stood, and Tralane felt a strong desire to touch her strong, lithe body. He struggled with a rush of emotion, thinking of her sad invulnerability to all the work and misfortunes which had hardened her body and mind, but not her heart. If he could touch her, offer her some kind of love and comfort, she would reward his sacrifice with the blessing of her strength. With Marzen by his side, choices would not matter. The loneliness would not be so overwhelming.

"What about my husband and his friends?" she asked at last. "Do you think they'll believe you? I doubt you'll even have the chance to speak. It's a miracle nobody saw you when you came in. But my husband will be coming up sometime to see the old man, and then what will you do?"

"Perhaps I'd best leave now," he said, reluctantly. His old plan of flight was not as attractive as it had once been.

"No, my husband's asleep downstairs and the tavern

is almost deserted. The few customers and servants moving about would spot you right away, even with a disguise. You'll have to wait until tomorrow evening, at the busiest hour, to try to get away. And pray you have the same good fortune you had tonight." She reached for the candle and started down the ladder.

"Will you be back?"

She glanced at him for a moment, not long enough for Tralane to understand the look on her face. "Just leave—and don't come here again."

Tralane sat in the darkness, listening to Marzen descend. Only when she had left did he think to ask her to come with him. As he was about to go after her, he heard the trap door close, and then two voices talking. Crawling to the vertical passageway so he could hear better, he recognized Marzen speaking. She was shouting, protesting. He heard the words "honor" and "betrayal." A man answered, one whose voice he also recognized. He remembered, in particular, the powerful forearms and hands. Tralane returned to his sleeping mat. Perhaps Marzen's advice was for the best.

A rustling against the far wall, followed by soft footfalls, told him Gibron was awake and heading towards him.

"So I'm not the only one who can't sleep tonight," the bard exclaimed. The room's candle sprang into life. Gibron was drawing back his hand from the flame. Tralane sniffed at the scent of the simple magic. He had used such spells every day during his apprenticeship with Mathi, and just as effortlessly. He had not used them since.

"I like to lie awake and think late at night, too, young one," Gibron said, sitting beside Tralane. "I heard your little conversation with Marzen and, though I may not smell as nice or feel as good to the touch as she, I believe I can be of more practical service to you."

Tralane remained quiet, avoiding Gibron's eyes.

"You've spoken of another world, yet you know the Sky Speech and dress and act like a mortal man. You have an aura about you that is not a wizard's nor a god's, but which tells me you've been nurtured in more than simple spells. These are mysteries which, perhaps, you might be able to explain?"

"Why?" Tralane was prepared to say more, to expound on the old man's foolishness and bothersome curiosity, but he satisfied himself with the single, curt question. He did not want to give the wizard cause for sorcerous retribution.

"Ah, no reason. None at all, for you. But you see, I believe you have come into the possession of a charm. No, not a mere charm, but a source, a point of focus for magic. You have power buried deep within you, but no skill in the arts to make it work. Yet you have something that sets you above the artless and apart from the practitioners of the art."

Tralane rolled away from Gibron and stood. His head touched a beam, and he wished there were a window in the room so that he might look out into the night. He yearned to see the moons, the stars, the infinite space. He said nothing and allowed the wizard to continue.

"We call such people Keepers, though they may be known by different names where you come from. Or do they know of such things in your world? No matter. No matter. I, with some few of the other mages, have long suspected that there are multiple consequences to each decision we make and that, at each fork in reality, a split occurs. Every decision creates a new world, a new dimension in which the consequences of a particular action are developed, and each new world splits further as new branches are opened up and alternate possibilities established. Can you imagine, Tralane, the number of earth-reflections that have been and are being created if, at every fork in every path of every living being, at least two new worlds were created—one for each alternative that we might have chosen? And you have the power to travel from one possible reality to another, do you not?"

Gibron's words were translated into a vision of a leafless tree, its branches growing by the moment, splitting, entwining, filling the void of Eternity.

Tralane, shaken by the vision, asked in a trembling voice, "Will you take it from me?" He was not sure if his question were not truly a plea.

The mage laughed softly. "No, I would not. My hunger is not for such things, and I suspect I would be interfering with a scheme of existence which destined you to come into this power's possession. There is something that binds you to this charm you carry, so that two fates have been inextricably woven into one that has yet to choose a direction. I believe if I were to take it, my fate would soon be decided in favor of doom."

"And what is my task as a Keeper?"

"Merely to live. You stand in the shadow of Life and Death, Order and Chaos. Stray too far from the shadows, and you might well die. And your death would affect the Balance of all Being."

Tralane stared up at the sloping ceiling. A huge weight seemed to bear down on the ceiling, making it close in on him. The fear that he could not decide the nature of his own actions and that some unknown force was leading him on took on greater substance. His hopes and ambitions seemed insignificant. He had worked a pretty theft, but had stolen more than he had bargained for.

"You won't speak?" Gibron stood, stretched, and sat again facing Tralane. "Do not be dismayed. There are many Keepers and many fulcrums in the Balance of Being. Yours is not the only life to be so burdened. Now, tell me, how did you come upon this object?"

In a rush of words scrambled into one long sentence, Tralane told Gibron about the coming of the Sorcerer King and how he had stolen the amulet that was Agathom's means of escape from a dying world. Without justifying himself, he told his listener about Oram and the companion in thievery he had left behind. The tale did not seem as bold as he had imagined it to be. Gibron was not Mathi, who had been only too willing to believe the fantastic over the real, so long as it allowed him to pursue his mysterious paths. In the solitary peace of the attic, Tralane's words rang hollow.

Gibron retreated to his own place against the far wall and lay down on his sleeping mat. He closed his eyes and asked, "What drove you to steal this amulet?"

Tralane shrugged uncertainly. "I had a desire for adventure. I wanted fortune, a kingdom. I had to escape. I don't know, really."

"Neither do I," said Gibron, sighing. "I am certain you are the amulet's intended Keeper and that one of the Sorcerer King's functions was to deliver the Eye to you. But beyond that, I am at a loss. Perhaps there is more to this than the amulet. Perhaps Wyden's Eye is being used as a link between you and some manipulative power which is drawing you towards it. Why such a link would exist and to what purpose, I cannot even venture a guess."

Gibron opened his eyes and looked at Tralane. "I am curious about this mystery. Will you let me travel with you? I can be of assistance and perhaps I can solve the riddle that surrounds you."

"Yes, I'd like that," Tralane answered. He did not know what other course of action to take, and he needed someone to share the responsibility of having the Eye. "I need a guide."

"Good. Tomorrow we'll make our plans. For now, I'm too weary for any more thinking and I suspect you also need rest, eh?"

Tralane snuffed out the candle flame in response. He stretched out on his mat and began to doze almost at once. He thought he heard Gibron pose another question, concerning why he had not asked Marzen to join him in his travels. But the bard could no longer distinguish dream from reality. The demons rose to resume the chase, and he forgot all questions and answers.

Chapter 6

Tralane woke feeling refreshed and unburdened. He sat up, leaning on an elbow, and saw Gibron underneath the candle, in the position in which he had first met him.

"Pleasant morning," Gibron greeted him.

Tralane gave him a nod and reached out for the sack Marzen had brought up the night before. He chewed on a strip of camulet while he broke the bread and cut cheese. As he ate the latter, he found a water bag containing sweet juice he had overlooked in his first examination of the sack's contents. He took a long draught.

"Not bad. Certainly a pleasant change from the dull poison I've been eating lately."

"I hope you've recovered from last night's conversation," Gibron commented, taking some of the fruit.

"Why yes, I feel much better this morning. It must have been fatigue and all the ill fortune I've been getting lately that made me so moody." Tralane reached over his quiver of arrows and grabbed his pouch, from which he drew out a smaller pouch drawn shut by string. He tossed it to Gibron. "There's the cause of all my troubles," he said carelessly.

Gibron took Wyden's Eye out and examined it. The central jewel, glinting green and blue, was as large as an average man's palm. Strange shadows and angles played with light. With every movement of Gibron's hand, the lights and shadows shifted into unexpected positions. An intricately fashioned silver setting held the jewel.

Gibron replaced the amulet in the pouch and returned it to Tralane.

"You are a strange young man. Last night, I thought I saw you as you truly are, confused and frightened. Now you're back in your flippant mood."

Tralane continued eating. "Perhaps," he said at last, with caution, "you seek to know others too well."

"But if I'm to help—"

Tralane held up his hands in mock surrender. "You're like an overprotective parent, Gibron. You want to know, to help, to do everything for your ward. But I've been on my own for six years. I can handle myself very well. Now, you said we were going to make some plans this morning?"

Gibron let out an exasperated sigh and opened his mouth to say something, but thought better of it and ate a piece of bread instead. "All right, I'll let that pass for now. Last night, I heard Marzen say that the evening would be the best time for you to try to escape. Tonight, I can go down first and distract Rimskiel, while you don a shawl, hunch over, and try to slip out unnoticed. I can follow shortly afterwards, by which time you will have procured some fast thorts."

"No sorcery?" Tralane asked, disappointed.

"You forget I'm running from the Golden King. I dare not use strong spells of deception, for that would summon his searching spells to me, and they would destroy us."

"We could use the amulet up here, though it might be a bit of a fall if there's no tavern on this spot in the world we wind up in."

Gibron brushed the suggestion aside with a wave of his hand. "From what you've described to me, it is not so easy to cross from one world to another. The doorway is long and the changes gradual, requiring some travel. No, we must wait until we've gained the streets before we can use Wyden's Eye. Hopefully, the Golden King's spells won't be able to follow us through."

"If Agathom could not reach me as I escaped, then your enemy will not be able to, either."

"Then let us save our strength for now. I don't think we'll get much chance for resting tonight."

Gibron finished his meal in silence, then went back to his sleeping mat, crossed his legs and arms as he sat, and withdrew his attention to inner matters. Tralane, shunning such activity, quietly sang a song about his future, Wyden's Eye, and the aspects of life which his companion might be contemplating.

The day passed like a thick, slow-moving fog, and night fell with an almost imperceptible change of atmosphere. Tralane gauged the time by the angle and brightness of a beam of light which slipped through a crack in the ceiling. He slept fitfully and remained with his dreams even when he was awake. He ate again and took up the time by lazily playing with the straw on the floor, designing intricate mazes. He had learned how to occupy his mind and prevent himself from becoming restless in the small, isolated confines of town prisons and dungeons, where he had spent parts of his youth paying for his inexperience. With Gibron uncommunicative and the mounting volume of noise from below only a reminder of the danger to come, Tralane found the memory of his incarcerations to be his solitary comfort. At least imprisonment had guaranteed his safety and a return to freedom after a moderate sentence of penitence had been served.

Eventually, Gibron rose.

"It's about time we left, Tralane," he whispered. The mage wore a dark cloak and carried a small pack over his shoulder.

Tralane grunted, surprised that he had missed his companion's preparations, and rose to his knees. Gibron went to the ladder and began to descend while Tralane gathered his belongings and straightened his wits.

He did not feel better for the day's idleness. The morning's freshness and bravado had worn away, to be replaced by doubts and fears. He could not recapture completely his old arrogance.

He stood, swayed as if pushed and pulled by the contradictory thoughts and feelings he could not quite grasp that were swirling in his mind, and finally followed Gibron into the dark hole, his pack, quiver, and bow strapped to his back.

Voices in revelry echoed in the passageway, and the wall to which the ladder was attached shook with the pounding of feet dancing to wild music and singing. Gibron whispered something to him, but he could not hear. He continued downward until he heard the trap door mechanism creak into operation. He froze as light flooded up into the secret passage from below.

Gibron motioned impatiently to Tralane. "Hurry up, I said," the mage reiterated, crouching by the trap door. "Go on down. If there are any servants in the room, they'll be wondering why I'm coming down from the attic. Subdue them, quickly."

Tralane slid down the remaining portion of the ladder and fell into the room. His muscular frame absorbed the impact without injury.

A woman servant was standing by the cauldron, wide-eyed and open-mouthed. Tralane rushed towards her and knocked her head against the wall before she could scream. A male servant was snoring in a corner, and his slumber was deepened by a blow from a stoking poker.

Gibron came down gingerly. He pressed the panel on the wall that sent the ladder extension back up and closed the trap door. Then he walked stiffly to the serving maid lying unconscious against the wall.

"Did I ever tell you this place was once an old king's summer residence?" Gibron asked airily as he inspected the woman's head. "The secret room did not serve him when his time came, though. His belongings fell into the hands of common folk like Rimskiel and his wife. Rimskiel handles the place well, probably puts it to better use than that king ever did. History takes many strange turns, don't you think?" Gibron sighed and pulled some leaves out of his pack, and applied them to the woman's forehead. "You didn't have to hit her so hard, did you?"

Tralane threw Gibron an exasperated look. "You talk of history now? And why does the girl matter, when her master will probably take great joy in roasting me with his other meats, if he ever catches me?"

Gibron laid the girl's head on a pile of rags. Then he hurried to the door, placed his ear against it, and turned to Tralane.

"I was merely commenting on your new position in life, Tralane. You've gained power, and ruin often follows in the wake of power. Even Keepers pay for their privileges, if they can't learn to maintain the Balance. It is not wise to abuse your place in the center of Being by hurting those who are not your enemies."

"Yes, yes, I'm a heartless knave. Tell me about it tomorrow. Right now, let's get to safety, so you can begin your lessons on morality."

Just then the door opened, sweeping Gibron aside. Rimskiel walked in, talking to a servant.

"When the King's man comes, just show him the way up the attic," he was saying. "There might be some spell work or blood, so leave this room as soon as he goes up, and tell the others to stay away. But don't forget to take the money—"

Rimskiel stopped in mid-stride as he noticed Tralane. He whirled about in time to see Gibron closing the door behind him.

"You?" he cried out indignantly, turning back to Tralane with a look of menace clouding his face. "They sent you to capture the old one? But where are your men, and what are you doing in those clothes?" He reared up to his full height and balled his hands into fists. "Are you trying to cheat me out of my reward for the old one, as well as of my wife?"

Tralane coolly took in the innkeeper's apparent betrayal of Gibron as if he had been expecting it. What disturbed him was his entrapment in a double's identity. A mage like Gibron could understand the subtleties of existence and accept Tralane. Marzen might know him by his dissimilarity to the original she loved. But Rimskiel's hatred was indiscriminate. Reason would not satisfy the innkeeper, and the bard was limited in playing out his role as Detrexan. He was not in the Golden King's service, so he had no gold to offer as reward and buy his way out of the situation. Nor did he fully know the intricacies of the relationships in which he was enmeshed, so he could not play on weaknesses that might otherwise have saved him. Somehow, Tralane had stripped himself of his identity in coming to Fargouet. He was naked, imprisoned by physical appearances, and caught without the words that would sway Rimskiel.

Gibron broke in, his quavering voice harsh with rage. "You scum," he spat, his eyes and veins standing out. "You would betray me? Can even a simple peasant not be trusted in this world?"

Rimskiel smiled and said, still looking at Tralane, "We are not so simple as you seem to think. We don't live in cities or frequent the court of the Golden King, but we know the value of coins. And we are not so ignorant as to let other men steal our wives."

"Then perhaps you would like to feel what happens when fools play with life, in their delusions of power." Gibron raised his boney arms in preparation for the unleashing of sorcery.

"No!" Tralane shouted. "Remember Sagamourin's searching spells. You'll give us away."

"We've already been betrayed. It's only a matter of time before they, too, arrive."

"But we've still got a chance."

Gibron stopped, his mouth open as if about to speak. Rimskiel glanced back and forth at them. His face was still red with anger, but his motions were confused.

Tralane slipped of his pack and threw it at Rimskiel, then lunged for a meat knife that was lying on the table by the hearth. The servant who had entered the room with Rimskiel went after Tralane, but the bard reached the knife first and flashed it in the servant's face. The servant backed away, but Tralane came after him, brushed aside his outstretched hands, and planted the knife in his throat. Blood spurted out, covering Tralane's face and hands.

A cry pierced through the background noise made up by tavern-goers, but Tralane did not know if it came from the main hall or the room they were in. Blood clouded his perceptions. He looked for Rimskiel and saw him advancing. Tralane stepped back until his back struck the side of the hearth and he could go no further. Rimskiel charged, yelling inarticulately, and Tralane crouched, watching his opponent's arms close in on him like avalanches from two directions.

The heat from the fire scorched the back of his legs, and quickened his mind. He reached into the hearth and pulled out a burning log with his left hand. Gritting his teeth against the pain of the flames that had licked his fingers, Tralane tossed the wood into Rimskiel's face. The innkeeper stumbled; the twin avalanches of his arms hesitated. Tralane gripped the knife with both hands and lunged once again, this time sending the blade its full length into Rimskiel's stomach.

Rimskiel closed his arms around Tralane as the bard twisted the knife. Warm blood soaked his torso, arms and legs. Life pulsed rhythmically into his hands. For a few moments, the bard and the innkeeper were face to face. They looked at each other, into each other, with nothing but life and death separating them. In the darkness of Rimskiel's eyes, Tralane saw the reflection of his face and gasped in shock. Then Rimskiel collapsed. The strength evaporated from his arms and legs and he fell to the floor, dead.

Tralane leaned back against the side of the hearth, breathing hard and staring at the ceiling to focus his eyes back on the real world. Though he had served with armies and was accustomed to death, he had never killed a man in close combat with his bare hands. The bow was his weapon, the arrow his instrument of death, and a line of stout men-at-arms his armor against retaliation. He avoided looking at Rimskiel's body.

His left hand was burned. Though it was only a minor wound, it was painful enough to prevent him from using his favored weapon. He cursed as he felt blood trickling down his limbs, and remembered the look in Rimskiel's eyes as death had stolen the light from them.

"Who cried out?" he asked with a tremor. "I heard someone cry out..."

"It was you," the mage replied, perplexed. "Are you all right? I thought you had seen action before. I thought you were a warrior, but you're still only a boy."

Gibron clamped a firm hand around Tralane's forearm and led him to the door. He returned the bard's pack to him, then tied the pouch with the Eye around Tralane's neck.

"I only hope nobody comes in to investigate the noise. I should think these people are used to strange happenings in the back rooms."

Once again, Gibron put his ear to the door and listened for nearby revelers. Then he opened the door slightly, glanced through the crack, and motioned for Tralane to follow him. They stepped out into the main hall, where Gibron quietly slipped a cloak off a hook and handed it to Tralane. Marzen saw them through the crowd from her station by the ale kegs, and sliced her way through masses and ushered them into a curtained alcove.

"I tried to go up and warn you," she said in a hurried whisper, looking from one to the other, "but Rimskiel wouldn't let me out of his sight. I only found out last night, after I left you. He plans to betray you. The guards are coming tonight. I'll try to delay them as long as I can—"

She broke off suddenly as she glimpsed the blood covering Tralane's clothes through a part in the cloak. He had already wiped his face and hands clean on the lining.

"Gods," she croaked, "what happened?"

"Your husband is dead," Gibron informed her coldly. "He tried to stop us and Tralane killed him. We must go now. Do whatever you can to slow down pursuit." The mage turned to leave the alcove, still holding on to Tralane.

Marzen stared absently at the curved wall of the alcove, her face a pale blank. "What will I do now?" she asked of no one in particular. "He's dead . . . how can I run the place myself . . . they'll have me like a serving maid . . ."

Tralane, still shaken from his battle, reached out and pulled her after him. "Come with us. You'll be safe. We'll escape."

"Escape? How can I? Can I?"

She followed them out, still in a daze.

The three pushed their way through the tavern crowd, but not so hastily as to attract attention. Somewhere behind them a tray was overturned, and voices were raised in anger. Tralane asserted his remaining strength in helping Gibron lead the way to the tavern door, grateful for the momentary distraction.

Despite their precautions, a pair of men who had turned at the sound of the tray spilling had taken notice of them and were now following. Eyes flicked uncertainly over the room as people sensed something amiss, but were not quite sure of the source of trouble.

"Speed is everything now," Gibron said as he opened the tavern door and rushed out. Tralane, hunched over in his cloak, did not dare look up. But he saw by the shadows in the street that this world also had two moons and that both of them had risen. The knowledge was small comfort.

They rushed up the street to a stable. Tralane found the owner looking over some thorts for signs of injury and tried to bring him down. They scuffled in a flurry of dust and straw until Gibron grabbed a length of wood and ended the fight with a blow on the proprietor's head. Tralane glanced with surprise at the old man. Gibron's smile was thin.

"You shouldn't let appearance deceive you," he said, discarding his makeshift weapon. "An old mage has had time to learn many disciplines, including those which can draw strength from an aged body."

Tralane was impressed by Gibron's calm. There was strength in Gibron, as there had been in Mathi, but his new-found companion seemed better grounded in the problems and feelings of daily living.

The bard brought out three thorts and saddled them while Marzen and Gibron kept watch. Then they mounted and rode out of the stable towards the edge of town. Marzen glanced furtively behind them and gave a small warning cry. A band of men had just left the tavern and were running towards the stable.

"I fear we've been discovered," she said, her voice wavering in the winds of confusion.

"Then we'd best ride hard," Tralane responded. He took out Wyden's Eye in preparation for the ride through the door between worlds.

Gibron held up his hand and stopped, listening to the night. Marzen and Tralane followed his example. They had reached the outskirts of the town. The buildings were small and makeshift compared to the sturdier frame and stone structures they had just left behind. Ahead of them lay a long, rolling plain of grasslands where, not too far off, could be seen a sleeping herd of shui illuminated by twin moons. Beyond them, the faint trace of a mountain range outlined against a star-pricked sky could be seen. The great cities and empires of the world lay behind that distant barrier. But between the mountains and the last straggling shanty that could be claimed by the town, on the road that wandered in and out of sight, depending on the roll of the plain, a band of dark shapes was moving.

"The King's warriors," Gibron exclaimed. He bowed his head. "By all the gods and demons, Tralane, if I knew nothing of the arts, I would still say some death-laden curse follows you, throwing your past sins across our path."

Angry shouts rose up behind them. The men from the tavern had discovered the senseless stable owner and were rushing out of the barn. Some ran back to the tavern, calling for their friends, while others drew swords and knives and came down the street after Tralane and his escorts. The night breeze carried oaths and threats, and the name of Detrexan.

"We're caught between two swords," Tralane cried out. He reached for his bow, but the pain in his hand reminded him of its uselessness.

Gibron dismounted. "Then it is time to show these worms the meaning of power," he said harshly.

"But your fight will be doomed," Tralane protested. "There's still time. We can take to the fields and use the Eye before the warriors cut us off."

Gibron the Mage looked small and weak beside his thort, and it seemed incredible that he had been able to move and strike with swiftness and strength. The last stroke of betrayal had drained him of his vitality. Pale resignation relaxed the firm lines of purpose on his brow.

"No," Gibron replied. He stripped himself of his garments and stood naked, bathing in the light of the moons and stars. Protruding bones cast angular shadows across his torso. "My fate no longer matters. This will be my last battle. Perhaps it will allow you to escape and pursue your destiny. But I will die. I have been betrayed for the last time. Let the gods, the fates, the movers of the universe do what they may—I have had enough."

Gibron knelt on the dirt road and began to chant in a language that had never been meant for the human throat. Yet Gibron spoke the alien sounds with apparent ease, and Tralane felt the air shiver and tremble with the power of those words.

The bard tried to break through Gibron's concentration, exhorting the mage not to surrender his life. "What do these people matter? Don't let them destroy you ... there's still time ... yes, there is ... you said you'd be my guide ... I need a guide, I need someone—"

The broken phrases were lost on Gibron, and the pounding of hoofs and the clatter of armor drowned his words as the Golden King's warriors approached.

They were charging up the road, their mounts panting

and snorting. Cloaks flew out behind them, and their armor and weapons glinted coldly in the night's meager light. These were not mere adventurers or mercenaries, but warriors with a stake in the Golden King's empire. They were mortal men who had been sent to flush out a mage, blind to the dangers of the task and eager only for the rewards of advancement in the ranks.

Yet for all their eagerness, they were not the first to reach Tralane and his group. The vanguard of the town mob that was spilling into the streets were already circling the bard, trying to drag him down from his thort. Tralane kicked his mount's flanks and charged into his attackers, but strong hands grabbed his legs and he was quickly brought down. He cursed and flailed out, gouging and kicking at his opponents even as they beat him with clubs, fists, and the flats of their swords. The amulet was struck from his hand. Pain stabbed him in his back, groin, and head. His injured hand throbbed with the racing beat of his heart as some of his assailants tried to pin and tie up his hands and feet. He heard Marzen scream as shadows began to draw over his eyes.

Tralane hovered between the twisted nightmare-reality that had engulfed him and the darkness of dreamless sleep. Slowly, blackness crept into his mind, swallowing his thoughts and his will to survive. Then the earth trembled as if a god's fist were striking it in anger, and people shouted out warnings and abandoned their beating of Tralane. He ceased his convulsive struggles as hands released him. He fought back the encroaching oblivion, remembering the amulet, Marzen, and Gibron. The image of Wyden's Eye burned through his closed eyes; when he opened them he found the amulet to be only a few arm's lengths away. Oblivious to the events occurring around him, he crawled forward until the amulet was firmly in his grasp again. His strength seeped back into his body until he was able to stand. He steadied himself, fighting the pain in his head and eyes, and surveyed the area.

He seemed to be in the quiet heart of a storm. Townsfolk were running towards their homes, pursued by a few warriors yelling taunts and brandishing their swords. Several bodies were strewn on the ground, crushed and battered beyond recognition. The King's warriors had charged the crowd and dispersed them, saving Tralane and his party.

A wave of gratitude towards his saviors broke against the hard shoals of the reality he saw next. Gibron was still kneeling in the middle of the road, but he was not alone. The Golden King's warriors had surrounded him and were nervously circling him. The last sounds of the fleeing townsmen diminished, leaving the night silent except for the groans of some of the wounded and injured and the hesitant steps of fearful kruushkas.

One of the warriors urged his mount forward, and the others watched his approach intently. Some cried out while others contended with their panicking mounts when their comrade was annihilated in an explosive flash of light. A dark, boiling cloud rose and dissipated slowly into the night.

"Get away, he's spell-working," one of the warriors shouted. The red and gold plumes emerging from his helm and the tassels on his saddle marked him as the troop's captain. "Let Those-Who-Search come and do our work for us. We'll collect our due for flushing him out."

Tralane opened his mouth to warn Gibron, but stopped as he realized that the mage could no longer hear him. Surrounded by forces of invisible magic, the mage was beyond the reach of mere mortals. Still, Tralane cautiously approached the mage, hoping to be of some help.

A woman's voice calling his name stopped his advance. He scanned the ground and saw Marzen lying by the road between the town and the warriors. Her head was bloodied and her leg was twisted into an unnatural position. She called to him again, between sobs, and he ran to her.

He knelt beside her and gently felt her injuries. She could no longer walk; indeed, if she survived the night, she would be a cripple for the rest of her life. Escape for her, Tralane realized with a surge of nausea, was impossible.

"Tralane . . . please, help me . . ." she croaked.

Tralane was at a loss to comfort her. His own pain and confusion tripped his thoughts and tongue. He could only stroke her face with his useless left hand and look on. "It will be all right in a while," he said lamely.

The sound of a footfall behind him made Tralane whirl around, expecting to see the edge of a sword streaking toward his head. Instead, he saw the captain of the troop standing over him, his sword sheathed. Tralane stared up at the captain's face, seeing something familiar in it, something he had seen and studied before in pools on cool spring days. Then recognition struck him like the sword he had been expecting—the man who stood so close, who was staring with such concern at Marzen and ignoring the bard, was the perfect image of Tralane.

"Marzen," his twin said, crouching beside Tralane and lifting the woman's head. "Gods, but what are you doing here? This wasn't in the plan, you should have stayed in town. Where's Rimskiel? I was hoping to slip in and out of town quietly, but I find a mob and a wizard waiting for me on the road. What happened?"

Marzen did not answer. Her eyes darted back and forth between her lover and Tralane. Her lips twitched, forming soundless words. She moved her head towards Tralane, then sobbed, her face breaking into a mask of pain. Finally, she sank back into the captain's arms.

Tralane stood and backed away a few steps. An eerie silence had descended over the road. The wounded were no longer crying out, and the warriors had dismounted and allowed their kruushkas to maintain a tolerable distance. They were arrayed in a wide circle around Gibron, who had stopped his chanting and was simply rocking back and forth, head down and arms in the air. He was oblivious to the actions of men and had isolated himself in a semi-globe of glowing light. Now was the moment for Tralane to make his escape good, but he could not bring himself to move. He was staring at his twin.

The captain placed Marzen's head on the ground and

then stood. He frowned, then glanced up at the bard, surprised at seeing someone so near.

"Detrexan," Tralane said simply, as a way of greeting.

"How did you know—" his twin began defensively, and stopped abruptly.

A flood of questions entered Tralane's mind as the two faced each other. Did this double have his manner of walking and talking, or was the man a stranger in more profound ways? He wanted to talk with this man, to find out if their histories matched, if they had the same hopes and dreams. Did Detrexan know the identity of their mutual parents? A longing came over Tralane for the warmth and closeness of a friendship he had never been able to hold with anyone he had ever met.

But Detrexan's eyes widened with terror, not curiosity. Tralane's clothes were doused in blood, and his face was cut and bruised with the beating he had taken. He was a perverse reflection of his own physical appearance.

"Demon!" the captain screamed, drawing his double-edged sword from its sheath. "The mage has summoned demons to replace us! Beware, look out for yourselves."

Tralane backed quickly away, having no sword to parry Detrexan's attack. He turned and ran towards an unattended kruushka. Detrexan followed him with long, purposeful strides, holding his sword high for the kill. Tralane stumbled over a body as he looked over his shoulder, fell, and rolled, trying to crawl away from his pursuer. The captain waved his troop off as he caught up to Tralane and sent his sword whistling down at the bard. Tralane twisted away but felt the edge nick his right arm. In desperation, he lashed out with his leg and tripped Detrexan, knocking him off balance. He heard a thud as the captain fell, and then a gurgling sound. But before he could see what had happened, a tremor shook the earth so violently that all the warriors were thrown to the ground. Tralane buried his face in the soil and cringed as an inhuman roar deafened him.

The roar was continuous, like an angry storm wind that refused to die. Its unrelenting savagery forced Tralane deeper into the ground, until he thought he would bury himself. After a while, when he had become accustomed to the din, he turned his head sideways, expecting to see Detrexan's men mustering their company and coming at him.

Instead, he saw that the world had been cast into utter darkness. The moons and stars were gone, and he could not even see his own hand that gripped the earth next to his face. His eyes searched desperately for some hold on reality, until he found Gibron in his dome of light. Yet, as he studied the mage, he found this was not the reassuring sight he had been seeking.

The mage's mouth was twitching spasmodically and his eyes were bulging. If he was screaming, his voice was lost in the roar. Around his globe of light darted intangible, wraithlike figures which defied the cohesive focus of human sight. They splashed against the mage's light; with every strike they weakened the shield. The Golden King's sorcerous allies, Those-Who-Search, had found their quarry and were tightening their circle around Gibron. The light grew fainter and the wraiths more numerous until, at last, Gibron could no longer be seen. The darkness was total, consuming even the roaring sound. There was no final cry from Gibron, nor any calls from the flattened warriors or the injured. Tralane at last gave up the struggle to remain conscious and allowed the darkness to envelop him, also.

It was still night when Tralane awoke. Star Speaker had set and the half-full Wanderer was making its way towards the horizon through the clear night. Tralane turned over on his back and welcomed the sight of stars and the peace of a natural night. His hand touched something metallic, and he shifted his gaze to see Detrexan beside him, his armor still bright and an edge of his sword buried in his throat. Tralane grunted in shock and sat up.

Bodies were stretched out across the road and surrounding fields like dead carcasses. Down the road, the town's doors and windows were shut tight against the events that had recently transpired. Gibron was nowhere to be seen, though Marzen was still by the roadside, unconscious but breathing steadily. A few kruushkas were grazing or sleeping in the fields.

Tralane rose to his feet and held his head to stop it from spinning. He was still holding the amulet in his hand, though his fingers ached as he relaxed his locked muscles. He could not find his pack, though his bow and quiver had survived. He gathered his weapons and headed for the kruushkas without delay.

He passed Marzen and began to sing a lament, remembering another he had passed without such consideration. He sang to escape the unfulfilled plans he had made for the both of them, but his efforts opened the way for sadder thoughts. The song stayed with him as his stride became steadier, and he was soon mounting a kruushka and urging the beast forward. He touched Wyden's Eye in the way he had been taught, and it was not long before the first changes—a shifting of some stars, the gradual appearance of clouds, a subtle change in the mountain range outline ahead of him—occurred. He entered this new world singing the lament, hoping soon the period of remorse would pass and he would forget. But even as he rode, he perceived the ghosts from his past flickering in and out of sight at the edge of his vision, following him as carrion-eaters follow the dying in the wastelands, goading him on even as the future taunted him with its unpromising vastness.

Chapter 7

The mountain stream's water stung his wounds and numbed his flesh, but Tralane did not mind. He continued to swim back and forth between the two banks, letting the calm of valley and the brisk current soothe his body and troubled mind. He stopped beneath an overhanging tree and watched a school of tiny, red and gold fish dart through his legs. Then he submerged and crawled upstream along the bed, studying the pebbles as if they were gems of knowledge. He grabbed a handful of stones, surfaced and climbed up on the bank on which his kruushka was contentedly grazing. Without bothering to dress, for his tattered clothes had still not dried from the wash he had given them, Tralane collapsed wearily onto the grass and spread the stones before him.

The mountain air chilled him as a breeze blew down from a high pass, and the grass caressed him. But the pattern he was laying out distracted him from the elements. On the previous night, while crossing over from Fargouet's unhappy world to his present locale, the bard had taken to staring at the sky. He had been praying, silently, to whatever gods were looking down, for deliverance from the curse that seemed to hang over him and which Gibron had sensed. He had found, instead of answers and aid, yet another mystery. The stars had moved.

Cuelon the Slayer had crumbled before his eyes. The Door to Heaven was warped beyond recognition—only the key star Dothos remained to show him where all sacrifices and incantations had passed on their journeys to the gods. Mophos taming the kruushkas, Alysis herding the shui, the goddess-star Aralaela guiding sailors to land, Wyd Win weeping in atonement for his brother CuChani's treachery—all these symbols of the world in which he had been raised had dissipated into the vast night. Mathi's teachings were useless; even the little magic Tralane remembered would not work if he were not secure in his knowledge of the forces and influences around him.

With each crossing Tralane made, Wyden's Eye took him farther away from his own familiar universe. The subtle changes were accumulating into drastic differences. Gibron's assumption that Tralane had no control over his journey had turned out to be unpleasantly true, and the ramifications—that he had no gods to call on, no spirits to comfort him—were only now becoming apparent. The soil he rested on was alien, as was the grass, the trees around him, the birds and sky above. The gods had not witnessed his birth on this world, if indeed they had done so on his own. But at least he belonged on his home world. Here, he was truly alone, with not even a pebble or a handful of soil to care for him. Mathi had taught him that the power of sorcery was in the merging of oneself with the world. The greater the understanding of the world and the self, the more formidable the power gained. Tralane had no understanding, no power, not even identity.

The urge to leap back into the stream, to breathe the water in, and to let the stream take him made his limbs tremble momentarily. He closed his eyes, shutting out the ancient, now nonexistent star patterns he had laid down with the stones. He breathed deeply, sucking in air instead of water, and allowed himself an ironic smile as the compulsion subsided. The water he had hoped to join, even the air he enjoyed instead, was a stranger to his being.

Death would not make him any more a child of this world than living.

He was nothing more than a vagabond orphan to the gods, and so his prayers for guidance went unanswered. He was an unknown element to the waters of this world, so the rites of absolution he had performed in the stream had washed him of only physical stains. The bloodshed he had caused in Fargouet and Agathom's camp was still with him, seeping deeper into his being, untouched by forgiveness.

He resolved never to use the Eye again. He had strayed far from the usual sources of comfort he relied upon in moments of crisis. Also, the vegetation and land formation had changed beyond the range of familiarity, following the transformation of the heavens. The further he drifted from his native reality, the more disoriented he would become.

Tralane began to reason that perhaps it was Wyden's Eye that was cursed and not himself. He regretted the rash theft that had launched him on his current path, but, after all, it had been a necessary act for his survival. The vision of adventure that had struck him in Agathom's camp no longer blinded him. Now all that mattered was peace, security, and the firm rule of the gods. Better never to act again than to have his desires warped out of shape and his actions loaded with unforeseen repercussions by sorcery he could not fully control.

So if he settled on this world, he would need a new purpose in life to protect him from his own frailties and inadequacies that had brought him to Agathom's camp to begin with. If he had learned the spells and incantations of his own world, he could just as well be tutored in the ways of the gods in his present home. A few years as an acolyte in a priesthood would teach him all he needed to know. With the judicious sale of the Eye, his knowledge would be put to good use. He would build a temple in some remote area where visitors were infrequent and unwelcome, dedicating it to a forgiving god, and there

spend the rest of his days in isolated worship and medi-
tation.

A simple life harbored no evil or, as the Karthasian
saying went, a shadowless sword did not shed blood. His
life from that moment on would be free of shadows and
blood. Plots, court intrigues, even the glory of archery in
a king's army, were all pleasure of the past. A place would
be set aside for him. Once he was rid of Wyden's Eye
and its interfering curse, he would be able to lose himself
in the intricacies of an idyllic spiritual existence, dedi-
cated to the service of a god who must, if accepting his
worship, accept him. Satisfied that because his dreams
had changed, he had transformed himself from a burdened
knave to a free and noble spirit, Tralane abandoned
thought.

He let his mind wander, releasing his heart from the
tight confines of plans for the future and trusting that
restless part of his being to find its own answers to the
questions and problems troubling him. He listened to the
strange bird calls and hummed along with the stream's
bubbling song. He drifted into the shifting seas of sensation, relaxing, absorbing the new, and carefully savoring
the different, secure in the knowledge that he would belong,
once he had mastered the proper disciplines and ceremonies.

Detecting something familiar but almost imperceptible,
Tralane struggled out of his half-dreaming, half-waking
state and clutched at the fleeting memory. Musical notes,
hauntingly evocative. When he had wrestled them into
the light of awareness, he cried out weakly. The song was
a lament, the voice Gibron's.

Cursing, he sat up and glanced nervously about. Everything was as it had been. The kruushka stared at him for
a moment, curious, then resumed grazing. He could still
see the school of fish, darting from one end of a backwater
eddy to another, moving as one. The pouch containing
Wyden's Eye caught his attention; for a moment he considered dropping the amulet into the water. He would be

rid of it, as he had wanted to be rid of himself. He did not move to act on his impulse.

Sighing with disgust, Tralane rose and, prompted by the sudden awareness of irritating sensations, examined his body. His skin was broken in many places, the cracks filled with blood dried black. Purple blotches marked deeper sources of pain. Even the scar on his right shoulder, which he considered Mathi's gift to him, was sore.

Old wounds never heal, he remembered bitterly—another thought someone else had said more eloquently, though probably less pithily, in some proverb or other. And again he thought of Mathi, but this time without so many of the recriminations that had colored his previous recollections. The curiosity of his childhood returned with all its fresh inquisitiveness, directed at Mathi.

What had made the old one adopt him, out of all the foundlings he must have been offered in his life? Was Tralane a nobleman's son who had forfeited his rightful place on some tottering throne because of his abandonment of Mathi? Or was he some unwanted child taken from doomed peasants? Certainly there were many reasons why parents would have wanted their child to be sent away with a wizard going into a retreat during the chaotic Karthasian civil wars. In those days, with gods, wizards, and mortals battling for supremacy, the future was not something to be counted on. Had Mathi known his parents and taken the child in as a favor in their memory? If so, why had he never spoken to Tralane about them? Was Mathi even still alive? Did some old wound hurt him as well as Tralane, or was the bard's disappearance from the wizard's life the first real brush with another's feelings he had ever experienced?

Once the flood was loosed, he could not hold back the questions that had gnawed at him during his childhood. The boiling inferno that had seared his emotions growing up, turned his love to anger and distrust, now bubbled over the rim of his soul. The tight lid he had kept on that cauldron—his stories, his minor competencies in archery and intrigue, and his wanderlust—crumbled into meaningless fragments. There was no one to catch the overflow. He had run away from Mathi. Gibron was dead, and Marzen was crippled or also dead. There was a tiny, weeping figure, mourning the loss of the mighty Oram, huddled over the giant's smoldering ashes. He had done nothing and received the same in kind.

Tralane wanted to cry, alone in the wilderness and for the first time knowing what it was to be alone, realizing that solitude was not a condition of the present but a product of the past. Even the gods, had they been there, would have been cold comfort. After all, they were immortal, encased in eternity. The twitchings of human feelings were incomprehensible to those who were not bracketed between life and death. The gods and spirits of any world were, in the final perspective, immune to understanding, much less comforting and forgiving the petty lives of humanity.

But Tralane did not give in to despair. If he had asked no questions, there would be no need for answers. Yet his very existence was a question, so he could not believe there were no answers. He did not cry. He looked, instead, to the mountains around him. Among them he saw the stranger, riding down to meet him.

His reaction was instantaneous. He ran to where he had left his bow and quiver and quickly strung an arrow. Disdaining clothes, he retreated from the camp by the stream and hid in a cluster of trees. On the rim of the cluster, the kruushka tugged on its reins, which were firmly tied around the base of a trunk. The animal could not set itself free and did not seem to want to exert itself, so it settled down for a rest. Meanwhile, the stranger had disappeared into the cover of the forest that blanketed the mountains. Tralane followed the example of his mount, sitting down to wait, patient, almost happy, for the real and physical danger to make itself manifest.

The remainder of the day passed uneventfully. Evening began to close in. Enough time had gone by to consider it safe to come out of hiding. Then Tralane heard a noise behind him.

Tralane fell forward, rolled, and came up on his knees with an arrow a finger away from being loosed. The pain in his hand was unbearable, yet he did not release the arrow. He realized the stranger had maneuvered behind him, caught him of guard, and that those who practiced such stealth rarely had good intentions. Instincts cried for violence. But the nature of his antagonist penetrated his reason and instincts and dampened his will. He dropped his weapon.

The stranger was not made of flesh, as he had assumed, but rather resembled nothing less than an animated jewel, man-sized and cut to human proportions. The stone surface of the chest rose and fell in a mocking imitation of breathing. Fault lines beneath were throbbing, like veins and arteries carrying blood. And the eyes were cold, many-faceted rubies, set with malevolent purpose in the bald, humorless face of the shimmering green warrior.

An object struck the ground near Tralane's feet. A few moments had to trickle by before the sound registered in the bard's mind. When he finally recognized that the stranger had given him something, he could only stare at the object.

By the time the stranger had dismounted from his strangely shaped thort—it was taller and more muscular than the mounts he was familiar with, though not as massive as a kruushka, and its eyes glistened with intelligence—Tralane had finally seized the meaning of the object at his feet. It was his pack, which he had thought lost on Farguet's world. Oram's white furs squeezed against the netting, protecting the bard's supplies.

"Where did you find it?" In his amazement Tralane forgot the usual amenities exchanged by strangers in the wilderness.

"Where you left it," the stranger replied coldly. His voice was as hard as his body, filled with long, sharp edges which cut at the expression of a simple word.

"Who are you?" Tralane asked in low tones.

"I am a warrior, the Jade Warrior." His answer was condescending, hostile.

"In whose service?"

"One who watches over you."

The stranger's intimidating presence was forgotten momentarily as a host of fearful implications overshadowed Tralane.

"Who watches over me?" Tralane stuttered in a panic. "Who? Is it Agathom? Are you one of his—how could you follow when I have the amulet? The Sorcerer King? I had nothing to do with him. I didn't know Gibron, I only met him in the attic. How could you follow? Are you a god? Have the gods, has Pichen-ma-thele, sent you to bring me back? Are you a guide? Please, tell me, who is watching?"

The Jade Warrior laughed, and his laughter was like the clashing of angry swords on a warm summer's day. The sharp edges of his skin rippled back and forth across his body, like the folds and creases of ordinary flesh, as he walked towards Tralane. His sword's black scabbard, inlaid with a series of complex, interlocking golden runes, tinkled against his leg. He stopped an arm's length away from the bard.

The Warrior's eyes were blank, inhumanly deep pits, level with Tralane's. They were both similar in height and build, but though Tralane's search was desperate, there was no resemblance in the Warrior's frozen, emotionless face to Detrexan's visage. The Warrior was too unlike anything that had ever lived to be recognizable as another aspect of Tralane.

They stood facing one another for a while, and neither broke the silence which bound them together. The Jade Warrior did not betray any thoughts or feelings. Tralane did not think to mask his confusion and fear.

Once again Tralane was reduced to helplessness in the face of his own actions. The theft of Wyden's Eye, the abandonment of his world to the Sorcerer King, the deaths in the recent and distant past, both of his direct and indirect doing, spread around him like a vast and devastated plain of isolation. Without action, without plans and schemes for the future which served merely to bury the past, he was a broken, pillaged fortress, useless in his vulnerability. The Jade Warrior had appeared like a grave marker, sealing off Tralane's return to the living world. He had nowhere to go for refuge in illusion.

"I am your companion, Tralane," the Jade Warrior said at last, after their shadows had moved into and merged with the encroaching night. "But of course, you know that."

Tralane slowly picked up his pack and shuffled back to the camp. He did not look behind him, knowing the Jade Warrior was soundlessly following him. His breath escaped through slack lips to form momentary clouds of frosty moisture. He shivered as he put on his clothes and broke out Oram's furs to warm himself for the night. Despite the cold, his wounds and bruises were not numb. Indeed, they burned and ached all the more, reminding him of the fragility of his flesh. For some reason, as he curled into a ball to ward off the night, the sight of the Warrior standing in the starlight by the stream set the scar on his right shoulder flaring in agony.

Chapter 8

They rode together silently, Tralane's kruushka still not accustomed to the Jade Warrior's unearthly presence as it occasionally shook its head and snorted in protest or stumbled with nervousness. Tralane had been equally disturbed during the night, his sleep tortured with the dreams that had haunted him in Rimskiel's attic. This time, however, the nameless, devouring demons had merged into one creature, endlessly pursuing yet always allowing the prey to escape the final doom of death. The teasing game between past and present was now being played between Tralane and the Jade Warrior.

The game continued into wakefulness. The Jade Warrior had been standing where Tralane had seen him last, by the stream, when the bard awoke. The morning meal was finished uneventfully, the only unusual behaviors being their mutual silence and the Jade Warrior's refusal to eat. He merely stood, to the side and slightly behind Tralane as the bard ate, staring at a mountainside. His brooding, self-contained demeanor had ruined Tralane's appetite. Nausea turned his stomach, weakness made his limbs tremble. The bard's thoughts ran into each other, producing an incoherent jumble of words, ideas and emotions that occasionally bordered on hysteria. He felt as he had in Agathom's camp, only this time there was no escape from the source. The Jade Warrior was wrapped in potent sorcery which, along with his manner of hostility contained by an attitude of condescension, prolonged Tralane's journey through uneasy dreams into day.

The bard had continued following the course he had taken when he first entered the mountains, picking his way through a winding trail of passes and valleys. As the sun rose, Tralane's patience shortened. There were no signs of settlements, and he was anxious to find human company, hoping the familiarity of a crowded tavern would help diminish the Jade Warrior's effect. He decided finally to break the silence between them and ask his companion for directions to the nearest habitation.

"Anxious to see another mortal, Tralane?" the Jade Warrior asked with obvious amusement. "I would have thought your preference to lean more towards isolated temples and mumbled prayers to archaic gods."

Tralane's surprise at the Warrior's knowledge of his recent fantasy turned to anger. Heedless about arousing the Warrior, he answered sarcastically, "Mortals at least make better company than stone gods."

"But at least stone gods don't die as easily as mortals when they are in your blessed presence, eh?" The Jade Warrior smiled, and his dagger-teeth were as red as his eyes. "If we keep following this trail, we will meet a river. If we follow the river downstream, we will come upon a village."

"How do you know? Have you been here before?"

"You asked me because I am a creature of sorcery, having access to knowledge you do not. You were right. I do not need to have been in a place before to know it."

It was not long before they found the river.

The water tumbled from the mountains on their right, gaining momentum as it surged down the length of the valley. Deep in the mountains a cloud of mist marked a spectacular waterfall. Downstream from where Tralane and his companion stood, a flock of white- and blue-feathered birds, whose great wings were like plains of snow and ice, frolicked in calmer waters. Overhead, a faint black dot circled. Another joined it, having launched itself from a mountain peak. Then the two dove straight down, towards the flock on the river, and they quickly became recognizable as sleek, dark hunting birds.

Screams of alarm greeted their arrival, and some of the flock managed to fly off. But the hunting pair were among them before most could free themselves of the water. Two piercing shrieks signaled the kills, and when the raid was over two limp, blood-stained forms hung from the talons of the attacking birds, who were returning to their mountain lair. Behind them, the flock wheeled away in the opposite direction, a harmless cloud blown away by a gust of cold wind.

"They, at least, are honest about their killing," the Jade Warrior commented. "They do not pretend to be other than what they are."

"They are animals," Tralane said flatly, dismissing the scene and urging the kruushka on.

"And what are you?"

Tralane turned his mount around and glared at the Warrior.

"Do not say you kill to survive, Tralane, for that, at least, would make you the equal of those you call animals. There are too many corpses on the road you've traveled to justify the bestowal of that title on you. And though you may pretend to be other than what you are, you lack the finer self-deceits that would make you fully human. You are a curious anomaly, young one, a strange new form of life destined to sink back into the mud that spawned you."

Tralane's rage grew to monumental proportions, filling him with recklessness. Yet fear opened a pit beneath his towering rage and swallowed it, even as he felt compelled to answer the Warrior's insults with blows. All his pride and indignation could not fill the bottomless cavern that had been created. The rent in the fabric of his being threatened to consume him.

"My bluntness does not please you? How unfortunate, considering the position you now find yourself in." The

Warrior's mount started forward, and the creature glided by the bard without a glance at him. "You see, I will not leave you. You have my company, whether you like it or not."

"And what if—" Tralane began to growl rebelliously.

"I would not try too hard, unless you've grown weary of what few pleasures you can appreciate."

Tralane caught up, but did not reply. They rode at a pace that served to preserve the kruushka's strength while the river, speaking its own language, rushed before them. The bard refused to look directly at his companion, satisfying himself with peering ahead to scout out the terrain while privately dwelling on the Jade Warrior's nature and origin.

Direct inquiry seemed inappropriate, considering the Warrior's aloofness and cutting remarks. Indirect reasoning and intuitive powers, talents the bard had always relied on in times of stress, were both disrupted by the thick, choking atmosphere of sorcery which followed the Warrior. Tralane could not understand his sensitivity to magic, since he had been raised with it. But then, perhaps the powers that had been awakened by Mathi in his pupil and which had consequently been rejected by Tralane after the grotesque monstrosity he had called back from the Dead had attacked him were being reawakened by the constant presence of the Eye and the Warrior. Working in tandem, they recreated Agathom's indomitable sorcerous influence. And the sorcery, like strong wine, clouded his mind.

However, his reaction did not explain where the Warrior, and indeed, where Wyden's Eye came from. The resurrection of an ancient fear of sorcery only served to complicate matters by involving the unanswerable question of his parentage in the general mystery. Events had taken a sudden, inexplicable turn. Uncertainty had always been a source of inspiration for new feats and adventures. The challenge to survive, no matter what the danger or cost to himself or others around him, was the only game he had ever considered potent enough to soothe and distract him from doubts founded on an unknown past. Now he was at a loss for a course of action. His resiliency was a weakness in the face of the implacable Jade Warrior; he sought, but could not find, the firm footing he needed for his struggle against this being. All the mysteries and their solutions were bound by the common thread of origin, and it was the answer to this question that Tralane had spent his years both in seeking and avoiding.

Out of the multiple ripples of frustration, a whirlpool of anger came into existence. As the morning bloomed into midday, the anger grew into a storm raging with darkness and blind fury, even while the sun shone brightly in Tralane's eyes. He had never experienced such anger; it was as if all the forgotten, dismissed, or denied moments of irritation or disappointment had been swept up from his past and hurled against the walls of his soul. No battle, no betrayal, no real or imagined wrong had ever sparked such deep and murderous hatred as that which he harbored in the presence of the Jade Warrior.

Consumed in the emotion, Tralane did not at first hear what was being said to him. He turned to the source of the words, to see the Warrior pointing ahead of them.

"Do you plan to ride calmly into the middle of a battle?"

The Warrior's words cleared the way for the sounds of men shouting to be heard. Tralane shook himself out of his revery and focused his eyes on the scene ahead of them. On the same bank of the river they were on, the bard could see over a hundred men engaged in a battle. They were armed with clubs and shields; some brandished spears, and a few waved swords in the air. Roughly half were dressed in red and black cloth kilts and black skin shirts, while the rest wore simple loincloths and had painted their torsos and faces with colorful runes. There were only a few casualties lying on the ground or hobbling to the edges of the battleground. The leaders of the two forces, recognizable by their elaborate head pieces and masks, seemed unwilling to commit their followers to a full melee. Instead, the two groups mingled and broke like two waves running into one another, waving their weapons more to ward each other off than to strike deliberately against an opponent's defenses. There were no archers, nor was there any cavalry waiting to charge down from the foothills. Elaborate curses and insults drifted into hearing in what was easily recognizable as the Sky Tongue.

Beyond the battle site, nestled between two hills which closed in to pinch the river's exit from the mountains out onto the plains beyond, lay a village of thatched huts, huddled on both sides of the bank. A string of figures, mostly elders and children, stood on the river bank, awaiting the outcome.

"Of course, if you like," the Jade Warrior continued, ignoring Tralane's questioning glance, "we could go in at a trot. They can't harm me, but you might sustain some additional injuries."

"Who is fighting?" Tralane asked, speaking simply instead of taking the chance that too many words might jumble his meaning into an expression of hate.

"The villagers—those red and black warriors—against some mountain tribe. They're still in the preliminary stages of battle. The true warriors, the clan magicians, haven't exposed themselves yet. They've been buried underground by both sides, and are awaiting their time. I suppose you'd like to stay here and see which side is winning before—"

With a swift motion that did not startle the Jade Warrior, but which did halt his speech, Tralane grabbed the pommel of the Warrior's sword and pulled it free of its scabbard. For a moment the two were frozen in motion, their mounts still, while men fought below. Tralane considered the sword, ran his appreciative eyes over the sharp, double edges, and sensed its sorcerous power pulsing against the palm of his hand. The pain from his wounds subsided, and the stiffness in his joints and muscles relaxed.

He met the Jade Warrior's eyes; for a moment he thought he had discovered a way to destroy him. But the Warrior's smile, arrogantly superior, dissuaded Tralane from trying the sword against its owner. No doubt the sword, whatever its qualities, would not harm its master, or the Warrior would not have allowed Tralane to take it from him so easily.

Instead, Tralane kicked his kruushka into a charge and held the sword poised over his head. He screamed out the Karthasian war cry, which he had learned in the Empire's service but had never had the opportunity to use, since he had never taken part in a charge. Now Tralane smashed his way into the heart of the battle without even a thought to his bow and arrows. Here, at last, was honest bloodletting to be done. His anger alone could turn back the hill tribe, and the villagers would no doubt have the greater resources with which to repay him for his service. Instinctively, he knew on which side he would fight.

The battle disintegrated at his approach. War chants and shouts were choked off, and a quiet descended over the field, broken only by the mild tumbling of the river waters over rocks and the exploding hoof beats of Tralane's kruushka. Through a haze of blood, he saw the incredulous expressions on the faces of warriors from both camps as he bore down on them. Even the leaders turned their attention away from each other, their terrifying masks and the ceremonial batons and spears they carried rendered absurd in the stillness. They watched him without knowing what to expect or what to do.

Only when Tralane was deep in their midst and had lopped off a hill tribeman's head with a smooth sweeping motion of his sword did the battle regain its vitality. However, recognizing the threat Tralane posed on the outcome, the hill warriors concentrated their efforts on bringing him down, even as the villagers abandoned their leader and rallied around the bard. The battle lost the mood of cautious, almost ritualistic combat and settled into an uncompromising death struggle. Tralane killed two more tribesmen before he was surrounded, and then he resorted to urging his kruushka into short charges and retreats while he twisted around in his saddle and hacked at his attackers with steady, rhythmic strokes.

His arm did not weary, as he had feared. The sword seemed to be keeping his strength up so that it could play out the only role it knew to perform. The shouts of the hillmen soon became cries of terror; instead of being surrounded by desperate enemies, Tralane found himself riding down fleeing warriors. The villagers followed him, finishing the wounded with swift blows from their clubs. He caught many of their glances as he searched for enemies to slay, and a distant part of him puzzled over their expressions of astonishment over what they found themselves doing.

Tralane knew now the battle rage that overcame the champions of the armies he had served in and fought against. He understood the satisfaction of wielding the terrible power of death, of crushing life with a blow, and of seeing a field muddy with blood and knowing he had caused the souls of men to flee into the House of the Dead, leaving only battered, broken corpses to appease his wrath. The path of war was revealed to him in all its glory.

He gave up the pursuit when most of the surviving tribesmen had crossed the river. They were joined by their magicians, who rose from the earth, glowering at Tralane, and together ran back towards the protecting mountains. Turning around in the saddle to survey the field, Tralane recalled the resentful jests warriors of his world made about archers. They were a cowardly lot, staying in the rear and picking off enemies from a distance, while refusing to join in the face-to-face work of combat. He laughed with them now, and shook his head disparagingly at the Tralane who played games of chance with death, yet was careful to change the rules to favor his survival. What wholesome satisfaction had he missed when, instead of partaking fully in joys of blood and death, he had hidden in the rear lines, protected by foot soldiers and horse, launching frail missiles that robbed him of seeing the instant his long blow fell. How much pleasure had he sacrificed, in both life and war, by maintaining a distant and detached attitude towards the people and events occurring around him? He would abstain no longer.

He dismounted and led the kruushka through small

mounds of the dead and the wounded. He walked with new-found confidence towards the village war chief, who had remained standing after Tralane's intervention and observed the turn of fortune.

The feelings of doubt and guilt over Rimskiel's and Detrexan's deaths now seemed to Tralane petty and childish. They had been his enemies at the moment of their deaths. The others who had died were victims. Perhaps they would have lived had he felt his anger earlier, and allowed a sword to speak for him. But that was in the past. He was a man, a warrior. He would bend no more to the wills of others, nor would he use cowardly deceit or trickery to satisfy his desires. He would take what he wanted, what was his, and what he chose to be his boldly and with force, if necessary.

The legends and deeds of warriors he had often recounted to barroom audiences for pay swirled in his mind, like the bright leaves of the fall season caught in a pool. CuChani was a weakling's god, a sneaking immortal thief. How much more worthy of respect and admiration were the mortal and demigod heroes of action. It was not by accident that Cuelon the Slayer ascended to his rightful place at the apex of all the other star constellations every year.

Drunk with pride and the surprise of discovering a new aspect of himself, Tralane reached the village war chief with a swagger in his stride.

"I am Tralane," he said easily, though still out of breath. "I hope you can give me shelter and food for my services in your quarrel with the hillmen."

The chief removed the mask—a construction of feathers, wood and hide—that had hidden his features. The fierce-looking insigne painted on his cheeks and around his mouth reflected Tralane's own anger as well as the symbolic outrage of the villagers. But beneath the paint there were other feelings. Awe, wonder, and fear danced in perfect synchronization across the chief's open face. Tralane basked in these reactions as he would in front of a warm fire after a cold night's outing. If even the war chief was overcome by admiration and respect, then how much more of the comforting emotions were being generated by the warriors gathering around him? Even his most finely told tales had never won him so much acceptance and approval from his fellow men. He had found another, more satisfying way to gain access to the hearts of others.

The chief reached out and touched Tralane's face, drawing the bard out of his self-satisfaction. When he withdrew his hand his fingers were bloody, and Tralane realized he was once again covered with blood. His sword's black blade was still dripping with gore, which splattered onto the ground even as he stood, forming a thick, grisly pool. The men surrounding him murmured in frightened tones.

"You speak the Sky Tongue strangely," said the war chief at last, with an accent equally difficult for Tralane to understand. "Your skin is paler than ours, but your strength is mighty. Are you a god?"

Tralane threw back his head and laughed.

"No, but by Cuelon and old bearded Pichen, I feel like one."

The chief nodded, then led the way back to the village. The line of observers had disappeared and the way was clear all the way down the main thoroughfare.

Tralane followed with the other warriors trailing behind him. He turned and searched for the Jade Warrior further up the river, but could not find him. All he could see were the village magicians, climbing out of their beds in the earth and returning his gaze with puzzlement and suspicion.

Briefly, he wondered what had happened to his companion. Perhaps, once the Warrior's sword was in Tralane's possession, the sorcerous being's mission had been fulfilled and whoever was watching over the bard had recalled him. Or perhaps Tralane's battle madness had given the Warrior cause to doubt the wisdom of harassing the bard. Anything was possible, in that moment of intermingled dream and reality in which Tralane found himself living. And if his physical stature was not truly that of a warrior born, and if his admirers hung back further than they normally would have had they thought him human, Tralane dismissed these negatives without much further thought. To march into a place, knowing he was its savior, was an event he had only dared dream through the telling of tales. He was not about to let that moment pass without savoring it to the fullest.

Chapter 9

The village resembled a Tribe Nations' encampment, though the huts were larger and sturdier than the shelters of that race on his own world. Apparently, due to some political situation in the northern kingdoms and empires that prevented them from expanding southward, this world's version of the Tribe Nations had spread into the Rechochoake Mountains and begun to settle there as hunters and farmers. The stronger tribes held the valleys and river land, while the weaker nations hid in the mountains and, presumably, when hunting in the Plains was poor, descended to the valleys in raiding parties.

The people were darker in complexion than most of the Tribe Nations in Tralane's experience and they spoke a dialect of the Sky Tongue among themselves which he could not understand. They painted themselves more than was usual and were more involved in readily apparent ways with ritual and ceremony than their nomadic, shui-herd-following brethren. As he walked between their dwellings, heading for a large wood-and-thatch dome which appeared to be the war chief's destination, Tralane caught the secretive stares of the village's population in the shadows of doorways and windows.

Their shelters and dress styles were still better suited for the Ousho Plains than for hill living. They had not

102

lived in a settled manner for long, perhaps a generation or two, and they were not fully adapted to their new environment. But already, the wild freedom that had made the people of the Tribe Nations such novelties at court and the feared enemies of southern kingdoms was transforming itself into something else, something complex, involuted, and hidden.

It was as if to stay in one place and master the land was to be burdened by all the life that grew and died around them. The rhythms of the earth infected them; they were learning to till the land, plant the seeds, and gather the harvest. When they listened to the earth, it was no longer to hear the wild throbbing that represented galloping herds of shui in the distance, but to listen for the stirrings of a gentle, more intimate kind of life. They were learning to love the land, care for it, and coax its richness out into day. They watched the cycle of life from beginning to end, death bringing life and regeneration, and no doubt pondered the secrets they glimpsed. Their children grew like the crops, tall and swift, and those that died were still among them in the surrounding fields and hills, their souls mingling with the earth and rooting the people of the Tribe Nation to this place.

As the warriors of the village stood in awe of Tralane's feat, so did the bard slowly awaken to the wonder of the metamorphosis that had occurred. He loved the brash, proud independence of his native world's Tribe Nations. They learned from technologically advanced neighbors, taking such useful tools as wagons and harnesses. But their way of life was not traded away in the exchange. Skins, meats, herbs, and roots found on the Plains, delicacies found grubbing in the mud after a sudden rain, and even the deftly woven figures of deities made of grass and the blankets which described the cosmology of the Plains were all fair trade items. Their spirit was untouched.

Yet on this world, there was something in these people's lives that was like the blooming of a flower long held in check by the night. Tralane regretted the loss of the Nations' freedom which, ironically, had been averted on his world by the avarice of petty kingdoms. These people had surrendered the past for the sedentary security of the river valley, and in this there was an admirable quality of courage in the face of newly discovered mysteries that was unfamiliar to Tralane. They had come upon a world they had never before experienced, thinking to find safety, and then finding the circle of their lives rimmed with questions. They had developed the courage to look within that circle for answers and not scoff and continue in their old ways with the foolish bravado of the unquestioning. Tralane wished to fill himself with the answers they had found. The honesty with which they approached and resolved the paradoxes of life would surely turn out to be the balm to soothe his inner wounds.

Tralane, in the tumultuous wake of his rage, had found a home.

He entered the domed hut after the war chieftain. The thick smoke and heavy aromas assaulted him immediately, causing his head to swim, but he remained standing steadily, his face set, his eyes calmly taking in the new environment.

To either side stood or sat—depending on their nearness to the central aisle—a horde of men and women, all older than the warriors who had taken the field. They whispered to one another as they bobbed their heads together and blew out smoke from pipes with each word they spoke. Some of the elderly who sat on blankets in the first row, in front of their children sitting on long benches, pointed at details of his appearance they found peculiar, nodding their gray-haired skulls as if he were meeting some previously specified regulation of appearance. Their middle-aged descendants, wearing the tokens of their crafts and trades around their necks like pendants—a wooden wheel, a bright red triangular piece of cloth, a square of leather, and other symbols—were more concerned with the events that had just transpired at the battle site. A few wept and were consoled by their neighbors for the loss of their relatives and friends, while others exchanged views on trade, weather, bandit hillmen, and gods.

Tralane suddenly remembered Wyden's Eye, still hidden in the pouch around his neck. He rebelled against the analogy between his pouch and the villagers' pendants. Once, he knew, he would have reveled in the symbolic ties between the stolen Eye and the craft of thievery and mischief, but now he wanted it understood by everyone, especially himself, that the honest edge of a sword had replaced and cut the bonds to an unfortunate past.

The warriors, filing in behind him, took up the rear behind the people of the crafts. They stood next to women wearing tunics and bands of metal around their necks and arms. He, too, would soon have a priestess for a wife and join the village's hunters and warriors in the community's high esteem.

He looked ahead and saw the war chieftain engaged in earnest discussion with a young woman. She was tall and darker skinned than most of the other people, clad in a tunic of brightly colored, complicated beadwork patterns. Black hair burst from the edges of a gold mail helmet, settling on her shoulders. Around her hips, a wide belt was snugly drawn, from which hung a broad sheath housing a sword with a pommel of glittering jewels. Next to her stood a man in black and red robes, with a golden band encircling his forehead, peering at Tralane with the unmistakable eyes of a sorcerer.

Tralane could barely hear the chieftain and high priestess converse, since the background of susurrant voices with their fragments of meaningful words and phrases vied for his attention. From what he could gather, he understood there was general puzzlement over his appearance on the battlefield and questions concerning the meaning of his arrival and his nature—mortal, demigod, or god.

In their well-ordered world of succeeding nights and days marking off the steady passage of seasons and setting the tempo of their existence, he had arrived with no warning or precedence. They believed in predictable gods and a smooth flow of magic between the planes of existence, not whimsical, autonomous entities who watched them dispassionately and appeared among them, out of boredom, with aloofness or, out of fear, with anger.

He walked the length of the aisle leading to the woman who now appeared to be not only the high priestess of the warrior's wives, but also their queen. With their curiosity satisfied and their suspicious natures appeased, Tralane hoped he would then be able to exchange his services as their protector for their acceptance into their community.

A hush fell over the enclosure when he moved forward. The smoke from the torches seemed to clog the roof openings, blocking out the natural light. The gloom thickened, clinging like fog to Tralane.

When he ignored the chieftain's warning signals, the queen sprang up from the throne that seemed to be carved from a single, giant piece of wood. She drew her sword, which looked far heavier and more imposing than Tralane's black blade, with the practiced ease of a warrior. The sorcerer stepped up behind her, a tall, menacing shadow. The war chieftain retreated to the side of the aisle, where his warriors stood after having filtered down through the crowd.

The queen lifted the sword over her head, holding it horizontally with only one hand. Her face did not show any strain of effort, nor was there any consternation over his approach. Her eyes were locked to his as the sorcerer made a sign over the sword's point, sending bolts of brilliant light flashing along its double edges. Tralane's mouth went dry. Magic charged the air.

"This is the Sword of Ara, vanquisher and giver, punisher and replenisher. Stay where you are, demon, unless you are prepared to force the death fight here and now."

The queen had spoken, her voice sharp and clear, though tainted with the same foreign accent as that of the other villagers. Tralane replied slowly, careful to enunciate his words so he would be understood.

"I am not a demon, I am a man. My name is Tralane, and I come from a land far from your home. I would like to settle here, to help you master your enemies and live in peace. I am a bard and a warrior." He said this last with new-found pride, then regretted its vanity. He quickly added, "I have been to many places, seen many things. I can show you how to live better, how to please the earth so it will share with you more of its treasures. All I ask is the warmth of your hearts."

The queen was immobile, her face hardened into a mask which kept the fierce wildness in her eyes from spilling out and overwhelming him. She was the repository for the tribe's untamed spirit. These men had not yet forsaken their heritage, after all. They had only placed it aside so they could contend with the day-to-day demands of life. She was the vessel, containing in her sturdy, feminine form the wrath and power of their traditions. Yet she did not speak. Instead, the sorcerer answered.

"You are a plague," he said icily.

Tralane was caught by surprise, but did not give ground.

"I have destroyed your enemies," he said indignantly. "They broke and ran before me like your river birds before a predator. I saved the lives of your young warriors, who deserve life in the families of their village rather than death at the hands of barbarians. I can rout these outsiders again, if you wish, whenever they show themselves on your lands. I am your protector, yet you call me a plague?"

This time the queen replied. "There was no need for magic or for blood. The time had not yet come. The hillmen were only testing. You disturbed the pattern."

"You have power," the sorcerer continued for her. "It does not have the taint of hillmen, but that does not mean you are not also our enemy." There was a tone of distaste in the sorcerer's words.

"Then let me repair the pattern," Tralane appealed to the queen.

"How?" the queen asked.

Tralane could not find the answer.

Before he could cover himself with a blanket of words, she had asked another question. "Where were you born?"

Again he was left speechless. Mathi's tower was the

only home he had ever known, and that, in the end, was a place to avoid, not to seek. Yet she was probing for that place for which the tower was only a shadow. And he had run away from that shadow, turning his back on the source.

"You do not know that, either. Were you born of mortal woman? Or goddess? Are you a dead man's restless soul cursed with the wandering fever?"

"He is not a ghost," the sorcerer interjected, and the queen turned sideways to look at him. Her expression softened as they exchanged glances, and Tralane was unaccountably envious of the sorcerer. "A spirit occupied the ghost hut when this one entered our village."

"Then you are haunted and evil," the queen exclaimed, facing Tralane again.

He gleaned their intention. They were attempting to trap him into a category so as to compel him to leave under the laws of the community. To join them would automatically mean exile.

"No, I am a man. I am Tralane. I can help you."

The queen lowered the sword, which still gleamed with restless energies. The priestesses had begun to chant a low, ominous prayer in the unknown tongue he had overheard the warriors speak. The queen joined them.

"You desire land space in our community," the sorcerer said disdainfully, "yet you know nothing of our ways, our gods, our magic. The hillmen are barbarians, but they share with us the knowledge of Ara and the other forces of the elements, though they may name them differently. You are worse than they, Tralane. You are a death carrier. Your help is unnatural."

Tralane's strength and self-confidence withered before this rejection. They were protecting themselves against his presence, using words and spells to drive him out, raising the solid wall of their commonality. As he stood his ground, still refusing to give up the chance for the settled, secure life he craved, tendrils of smoke rose from the ground and entwined themselves around his legs. They grew like vines, spreading, constricting, rooting him to the earth. His hands passed through the smoke tendrils, shattering the illusion of their physicality, but not their effect.

"Do you know what it is to be born and raised on the land belonging to your family? Can you tell me the laws that govern your people, the questions they seek to answer? Can you tell me the purpose of your life? Or will you confess that you are a lawless demon of chaos, that you have no people, no land, no gods to protect you?"

The sorcerer had stepped beside the queen, who was lost in the singing of the chant, her eyelids trembling and body swaying. The smoke still oozed from the earth, climbing up the length of Tralane's body and reaching for his throat. Its tendrils tightened around his chest so that simple breath became a violent struggle.

But when the smoke reached the pouch in which Wyden's Eye was kept, the tendrils dissipated and released their crushing hold on Tralane. He stamped his legs and moved his arms to restore circulation. A ripple of dismayed mutterings swept through the crowd on both sides of him. In their momentary surprise Tralane might have easily forced his way out of the hut and escaped, but he did not take advantage of the opportunity.

"Sky magic, wind magic," the sorcerer exclaimed with consternation. He retreated to his previous position behind the queen.

Magic, whatever its source, had proved antipathetic to the tribe's earth-based sorcery. Wyden's Eye had defended itself against an entire people's power. The depths of the amulet's strength, summoned without Tralane's call and protecting him in the heart of an opposing force, shocked him. Whatever its origin, Wyden's Eye was a mightier enigma than he had ever imagined. And if the Eye could act of its own or some controlling agent's volition, then were not Gibron's warnings far more serious than he had first taken them to be?

"Plague, disrupter of death. Unnatural demon! What do you want from us?"

"The warmth of your hearth fires, the smiles of your children, the friendship of your elders."

The queen came out of her trance, and the last of the chanting priestesses fell silent. The crowd stirred nervously, impatient with the failure of their leaders to expel the outsider. The sorcerer was silent, his mouth turned up in scorn for the intruder.

"If you truly wish to be with us," said the queen wearily, not quite focusing her eyes on Tralane, "then you must be tested in other ways. Your magic is strong, but it is not our magic, and perhaps it is not even yours. There are forces within you, though, which can be drawn out. There are signs within you, omens and portents which can answer the questions which have been posed and for which you have no tongue. Both you and I will discover your purpose in coming here and whether you are truly destined to stay or to leave."

The queen sheathed the sword, turned, and departed through an exit behind the throne. Warriors sealed her departure and began herding the villagers from her house. The people left unhurriedly, without complaint. The priestesses remained, straightening and refurbishing the queen's quarters while Tralane followed the villagers out. Four warriors closed in around him as an escort. Tralane cast a quick glance over his shoulder and saw the sorcerer standing by the empty throne, staring coldly after him. Then he left the hut, and the brisk evening air awakened his spirit to the coming ordeal.

Chapter 10

Tralane was brought to a hut on the outskirts of the village, towards the pinched end of the valley through which the river squeezed to reach the flat lands beyond. A huge bonfire was burning on the site of the day's battle, sending thick columns of sinewy smoke coiling into the evening sky. His heart jumped when he saw a moon standing out among the stars. It was the first glimpse of the familiar moons of his world. But before he could identify the body, smoke had engulfed the heavens. He searched for another moon, but could find none.

He stood at the doorway of his hut, quickly checking the inside and finding only a sleeping mat of woven grass and a blanket. Instead of going in, he turned and watched the fire from across the village. His warrior escorts were walking towards the conflagration, and one of them glanced back apprehensively at the sword Tralane still clutched in his hand. There was no point in guarding what they regarded as an inhuman creature capable of destroying so many of the enemy and resisting their most powerful magic. If he wanted to leave, he was free to go. He was granted the freedom of the village, since there was no one to oppose him. Meanwhile, the villagers had abandoned their sacred hearths to him for a victory celebration, commemorating a battle he considered he had won for them.

He scowled with disgust, but did not venture out of his designated area.

He settled into the hut, laying down his sword and wiping his face with the blanket. Dried blood and dust, caked on his skin like scales, clung to the blanket's sophisticated weave. A slight sound near the doorway startled him and, grabbing his sword once again, he peered out carefully, fearing treachery. Instead, he could make out only the slim figure of a girl in a priestess' robe, running up the street. At his feet lay a pile of clothes and blankets, a basket of meats and fruits, and two jars of liquid that had been placed as an offering. Tralane took the goods inside.

One jar was filled with water, so he washed as thoroughly as he could. He noted that his wounds had healed remarkably and that his aches and pains had diminished, as if his body had sucked regenerative energy from the sword's life-taking. He changed into the loincloth, hide leggings, and jerkin that had been given to him. He ate quickly and voraciously, drinking the rich, mildly intoxicating contents of the second jar with deep appreciation. Only after the meal did he spread himself out on the mat with a groan and allow himself to relax. Though his body had begun to heal from the beating and cuts he had suffered in Fargouet, new aches were awakening as his muscles protested the exertions of the day. However, they were a welcome testimony to his prowess. He drifted pleasantly into sleep, relieved that at last the Jade Warrior had disappeared and trying to decide whether the courtesies he was enjoying were an attempt to appease him or a kindness dispensed on a doomed traveler.

He was dreaming when a blow, like a far-off warning at a gathering of thieves, woke him into tense wakefulness. He tried to recall the fleeting images his mind had conjured during his sleep, seeking to embrace their comforting aspects and drag them into the real world. But they fled precipitously before a chilly breeze and a sudden sense of danger.

His eyes still not accustomed to the dark world around him, Tralane rolled off the mat and lunged for his sword.

He became entangled in the blankets covering him, and something long and hard tumbled from his chest to the floor. His own weapon had been placed diagonally across his torso. A laugh, unpleasantly familiar, grated on the bard's ears.

"Brave warrior, what is a sword without a sheath?"

Beside him, Tralane's hand fell upon a casing for his sword.

"Unless, of course, you plan on using your weapon on every possible occasion."

Tralane squinted at the Jade Warrior, who stood framed in the starlit doorway. The being held up a hand; when the hand was lowered, a green glass ball was floating in mid-air, its glow permeating the hut.

"Here is light," the Warrior continued, squatting, "so we may all see the mighty Tralane in his finest glory."

"Shut up," Tralane spat, recovering his sword and disentangling himself from the blanket. He sheathed the weapon, then noticed the Jade Warrior had somehow acquired a duplicate.

"And here's a belt to hang your sheath on. You'll need that, too."

"What are you doing here?" Tralane asked, disdaining to respond any further to the Jade Warrior's sarcasms.

"I'm your companion. I told you it is not so easy to rid yourself of me. I am your aide, I facilitate the course of your adventure."

"Well, my adventures are at an end."

"Oh?"

Tralane rose and walked by the Warrior to the doorway. He looked out across the sleeping village to where the bonfire had been. There was no sign of life on the field; he had slept through whatever rites the villagers had performed.

"Were you in their ghost hut when they took me in?"

"Yes," the Warrior replied without turning to face Tralane. "These villages always provide my brethren with lodgings. I merely availed myself of the convenience."

"They took you for a spirit haunting me."

"Who is to say that is not so?"

Tralane snarled and whirled about to find the Warrior facing him, feet firmly planted apart.

"You almost ruined my attempt to gain a normal life here," the bard exclaimed bitterly.

"Do not blame me for the harvest your own actions have reaped."

"Don't try to fool me. I saw them celebrating their victory out there, and I'm the one who made that victory possible. I am their hero. It was that jealous sorcerer of the queen's, and your poor choice of lodging—"

Tralane stood and glared at the Jade Warrior, emboldened by a new thought.

"You and the sorcerer are in league."

The Warrior shook his head. His eyes gleamed maliciously. "No, Mascu and I have not allied ourselves against you. I would not stoop to aid his kind, and he would never dare call on me. He hates you quite naturally, without instigation on my part."

"Why? What have I done? I'm not interested in his queen or in his position in the village. I don't want to take what is someone else's. I want to earn what is mine."

"The queen, Lisakeness, is not his for you to take from him. Nor is he fearful that you will take his rôle in the life of the village. His animosity has been raised because you are alien and evil. The fire was not a celebration, it was a purification. You have disrupted their order—the battle had not even commenced. I told you the magicians had not yet made their appearance. Your presence, with its accompanying aura of violence, hatred, and gratuitous death, along with your refusal to leave, forced them to make a sacrifice of their dead in the hopes of cleansing the earth and their souls of blood. Mascu hates you because you do not fit into the pattern that has been laid out for the village. You will never belong, yet you refuse to leave. For them, that is an attack."

"But I want to try to fit into their pattern," Tralane protested, catching his childlike whine too late.

"Why?"

Tralane frowned, struggling with the words to convey his feelings. Not only were his emotions strange to him; but the need to express them was also a new aspect of himself that had never been open to examination. He went back to the mat and seated himself.

"I'm tired of deaths and running."

"Deaths never disturbed you before." The Jade Warrior spoke with a hint of amusement, as if Tralane's confession were a source of entertainment. The bard, aware of the attitude, replied coldly, trying not to reveal too much emotion in his statements.

"Only because I didn't have to see them."

"Yet you caused so many, Tralane. Did you ever think that your abandonment of Mathi might have broken him and caused his death? You were his pupil, his hope for the future of the knowledge he was accumulating. All that he strove to gain would have been yours."

"But that was not what I wanted from him," Tralane cried out.

"Does that justify his death? And in the kingdom of Corru, did you not know that your sudden departure would implicate the princess Amalkys in a plot to overthrow her own father? What do you think happened to her in the hands of a king feared for his savagery? When you played the fool in Lord Yshaleth's court, watching his seven brothers who had placed their faith in you vanish one by one after you reneged on your promise of providing them with an escape from their mad brother, did you not ask yourself what the Lord had done to them? Were you not weary of death then? But we need not go so far back into your past for examples of your noble character. You could have cared for Oram and given him the few extra days of life he would have needed for the two of you to escape Agathom's camp. Crecia, I hear, did not fare too well either, nor did Fatome. Where four could have lived, only one survived unscathed. Curious."

Tralane, shocked by the revelation of a past he had conveniently forgotten or passed over as playful incidents, whispered hoarsely, "How did you know?"

Ignoring the question, the Warrior pressed his point. "Did you care?"

"No." The truth of his admission made his voice barely audible.

The Jade Warrior laughed, rocking back and forth, his hands resting against his hips. "Then don't be a fool and care now."

Tralane stared at the ground, guarding his shame. He did not admit to the Warrior that he had never thought about the people he had been involved with enough to care about them. They had all seemed selfish, concerned with their own survival, so he had felt no compunction in placing his own well-being above that of others. That they might have had better reasons than he to be so concerned about their lives had not occurred to him. Like his involvement with Crecia, he had understood what the people around him felt, but had not judged the sincerity with which they came to him for help. The hard ones like Crecia, as well as the vulnerable ones like Princess Amalkys, had suffered indiscriminantly. He had not realized what it was to hurt others, having wrapped himself in the invisible cloak of his own pain and the suffering of real and imagined wrongs.

"But I do care, now, and I wish the gods of this place to forgive me. I want the people of this place to accept me into their midst."

"You show more faith in gods and people than you have done in the past."

Tralane shrugged, then looked up. "Will you help me?"

"No."

"Then if you will not be my aide in this new course of my adventures, why are you here?"

"Because the course of a river does not change with a wish. I am with you, as you have been with others."

The Jade Warrior reached out and took back the green globe. The glow faded as he wrapped his hands around it, and Tralane's hut was dark once more.

"I would sleep if I were you," the Jade Warrior advised, turning to leave. "You will need a clear head for what they will ask of you. When you have finished, I will be waiting by the river with your mount. If you are still alive, we will move on."

The Warrior passed through the doorway before Tralane could question him further about the next day's events. By the time the bard reached the opening, the Warrior had vanished without a trace. He decided the search for the ghost hut would be a vain one—the Warrior appeared to have little inclination for revealing anything that might help him.

He returned to his mat, glanced at the sword which lay beside it, and wondered what had driven him to take it. The mystery surrounding the Jade Warrior's existence was even more troubling after the brief respite from the being's pointed comments. The illusion of freedom had evaporated, burned away by the questions to be asked about the Warrior and about the bard himself. Only when there were no more surprises within him, Tralane realized as he drew the blanket around him and closed his eyes, could he face the Warrior on his own terms.

But all these doubts would prove to be unnecessary, for in the morning he would rise and face the test the villagers had proposed. After the villagers' fears were erased, the secure welcome of the people would embrace him.

Chapter 11

Two young warriors, one wearing an unhealed scar across his cheek while his shorter comrade limped slightly, came to escort Tralane to the place of trial. They stood outside his door impassively, their stoic faces and averted gazes cutting off Tralane's unspoken desire for a morning meal.

He emerged from the hut in the shadow of the rising sun. The village was deserted, as it had been since his arrival. Those who worked the fields, as well as the herd animals, household pets, fowls, and even stray animals foraging on the village's wastes had been sent somewhere out of sight.

Angered by their avoidance of him, Tralane stopped suddenly and put a hand on his sword hilt. He surveyed the village with deliberation while his escorts waited patiently, without urging him on. Since they did not respond to his provocation, he continued sullenly to follow their lead.

He was unsure of his new-found emotion and the ease with which he could express it. Anger had given him an unaccustomed feeling of mastery and power the previous day. He was not as weak and vulnerable as he had once thought he was, and yet he could not believe he was as strong as he now seemed. His bow and arrows were forgotten; his clever and wily guiles, strategems, and maneuvers were not necessary to his survival anymore. Having contained his anger for so long while letting it seep into the world through intricate, quietly executed plots and manipulations, Tralane did not fully trust the new form the emotion had taken, nor the new perspective in which frank anger now placed him. Before he had never thought of himself as angry and now he knew that was all he had ever been. Uneasy with himself, he wished more than ever to sink back into the warmth and security of lively fellowship, where often such knowledge is inadmissible to others and to one's self.

But his memory cursed him. As they left the village, heading for a hut he had not noticed the day before further along the river, the lumbering figure of Oram loomed over the walls of Tralane's feigned ignorance. The white-haired giant had also suffered loss, privation, and loneliness, and a Tribe Nation had taken him in. Could these sedentary, subdued people, who had settled land and understood the agony of rootlessness better than Oram's adopters, truly drive Tralane away? Or was the earth still too new; was their wildness, unbridled from the demands of nomadic life and still not wholly accustomed to the new routine of life, rebelling against the shifting of laws that governed behavior? Tralane studied the shoulders of the warriors walking in front of him, but the answers were not painted among the designs of bright colors, which decorated the youths.

Perhaps the differences lay not in the people who were in the position to accept strangers as much as in the strangers themselves. Oram had drowned himself in a flood of emotion, while Tralane could only sip momentarily at a well of feeling before continuing his trek across a vast, inner desolation. Others had reached for Oram and touched a living, responsive spirit—Fatome mourned for his passing. Tralane did not know of anyone who would mourn his own death.

His mood was still wavering between uneasiness and self-pity when the group reached the hut. Upon close examination, the shelter appeared to have been newly constructed, perhaps built overnight. Apparently, after the bonfire, the villagers had crept downriver and raised the hut. He suspected they had picked a site outside the sacred confines of their home territory.

The two warriors pointed to a spot before the entrance, which was covered by a black blanket, then ran off in the direction of the village. Tralane stood on the place that had been picked for him and waited. He lowered his eyes to the blanket, thinking only of his immediate environment, and tried to relax. Then the fading footsteps of his retreating escorts suddenly stopped as if they had sprouted wings and flown away. Tralane did not turn around to see what had happened. Wyden's Eye hung heavily around his neck.

Finally, the grim figure of Mascu stepped out from the hut. He barred the entrance and ran his eyes over the bard, noting every minute detail as if to catch some physical flaw which would disprove Tralane's claim to humanity. He sneered at the village-made clothes Tralane wore, but failed to find any gross irregularities. He stepped away from the door.

"You may enter, Tralane. Our queen waits for you."

"My thanks, Mascu," Tralane replied flatly. He stopped when, taking notice of the sorcerer's surprise, he remembered the source of his information concerning names. He answered Mascu's startled expression with one of cool bravado.

"I see Lisakeness has gone to some lengths to prepare for my reception," he said, gesturing at the hut.

Mascu's face hardened, and he said in a whisper, "You are a demon."

"No, merely well informed." Tralane could hardly keep himself from laughing, and he felt the old satisfaction of a ploy successfully executed filling him with confidence. "Why have you sent the people away? I mean them no harm."

The sorcerer shook his head vehemently and took a step away from the bard. "They are in the Nushu Land, the world of the dead. There, even you may not touch them. Nothing living that belongs to us will be touched by you."

This time Tralane did laugh as he reached for the hanging blanket to brush it aside. "Mascu, you both underestimate and overestimate my power."

Without further words, Tralane entered the hut. His freshly won confidence immediately evaporated as he found himself in total darkness. The door was effectively sealed against light, and the usual smoke hole had not been built into the roof. Tralane groped for a proper response to the situation, a way to gain control over what was happening; but without a guide to help him forge a new course of action and without the old fortifications of his mind which had invariably protected him from the consequences of his actions, he was at a loss. He cursed his companion, the Jade Warrior, who seemed totally disinterested in his fate.

"Sit, Tralane," came Lisakeness's voice from somewhere in front of him. Tralane obeyed.

A glow emanated from a small pit when a flat stone was drawn across the floor, uncovering the hole. Coals piled at the bottom of the pit provided the light in which Tralane could make out the queen, sitting naked on the earth floor on the opposite side of the glow's source. The walls were indistinguishable from darkness. They might have been sitting in the cramped night of another world.

"You and I will talk, Tralane," the queen affirmed in a matter-of-fact tone. "Mascu has left, your spirit has abandoned the ghost hut. We are alone. No one will interfere. We can speak freely."

Tralane nodded, puzzled by the shape his trail was taking. He had been expecting something more physical, like one of the initiating rites he heard the Tribe Nations favored.

"I will tell you I am Lisakeness, daughter of Lysaka, guardian of the gate to the Nushu Land. I have loved her with my heart, as I now love Mascu, and as I will love my children."

She swayed in a circular motion, staring into the pit, awaiting his reply. He was expected to answer in the same formula of speech, but there was nothing he could say.

"I will tell you of the beginning of all things, so it may be known how the People of the Plains came to settle the valley," she continued, without looking at him. Already, Tralane was losing the battle.

"There was a place in the west, beyond the marshes and seas, where lived the Twelve Mothers and their consorts. These couples had children, the Sons of the Plains, and the Daughters of the Earth. These children traveled east over ice, sea, fire, mountains, and unfathomable chasms, all to satisfy their lust for wandering and to rid themselves of watchful parents. The first land they saw when, at long last, after much in the way of suffering, they broke through the barriers the world had thrown across their path, was the wide rolling plain. Herds of wild shui, tawwas, thorts, kruushkas and other beasts, large and small, made the ground tremble with their multitudes. Flocks of wenoths, as well as the predatory shyn and bokkara, wheeled across the sweeping sky, borne by the strong winds that carried the clouds before them and caressed the earth below. The Sons, with a shout of joy, rushed out into the open expanse, each with a sister trailing behind uttering unheeded warnings. Soon the Sons lost sight of one another. As the great bowl of stars closed over their heads they spread out in all directions. They could not even see each other's camp fires.

"The sisters caught up to the brothers, and every couple beat back the whisper of loneliness that had worked itself into their souls. The twelve brothers and sisters lay with one another, and on that first night in the living lands the race of men was conceived.

"As the grass grew and was felled by winter, the sisters gave birth while the brothers stayed out on the plain, hunting food and seeking one another. The brothers came home to their makeshift shelters, to the blood and life around their sisters, and cried out. And the sisters, on seeing the new spears and knives the men had fashioned for their hunt, also cried out. From then on, the knowledge of womanhood and manhood has been kept a secret with all twelve lineages, and taught to the children with the dignity of ceremony befitting such terrible knowledge. And the sleeping together of brothers and sisters has been forbidden, so as never to recall those days of isolation on the plains.

"But in those days the children grew without restraint, and the pattern set by the twelve sons was woven again by the male sons, while the daughters could only do as their mothers had done and follow. The parents died as time wore down their spirits, and their children had children. And now, with the plains more populous, the grandchildren began to meet one another as they hunted and wandered. They began to gather and follow the herds. As they did, they fell into clans to protect their child and hunting rights, and to guard against the rashness of desire that had moved their grandparents. Families moved and merged, split and reformed, as herds diminished or were discovered. Nations were founded as the clans banded together so that more hands might be able to feed more mouths. For generations upon generations, until the Daughters of the Earth were almost forgotten and only the Sons of the Plains were revered because they had led while their sisters trailed behind, the people wandered across the land.

"But the ancient spirits of the Twelve Mothers had not forgotten their children. They sent the winds and rains driving across the plains. Ice and snow fell during the winter, and with each passing year the air was colder and the game scarcer. Many died, more were never born. The plains were cursed with affliction, and the people became weary of the endless pursuit of life. They traveled north until they were met by the mountains, and then came the time for the Sons to rest and the Daughters to take up their right.

"The mysteries of life and blood replaced those of the hunt and the kill. What was needed came to the fore, what was not fell back. No longer do the Sons lead and the

Daughters follow. Now the time has come for the Daughters to build and grow, to reach down into the depths of the earth for the warmth and life buried there. The Sons leave, but they must return. The search for sustenance is at an end, it is here, where all life begins and ends. It is within me, beneath me, about me. The life of the Shosheya people beats around us. Hear it? The sustenance feeds all and attracts all, friends and enemies, saviors and jealous demons. All follow the sweet scent and the filling light to us. And here we stay, to greet them or destroy them."

Tralane's head was pounding by the time Lisakeness finished the tale of her village. The smoke from the coals, as well as her hypnotic intensity, clouded his senses. Her silent swaying indicated a response was required of him, but again there was nothing for him to say. Hers was a story of life, a history of her own people. She had given him the reason for her existence and for the existence of her world. In the stock of tales garnered from the finest courts of his home as well as those taught to him by Mathi, there was nothing of equal personal value for Tralane to offer in reciprocation.

"Now let me tell you of a savior," she went on, firmly cutting the silence. "When first the Shosheya came to the mountains, following the river with the hope of finding a haven before the winter closed in, they came upon a hut built on stilts over the river. In the hut they found an old woman, and by the woman they found a chest. But before they could touch the woman or the chest, she woke. Upon seeing so many people in her hut and on the shore, she cried out and, clutching the chest to her bosom, leaped through the door and disappeared into the waters of the river.

"The Shosheya moved on, deeming the place to be cursed, and continued on their quest. Many days later, when camp had been made and the fires were beating back the fearsome night that poured down the mountainsides, the woman appeared among them. She carried her chest under one arm while holding a talisman in her hand. She sat by one of the fires as if it were her due.

"The people greeted her with food and drink and let her sit by the fire alone until she had her fill of rest and refreshment. They thought her a spirit of the river, demanding repayment for being disturbed in her home. For the respect and kindness they showed her, the old woman promised to lead them to a place which would shelter them from the winds and storms and teach them new ways of gathering food and living from the land.

"There were more days of travel, and they parted from the main river to follow the streams as the old woman told them to do. Then she said stop, and our ancestors did. They settled on the quiet banks of the waters that run outside, and which have swollen with the years of settlement. The old woman showed what fruits could be raised from the earth, when to sow, and when to harvest. She taught new weaves to the women, and gave men power to master and herd more animals than they had ever thought possible. The Shosheya celebrated their gifts with great fires and magics, and even the smothering night held back its gloom before the joy and health that glowed within the people's hearts.

"The old woman was asked to stay in the village she had helped to build, but she refused. Her time in the world was nearly spent, and she preferred the deep, lonely silences of the rivers and mountains to the daily reminders of fresh life and promise which the children of the village held. But before she left, she buried her chest at the village's center, that the place might be made sacred and a source of supernatural might. For at the call of one who knows the soothing words, the chest does open, deep beneath the earth, and out of the eternal depths of that box the souls of all those who have lived and died among the Shosheya answer. Though no loving creature may know of those depths where the dead rest and answer the call of their children, the old woman unlocked the door to the place where we might be closest to our ancestors. Thus was the Nushu Land made open to use, power bestowed, and the secrets of life given to the people of the Shosheya."

When she had finished, Tralane had only a question to offer in response. He did not want to ask it. A bawdy story from his bag of entertainments might break the web Lisakeness had spun around him. Seduction, violence, and rape were other options to be considered. What he could not gain by the old, subtle tricks that had carried him through his youth, he could now have by sheer brute force. His palm itched for the feel of the black sword's pommel. But his violent fantasies could not break the chains that bound him. The point of his anger pricked only at his own heart.

"How did the woman open the way to the Nushu Land?" he asked, his voice cracking and his eyes tearing from the smoke.

"Her talisman shattered the barrier between worlds, and she found that realm which is closest to the end of all worlds. She worked powerful spells and drew forth the hidden energies of her instrument to break down the door permanently, so that only a thin veil of illusion separates this earth from the Nushu Land. She gave the illusion-shattering words to the Shosheya and placed barriers so that none but the Shosheya could venture to that other land. It is grim and shadowy, with little light or life. My people are there now, because of you."

Tralane met her gaze steadily. "And what happened to the talisman?"

His curiosity was reflected in her eyes. The air hummed, as if with many voices chanting in a secret tongue.

"She took the talisman with her when she departed. But the old woman left behind her a warning. If ever the Shosheya should see that talisman again, they should call on all their powers to bury it in the chest at the village's center. She called it an evil thing, and destined to bring suffering and death to all who surrounded its carrier. She was a sorceress and so knew ways to twist its evil predispositions to suit her will. But there must have been a price, or she would not have chosen to live alone by a river deep among the mountains."

Over her words and the ever more distinct ethereal chanting came the mage Gibron's name for people such as Tralane—Keepers. There had been, Gibron said, many of them.

"And so what price have you paid, demon?" The queen leaned forward, and her entire body seemed to be lighted, as if from fires burning within her. Her eyes lost their humanity, becoming more like angry suns than soft, sympathetic reflections of moons that Tralane expected.

"What sacrifice have you made to return the curse to the Shosheya, who are prepared to put this evil to rest?"

The chanting became deafening. No matter how hard Tralane pressed his hands to his ears, the sound came through. The walls of the hut trembled. A strong breeze slapped his face.

"Go join your brothers and sisters beyond the Nushu Land, demon Tralane. Be taken to the village center, be buried deep, deep beneath the earth. Fall into the chest that holds all the souls of the Shosheya. Put to rest the talisman of our ancestors, the instrument of our savior, the curse of our future. Do these things, and your wish will be granted. Join our ancestors, and you will be accepted."

"No!"

Tralane's refusal was swept away by Lisakeness's many-voiced scream. He stood to leave, not sure of where he would go, when a sudden blow to the chest knocked him through the black curtain and out into the natural world.

Awareness of every curve and point, edge and line, flooded Tralane's mind. The mountains and trees, even in their distance, staggered him by the sharpness of their definition. The river's water trickled by as if it were inside him, flowing through him. The smells of the earth and vegetation and the scents of animals and men were each clearly distinguishable. He could almost picture the appearance of each thing he smelled.

The Shosheya's village and lands became the focus of

reality, and the rest of existence was transformed into a dense fog. All that belonged to the Shosheya assumed more than its share in a physical state; their belongings emanated the sense of interconnection, of sharing, of being in a state of one and many at the same time. Each thing cried out its own special name, and the many voices merged to form a song in which every part was distinct yet merged into a whole. Tralane was not a part of that song. Already, he was becoming physically indistinct, a part of some other existence beyond that of the village and its surrounding lands.

Tralane tried to take a step, and found himself being half-pushed, half-carried towards the village. The clarity with which he sensed was dizzying. He could not grasp what was happening to him. Huts passed, achingly empty; cooking utensils, unfinished carvings, tools, and other paraphernalia of craftsmen and workers were strewn about, abandoned. The chant that had deafened him in the hut followed him, the unseen voices rising in intensity as he approached a circle of huts ahead. At the center of the circle, a mound of earth boiled.

Clumps of soil leaped into the air, and rocks flew out like startled birds. The mound spread. At its center, a pit was being widened by desperate but invisible hands. Something was digging itself out of the ground, something which, for all of Tralane's sudden clearsightedness, he could not make out. A mere shimmering of the air, like heat rising, was what penetrated his jumbled senses.

The forces pushing him now grabbed hold of his limbs as he struggled against his relentless advance. He was lifted off of the ground and carried to the pit. He struggled with increasing ferocity, fear swelling to take control of his mind and body. The pit seemed to be more than death, which perhaps he would not have tried to fight off with such determination. Mere annihilation and the eternal blackness of nonbeing were welcome fates compared to the thing waiting for him in the depths of the mound. There lay the Shosheya soul, the Tribe's collective spirit mingled and rooted in the spirits of the earth, seeking to grasp him forever to its bosom.

Life in its power would not merely be extinguished; it would be petrified in a prison of rigid law and ceremony. He was being sucked into the chaos that lay at the heart of every order, bound and hidden beneath the everyday world where it would not disturb the smooth functioning of material reality. He would be part of that thing which only emerged when called upon, when survival of order meant the unleashing of chaos to destroy the greater threat of nonexistence. He would belong to a spirit which was never fully acknowledged, only fed and used. His individual being, transformed into a mere source of energy, would be worse than crushed: it would be denied the fact of its existence.

He screamed, and his voice was as steady and undying as the chanting of the Shosheya spirit.

He was at the mouth of the pit, and all the world was being drawn into the confines of that hole. Wind rushed by him, funneling into the depths of the mound, twisting his limbs and torso as it tried to make him tumble down. But Tralane resisted the wind, the invisible hands, and the trembling, ever-shifting earth. Still screaming, Tralane looked down into the hole, into the darkness. He quickly turned his head when his eyes stung with pain from the needles of blackness that were flashing up, enveloping his head, cutting him off from the diffused light of day.

In a desperate attempt to free himself, Tralane reached for the pouch containing Wyden's Eye. He tore it from around his neck and was about to cast it down into the pit as a sacrificial offering to substitute for himself when a surge of power coursed from his hand through his arm. He held the amulet with both hands, and the awareness of external reality suddenly inverted. Every muscle, bone, vein, and fiber tingled with new life. He knew his body's every strength and weakness. Control of his actions returned to him, and the hands of the Shosheya spirit sloughed off as he regained firm footing. The wind lashed his face, and Tralane could taste the blood oozing from his open mouth and trickling from his eyes and nose to his lips. His clothes ripped, his skin was raked and punctured. Blows from unknown quarters landed on his chin and back and across his shoulders. His legs, however, were unshakable. Turning his back to the pit, he made his way down the side of the mound. His hands were locked around Wyden's Eye, as both he and the amulet, momentarily welded into one creature with the common goal of survival, struggled away from the village center.

Tralane reached the outskirts of the village with no idea of how much time had elapsed. He gauged his life by the diminishing force which resisted his departure; nothing else mattered. Once the hut in which he and Lisakeness had conferred was behind him, he found his stride lengthening as the Shosheya spirit's strength weakened with every step he took. The village was a distant cluster of huts when Tralane stopped and looked back. There was no sign of life or movement. Birds had left the area, and even the insects and brush creatures were silent where Tralane stood. Only a cool breeze blew along the river and ruffled his hair on its way to the village.

Dusk was creeping into the valley. He was free of the Shosheya, as they were of him. He shivered and tried to arrange his tattered clothing so that he would be protected from the evening air. He moved on, scanning the hills for a refuge and wincing from the new series of injuries he had sustained. He was not surprised when the Jade Warrior appeared ahead of him, leading the kruushka carrying Tralane's few belongings.

"You knew?" Tralane asked, as the Jade Warrior rode up to him.

"Yes."

Tralane fell to his knees and collapsed forward, letting his forehead lean against the ground. He was exhausted, and now his limbs shook, not with fear or cold, but with weakness.

"Then why did you let me go in? If you knew I was carrying Wyden's Eye, and that it had passed this way before, that it was cursed in this place, then why didn't you tell me?" Tralane spoke to the ground, breathing its rich aromas. In some detached portion of his thoughts, he realized the season was changing. The earth was cold, and the chill bite in the air was as sharp as the Jade Warrior's reply.

"You did not bother to ask, and I am not bound to warn you of the consequences of your actions. It was your choice to enter the village and to stay when you were not welcome."

"Get away from me. You're trying to kill me. Leave me alone."

"I cannot do that, nor am I seeking your death."

Tralane did not stir. He was in the process of surrendering, both physically and psychically, to the weariness assailing him in the wake of his conflict. He wanted to rest, but the presence of the Jade Warrior troubled his entry into slumber. A hard, unyielding figure stood at the edge of his sleep, waiting for him to cross the border into the dream reality. There were shadows of demons seeking to pursue him, and the stirrings of another pit in which would be exposed horrors Tralane would be unable to escape. Tralane grunted and roused himself, looked up at the Jade Warrior, and tried several times to stand before he accomplished the task.

"You led me to the village," Tralane said finally, in an accusatory tone.

"And you stayed there," the Warrior replied flatly.

Tralane swayed from side to side, then staggered to his kruushka. As the Warrior watched, the bard pulled himself up into the saddle, almost falling several times. Once mounted, Tralane unclenched his fist and saw the pouch and the Eye in his hand.

"Is this what you're after?" Tralane implored, hoping to be relieved of the burden Wyden's Eye was turning out to be.

The Warrior laughed and shook his head. "No, hardly that."

"Where does it come from?"

"From one who watches over you."

"Who watches over me?" Tralane asked. His words were hollow croakings. He was too weak to express the passionate despair that moved him to speak. "What does he want? Tell me, what must I do to rid myself of this thing, of you, of everything. Tell me."

"Let us go on, Tralane. You have your magic. Use it."

The bard kicked the kruushka into a walk and, while laying his head against his mount's neck, made the motions he had sworn never to make again. The Eye responded willingly.

He was glad to leave this world that had promised so much but had finally disappointed him. Or had he been the disappointment? His happiness was a spark that could not find fuel to ignite. The amulet, cold metal and jewel in his hand, and the Jade Warrior were still with him. He was being led, but for what purpose he was too weak at the moment to attempt to discover. His only comfort, as he rode through the night and the doorway between worlds with nothing but the Warrior discernible around him, was his own sense of desolation.

Chapter 12

There followed a week of silence. The season was indeed changing, and in the world the pair now traveled winter was settling into the air. Oram's furs warmed Tralane, but the nights were long and storms descended on them with frequent fierceness. Roads were hidden beneath the white expanse of snow covering the ground, and the hills carefully hid their human settlers so that solid shelter and a blazing fire were impossible to find. Tralane fell ill and sullenly kept his thoughts to himself. The Jade Warrior said nothing, content to follow wherever Tralane led.

One evening Tralane had his sights set on a small, delicately built creature with brown and gold fur and an intricately woven pattern of horns emerging from its skull like a crown. He had never seen such a creature before. Had illness and hunger not ruled the hands holding the bow and arrow, he might have found it beautiful. As it was, his hands were not steady, and what he might have once spared through a sense of displaying his aesthetic appreciation, he now missed because of the frailty of his health.

He threw his weapon to the ground and cursed.

"What am I doing here? Why am I doomed to this petty existence?" He gave the Jade Warrior a venemous glance. "And you, you don't eat, you don't feel the cold, you don't care about anything. What good are you?"

"Now you'll have to dismount," the Jade Warrior said laconically, watching the bard's meal bound towards the cover of trees, "pick up your bow, and mount again, wasting your strength on a childish display of frustration. You have done well, Tralane. At this rate, I shall be companion to a corpse."

"Then why don't you help? Why don't you lead? Make a few decisions?"

"That is not in my nature. I am a follower."

"You follow better than most can attack."

The Jade Warrior laughed, and his merriment echoed under the snow-capped trees which covered the hills around them, rolling back to douse Tralane in scorn.

"You are becoming wiser," the Warrior replied, after his amusement had subsided.

Tralane's stomach suddenly heaved. He coughed up bile, which he spat into the snow. He lost control over the focus of his vision, and the world around him doubled and blurred, as it had done from time to time in the past few days. His head throbbed, his body ached, and his thoughts were sluggish. Finally, after the spell of nausea passed, Tralane caught his breath with heaving breaths and posed the series of questions he had been designing in his mind to the Jade Warrior.

"Where is the nearest town?" was his first query, which he asked while facing the Jade Warrior, but looking past the creature, as if the crystal being were not really so close by.

"There," the Warrior answered, pointing.

"How far?"

"A few hours."

"Are there dangers to me on the way?"

"Yes."

"What kind?"

"The kind you would not be able to fend off in your condition."

"And if we stay here the night, will there be danger?"

"Yes."

"The same as on the way to the town?"

"Yes."

Tralane was surprised by his own patient probing. The Jade Warrior was not an inspiration to trust or patience, and people with whom Tralane had experienced similar attitudes of insolence, arrogance, and condescension had never been used by him as sources of information on which his life depended. But necessity made Tralane compromise in a way which he would never have conceived possible.

"And does this danger also exist in the town?"

"No, not yet."

"Will the danger soon pass there?"

"That I cannot say. Too many factors are in the balance."

"If I go to the town, will the danger avoid me?"

"This is not a danger that can be so easily eluded," the Jade Warrior said wearily, tiring of the game.

Tralane felt a tiny exultation of victory at the Warrior's reply, as if he had won an edge. But he still had questions to ask. He would not be accused of ignoring the wisdom and warnings that were waiting to be dredged up from the Warrior.

"Are there other dangers in the town?"

"Yes."

"What are they?"

"The kind that can cure you."

Cure him of what? But he did not go any further with his inquiry, though he was beginning to enjoy, in a petty way, his contest with the Warrior. The time spent in brooding silence, thinking about his companion's logic, had been rewarded. However, time was also important, and the Jade Warrior was still answering in cryptic riddles. Tralane did not have the time to unravel them or to ask for clarification. With the vague promise of food, shelter and warmth, and an ambiguous cure for an undefined illness waiting for him after a mysteriously perilous journey, Tralane set out for the town. As evening turned to night, Tralane listened carefully for any sounds other than their mounts treading across the treacherous, snow-camouflaged ground.

Lights from the town became visible as they crested a hill and gazed down into a valley. Tralane was unsteady in his saddle and eager to reach the haven, but straightened suddenly when a howl slashed the silence. He drew the black sword and prepared for an attack, glancing in every direction. The howl, long and high-pitched, came again, so near that the bard was afraid he would be set upon before he could strike to defend himself. Then an ice storm shattered the sky, instantly coating the ground with a crystalline shell. Darts of ice blinded Tralane as he searched the darkness, seeking the source of the howl. The hills did not reveal their secret.

Tralane sheathed his sword and urged the kruushka down the pass into the valley. The cry, savage and desperate, was that of a predator. The storm would stave off the animal's attack long enough for Tralane to reach the town. Yet as he rode, Tralane listened to the reverberations of the howl in his memory and heard the anguish of a beast unjustly wounded. He glanced back at the Jade Warrior, whose rigid visage expressed only an uncommon degree of disdain for elements and emotions, and decided the echoes he heard were not so laden with meaning as he had originally conceived.

The storm was still rising in pitch when the pair reached the main street. The town's outer buildings were abandoned, their walls broken and breached by the season's snow. Carts had been stripped of their wheels and lined up to form a ramshackle wall between the gaps in the houses, but they were almost buried in snow and had been shifted by the wind to open many holes in the defensive perimeter. The town had the bedraggled appearance of being under seige by more than a harsh season and losing the battle of attrition to its enemies. Tralane gave the Jade Warrior an uneasy look.

"Is the danger you spoke of near?"

"No, we've already passed it."

Somewhat reassured, Tralane stopped in front of a two-storey building on whose double doors were painted two large-petalled flowers in red, yellow and green. The emblems were meticulously clear of accumulated ice and snow. The colors glistened in the dim light leaking from windows across the street. Tralane dismounted, gave the reins of his kruushka to a startled livery girl who came running from the stable next to the building, and ploughed through a snow bank to reach the doors. He pushed one of them open with his shoulder and stepped inside.

Tralane had forgotten his appearance. The white furs, loosely knit into a jacket, made him appear bulkier than he really was. His leggings were darkened by moisture and mud, contrasting sharply with the lighter top. His cap and the hair which stuck out from it was matted, like the rest of his clothing, and covered with clumps of ice which began to melt from the heat of the hearth fires situated around the room. His eyes were red from exhaustion and fever, and his face and hands were bloated by exposure and illness. Scars lacerated his exposed skin, and the sword which hung ominously at his side proved that he had survived wounds when his enemies had not.

The tavern was almost empty, the townspeople obviously preferring the company of their own families on such a night. The few who were present were divided into two groups, one sitting around a table against the far right wall and the other standing at the counter against the back wall. They stared at him with wide, shocked eyes.

The tables were round, and the unused stools were placed upside down on the tops. Through the jungle of wooden legs, Tralane returned the stare of the people with a silent plea.

Their eyes shifted as the Jade Warrior arrived behind him. The emerald, crystal-cut body was coated with sheets of ice which slid across the Warrior's skin like interlocking plates of armor whenever he moved. A thin ruby crescent between his lips indicated a slight smile. Upon seeing him, the men in the tavern rose, some backing off, while others fumbled for swords, daggers, and staffs. The man behind

the counter—short and balding but robust nonetheless—
pulled out a bludgeon and leaped over the countertop with
efficient agility.

Tralane looked frantically from face to face, seeking a
way to head off the impending brawl. He said nothing;
he was at a loss to speak about anything other than warmth
and rest. In turn, the men of the inn stood their ground,
once they were unified in a common front against the
strange intruders. The tension from the deadlock mounted
as the silence continued, until Tralane felt as if he would
collapse under its weight.

Then a woman entered through a door behind the
counter. She stopped short, holding a small barrel in her
arms. Her black eyes energetically surveyed the room.
Her chestnut hair fell in loose curls over her forehead and
ears, accentuating her high cheekbones. The curls blended
with the rich brown and tan work frock she wore. She
had the demeanor of a bright and curious child.

After her appraisal was completed, she calmly placed
the barrel under the counter and, distractedly brushing
herself off, wandered up to Tralane and the Jade Warrior.
While still a few arm lengths away, she looked up suddenly
and, as if taking notice of them for the first time, smiled
heartily.

"Well, now, you've picked a fine night for traveling.
What brings you two here at this time of night, in the
middle of a storm?" She was cheerful, and her inquiry
was made disarming by a coquettish turn of her head and
a fist propped against her hip.

"Sleep?" Tralane croaked uncertainly, holding out his
hands hesitantly, palms up.

The woman nodded, then eyed the Jade Warrior. "And
your friend?"

The Warrior retreated to the near left-hand corner of
the room, diagonally across from the group seated around
the table. He took down a chair and seated himself. He
remained immobile, fixing his gaze on the emptiness in
the middle of the room.

"Cumulain!" exclaimed the balding bludgeon-carrier, holding out his free hand as if to stop her.

"Don't worry, Jax. The green one's beginning to look like a statue, and a statue's harmless enough. This one," she said, cocking her head at Tralane, "is certainly in no condition to be any trouble. He needs help, and the Wilderness Flower has few enough visitors to start turning away half-dead men now."

"No, they're sorcerous," Jax protested. "The Beast will follow them in. He'll try to take them."

"Send them back out," another muttered, while a third chimed in, "What are strangers doing here in this season? It's a trick or an evil omen!"

The woman's face reddened and the muscles of her neck constricted.

"They are my charges," she shouted, "and the Wilderness Flower is my tavern. You are welcome to the snow and the Beast outside if you don't like the way I run things."

Again, there was a tense silence in which the men and the woman glared angrily at one another. The quiet was broken when Tralane, too fatigued to stand and wait for the outcome of their fight, collapsed onto the floor. A couple of men instinctively took a step forward before they held up their weapons in defense against their compassion and rejoined the group in surprised confusion.

Cumulain bent over Tralane and loosened his clothes.

"Brother, help me bring him upstairs," she said over her shoulder.

Jax hesitated, gripping his bludgeon until his knuckles were pale. She twisted around and cried out, "He's not the Beast, nor is the green thing our enemy. Are you just going to watch him die?"

Jax shook his head vehemently and opened his mouth to say something. He changed his mind abruptly, threw the bludgeon aside, and reluctantly joined his sister. The inn's customers started at the sharp crash of the weapon's landing.

"He may be a hero, or a god of some kind," Jax grunted

as he helped Cumulain lift Tralane, who remained passive. "He has enough wounds to be taken for a battler, at any rate. Whatever his birth and station, he'll pay for his care and lodgings by going out to hunt the Beast."

"If he's a god," an onlooker snorted as Tralane's limp body was carried by him, "they're making them poorer and frailer than they used to."

"Maybe," Jax replied in a whisper, casting a worried eye at the Jade Warrior, "but his friend seems a bit sturdier. I don't think we could get rid of *him* so easily."

"And he might stand a better chance against the Beast, eh?" Cumulain said with bitter resignation. "There's always the Beast to think of."

"Yes, there is always that. There is nothing else for us but the Beast."

The words drifted down to the level of Tralane's consciousness, barely audible, with meanings difficult to grasp. He heard the Beast named over and over again, spoken by stoic voices weary with the endurance of suffering and taut with the contained rage of helplessness before an overwhelming power. Something monstrous, something terrible and feared, lurked in the hills surrounding the town. Had the howls signaling the sudden ice storm been its cry?

He was carried through a dark hall and up a flight of stairs. A green haze began to settle over Tralane's perception of the world, and rivers of molten metal cut through the thickening fog like lava running through a forest. A figure coalesced, shimmering emerald in a bloody mist, and Tralane sank into the fitful other-world of his sleep where his own beast lay waiting. A scream was on his lips.

Chapter 13

They were facing one another on a desert plain, sand trails whipping across their feet and calves, wrapping themselves around flesh and cold rock crystal. Tralane watched himself, a black sword sheathed in a bright aura of silver light in his hand, standing before the Jade Warrior. Tralane could not tell if he had initiated the confrontation, or if the Jade Warrior had finally decided to end his tactics of harassment and commit himself to a direct assault on the bard.

The Warrior struck first and beat Tralane back. As Tralane's other-self perspective sank to the level of the battle, the sands parted beneath his feet. He fell back, retreating down a ramp into a cave, the mouth closing after the Jade Warrior entered. Tralane turned and ran. The walls and floor of the cave were cold to the touch, yet he stuck close to them, wanting a firm wall against his back when it came time to fight. His two selves were merged; he had lost the position of detached observer.

Tripping once on an unseen object, he lost his equilibrium and started to fall. He twisted and turned to keep from striking the ground. For a moment, he was frighteningly dizzy, on the verge of collapsing into a pit he could not see. He could only sense a vast openness waiting to engulf him. He managed to regain his balance and rested, leaning on a wall and breathing hard. The wall collapsed and he fell through the opening, landing on a paved stone floor. He looked and listened for the Jade Warrior's pursuit; on seeing and hearing none, he scrambled to his feet and started running along the paved corridor. There were torches on the walls, set at regular intervals and held by mangled arms with rotting flesh jutting from the massive blocks of cut stone from which the walls had been constructed. Soon there were doors, heavy iron and bolted, with portals rusted shut. They alternated on either side of him. He stopped in front of one and opened it. He cried out in terror as the ghostly apparitions of his mother and father spread out their arms to him. They were hanging from the vaulted ceiling, the nooses tightly drawn around their necks, but they were still alive, pleading for him to join them. Again he cried out and tried to close his eyes. Instead he found that he had just opened them.

Chapter 14

Cumulain's concerned face hovered over him, dissipating the nightmare images like a morning sun chasing the fog across the land, driving it from the paths of civilized men. The faces of his parents vanished, though he tried to hold on to them. The stone walls melted, and the dungeon doors receded into the unknowable.

"You were shivering, so I added some more blankets to your bed," Cumulain whispered with sympathy.

Tralane groaned hoarsely and tried to pass a hand over his face, but found his arms weighed down under several thick fur covers. Despite their number, a cool breeze was still gently caressing his skin, sending shivers down his spine. In an odd contradiction he could not wholly grasp, but which seemed important for him to understand, his eyes burned like coals set in a pit of warm ashes. The room was indistinct beyond Cumulain's face, revolving around his head until it was nothing more than a blur. Breathing was a burden.

Cumlain offered him a cup of steaming, herb-scented liquid. Holding his head up, she poured the beverage into his parched mouth. After a few moments, the nurturing heat of the liquid spread throughout his limbs. But along with the warmth came the awareness of pain as wounds, festering with infection, and bruised bones were remembered. Again Tralane groaned, and Cumulain let his head rest on the cushions.

"You've been in delirium for a week, Tralane," Cumulain told him, her forehead creased with anxiety. "My mother Camala and I have watched over you, fed you, and applied all the balms and potions in our knowledge to heal you." She shrugged her shoulders apologetically, her eyes studying him for signs of consciousness. He tried to speak, but the vague words died on inarticulate lips.

"You're weak and very ill. Our magic has not healed you, but at least it's kept you alive. The strength to outrace death must come from you, Tralane. Can you hear me? Can you understand? Your wounds have not gotten better or worse, your sickness steadily consumes the medicines we've given you. The balance is yours to change."

He remembered that her eyes had seemed black when he first met her, but now they were green, the color of summer forests, inviting, comforting. Concern flowed from them into his exhausted spirit. Her eyes anchored him to a reality which resisted the surges and eddies of disease. The frigid, crystalline beauty of emerald, precious stone of rulers, symbol of power, no longer haunted him. The green he saw now was lush, overflowing, invulnerable in its magnitude.

A green mist descended over his eyes, but this did not signal the arrival of demons, their sharp talons clawing and clutching. The field of his vision was free from ominous shadows. There was quiet; in the serenity, the nausea and pain that wracked his mind and body began to coalesce into a fiercely glowing jewel, its countless facets shimmering with the intensity of his suffering. Around that jewel gathered an invisible force, enfolding and crushing the blight. He closed his eyes, allowing something within to tame the chaos, to channel the frenetic energies into life-preserving duties. Relief settled over his troubled mind. He fell into dreamless sleep.

When he awoke, he felt as if time had not passed. Yet he was stronger, and he could see his room clearly by the light of a lantern standing like a sentinel on a table by

the door. He moved his head from side to side, taking in
the log walls, low ceiling, and single window looking out
onto the night. As if by a prearranged signal, the door
opened and Cumulain stepped in. She immediately noticed
his open eyes and looked at him questioningly. He nodded, croaking words even he did not recognize. She quickly
came to him and brushed hair from his forehead.

"I only stepped out for a moment, Tralane. I didn't
mean to leave you alone." Her face was pale, drained of
vigor. Worry lines seemed permanently etched into the
folds of her skin.

He closed his eyes briefly and nodded once. He managed to move his hand from beneath the covers, and
touched her face. Her expression did not change, and
from his cold finger tips he feared she might be frozen.

"You understand what I'm saying now?" she pleaded.
To his puzzled grunt, she replied, "Good, I'm glad something has finally turned for the good. You've been here
for over three weeks."

Tralane started at the length of time he had been engaged
in his dream battle against illness. Two weeks had passed
since Cumulain's last exhortation. Two weeks for the foul-
ness within him to gather into the jewel, to be crushed,
and then redirected. He wanted to be tired from the effort,
but his thoughts were becoming clearer, his attention rising to absorb Cumulain's words.

"Yes, three weeks. And a few days, I think. I've lost
track lately. The others, the townspeople, they're becoming impatient. More were taken in broad daylight. The
Beast uses us like a store of food. The heavy snows have
cut us off from the other towns. We're penned in. We
can't stop it; we're helpless. It can't die by our swords.
The men are not skilled enough as fighters to discover its
weakness." She paused, glancing at the door.

"I was afraid they might take you and offer you to the
Beast. They tried with your friend, but they couldn't budge
him. He just . . . sat, and when they tried to force him
up, they cut their hands and notched their swords on
his skin. Even the Beast bleeds when cut by a sword, but

your companion is as invulnerable as he is immobile. The men have been driven away by his constant presence; they call him another Beast and shun my house. My brother is with them, but my mother and I have tended you despite their threats. They don't dare come for you while one of us is with you—not yet. But now with your wounds finally beginning to heal and the sickness turned back, you'll soon be able to fend for yourself. Don't worry, my arts will take hold now and speed the process."

She rose suddenly and left the room, leaving Tralane dazed by her breathless speech. Without her to distract him, the dim memories of his arrival began to coalesce. Brief moments of consciousness also returned to him, and a pattern emerged with the repetitive motif of the Beast. The townspeople were terrified of this monster they could not destroy. Like the Jade Warrior in relation to Tralane, the Beast seemed to have fixed itself upon a victim, relentlessly stalking, waiting to strike, hovering on the borders between life and death, awareness and dream. The Warrior and the Beast were of a breed. They were the implacable enemies of life. And if they were kin, then so were Tralane and the townspeople. If they considered the Jade Warrior another Beast, then he would view the Beast as another Warrior. Cumulain's enemy was also his.

By the time Cumulain returned, carrying a tray piled with food, across which lay his sword, Tralane had resolved to return the aid that had been granted him in restoring him to health.

"Here," Cumulain said nervously, laying the tray on the table and bringing the sword to him, "a warrior should not be without his sword. And this," she said, taking out the pouch containing Wyden's Eye. "You should not be without this, also. It is a powerful source, Tralane. You must be mighty indeed to have mastered such a thing."

Tralane laughed, and coughed up phlegm. He wanted to tell her he was nothing more than a thing called a Keeper, a mere playing piece in a game he could not control. The Jade Warrior was not his friend, but a strange, passive kind of enemy who would watch Tralane die without coming to his aid. He needed protection and sanctuary.

Fates, gods, demons, and spirits all reached into the soul to light fires that drove men into the pits dug by these same immortal forces. There was no such thing as mastery; did the scar on his shoulder not prove this? One could manipulate and deceive, and thus win a few short moments of power. But the end always came. The artifice of lies crashed, revealing the bitter core of helplessness in the face of an ancient, malevolent universe.

His confessions died with his voice. With the tokens of his strength by his side, Tralane watched as Cumulain dragged the table across the room to him. Despite her obvious exhaustion, she was still strong, driven by an iron will towards the preservation of life. She was not crumbling; she was a mountain whose face might be changed by a storm, but remained unmoved. She gave him bread, cheese, and meat, along with small draughts of strong wine.

"You haven't eaten anything solid since you've been here. You must build your strength."

Tralane nodded gratefully and offered her some of the food. She hesitated, then let her own hunger dictate her actions and shared the food with him. As they ate, she looked at him with curiosity.

"You are so strange, and your friend is different from anything spoken of in the legends, or even in texts of magic. Where must you come from? Surely not this world?"

Conflicting emotions struggled for access to the frigid portals of his flesh. Tears stung his eyes. Another jewel within him shattered, flaws branching through its core like lightning in an ominous sky. Another sickness collapsed into itself, disintegrating into a galaxy of myriad fragments.

There was a brief flash of light, in which could be seen a cowering, fearful thing, stripped of the accoutrements of meaning, kneeling over the blasted ashes of a dead self, as Fatome had knelt beside the smoldering earth that had taken Oram. The triumphant joy he felt after such fantastic escapades as the theft of Wyden's Eye, the transient moments of security before the visions of a future tamed and uneventful, and the profound depths of hopelessness he experienced when the world within him conflicted with the world around him were all combined and transformed into one swirling truth. There was sadness and bereavement over the loss of some part of him. But with that loss another thing was gained, another self born. The cowering, fearful thing stood, naked, without the veils of imagined power and glory beautifying its existence. In its nakedness was its strength.

The light vanished, and reality seeped back to replace it. The broken jewel fragments were swept away as waters bubbled from a well, irrigating a hard, parched surface. An old suit of armor split, and the skin beneath was raw from the chafing of new flesh against the walls of an unyielding container.

"He is not my friend," Tralane cried desperately, pleading for her to understand.

The lines of anxiety on her face softened. Whatever pressures had been brought to bear on her by angry neighbors, worried and endangered relatives, and the piercing howls of the Beast were momentarily dissipated as she drew from Tralane the few drops of strength she had craved for.

"Yes, my warrior," she said, laying a hand across his chest. "There is no need for shame. He is not one a mortal could ever befriend. But rest, Tralane. Nourish yourself and sleep. Tomorrow we will talk of our dreams and our lives, of hopes and enemies." And she smiled as she brought a cup of wine to her lips and drank from it deeply.

Tralane relaxed, relieved. A burden he had never known he was carrying was suddenly made lighter as the load was shared by another.

Chapter 15

The next day Tralane was torn from his sleep by a shriek which seemed to originate from beneath his window. Dawn had not yet completely lightened the air. Tralane sat up, feeling the emptiness of the room after the unknown voice had filled it. He wondered where Cumulain had gone to, then worked himself free of the covers. He walked on shaky legs to the window, where he leaned heavily against the wall and peered through the glazed facade of the shutters.

A moon in three-quarters was vying with the still-slumbering sun for the role of light-giver. In the street below, stark against a new layer of snow, was the carcass of a thortlike animal. Its snout was longer, as were its legs, and a mane of hair covered the back of its neck. Beside the slain mount stooped a huge, white-furred creature. It stood upright suddenly, carrying the bloody, mangled remains of a man under its arm. The monster quickly glanced up and down the street, then half-jumped, half-limped away into the whiteness.

The door behind Tralane burst open, and Cumulain rushed in, out of breath.

"Did you see the Beast?" she yelled hysterically. "In front of the Wilderness Flower! It took a man right outside! Did you see who it was? No one will ever cross our threshold again, stained with such evil blood—"

Steps reverberated outside the door; before anyone entered, Tralane was already diving back to his bed to take up his sword. Jax entered, saw Tralane sprawled sideways on the bed fumbling with the handle of the sword, and started forward. Cumulain dove after her brother and held on to him with a tenacity which surprised Tralane as he finally freed the black sword from the sheath. Though he was weak and could not make the anger in him rise to give his body strength, Tralane hardly needed any effort to lift the sword. Again, the weapon was drawing on unknown sources of power.

Jax halted when he saw the black sword and the way it swayed effortlessly to and fro in a defensive arc.

"What are you doing?" Cumulain cried, still venting her fright uncontrollably.

"He was the cause," Jax shouted, pointing his short sword at Tralane. Caught between fear of the Beast and the sight of a man who had just escaped death handling a blade with apparent ease, Jax remained immobile. He allowed Cumulain to stand between him and Tralane.

"The Beast was coming for him," he continued, his voice edged with the hysteria his sister freely expressed. "But he took poor Lythgar instead. Let me send him out now, before someone else dies because of misguided mercy to strangers."

"The Beast was with us long before Tralane arrived," Cumulain said, her will and anger starting to assert themselves over fear. "Don't . . . you can't abandon him to his death now, so soon after his recovery. He doesn't have the strength yet. Don't join your enemy, Jax, don't help to feed it."

"I'll hunt your beast down for you, Jax. By the sword in my hand," Tralane heard himself saying, as if he were a stranger to himself, "I swear it."

Jax looked at him uncertainly, his eyes weighing the contradiction of man and sword. Suddenly he turned, ignoring his sister, and stalked out of the room.

When he had left, Cumulain's shoulders sagged and she stood hunched over. Then she took the few steps between her and the bed and collapsed on its covers, weeping.

Tralane dropped the sword and crawled across the bed to where she lay. He caressed her head, her hair, and stared absently at her shuddering back. She was so different from the women Tralane was accustomed to dealing with, ladies of the court and their coarser counterparts in the taverns. The range of feelings and their depth was greater than Tralane was wholly comfortable seeing. If he had met such people in his past, he had not thought much of them and had disdained their company, making them his victims rather than his allies. But now he did not feel the need to victimize in others those aspects of himself he despised or could not face. The loneliness of detachment was no longer a prize. He cradled Cumulain's head with his other hand.

"Your brother is frightened," he said gently. "Why? Why can't the creature be killed? What is the Beast?"

Cumulain spoke into the bed, looking away from Tralane. "My brother is afraid? We're *all* scared, Tralane! It haunts us, it can't be killed, and it won't go away. Do you know what that's like, to live in terror from day to day, waiting for the blow to land? Do you know what it feels to have the life drained from you as you watch something approach you, feeding on you even without touching you? You can't stop it, you can only watch, watch, I tell you! You can't even see it, but you can watch. The bodies drop, the houses become empty. The corruption spreads, invisible, except for the eyes. You can see it in the eyes of the survivors. There you see it, so when it comes for you there is recognition. Because you've watched, and you haven't been able to do anything against it. Yes, Tralane, we're afraid of the Beast, afraid to recognize it."

She turned her head and faced Tralane, her eyes puffy and red. Defiance was mixed with horror in her expression.

Tralane tried to touch her but she backed away, still

staring at him, as if he were the monster. Despite the heat rising through the vents from the hearths below, Tralane felt a chill.

"Is the Beast immortal—demon or spirit? Is he a sorcerous creation, or a mortal animal?"

"The Beast," she recited, releasing an inner litany of unreason which had apparently been repeated often and in private, in the hope of finding an underlying foundation of logic and justice, "is part animal, part human, and part sorcery.

"Many years ago, this town was an outpost for the northern kingdoms seeking trade routes south through the mountains. We were a prosperous town then, and this tavern, which was built by my father and uncle, was always filled with the restless breed—traders, hunters, caravanners, and soldiers for hire. My family called this place the Wilderness Flower—wild for its location and patrons, and flower for the hopes they had for their future. But then the winters became harsher, as if the years of relatively mild snows were a lure to bring people to their ruin. The passes south were choked, and the caravans and soldiers left. A few hunters, trappers, and small traders stayed, for habit's sake, but they could not keep the town alive.

"Then a sorcerer came, worn and hurt, much as you arrived. But he was far older and weak by the nature of his body as well as the weather. He had been defeated by a rival, and strange wounds—cuts which glowed, movements under his skin as if maggots rifled his inner being, and palpitating, dark green growths on his limbs— marked his nearness to death. He railed against kings and nobles, petty warriors, and insane magicians. He refused to appreciate the town's help; indeed, he seemed to think our care for him was his right. His temper became fierce, and he claimed we were holding back our healing arts when he realized we could only slow the approach of his impending doom. Children suffered burns by his spells, women miscarried and were strangely infected, and men were stricken by weakness and fainting. This wizard was a disease, corrupting us from within, so we ceased our attentions and turned him out of the Wilderness Flower. That night there was a storm, and we thought it would end his misery, for he had taken his bitterness and hatred and carried it up into the mountains, where the winds and the cold were at their worst. It was soon after he disappeared that the Beast took its first victim."

"How long ago was that?"

"Before I was born. Twenty years ago, maybe more. The Beast would take only one victim a year, and the townspeople, feeling unclean over their turning out of the wizard, did not find that too great a price to pay for their unity of passive purpose against a common enemy."

"All this time, and no one fought back?" Tralane asked, disbelieving.

"Tyranny is best imposed on oneself, Tralane. There was no courage to face the wizard directly when he was among us and put him mercifully out of his misery. I think that's what he wanted done. He goaded us and jeered at us, probing for the strength he himself lacked and uncovering only cowardice. He was beyond the medicinal power of anyone, yet there were those among us who would not admit such a thing as death, for to do so would have been to acknowledge this town's and their own eventual doom. So they prolonged the wizard's life and, under the mask of caring, fed their own delusions. In turn, this wizard's madness and desperation grew as he was not allowed to die. He was the prisoner of his own and the town's denial of death, just as we are now imprisoned. We accepted our fate, for that, too, distracted us from the town's eventual demise. The tyranny was steady, but undemanding."

"But people were sacrificed! Isn't that a demand?"

"A stranger, a criminal, a stray or deserter. Oh, it was not fair, Tralane. We did not ask permission from our sacrifices, especially when the sacrifice came from our own people. We kept it a secret, and not even the trappers and hunters who settled in the town to marry our daughters were informed, for they might one day be chosen. The secret united the town, and the bond that had been formed to turn out the wizard became unbreakable. What had been founded on hope was now resting on collusion to deny the inevitable. The town was preserved, and the Beast satiated every year."

"Until?"

"Until only recently, in the past year. The Beast is apparently tired of the game. It is hungry for flesh and power. It taunts us, flaunting the strength we allowed it to gain all these years. Now we are even more its victims."

"Then the Beast is really the sorcerer?"

"No, the sorcerer died. But, according to my mother, who along with a few others here is knowledgeable about magic, it is driven partially by the sorcerer's will. You see, the sorcerer died in the snow, and was probably stalked by a hunting animal—by the look of the Beast, a cthan feline. There must have been one last spell before death took the sorcerer, merging man, snow and cthan into one creature. It is mortal—animal and human—hence it can bleed. But the Beast is also snow, elemental, limitless, easily replenished, and it is also magically endowed. We can wound the flesh, but that is not what holds the Beast together. Winter and the sorcerer have allied to keep us in the borderlands of death, just as the townspeople must have kept the wizard."

Tralane crawled back under the covers and rested his back against the headboard. His gaze wandered away from her.

"Does the Beast frighten you, too?" she asked, her face softening a shade.

"I'd be a fool to say no," Tralane replied, irony adding the edge to his voice.

"Would you have said no, once?"

"Yes, once. And then run away."

"Will you run now?"

"No."

Cumulain approached Tralane, moving his sword aside to sit beside him. She ran her fingers along the weapon, touching the amulet's pouch lying beside the pommel.

"What else do you fear, Tralane?" she asked with deceptive naïveté.

"Too many things," Tralane said, turning to look at the shuttered window.

The young woman rose, closed the door Jax had left open in his retreat, and returned to sit on the edge of the bed. Her mood had changed; her face was still shadowed by the shock of the killing just outside her door, as well as her revelation of the town's darkest secret, but now an intense curiosity renewed the color of her skin. Yet Tralane sensed that hers was not the inquisitiveness of an observer interested only in the entertaining details of a story. She had trusted him enough to lay before him the source of the town's present curse. She had protected him from people who no doubt had their fill of sickly strangers and who, until lately, had sacrificed those passing through their lands to the Beast. Now she wanted reciprocity. She rested a hand on Tralane's chest, leaning on him slightly, and gazed at him expectantly like a woman waiting for her lover to divulge his intimate secrets.

"Your friend downstairs?" she offered. "Is he really a companion?"

"No," he said hoarsely, fixing his eyes on her hand resting on his chest. He had difficulty bringing up the words. It was simpler to imagine his thoughts flowing from his heart to her hand, and from her hand through her arm and to her heart.

"Where did you find him?"

"I didn't. He found me. He calls himself the Jade Warrior and was sent to watch me as I flounder in trouble of my own making."

"And there is no peace from him?"

"No, there isn't. His words cut me, his presence humiliates. He won't leave me, and I cannot avoid him. He's invulnerable, as far as I can see. He does nothing, yet I know he's toying with me. I don't know where he comes from, who sent him, or even why."

"Oh yes you do, Tralane. This," she said, holding up

the pouch, "is the bait which has attracted the Warrior to you, is it not?"

"How do you know that? No, it isn't true; he's not after the Eye. I've already asked him."

"I did not say he wanted the charm. I merely pointed out a bond. How did you get it?"

"I stole it. And how do you know it's a charm, as you call it?"

She smiled. "I'm not such a fool as to be blind to sorcery. And the fact that you've stolen this charm does not mean it is so precious that another would try to take it from you. Some things are meant to be taken, and I sense you were destined to come into the possession of this Eye—"

"Wyden's Eye, an amulet with the power to breach the walls separating existences from one another." He spoke authoritatively, seeking to impress her with his power.

"And who is Wyden? Why is his Eye in the hands of a stranger?"

Tralane's expression was blank. "I don't know."

"If you don't know the source of this magic, how can you control it?"

"I can't."

"Then whose purpose are you serving? Where are you going?"

Tralane shrugged his shoulders. "I want to be left alone. I want shelter, food, and peace. I want warmth and the beating of many hearts around me."

"A thief steals, then does not want to spend his prize?" she asked incredulously. "Where do you come from?"

Tralane grimaced at the question and turned his head aside. He rolled away from her so her hand could no longer rest on his chest.

"No past, no future?" she persisted. "Only the present, with power and no purpose. A stranger to whom you have surrendered follows you."

Her summary of his situation was of little comfort. He could not bear to hear such a concise encapsulation of the meaninglessness of his life, nor could he stay with people who, even if they were to say nothing, saw the emptiness within him. He could fulfill his obligation to the town and fight their Beast. Then he would leave.

"You are a dangerous man, Tralane," Cumulain said sternly, getting up from the bed. "You are more dangerous than the Beast, who to us is merely evil."

"An arrow unguided is deadlier than one shot in anger." He repeated the archer's proverb of his world with spiteful sarcasm.

"You know this yourself. Good. I'll bring you some food, and then help the others downstairs recover from their fright. Perhaps I can convince them to keep their wits collected, now that you have promised to defend us. Later, we will talk some more."

She left, to return shortly with a platter of tubular, almost translucent objects which he discovered, after tasting the sweet, juicy meat, were fruit. Again she left. As he ate with the sullenness of a punished child, he heard Cumulain's voice downstairs, shouting. She was arguing with a group of men, one of whom sounded like her brother. While he listened and ate, trying to make out their conversation, an old woman quietly entered his room.

The woman carried a stool, which she placed by the window, and sat so that the morning sun's rays could bathe her with the first light. He offered her a fruit, but she shook her head slightly in refusal and peered through a crevice in the shutters. She watched the street silently, the folds and wrinkles on her face immovable under the weight of time and experience. Her white hair lightened the grayness of her face. Though any resemblance had crumbled under the onslaught of years, Tralane took her to be Cumulain's mother.

A door slammed below them, and a few angry epithets accompanied the exit. The mother's expression did not change as her children bickered in the snow. Then there was silence. Cumulain's mother continued to stare out into the street as the sunlight began to emphasize the lines of her worn features. Tralane said nothing to her, retreating into his own thoughts rather than eliciting them from another.

Yet he felt the need to pry from her the wisdom she had no doubt exchanged for the youth that had been stripped from her by the elements. Cumulain had clarified many feelings and questions, but the resolution of the conflicts were still beyond his reach. The acknowledgement and expression of weakness was of small comfort if he could not also see, at least on the horizon, their elimination. He was afraid that if he fixed his gaze too long on these failings, he would withdraw again into the oblivion of feigned ignorance and pride. He saw only the endurance of an evil aspect within him and wished only for its utter destruction in himself and others.

But fear held his tongue. He could not summon the strength to hear what she might have to say. The paradox of wanting to protect and wishing to expose, of fortifying and tearing down at the same time, weighed his words until they sank to the bottom of his soul. He had to be free, yet someone else had to break the chains that bound him as a prisoner within himself. The old solution—a guide, a knowledgeable companion to direct and take responsibility—was the chief seducer of Tralane's will. Yet the price of this last solution was not to his liking, either, for with it he would forsake all hopes for independence.

A paralysis slowly settled over Tralane. He watched the old woman with mixed feelings of resentment—that Cumulain had stirred his thoughts and that her mother would not quell them—and hope that at last he had found a source of aid. He was like an exile at the gate of his own city, longing to go in, yet suffering from self-banishment. He could no more express himself than control his passage between worlds.

Cumulain returned when the sun was nearing its zenith. Her hair was soaked with moisture, and her face was covered with a film of sweat. Immediately, Tralane's doubts evaporated and his anxieties calmed. The old woman left, as silently as she had arrived, without a glance at her daughter or the bard. Whatever thoughts or judgments she had made went unspoken.

Cumulain fell on to the bed and lay atop the covers, next to Tralane.

"You must get well soon, Tralane. This last murder by the Beast has shaken the townspeople. They're restless, afraid. They'll be coming after you, and I won't be able to stop them."

"I'll go out to fight the Beast," Tralane said angrily. "Tell them—no, bring Jax here, and the others. I'll tell them myself."

"Don't be so headstrong." She sighed wearily. "I believe you. You've nothing to prove."

He raised his hand, hesitated, then caressed her hair. When she did not move away, he continued.

"Your mother said nothing to me. Is she like the others, like Jax? Does she secretly despise me?"

"She wouldn't have stayed with you all these nights if she did."

"Then why didn't she say something?" Tralane asked, piqued.

"Did you speak to her?" Cumulain was talking with a distracted air.

"No."

"Then why should she?" Cumulain retorted with irritation. "My mother's buried husbands and children, seen gods tear at the earth, and watched sorcerers transform men and elements into each other. She's lived in the mountains and in the cities of the north, and now she's watching her last two children threaten each other with death over a spindly stray with an animated green rock for a shadow. She has no words to waste on you, if you've none to offer." She rolled on her stomach and stared at him. He wiped the sweat from her face.

"There was a lot of work to be done," she explained, her voice softening. "Especially with Jax gone."

He acknowledged her statement with a distracted nod, then asked, "The Jade Warrior?"

"He's still downstairs. He hasn't moved—he doesn't eat or sleep."

"What must he think about?" Tralane wondered out loud. The same question had plagued him during their days of travel together and the nights in camp. Tralane would go to sleep only to wake up in the morning and find the Warrior sitting by the ashes of the fire, staring at the horizon, his position unchanged from the previous night.

"More importantly, what do you think, Tralane?"

Her query tore him away from the blurred but absorbing memories of long, harsh, lonely days and nights in the wilderness.

"Think about what?" he asked, perplexed.

"Yourself? Me? The Jade Warrior?" She paused, touched the scab of a wound on his chin, lifted the covers, and traced the path of the old scar on his shoulder with her fingertips. "You've been hurt before. You came to the Inn almost beyond life. How have all these things happened?"

Tralane considered the scope of her question and flitted over the surface of his memory for a place to dip in and start drawing out the past. There were so many things to say, and once cast into the frame of words and given to another, they would be solidified into an emotional reality that had so far eluded him.

"I dreamed last night about my parents," he began, speaking softly and avoiding her eyes. "I'm an orphan. I was given to an old wizard who knew nothing of children, to be raised as an apprentice sorcerer. He had also the need, no doubt, for some kind of unobtrusive company during the days of his dying. Why he picked a child, I shall never know. He never explained where I came from and how he came to have the responsibility of raising me.

"I imagine he wanted some breath of innocence in his life, steeped as it was in the dark ways of sorcery. But I have seen what pesky things children can be to those who do not have the patience or interest in caring for infants. And unlike the ladies of the court, my adopter did not surrender me to nursemaids. He took me into the wilderness and exiled me along with himself. Alone together, I must have been a bothersome distraction from his studies and pursuits of sorcerous power. It's a wonder he did not sell or give me away to some passing wizard or traveler; but then, perhaps he tried, and none would have me. He surely regretted his rash undertaking, for he rarely spoke to me of anything but sorcery, as if her were trying to mold me into his own image. Yet I was not made from his flesh and blood, so why should I have allowed myself to be his shadow? He did not treat me like a son but rather as a wayward pet who would not learn his master's tricks.

"So I rebelled and made his life even more miserable until I finally brought this injury on myself, though I was really trying to hurt him by gaining knowledge of my parents. I failed in my undertaking and raised some monstrous demon. He cared for me diligently, but I sensed his irritation with the reasoning behind my attempt and also with its failure. I had challenged him and failed. I was not worthy of being his apprentice, and he had no need of a mere adopted son. I decided to spare the both of us the irritation of our coexistence and ran away."

"You haven't mentioned your caretaker's name, Tralane," Cumulain interrupted.

"Mathi."

"Is it so painful a name that you cannot speak it?"

Tralane shrugged off the probe and continued, his voice a touch softer.

"I toured the royal courts of the kingdoms of my world, thirsty for people, knowledge, and experience. The wives of rich merchants took me in at first, until I learned to entertain the nobility with my tales and defend them with my bow. I slept amid the trappings of power and glory and I spoke only to the famous or powerful. I played for power, using the people around me like pieces in a harmless game. When I lost my pieces, I moved on, banishing myself for a while from the high places of rule and withdrawing into solitude to nurse my wounds. Of course, after a while, my solitude resembled my time with Mathi, and I could not stand that. So I returned to the kingdoms and gambled again. That has been my life, until just recently, when I stole this amulet from an invading Sorcerer King accompanied by a host. I abandoned my world and again set out for adventure.

"I, too, have seen gods rake men with sorcerous talons, Cumulain. I saw a wizard die, fought myself on a parallel world, allowed a creature to attach itself to me, and was almost slain by my own blind fears and desires.

"Yet all that seems as if it happened long ago, to another man, or rather to a boy. My history is to me like one of my tales—an artifice contrived to entertain and distract. And now I dream about my parents. I've never known them, but I saw their faces in my dream. I knew them. Isn't that strange?"

He paused, waiting for her to respond. She was silent.

"I'm tired, Cumulain," he said at last. "I want to rest."

Cumulain rested her head on Tralane's scarred shoulder.

"I know," she answered soothingly. "My mother has seen this in you, and she has taught me how to see such weariness. But you are young, Tralane, and still have things to do. My mother rests now, even though she would rather be pitting her waning strength against the Beast, because she has done the things she set out to do."

"I have no tasks to complete. I am adrift, useless. You said so yourself."

Cumulain sat up angrily. "I said you were a danger because you were adrift, Tralane. Do not twist my words to suit your self-pity. If you don't have a past, find it. Go back to your world, find your magician's dwelling place. There must be a record of your birth, or perhaps an agreement between your true parents and this adopter. Dig for your past, Tralane, and find the clues. What happened to your family? Why were you not placed in the care of someone from your birthplace? Why a magician? Why Mathi?"

Tralane rose to lean on one of his elbows. He spoke

loudly, looking down at her, beating back her words from
his vantage point.

"And how do I get back, little one? Should I survive
this Beast of yours, what am I to do with the Jade Warrior?
How can I travel back to my home world without mastering the Eye and freeing myself from the one who is
watching over me? And what am I going to do when the
sorcerer from whom I stole this little trinket discovers,
as he surely will, that I have returned? I am a mortal, not
some god or hero blessed with divine power."

"Are you? Then why does so much happen to you?
Why are you so important that a creature follows you to
your own destruction? Why must you die?"

"Who says I must die?" Tralane protested, knowing
he was denying his own thoughts. "The Jade Warrior hasn't
tried to harm me."

"Come to your senses, Tralane. You've seen enough
intrigue to know you're caught in a trap; you cannot rest
unless you wish to die. And if that is so, I should have
let Jax throw you to the Beast when you first arrived."

Tralane sank down into the bed and let his eyes roam
the ceiling. The suitable retort did not fly from his lips.

"There are only two paths to follow," she continued,
her anger subsided and her voice intense. "You can continue your wanderings and eventually destroy yourself.
Or you can stand and fight. I cannot say if you will win
or not, but at least you will have a chance."

"And how do I fight the invulnerable, the unseen, the
all-powerful?"

Cumulain smiled with disbelief. "You, a sorcerer's
apprentice, and you cannot see the way?"

Tralane glanced at his scarred shoulder. "I've shown
you the proof of my failure in magic."

"Indeed. Then I will teach you."

"With simple peasant spells I will conquer my enemies?"

"No, Tralane. With a little simple wisdom."

Then she stood and, to Tralane's surprise, began to
undress. Her hair diffused the light breaking in through

the cracks of the shutters, softening the contours of her head with a glowing aura of daylight. The aura trickled down the side of her body, accentuating the slimness of her waist, the flair of her hips. She turned slightly as she stepped out of the dress and exposed the dark triangle of her loin and her erect nipples to the sun beams. Her face was in shadow, but he could detect the glimmer of a smile on her lips as she looked at him with soft, dark eyes. He reached out with his hand, and she took it, intertwining her fingers with his. She joined him under the covers, embracing him with her arms and thighs. The tension produced by their brief confrontation flew out of his body with a breath. He stroked the creamy skin of her back and savored the warmth of her body pressing against his.

"It's not even the afternoon yet," she said, closing her eyes and arching her neck as she stretched, "but I feel as if I've already worked a full day." Then she laughed and squeezed his arms playfully, and he went to her with a passion he had never known before, until their love left them arm in arm in the gentle wake of affection. Tralane slept deeply and without dreams.

Chapter 16

Tralane gradually came out of his slumber, drawn by a flickering half-light, like a ghostly apparition hovering just at the edge of his field of vision. He hoped for a while that his waking was a dream, but the stirring of the covers near his foot alerted him to the reality he was slowly entering. He rolled over on his back and squinted through crusty eyelids to find Cumulain sitting up in bed, drawing up her feet to sit cross-legged, and studying Wyden's Eye, which lay in her lap like a piece of jewelry she was planning to wear. Outside the shutters, evening had fallen. A candle burned lazily on the table next to the bed.

"A fine piece of work," Cumulain said without turning around to look at Tralane, seemingly absorbed in the intricacies of the amulet.

"I've always thought so," Tralane replied in a light tone, though his response carried uncomfortable reverberations of a bravado he did not feel.

"Yes, but whoever made you forgot to let you cool long enough in water," Cumulain laughed and fell back on the bard's chest. He cried out but yielded to her weight, stroking her hair with one hand, her throat with the other. She held the Eye aloft, letting the candle light catch the flowing lines of the emerald jewel in its silver-woven web.

"What do you make of it?" he asked, after they had listened for a while to the wind blowing outside.

"It can be mastered, Tralane. You've been trained for the art, though you may never have exercised the will to control the forces you've been taught to call. The problem with you, dear Tralane, lies not so much with what you can do as with what you want to do."

"Oh yes, I've always wanted to do a lot of things, and I never seem to manage them all."

"Please wake up, Tralane," she said with exasperation, "and join me in this world. You've never really wanted to do anything but run."

Tralane thought for a moment. "I do that well," he commented.

"I'm sure. But there are better ways to pass the time."

"You, perhaps?" Tralane was aware that he was slipping into glib seductiveness. He had already had the woman, but now he felt the urge to keep her. He did not want to leave her or give her up to anyone else. Jealousy lurked on the fringes of his thoughts, prodding him to build a wall of fantasy around Cumulain, so that none but he could touch her.

Cumulain looked at him sadly. "Have you forgotten so soon what I said could be seen in you?"

"Is there a man who claims you?" Tralane asked, only partly in jest.

"There's been no talk of love since the Beast broke the bounds of tradition and claimed his own sacrifices. There can be no love until the seige is broken and the roads freed from ice, snow, and the threat of death."

"I know, I know. But afterwards—"

"We shall see. At this moment, no one has claims on me."

She turned her attention back to the Eye, holding the amulet in her palm.

"How did you learn to use the Eye?" she asked, her voice hardening to the tough, businesslike tone of a tavern keeper.

"The person—the woman—who helped me steal it showed me how."

"She taught you poorly."

"There were some loose ends on my part of the bargain, too," Tralane replied.

Cumulain ignored the statement and traced a sign in the air over the amulet, with no effect.

"There are webs of power surrounding this trinket. The trick is to find the one we want."

She moved her finger back and forth, up and down, searching among strands of sorcery for the key that would unleash its power. Tralane began to see the patterns she was tracing as his eyes adjusted in the way they had been trained to do when in the presence of magic. Memories of the old wizard explaining the principles of binding magic forces to particular tasks within such tokens returned to him. He recognized the sign he had learned from Crecia in the tangled web and realized Cumulain's probing fingers were dancing too near the locks that held back the threshold-breaking energies within the Eye.

"Watch out," Tralane cried in alarm, rising to stay her hand.

She leaned out of his reach. "I'm close to the door between worlds? Good, that means what we want is close by. Show me the sign."

With trepidations, Tralane worked the sign Crecia had shown him in the air before him, careful not to do it too near the amulet. She repeated his movements several times until she understood their nuances, then worked several variations over the amulet. After one of them, the air shimmered over her hands, lost its transparency, became a reflecting pool, and then shattered as ripples broke the surface and reformed into shifting shapes and colors.

"Willful purpose, a mind searching with intent, fills the emptiness with an image," she explained. "This thing is named Wyden's Eye, and whoever or whatever Wyden is, his Eye is still an eye. It can be made to see. The amulet has the power to cross over to other worlds, thus is must also be able to see them." She paused, waiting for Tralane's question. He understood, and so said nothing. She continued with a piece of advice.

"See as the Eye sees, and not as you would have things be, and you will master its power."

Her forehead creased, and a succession of scenes passed before their eyes. The last image was that of a vast city spread to the horizon of a plain, with broad avenues and majestic temples framing smaller streets and rows of buildings. The city appeared to be abandoned, and what structures Tralane could discern were in partial ruin. Then the picture faded, and with it the memory of the brief scenes that had passed before it. But the city remained in Tralane's mind.

Cumulain fell back on the bed, breathing heavily with her eyes closed.

"That's hard work. The amulet would be easier to control if one had a specific destination in mind. You remember the sign for the images?"

"Yes," and he repeated it, even though she could not see him. He executed the sign only once, as he had released his old skills from the bind of ignorance he had kept them under.

"Then at least you'll see where you're going and be able to direct yourself to a destination instead of being guided by someone else. And there is someone else," she said seriously. "I felt another will contesting my seizure of the amulet. But whoever exerts influence over this Eye, and thus you, is far away. He can be overcome."

Tralane was moodily silent. He was glad to have learned the more refined aspects of Wyden's Eye and its powers. Yet he was not eager to use the amulet, for to do so would be to abandon her.

"If I go," he asked suspiciously, already knowing the answer, "will you come—"

"With you? And how will poor Jax manage the Wilderness Flower by himself? Who will bury and mourn my mother properly? Only I was trained in sorcery, and only

I know how to protect her soul on its journey to other lands beyond the living. No, I will not go. But I've told you, there are duties which you must fulfill."

"Yes, yes, the Beast," he said.

"True, you must kill it for us, but there are others for yourself." She thrust her legs out from underneath the covers and sat on the edge of the bed. "I must speak to my mother about the possibility of getting you out of bed sooner."

"But I'm still hurt," he complained. "My wounds haven't completely healed."

"True, but perhaps we can remedy that."

Her hand searched through the folds of the cover for the pouch. Finding it, she slipped the amulet in and dropped the package back on the bed.

"Remember what I've shown you, Tralane. Use that hook of knowledge to catch whatever other lessons of sorcery are swimming in the depths of your memory. Don't forsake your past for illusory futures—you are what you have been, seasoned with the promise of what you can be."

She stood and dressed quickly. "I know you better now. My thanks for your confidence."

Tralane did not reply, uncertain of his feelings and the words with which to express them. She had grounded his ephemeral nature, which he recognized had reveled in the trivialities and superficialities of court life. He admired her wisdom, so much so that he wanted to tell her the many tales he knew, so that she might explain their meaning to him.

The old tide of loneliness slid over the exposed and shifting sands of his happiness as she made ready to leave. He felt abandoned, loved and cherished momentarily, only to be thrown back into the roaring sea to fend for himself. Her every rebuff was a dagger twisting in his stomach. She could not hurt him outright, he sensed. But she would not allow him to stay, to be nurtured with warmth in safety. He loved her, but in the source of that emotion were the flaws which could only tear at the bonds holding them together.

And she had sparked desires in him that were flaming higher than those for isolated self-protection. There were questions to be asked, starting with the amulet—the immediate, material mystery—and growing like a many-limbed tree into the nature of his origin, his parents, Mathi, the world of his birth, the parallel planes that were lined like tomes on an infinite shelf. A new curiosity, personal on one hand, visionary on the other, was born from the hard, dry wasteland of his past. This sense of mission filled him with satisfaction and hunger at the same time.

He was falling into a pit, but the hole did not darken and constrict around him, clutching him close to the soundless heart of death. Rather, the pit yawned even wider, the light growing brighter, as if he had fallen through a hole in the sky. He no longer felt attracted to mere adventure or petty schemes for self-aggrandizement, nor was he even struck with the urge to find one true pattern, one true meaning in all the events he had experienced. The absurd brevity of a meaning which could be encompassed by his mind was made apparent by the simple instrument of the amulet. Here were limitless possibilities and variations. All the gods, all the faiths, all the conquerors and heroes, were mere facets of a jewel and could not be seen all at once. To turn the stone was to fill the eyes with the gleam of a new facet. The whole concerned him only with its inescapable presence; it was the array of worlds and possibilities opened to Tralane that pricked at his attention. Life was not a state to preserve at all cost and to rush through as quickly and unconcernedly as possible.

Yet along with this need to expand, there was also the desire for Cumulain. For what the world of the senses and action could not provide, she could supply in ample amounts.

Tralane followed Cumulain eagerly with his eyes and she, seeming to sense his stare, turned to face him at the door.

"You must not think of me too hard, Tralane. I have

my mission, as you have yours. It would be a fine life with the two of us together, but that cannot be." She moved as if to leave, hesitated, and spoke again. "Always face your enemies, my dear Tralane, even as I and my kin face the Beast, though we are in terror of it and cannot defeat it. To turn one's back on an enemy and run is to be overwhelmed by that enemy, suddenly, and swiftly, sooner or later."

"A wise saying," Tralane replied, mixing sarcasm with respect.

"Then remember it in times of trial. Now rest, and we shall see how well a warrior can heal."

He watched her exit, closing the door silently behind her. He almost shouted after her, asking why she didn't stay with him. But her steps faded quickly, and the gloom leaked through the window shutters and the chimney vents, pressing the dwindling taper with shadows. He leaned over to the table and blew out the flame, then sank back into his bed and savored the moment of comfort.

He had forgotten the last time he had slept in a real bed. Weeks of traveling, predated by his brief tour as a campaigning archer on his home world, had not afforded him his usual access to the private bedrooms of those he was accustomed to serve. It had been awhile since he had even occupied private quarters, acting out the role of some noble lady's privileged entertainer and advisor. He had begun to take such luxuries as his due and whatever rough living he did between more comfortable lodgings he had considered a mere temporary inconvenience, a spell of rudeness that would renew his taste for finery. The cramped cot and the later stone bench on which he had slept in Mathi's tower had been forgotten until now. The unexpected warmth and softness of his bed, as well as the harsh wind blowing outside and the renewed vigor of his body, put him at ease. He allowed his disappointment over Cumulain's departure to slip through his dissolving attention. His mind drifted peacefully into the night.

Time was a tranquil pool, and night still reigned over

the world when Tralane began to see the darkness transform itself into colors that did not betoken the dawn. Startled, he reached for the pouch containing Wyden's Eye, and found it already in his hand. He took out the amulet as shadows clashed with shadows all around him. Colors bloomed in corners of the room, dark purples and blues, peppered with shades of green, yellow, and red that grew over his bed in the form of long filaments. Constantly shifting shapes of color flew around the room as if blown by a wind Tralane could not feel. They began to dance in a discernible pattern, pulsating, throbbing. At first he thought his eyes were playing a trick on him; then he doubted his mind—he feared a fever, or the rising of a mysterious, monstrous part of himself. Finally, he began to suspect the entire effect as being an illusion, a taunting thrust at his sanity sent by his nameless tormentor through Wyden's Eye.

Then he looked at the amulet.

The night convulsed. Waves of pressure passed over Tralane's body. He imagined himself being swallowed, head first, by an enormous serpent. The constrictions came with increasing rapidity, until their speed and force were crushing him. He twisted and turned, struggling to resist the darkness that was sucking him into itself.

Cumulain and all she had said to him echoed through the waves of pain, and he cast the line of his fading consciousness deep into the ocean of memory. He thought of Mathi, his stern, cold visage peering over open tomes of sorcery, the dry, cracked voice admonishing Tralane to concentrate, to focus his mind, to create an image of what he wished and make it happen. Magic. He thought of the art of healing.

The constrictions died down. Air whistled in his ears. Unseen hands buffeted him on every side, until he was flailing about like someone with the falling sickness. The covers were ripped away, exposing Tralane. Desperately he tried to take hold of the bedposts, but his limbs did not have the strength to obey. Like driftwood in a stormy sea, he was tossed out of bed and suspended in air, riding the violent waves of unknown sorcery. A cry struggled in his throat, close to the sound of panic, but it was unable to fight through to release.

Sorcery! Tralane held Wyden's Eye tightly and was aware that it burned in his hand like the scar on his shoulder when it had been a fresh wound. But despite the pain, Tralane held on to the amulet. He refused to let go, and tried to concentrate on healing.

The dance of colors stopped. Tralane was wrapped in total darkness. The buffeting, like the constrictions, slowly lessened in intensity and he floated back down to the bed. But he did not reach the bed. Before he could do so, something closed in around him. Successive layers of weight pressed in all around him, locking him in a spread-eagle position. Then, instead of convulsing, the darkness throbbed, the pulse of its life pushing Tralane closer to panic and madness.

Tralane's hold on his sanity was rapidly slipping. The helplessness, the surprise and complete mystery of his predicament spurred his thoughts on to outstrip his racing heart. Had he reached for, had he actually drawn on the magic in Wyden's Eye? The possibilities overwhelmed him. He lost his tentative grip on his self-control as power flooded through him, responding to his needs. He forgot Cumulain, forgot Mathi. Magic was lost in the maelstrom of panic that came with the remembrance of his shoulder, the wound, the mistakes he had made, and the controls he had never properly exerted. It would happen again; he would overlook the proper sign, his timing would be off— he was reaching too far, too quickly, asking the wrong questions, questions that should not be asked, beseeching those who laughed at his presumption and lanced shoulder, striving for his heart, with fire—

A coldness numbed his senses. Time lost its shape. The passing of moments was subsumed by the beats of throbbing darkness, each pulse a self-enclosed lifetime, gently caressing his body. The beats became his world, his reason for existing. But between the pulses of life there was emptiness, as if life had surged through him as meltwater inundates a normally dry creek bed. A void stretching infinitely into the past and future rushed in once each constriction of darkness. Tralane forgot the beat of life and allowed himself to slip slowly into the emptiness, but then the pulse returned and the solitude of death was just as easily obliterated from his consciousness.

Fluctuating between these two states of existence, Tralane did not at first grasp the meaning of the new sensation stimulating him. Then dimly he recognized sight. Streaks and blotches of color returned. Hanging on fragments of memory, pieces of ritual, and spell work, Tralane concentrated on their disquieting appearance. They were, he thought, his own injuries, which along with the rest of his body he could no longer feel. With that association, identity bolstered his will and purpose. The shapeless, mindless creature drifting in a void became Tralane again.

The suppurating wounds started to heal, closing in on themselves. The moist, infected borders crumbled before the invading darkness. The harsh red, purple, and blue splotches faded, their violent intensity dwindling as gentler, lighter shades seeped through from beneath. Fine filigree networks of red and blue lines meshed to form larger patterns, which were then subsumed by the night. Rustlings replaced the whine of funneled wind as the air settled into quiescence. Unseen structures moved and mended into predefined patterns. The pulsing beat dimmed along with the colors and the rustlings as time flowed with measured pace through Tralane's body, until the mechanics of life were set and coordinated and the groundwork of his existence was restored.

The night receded, assuming its proper proportions in relation to the rest of the world. Tralane found he could move at will again. He stirred, rolled to his side, rubbed his arm with his hand, and felt the scars gone. For the first time since he had awakened from the weeks-long sleep of sickness, he was free of generalized pain. He was stiff, not with sore muscles and stressed limbs, but with untried tissue. His nerves tingled, and his body was bathed in sensuality. It was as if he had been cleansed and washed ashore on a new land by a stormy, starless night. He stared at the amulet in his hand, and marveled as much over its power as at his instinctive use of that power to heal himself.

A shriek pierced Tralane's pleasurable indolence. He sat up and heard a long, wailing moan amid the scuffling of feet and furniture coming from beneath the floor boards. He grabbed his sword, which had fallen with the blanket during his thrashings, and stuffed Wyden's Eye back into its pouch. As he ran down the hall towards the glow which marked the stairwell, he noted with satisfaction that he moved with an energy and ease he had not possessed in a long time. He bounded down the steps, the chill air and unexpected smoothness of his motions thrilling him with their vitality.

The scene confronting him stopped him short. The main room was darkened, with only two hearths supplying light and the heat to the room he had been sleeping in. The fires painted a shifting backdrop to a set piece framed by the open door at the bottom of the short hall leading to the main room. However, this set piece was not a performance mounted as a spectacle to amuse those courtly nobles momentarily bored with their games for power.

Cumulain knelt, bowed over the head of her mother which lay in her lap. A few men, bundled in furs and thick leggings and heavily sprinkled with moist snow and blood, were clustered behind her, their gaze fixed blankly on the far corner opposite them. Tralane did not have to follow their eyes to discover the object of their fear.

Tralane descended the remaining stairs and walked to the doorway, where he stopped.

"Welcome back to the living, my dear Tralane," the Jade Warrior commented superciliously.

"Would you have it so, stone man?" Tralane responded in kind, eyes narrowed as he peered into the corner, barely making out the outline which framed the twin ruby stars glaring back at him.

"The trials of mortality are none of my affair, fleshly one."

Tralane smiled. "Keep it so, then, Jade Warrior."

There was a testing silence, in which neither Tralane nor the Warrior turned down their steady gaze.

"You stand before me anew, master Tralane," the Warrior said casually. "I have never seen you," he continued, with a shadowy wave of his hand, "quite so naked. You have these good people to thank for your new, soft, pink skin and mended bones. As grand a display of sympathetic sorcery as I've ever seen. Most diverting."

"I also found it so, Warrior. A rougher road, perhaps, than the healing with time, but there's a stronger sanctuary at journey's end."

One of the men standing behind Cumulain spat and, with his mouth turned up in a snarl, drew out his dagger. He faced Tralane, feet apart, defiant and angry.

"By Krasok and Gel, you're playing with words while these two suffer on your account. I'll gut you now, before we bleed for you again."

The others followed his example, forming a threatening semicircle with an edge of steel. The point of Tralane's black sword came up to meet the challenge, but he looked to Cumulain to stay their anger. She remained oblivious to the events occurring in her tavern, having spent the last reserves of strength. She had nothing left for her mother or for the hero in whom she believed. He could not look to her for protection anymore. He had to find his own formula for changing the hearts of men.

He took a step in retreat as they advanced. He was unwilling to shed the blood of Cumulain's neighbors, yet the choice was being taken out of his hands.

Suddenly the door burst open, and Jax staggered in, followed by a blast of frigid air and a swirling cloud of snow. His sword was notched and streaked with frozen gore. His left arm hung loosely as his knee-length animal skin coat flapped in the wind, revealing torn and bloodied mail underneath.

He whispered hoarsely, "The Beast . . . came back . . ."

His face was caked with frost, but his eyes were fixed on Tralane, questioning and accusing at the same time.

Tralane did not have time to ask what the Beast had returned for.

Jax collapsed onto the floor, the dull sound of his body as it landed on the floorboards sending dim reverberations through Tralane's mind. He took a step towards the fallen man, but another powerful blast of cold air and a faint shuffling sound outside the doorway brought him to a halt before he could go to Jax's aid. Acutely aware of his own vulnerable state, Tralane backed off and looked about for some garments for himself and dressings for Jax's wounds. The other men dropped or sheathed their weapons and gathered hurriedly around Jax, and even Cumulain stirred from her self-absorption to watch as her brother was lifted gingerly onto a few tables lined end to end and his outer garments removed. One of the townsmen went to shut the door and glanced outside as he laid his hand on the lintel. Tralane, keeping an eye on the proceedings as he searched the storage cabinets behind the counter for clothing, saw a flash of white wrap itself around the man's head. In a moment, the doorway was empty.

Cumulain had also noticed the action and she cried out weakly. The three remaining warriors whirled about, concern for their comrade fleeing before the terror of the empty doorway. With one mind, they retrieved their weapons and faced the storm that was lapping with rapidly increasing fury at their doorway.

Cumulain stood, took notice of Tralane's condition behind the counter, and motioned agitatedly for him to go upstairs. He had reached the first step of the stairs when a shrill, piercing ululation transfixed him to the spot. He looked over his shoulder, waiting for the next event to happen, gripping his sword tightly.

He was about to continue going up the stairs when a long, pale object flew into the room, leaving an arcing trail of blood. The dismembered arm struck one of the men who had recently challenged Tralane and knocked him backwards onto the floor. The downed man moaned with shock over the nature of the attack, while the others tried to help him up. Then a furry whiteness filled the door frame, and a stifling, fetid stench rolled into the room. Tralane gagged and retreated up the stairs, watching the townsmen falling back around the injured Jax. Cumulain knelt back over her mother, leaning across her face to protect her from the sight of the grisly arm lying on the floor. An invisible border divided the Wilderness Flower into two camps—fearful, mortal men against a white, murderous shadow.

The monstrosity darted a long appendage into the inn, searching, grasping the air. Its fingers and talons were covered with the same blood that matted its fur. Then a howl, like the one Tralane had heard when he had first ridden into town, was flung at everything that lived in the tavern. The rage and frustration impelling the voice drove Tralane and the others back a step. When neither the lunge nor the howl produced any overt panic, the white shadow disappeared from the doorway. But the tension did not end with its departure.

"The Beast..." Jax repeated. "Don't let... it..."

"We won't," whispered the man who had been knocked down. He rose to a half-kneeling posture. "Someone had better stay with Jax. I'm going to round up the others, before it manages to pick us off one by one."

Tralane did not stay to hear them discuss plans. He raced up the remaining stairs. By the glow of the hearth fires which followed him up the stairwell, he tried the three remaining doors besides his own on the floor. The first two were locked, but the last opened at his touch. In the room he found a chest full of clothes lying at the foot of a bed. Some of the garments seemed too large for Jax.

As he sifted through the collection, picking out what looked as if it might fit him, he began to feel jealous. Then he realized, by the age and condition of the oversized garments, that they had not belonged to one of Cumulain's lovers, but to her father. Feeling foolish over his needless burst of emotion, Tralane busied himself with donning shirt, jerkin, leggings and boots. As he turned to leave, he saw the remnants of his old net pack. Its provisions had been thrown away. His bow and arrows were propped against the wall behind the pack, and next to his old weapons hung a greatcoat put together mostly from Oram's furs. He took the coat, acknowledging it as a gift from Cumulain. He drew the hood up around his head, tied his swordbelt tightly around the coat's bulky waist, and went from the room. He left the bow and arrows behind.

By the time he returned downstairs, two townsmen had gone off to warn the neighbors and gather a hunting party. Only one man remained, sitting by Jax and idly staring at Cumulain and her mother. Tralane's appearance in the doorway drew the townsman to his feet, sword in hand. The bard and townsman glared at one another.

Simultaneously, the Jade Warrior and Cumulain stood. Cumulain approached her neighbor, who lowered his weapon when he saw himself bracketed between enemy and friend. She stopped a few paces away from the man and looked at Tralane pleadingly.

"Now is your time, Tralane," she croaked, her voice as old and cracked as what he had assumed her mother's to be. "Hurry, before the others find the monster and waste their lives. Next time, the Beast will not stop at the threshold."

She evaded his grasp. Her vacant eyes offered their depths to him. The cold suddenly penetrated his awareness, and he shivered. He remembered the task he had to perform. It was an obligation, and he saw in her eyes that there was no choice but to fulfill that moral call to duty. She had seen too many dead to allow anything but justice to be served. In her simplicity and purity of purpose, she was almost a stranger to him. Tralane, whole and solidly entrenched in life due to the workings of this woman and her mother, turned sadly away from her. Cumulain's only demand was the fulfillment of duty. That the duty was to himself as much as to the town awed him. Reluctantly, he put aside his childhood desires and went to meet the challenge.

He left Cumulain to look after the two survivors of her family as best she could. He stepped over the dismembered arm and crossed the invisible border that had marked off the safety of the inn from the dangers of the outside world. He passed into the night.

A green blur appeared at the edge of his vision. "So now we leave, eh Tralane?" the Warrior said over the screaming wind. "To another town, or another world?"

"Not yet," Tralane replied in a commanding tone. His eyes were slitted against the gusts, and he battled forward against the lacerating particles of snow to take the first steps of his hunt.

The outlines of buildings were hardly distinguishable in the furious descent of snow. Portals of light could be dimly made out, but the rest of the landscape was lost in the white haze. The wind blew steadily against Tralane as he made his way up the town's main street, plowing through the drifts and almost toppling over whenever a pocket of swirling air sprang up beside him, pushing him from a new direction.

The storm was at its height. Relentlessly, it pounded at whatever stood, quickly burying the fallen victims of its might beneath a heavy, frozen blanket. More than once, Tralane tripped over a buried object; when his hands came forward to break his fall, they struck hard flesh. Thorts, abandoned or lost as the storm's frenzy had rapidly increased, had panicked themselves into exhaustion and collapsed. No doubt, the two visits by the Beast had also unnerved them.

Tralane glanced over his shoulder as he approached the outskirts of the town. Anxiety was beginning to gnaw at his will. He dreaded falling across the remnants of the dismembered man's corpse, since it would only be a token of the creature's raw, uncaring hatred for the living. And in the storm, Tralane would be a victim of that hatred sooner than the Beast would become a prey to the bard's hunt.

Tralane was about to turn his attention back to the land ahead when he recoiled before a faint green shape looming close behind him. Then he recognized the Jade Warrior, faithfully following his charge. Ignoring the Warrior's

inescapable presence, Tralane resumed his fruitless probing of the white curtain that had fallen around him.

The last cluster of houses was behind them, and Tralane
found himself in the wilderness. He had never known the
fear of death when in the fields and hills of his homeworld,
running from a past adventure headlong into the next. He
drew his sword, hoping its black blade would drive the
fear away. Of course, the blade was no defense against
the Beast's coloring, which would camouflage it until it
was upon Tralane. Driven by the certainty of doom, but
disciplined by his new-found sense of duty and obligation,
his mind danced nimbly around the dangers, seeking a
flaw in the well-laid death trap he had freely entered.

Tralane settled down to examining Cumulain's words
more closely. The amulet was indeed a tool, as she had
said, and as such it could have many uses. The Eye was
a source of power; his will had already been able to channel that power, and there was more he could do if only
he knew the limitations of the magic and the laws governing its existence.

The amulet's origin was unknown, and thus its nature
and powers hidden. But Gibron had said he was a Keeper
and that a bond existed between him and the Eye. Even
without full awareness of the amulet's secrets, he had
access to its power. It was his choice either to face what
Wyden's Eye had to show him or to turn away and allow
the Eye and whatever entity influenced the Eye, to control
him. The strength had to be summoned from his being,
or that strength would be fragmented and turned against
him.

What truly great magicians possessed, Mathi had said,
were not the words which summoned the gods and demons,
nor the phrases and implements which invoked the underlying forces moving all of existence. These were all shov-
els and buckets with which knowledgeable fools dug
through the earth to bring up small doses of water from
underground streams. Such people were rare and potent
enough. But a sorcerer who wielded ultimate power, who
had tapped and could unleash not mere buckets but tor-

rents of power, knew himself in relation to that power. He knew and could call upon, by the action of his will, the forces governing existence. Such sorcerers had merged with the forces binding matter in the universe. They could transmute objects and substances, create and destroy whatever they beheld, and, most important of all, lose their physical selves and join that binding power. To know and mingle with a primal force was to survive the blinding light in which such a transformation had occurred. Sorcerers achieving this state were almost unknown, though it was the goal of all magicians who placed themselves, like Mathi, in exile. The price too often was paid with madness and self-annihilation. But the reward was freedom from the constraints of life and death.

That Mathi had failed in his endeavor and was embittered by his lack of success was Tralane's childhood perception, which he maintained even now. Perhaps this was the reason Tralane had refused to absorb the meaning of Mathi's lessons. For Tralane, Mathi had fallen before the naked glare of truth, and this had inspired contempt, not compassion, in the youthful bard. But he himself had not even possessed the courage to pursue the revelations of magic as far as Mathi. He had never tested himself, as Mathi had done, and found his true limits and nature. He had only followed Mathi's apparent path and achieved his tutor's end. Tralane clenched his teeth and closed his eyes tightly as he realized what he had been running from.

To see as the Eye saw, and not as he would have it be—that was the key Cumulain had given Tralane. His youthful years had been wasted fleeing and hiding, playing for power only to let it slip through his grasp. He had wanted his way, but without paying any price. He had avoided confrontations only to trap himself. There was no escape—what was left undone had finally caught up to him.

Tralane removed a glove and wormed his hand through the layers of clothing. He unfastened the pouch which hung around his neck and pulled out the amulet. Then, when its silver mount and hard green gem glinted in the snow storm, Tralane knelt, holding Wyden's Eye with both hands, and peered into its intricately faceted depths.

The Jade Warrior stood behind him, his leg almost grazing Tralane's back. The base of the bard's neck tingled with the close proximity of the creature. It was as if the Warrior were trying to distract Tralane's attention from the task at hand, as if the Warrior were guarding the gates through which Tralane wished to pass.

Tralane fought and conquered the Warrior's encroachment. As his mind began to concentrate on the amulet, shadows and light played a mad child's game of running and hiding from the world. Tralane repeated the sequence of mental steps Mathi had taught him to approach the paths of sorcery. He concentrated on the Beast and plunged deeper into himself and the amulet. He closed his eyes.

The wind ceased to howl; the daggers of ice pierced his skin, but not his mind. Yet he still saw Wyden's Eye in his hands. He caught in its myriad reflections glimpses of his own secret thoughts and fears, forgotten dreams and dreaded nightmares, the loves captured and then smothered in quick-frozen crystals of passion. Ancient, unhealed wounds whose scars Tralane had never perceived in himself reopened before him. For a moment he tried to see clearly the run of these dark scabs, fascinated by the aberrations and petty corruptions he had so quickly seen and cleverly exploited in others, and which he now readily saw in himself. The further back he traced them, among the flickering lights and shades of Wyden's Eye, the more tangled and obfuscated they became, and the harder he had to concentrate on tracking down their origin. He wanted to understand the injuries and discover what weapons had been used to make them. His curiosity picked at the incrustations, as it had done with so many of the people in his past, and he winced with pain and satisfaction at the ugliness he exposed. He began to take pleasure in the destruction, forgetting that the object of his cruelty was himself.

The unmutilated flesh of his self was disappearing as he delved further into the source of pain. The faint patches of white became tiny stars in the web of night, and these stars glowed brighter when his eyes came to rest on them. They shone with piercing whiteness, calling to him, urging him to explore their minuteness. A dim roar, gravelly, hungry, issued from the stars. They began to move, lazily at first, then faster, in circles, and finally in tempestuous chaos. He recognized the snow. He was back kneeling in a mound of snow, the Jade Warrior standing behind him. The Warrior seemed far away, yet Tralane could plainly sense the creature's nearness.

Then Tralane remembered he had closed his eyes. He had become the Eye, scanning across the horizon, the clouds of swirling snow a galaxy of stars by which he could see all the more clearly. The gate was crossed, its guardian safely bypassed.

Tralane sought, and found, the Beast. It was crouching not far away, as tall as a man in its hunched position. The eyes were red and white, filled with the primitive rage of a dozen wild beasts held captive and molded into one being by a single intelligence. Tralane could separate the remains of the sorcerer Cumulain had told him about, buried alive in the savage passions lending strength to and propelling the Beast. Vengeance had been its own curse. Sanity was absent from the sparkle of awareness; only the joy in the unleashing of murderous power remained.

The Beast watched Tralane, sensed the sorcery, and snarled. But with its maker no longer in control, and motivated by the single drive of bloody revenge, the Beast could not sift through the dangers it sensed and discover the true source of the threat to its existence.

Tralane's consciousness slipped partially back into his own body. He stood shakily, keeping an unsteady balance of awareness between the Eye and his true physical form. His right hand grasped the pommel of the black sword, and the weapon responded with a surge of strength racing up his arm. Tralane walked uncertainly towards the Beast, finding the balance between flesh and stone even more difficult to maintain when moving. However, his clumsy

movements managed to ally the Beast's suspicions. The
monster waited patiently for Tralane to stumble into his
arms, thinking the bard was blinded by the storm.

The Beast stood when Tralane was almost within striking range. It raised a huge paw into the air, then swept
down in an arc that would end at Tralane's head. But
before the blow could land, Tralane fell to one knee. He
watched the arm swing by him overhead, the momentum
of the missed blow forcing the Beast to fall forward, off
balance. With an upward sweep, Tralane sank the sword's
edge deep into the Beast's upper arm. A wrench with a
backward step made the sword bite deeper, almost severing the arm. The snow on the ground blossomed into a
scarlet bed, and the spraying blood transformed the falling
ice crystals into rubies.

The Beast's scream beat down the angry wind's voice.
Tralane took two steps to the side and let the creature fall
on its injured arm. Before it could roll over and attempt
to sit up, Tralane pulled the sword free from the arm and
pushed the point into its back, trying to sever its spine.
He missed the bone, but the Beast's shudder and spas-
modic flailing told him he had struck something of equal
importance. Then one of the Beast's legs struck him and
knocked him twice the length of his body's across the
snow, almost wrenching the Eye out of his hand.

The Beast's howl was incessant, evenly proportioned
with wrath, pain and fear. It began to stagger to its feet
and withdraw, seeking the path to some unknown refuge.
Tralane grunted with the effort of getting up. He lunged
across the distance between them and desperately sliced
at the Beast's knee joint, before it could make good its
escape. His blow landed, and the Beast collapsed in a
heap.

Tralane took a few steps back, breathing heavily. There
were some red stains on his coat, but the monster had
not touched him; the blood came from the Beast. The
Beast's gaze was resting steadily on Tralane as it pre-
tended to be hurt beyond action. The bard waited patiently
for the creature to make the first move. It did, whipping

the remaining arm at Tralane as it suddenly sat up. Talons emerged from the paw, ready to slice through his garments and rake open his body. Tralane met the blow head on with his sword, the hand holding the Eye backing his hold on the weapon. The black edge passed smoothly and evenly up the Beast's arm, through bone and sinew. The Beast fell on its side, again knocking Tralane away. Before the monster could rise again, Tralane leaped up and finished the battle with a swift downward stroke to its neck.

When the work was done, Tralane stepped away from the body. Wyden's Eye was not needed any longer to see the Beast—free-flowing blood marked the corpse, matting its fur and corrupting the pristine innocence of the snow-covered earth. He released his sensory hold on the amulet and took deep breaths, glad to have returned to his own form. Then he turned away with disgust from the sorcerous creature as it began to break up into its component animals. The town's spurned sorcerer had tormented many natural beasts out of shape besides the predominant cthan, to accommodate his plans.

He put the amulet in a pocket inside the lining of his coat and washed the sword with snow. The Jade Warrior emerged out of the storm. The Warrior's hand was on the hilt of his sword, but Tralane did not give any sign of his apprehension. For several moments the Warrior stood by Tralane, his crystal sinews tensed, the flaw lines in his limbs and torso refracting more light as they contracted to form bright, nervelike clusters.

Tralane memorized the location of the bright clusters he could see. They would make logical targets in the inevitable confrontation between the two of them.

His sword cleansed of blood, Tralane stood with the weapon held firmly in his hand. The Jade Warrior crouched slightly, anticipating battle. Tralane calmly sheathed his sword with one fluid motion. He had no intention of meeting his enemy on even terms.

"You've done more tonight than I thought you capable of, Tralane," the Jade Warrior shouted over a shrieking gust of wind. Though he had relaxed slightly, Tralane noted with satisfaction that the Warrior was not as arrogant in his stance as he had previously been.

Tralane started back in what he assumed to be the direction of the town, anticipating a hero's welcome by the townspeople. Surely now they would cease their cursings, set aside their hostility to strangers, and accept him into their community. At last he had proven his worth and lifted the doom from their lives. He had won a place among people.

But before he took a dozen steps, doubt dampened his enthusiasm. He was indeed a hero, a savior of the community. Cumulain had healed and strengthened him and sown the seeds of knowledge that had bloomed into the victory that was the fulfillment of his mission. She had prepared him for the task, but she had also cleared a path for his departure. He heard once again her evasive replies to his demands for commitment. She had met his desire for the security of protective walls with the freedom of the choices in his future.

He stopped and pictured the scene he would find in the Wilderness Flower: a group of men, quiet, sullen, fearful, waiting for the storm to end so they could go out and bury the remains of either their hero or the Beast. Cumulain would be hovering over her family, desperately pulling together the shattered fragments into a whole. She would have no time for the dalliance of courtship or extra affection for a young lover. The feeble strength she had left would be used to seal the rifts that had fractured her world. The townspeople would close in around her, protect her, and share their common grief over the loss of loved ones and the memory of cursed times. Already, she and the town were drawn together, trying to forget the Beast and sealing the grim reminders of their suffering from their reality. And he, as their hero, would only haunt them as a living memory of the past.

Tralane stood for a long while, letting the snow pile around his legs. The wind pushed him from behind, like the giant hand of a parent prodding a stubborn child towards an ambiguous goal. The cold seemed to have jumped through the layers of clothing and coated his stomach with ice.

He would live with them only in legend and song; perhaps, in a lonely hour, their voices raised in revelry would reach him on some distant world with the tale of his feat. The comfort, if it happened, would be small. Tralane turned his back on the town, as he must have known he would have to do.

The Jade Warrior had not moved from the spot Tralane had left him. The bard glanced at his companion's stony visage, detecting a hint of perplexity and suspicion. Tralane had changed, and the Warrior was revising his estimation of the man.

Tralane trudged resolutely past the Warrior without a word. He took out the amulet and began the motions that would open the door between worlds. Keeping his body between Wyden's Eye and the Warrior, Tralane altered his motions slightly and painted in his mind the barren world with its endless city that he had seen when Cumulain had tried her hand with the Eye's magic. The city began to appear before him, as it had done in his room at the inn. He concentrated on the image so that the right door would be taken. The site was ideal for the winning of answers from the Jade Warrior.

As they walked through the slowly dying storm, Tralane sensed the distant movement of another intelligence. Something stirred in the Eye, searching for the source of his subtle manipulation. He withdrew before he was discovered, satisfied that the Eye was set in the direction he wanted. He wondered at the Eye's power, that two wills could wander in its vastness without meeting each other. Then he questioned whether the vastness was not left deliberately unoccupied, so that Tralane might lead himself to where his enemy waited. But if this were so, it served Tralane's purpose as well.

Again reality began to lose its tangibility, and his feet trod on both the snows of the past and the soil of the future. The town behind Tralane was as nameless as the city before him. The comforts of the Wilderness Flower receded, and there was nothing ahead to replace it. Tralane welcomed the emptiness, for in it he would at last mold his own future.

Chapter 17

The city grew around them with the creeping appearance of dawn. The stars appeared briefly in the half-light, and Tralane was shocked by their scarcity. Even the day, when it had finally gained all the strength it apparently would ever have, seemed pathetically weak. The sun was a small fist of dull light, almost lost in the thin haze which covered the sky like a veil woven from the floating dust of the dead. The city's buildings, many-terraced, gilded with bright, precious metals, and interconnected by delicate spans of stone, appeared untouched by the general aura of decay. Yet when they passed near a cluster of tall, intertwining structures, the illusion of immortal beauty gave way to the reality of crumbling edifices and gaping holes, like the dead eye sockets of skulls, signifying the passing of an age. The city was rotted, ready to collapse, undermined by an unknowably long period of neglect. Even the ground they walked over was powdery, rising in scurrying clouds with every step.

The air was thin, and Tralane had some difficulty breathing. There was hardly the touch of a breeze on his face, and whatever movement of air existed was amply heralded by swirls of dust. There was no sign of life— even the ground was bare of the slightest form of vegetation. Tralane could not imagine that the city was inhabited. The fanciful buildings, towering and winding into space, had caught in their delicate dilapidation the strands of a funereal web of silence. There was nothing left to disturb the quiet work of corruption.

The avenue Tralane and the Jade Warrior found themselves traveling on was wide, with several lanes of paved stone separated by equal proportions of dusty earth which at one time must have nourished a rich abundance of vegetation. The unprotected openness, surrounded by distant borders of stone and metal, chilled Tralane. Despite the heavy clothing, he was colder in the city than he had been in the storm on Cumulain's world. He shivered and hunched his shoulders against the gnawing air.

"Would you not like to rest, Tralane?" the Warrior asked suddenly, shattering the grave silence between them that had been made nearly audible by the passive, quiet presence of the city.

Tralane was still strong from his healing and long sleep at the Wilderness Flower. He shook his head and directed them to a nearby complex of low, flat buildings. The streets narrowed until they were barely three man-widths across. The closeness of the walls did less to comfort Tralane than the wide expanse of the avenues. The air was musty, and the sense of entombment was heightened by the permanence of decay in the city. He wondered if he had not brought himself to the House of the Dead, the resting place of souls belonging to all the worlds existing and accessible to the Eye. But such a place would be teeming with some kind of activity—the spirits of the dead would be restless, especially with a living soul among them. In the city, there was not even the feeling of being watched. There was only the emptiness framed by skeletal monuments to loneliness.

"What are we doing here, Tralane?" asked the Jade Warrior. Even his voice was subdued by the silence.

"Searching for answers."

"What are the questions?"

Tralane stepped through an open doorway and quickly examined the room beyond it, finding it devoid of content, except for the hint of oddly shaped steps leading upwards in a recess at the far end of the chamber. He came back out into the dusky light, noticing that the Jade Warrior was keeping distance between himself and Tralane.

"Did you know, Warrior," Tralane quipped with a smile, "that you are terribly dull to look at when there's no sun to reflect on your many facets?"

"That seems a shallow enough question for a human. Is that all you hoped to discover?"

"Oh, no." Tralane began to walk, quickening his step as they progressed further into the complex. He wandered, doubling back, surreptitiously marking buildings as he passed and checking them as he came across them again. He appeared to be lost, taking streets and turnings seemingly at random, while he mapped routes and laid out his strategy.

"I have a few problems that need to be solved," Tralane added after a while, distractedly.

"You'll find no answers here. We are alone, the two of us. All the books and records have long since crumbled to dust and followed their makers into obscurity."

"Is that another one of your penetrating perceptions?" Tralane asked caustically, giving the Warrior a sneering glance.

"If you wish to call it such."

"You assume I need written words to satisfy my curiosity, when spoken words will do just as well."

"And who will speak these words?"

"You, my friend."

Laughter, like the sound of sharp scythes slicing down the long stalks of grain grass, hissed behind Tralane.

"You have learned a trick or two, my young one, but do not presume to think you can change your destiny with a little fakery and a few weak probes of the mind."

"Who gave me this destiny?" The question went unanswered. Tralane, still leading the Jade Warrior through the streets, continued. "It is true I cannot fight a destiny I myself have made, but one imposed from without can surely be sloughed off when its wearer has become too large for it to contain."

Again the laughter overtook him, but Tralane kept his eyes ahead. The time for a stand had not yet presented itself.

"You have imposed your own destiny from without," the Jade Warrior said enigmatically, still laughing. "How can you free yourself from what has been wrought by your own hands?"

"Whom do you serve?" Tralane asked forcefully, not liking the Warrior's smugness.

"Serve? The Jade Warrior is vassal to no one."

"Then why does such a mighty being choose to waste its time following me?"

"Ah, because we are allies, you and I."

"Allies? In what cause."

"Our own."

"We share nothing, Warrior. Not anymore."

"Renouncements come late in the game. They do not alter what has been agreed upon, and what has been set in motion."

Tralane was trotting through the streets now, giving the impression of searching desperately for something. The Warrior was following with long strides. Suddenly, Tralane darted into a side street, broke into a run, and wove a pattern of sharp turns and quick bursts of speed through the maze of passages. The Jade Warrior's steps dogged him, as he had hoped.

"You cannot escape me. I can follow your trail on earth, stone, or space."

Tralane gave a nod of agreement and continued to run. He came across the building with the open doorway and entered. He crossed the empty room cautiously, afraid the floor might collapse into a basement under his weight. He reached the recess with its stairs safely and sighed with relief. He began to climb the steps, stumbling over their uneven distribution but thankful that, like the floor, they were made of solid stone. Even so, he felt some of the stones tremble beneath his feet as he put his weight

on them, protesting the sudden strain of use. The very
elements of nature were weary of existence on this world.
Tralane unsheathed his sword, as if to beat back the closing twilight of being, and continued gingerly up the steps.

He emerged on the roof of a building which was level
with those of the adjacent structures. He went to the edge
of the roof and looked down on the street he had just
passed through. The Jade Warrior, stalking him with an
even stride, confident in whatever supernatural sense
allowed him to follow Tralane, could be heard several
streets away. Tralane backed off a few steps, then ran
and leaped across the narrow divide of the street and
landed on the opposite roof. He waited for a few moments,
listening for the Warrior's reaction to the sound of his
landing. But his enemy continued his straightforward pursuit, and Tralane wished he could be certain whether the
Warrior was really as confident as he appeared to be, or
whether the creature was taking the blunt approach to
tracking out of the same fear of a confrontation that made
Tralane's knees so unsteady.

Tralane crawled to the opposite edge of the roof and
lay at its edge. The Warrior appeared shortly, turning the
corner with his head bent down slightly to catch the path
Tralane had taken. The thin ruby streak separating his
upturned lips showed the Warrior's pleasure in hunting
down a seemingly panicked mortal. His senses were
focused on the particulars of Tralane's trail, and not the
whole of the quarter. The creature's rigidity extended
beyond mere appearance; whatever the Warrior's sorcerous origins, he had learned only too well the human traits
of arrogance and pride. There was no question of him and
Tralane sharing the wisdom of fear.

Tralane tensed as the Warrior passed below him, then
leaped to the street. The paved street crumbled under the
blow of his landing, cushioning his fall and raising an
exploding cloud of dust. The Warrior whirled about, his
sword raised in defense before he had completed the turn.
Tralane, his sword out, lunged forward through the dust
before the Warrior realized what had happened, and

pricked a point between two facets of the creature's crystalline torso he had previously picked out as a vulnerable cluster of nerves.

Before the sword could penetrate, the Warrior had parried Tralane's thrust. But the lunge had made him fall backwards and lose his balance, so that he could not take advantage of Tralane's momentary helplessness on the ground. The bard scrambled to his feet as the Warrior fell against a wall, but he held back his urge to charge forward when he saw the Warrior brace himself. They stared at one another, allowing the surprise to settle into reality.

Tralane examined his enemy's torso for any signs of damage, and was at first dismayed by the lack of apparent wounds. He had gambled on being able to strike first, to slow down the Jade Warrior so that a mortal would at least have a chance against the creature. Perhaps he had not struck deeply enough, perhaps the Warrior was safeguarded against the black blade. There were so many possibilities, so many chances for failure. But of course, in the end, Tralane would have lost anyway, so best to have taken the inevitable with his own hand, rather than waiting for it to be thrust upon him. He looked to the Warrior's face, expecting to see a sneer of contempt. He saw, instead, a blank, dull surface, like a dead lake beneath gray skies.

He looked again, and this time he saw, at the point where his sword had penetrated, a tiny black cloud that was slowly growing, disturbing the icy peacefulness of the Warrior's glittering torso.

The Warrior threw himself off the wall and glided with long, easy steps towards Tralane. The Warrior held his sword with two hands. As he swept by Tralane, he let it fall in a bewildering series of tiny, crisscrossing arcs, so that the bard was never sure where the blow would land. Tralane crouched and, as the Warrior went by him, slashed the creature's stomach with his blade. His blow bounced ineffectually off the Warrior's hide, and he cursed himself for not aiming more carefully at another set of nerves. He stopped cursing and greeted the street with his face when the Warrior's sword grazed his head, chopping a section of fur from his hood.

Tralane rolled forward, feeling the Warrior's sword point tearing through the back of his coat, just missing flesh. As he got up, he barely had time to put up his sword to avert the Warrior's next sweep. He stumbled backwards, and found himself against the same wall the Warrior had just launched his attack from. He was breathing heavily.

He was no swordsman, and the black blade, whatever its strength-giving qualities were capable of lending him, could not guide his hands with the skill to match the Jade Warrior's practiced limbs. The Warrior was not a badly armed hillman or even a towering but essentially slow-thinking monster like the Beast. Raw strength and stealth would not prevail against such craftsmanlike skill, backed as it was by near invulnerability and an equal, if not superior, degree of strength and intelligence. Tralane did not have the time to choose his target. It was all he could do to defend himself; he knew his chances of survival were better against the greatest champion on his homeworld than before this almost perfect fighting machine he had just set in motion. But strangely enough, he did not regret his action or feel pity for himself. He stood face to face with the certainty of death and found in the solitude of the dead city the strength to face his doom without cowardice or thoughts of self-betrayal.

So it was all the more shocking when, in bringing up his sword for the final death stroke, the Jade Warrior froze in mid-motion and remained standing like a waterfall in the heart of winter.

Tralane at first could not believe what had happened. He waited for the Warrior to complete his move, thinking he was being toyed with. But the moments stretched on, unbroken by physical movement, and at last Tralane moved out from the Warrior's path and stood aside, appraising the new twist in the course of events.

He was surprised at the deadliness of his perception, for the cloud that had marred the Warrior's crystalline lines was now ballooning into a massive black storm. His

eyes had, with a courtier's acuity for weaknesses, chosen
and memorized the precise spot that marked the Jade
Warrior's death, and with an archer's keenness directed
his weapon into that vulnerability.

Tralane was startled by the Jade Warrior's voice, which
was hoarse and grating.

"You have betrayed me," the Warrior whispered with
an effort. "I am stricken with the venom of my own cre-
ator."

The being's face twisted into a frightening range of
mountains and valleys. His eyes stared over Tralane's
shoulder, at spaces beyond the close confines of the street.
Tralane, confused by the Warrior's defeat and the mystery
of his words, chose to latch onto the last phrase and
pursue his own line of questioning.

"And who created you?" Tralane asked, his voice shaky.
He placed the point of his sword against the Warrior's
side, where another cluster of nerves lay hidden, accessible through the flaws of the joint where two facets of
the creature's body met. He kept the weapon steady as
a threat of more pain, though he was loath to inflict anything further on the Warrior. If he had not needed answers
so badly, he would have finished the Jade Warrior.

"I am the child of Wyden and the Emperor of Many
Faces."

Again, Tralane grasped only the familiar. "Wyden?"

"The serpent, whose coils can stretch across eternity,
whose Eye was cast into the Pool of Worlds to destroy
those who might prove to be the enemies of its master,
the emperor."

"Is Wyden a god?"

"The god of gods, whose fangs and poison can shatter
the unifying power of magic and spread chaos through all
the worlds."

Tralane glanced at his sword, then at the Warrior's.

"What swords did you carry?"

"The Fangs of Wyden."

The rent in his coat suddenly seemed to allow a gust
of cold wind to chill his spine. "And where is Wyden?"

"With the Emperor of Many Faces."

The black cloud was spreading with greater speed, like a flood wave gaining momentum as it rolled closer to the shores of death. Tralane hesitated before placing his next question.

"Who is the Emperor of Many Faces?" he asked finally, weakly.

"The ruler of the worlds beyond this one, where the suns have faded and the soil has turned to dust. A traveler, who came to the end of all possible alternate worlds, blinded and subjugated that last remaining god, Wyden, and then coupled with the serpent to people his realm."

"What is their interest in me? Why have I been chosen to be a Keeper of this Eye? Why were you sent to me?"

"You are a destroyer, brother and ally to the Emperor, and thus his most dangerous enemy. You are the last of his . . . enemies. You were drawn to the Eye, because you and the Emperor are part of one, and he called you through the thing you stole. I am . . . I was to retrieve the Eye, after you had destroyed yourself. But you . . . you betrayed me. You turned against me, against yourself . . ."

"Why did you name me as your ally?" Tralane asked, though the answer was on his mind.

"Because I am of the flesh of Wyden, and you are the Emperor's brother. The bond that ties them together is the same that lies between us."

Tralane was reeling from the Jade Warrior's replies, vehement denials struggling with more questions in his throat, when the creature suddenly slumped to the ground. The sword's venom had spread to the Warrior's arms and legs, transforming him from a creature of hard stone into a lump of charred, rotted matter. The Warrior was dead, if he had ever truly lived.

The Jade Warrior's destruction left Tralane unsatisfied and drove him into lonely melancholy. For all his hatred of the Warrior, there had been bonds between them. Now he felt them by their absence, for he had grown accustomed to the unfaltering presence of the Warrior. Now he had no one with whom to exchange even unfriendly words.

He felt as if he had been lured outside of himself to affirm his true identity, and then abandoned to stumble and falter through reality by himself. The shadowy ties to the Emperor, formed through the Warrior and the Eye, merely defined the craving in Tralane that needed to be satisfied. The hidden pattern in the recent events of his life, the faint sense of another while his mind sought to possess the amulet, and finally the Warrior's demise, were not answers or solutions, but bait that forced Tralane to explore deeper into realms that bore little resemblance to his native reality. He had to follow the wispy trail of relation to the Emperor, and hope the strength given to him by Cumulain's words of confidence and the two victories over the Beast and the Warrior would be enough to bring him through this next trial.

Tralane turned away from the corpse, gouged to hollowness by the thought of the new arena of conflict he saw ahead of him. He perceived clearly the strands of mystery emanating from his unknown parentage, running through his forced apprenticeship with Mathi to this moment. He cursed the old sorcerer again for not having been honest about how he had received Tralane into his care.

There had been brothers after all, Tralane thought bitterly, and perhaps sisters as well. Obviously, like himself, they had all been mortal, frail flesh and bone, except for one, the one who claimed kinship through the Jade Warrior, the one who lurked within the Eye, watching, waiting. But waiting for what? Were his mortal relatives a threat to his demigodhood? If this were so, then why was Tralane still alive? This brother had journeyed somehow to the ends of all worlds, won great power, and then surrendered it. Why?

Even the blood that pounded in his ears fed the strangeness of his life. Had his mother slept with a god and borne a child, only to be murdered and the family cursed by a jealous goddess? Or had his father lain with a goddess and won the son away from the mother, along with her wrath? He blushed as he recalled the many stories in his repertory that might have been the tale of his own family. Perhaps Mathi had, through the parable of such stories, told Tralane the tale of his origin, expecting his young ward to divine the true meaning of the tale and realize the danger implied in having an immortal for a brother.

Then for a moment Tralane despaired, for all this might also be a lie and the truth be hidden in some dark corner that would never yield to the light of day. But the despair lost itself as the dark corner merged with the gloom and became indistinguishable from sadness.

Tralane turned back briefly to the Warrior's sprawled corpse and bent down to retrieve the creature's sword. Only the Emperor of Many Faces held the answers to the bard's questions, and if Tralane were to unravel the truth concerning his origin and destiny, he would need all the power he could raise to compel his godling brother to give up his knowledge.

Tralane strapped the second belt around his waist, so that he had a scabbard on either side of him. He sheathed his own sword and walked through the narrow streets until he found the broad avenue where he had originally entered the city. He took the Eye out and gazed into its depths, his mind fixed on the Emperor of Many Faces and the god Wyden itself. This time he did not let the tantalizing glimpses of other realities lure him away from his quest. He rejected the false images of his desire, letting the temptations to discover and explore new sensations and experiences wither in the blaze of his purpose. Finally, amid the half-seen, flickering shadows of green and black, a masked and armored figure appeared. The figure flashed out of existence, but Tralane summoned it back. When he had it clearly in the amulet, reflected across its many facets, he saw the emblem of a coiled serpent emblazoned on its chest. Behind the figure, a mountain solidified, and on its uppermost peak clung a small city with walls carved from the rock and towers piercing the dead night sky. Below the city walls, a massive, glittering rope of green wound its way down the mountain to disappear in the valleys and hills below.

The Emperor was found but, curiously, only the hint of his form appeared. His mind, and that of the god, was still beyond Tralane's reach. But that did not matter now. Tralane opened the door between worlds and commenced the journey, the image of the city captured in the amulet in his hands. As he walked down the avenue, he felt the cold touching him again, tracing a raw edge along the length of his spine. It would be colder on this last of all worlds, and not all the fires and warm clothing would be able to keep out the frigid void he would find there.

The world of the ruined city began to lose substance, the glow of the dim noonday sun fading among the stars. On the horizon, a delicate tower broke and fell majestically behind a skyline of smaller domes and towers. The grave land silently accepted the defeated structure, its sudden collapse signaling the departure of life from that barren world.

Chapter 18

The darkness unfolded as the ground became rocky and treacherous. Tralane groped his way up a black mass of sharp, loosely packed stones and boulders, nearly blind in the deceivingly bright starlight. The unseen smiles of the night leering down at him from beneath the cold, derisive eyes that were the stars drove Tralane steadily upward. His climb was methodical—reaching, feeling for security, balancing, pushing and pulling with his legs and arms. He brushed aside the fears of darkness and high places, setting in their place the soothing balm of routine. His body worked forcefully against the near-vertical slope, and his mind and emotions shielded themselves from the maddening loneliness and danger of the place by allowing action to take precedence. Cumulain's healing powers had transformed his image of himself; where before he had been a lowly archer avoiding every possible chance to exert himself and usually managing to win through negligence a post guarding some noble of dubious honor, he now thrilled with the exertion of the climb and the smooth delivery of strength to his limbs. The chill, dead air biting along the trails of his sweat was a keener bait to life than any of the power and dangers his court machinations had led him into.

The rock surface he climbed suddenly began to take

on the chiaroscuro of detailed reality exposed to harsh
light. A shadow, his own, faced him. He looked up at the
sky and saw the craggy escarpment ahead of him, with
what appeared to be a shimmering wall of green, blue,
and white crystals jutting out from the rest of the mountain. The coils of the god Wyden were waiting for him.
Grimacing with disgust, he turned his head to find the
source of the new light. He opened his mouth to gasp,
but found he could only clutch at his hold on the mountain
until his hands ached with the strain.

A moon was rising on the uneven horizon behind him.
For the first time, Tralane understood the terror Agathom
must have felt at the falling of his world's moons. A body
was heaving itself into sight before Tralane's shocked eyes,
glowing as if subterranean fires were raging beneath a
translucent surface, and its widening semicircle was
already larger than both Star Speaker and Wanderer
together. The sky's face would be nearly obliterated by
the fully risen moon. Its mountains and craters were clearly
defined, marking out in curious runes the annihilation of
a world.

Tralane considered using the Eye to escape the baleful
scrutiny and doom of the moon that seemed to be falling,
even as it rose. He cursed his every past wish for a lucky
glimpse of Star Speaker or Wanderer. Then reason took
command, and he waited as the satellite freed itself of
encumbrances and hovered overhead.

There were no tremblings in the earth, no rifts or explosions, nor any great onrush of wind. The air thickened
and warmed with fog which flowed up along the mountainside, racing past Tralane. The rest of the world
remained as it was. Nature's laws were not being set aside
by wrathful gods; the moon was not falling. Reassured,
though still nervous over the proximity of his onetime
sign of fortune, Tralane resumed his climb.

The moon was full, but the fog dampened the sharpness
of light until a universal, hazy whiteness surrounded Tralane. A pale maw that was the moon above him was the
extent of the physical environment defined in the fog. The

slope yet to be climbed had disappeared, this time not into darkness but into scattered light. Swirling tails of mist trailed after his hands and feet as he moved, and clouds of moisture exploded from his mouth and nostrils as his breath became increasingly labored. By the time he had reached the wall of crystals that was the body of Wyden stretched out on the earth, he was almost overcome with weariness. The rapid embracement of the moon by the cloying, damp cloudiness was draining the vitality from him, just as it was diffusing the light. Again he cursed, and this time the object of his anger was the amulet. He had been allowed to enter the world of the emperor, but his route had been deflected so as to weaken him for the final confrontation. He did not have to wonder who had caused the diversion.

Tralane brushed his hand cautiously across Wyden's impenetrable hide and studied the now milky jewels which composed the skin. He revised his initial assessment of impenetrability, since the Jade Warrior, at one time, had also seem impervious. But the vulnerability of the living wall did not for the moment interest him. He had to climb over the protruding mass, yet the few handholds the crystal-incrusted surface offered would tear his flesh, and bleed more strength from him. He thought of climbing down, using the Eye to back away into another world and try a new approach into the city itself. But the mind sharing the Eye with him would not allow him any such easy convenience and might lead him into an even more dangerous approach.

He crept sideways underneath the overhang of godhood, sometimes approaching and at other times retreating from the wall, depending on the location of the holds he could find. His purpose was to avoid beating himself fruitlessly against the barrier. He sought, rather, something inexplicable, and he would follow the serpent's windings around the mountain until he reached the city's wall, to find the core of his mystery. His progress was slow, until the fog momentarily parted around a dark crevice partially hidden by Wyden's body. He made his way towards the crack and squeezed through the opening, until he was inside the mountain. He rested awhile, trying uselessly to catch his breath and not dwell on the task ahead. Then, before doubt could unseat his courage, he crawled up into the crack, Wyden's body at his back and the mountain in his face and on his sides.

There was the smell of dank, uncirculated air, like that of the deepest dungeon of a fortress. He had been in enough of such places to know the aroma and dislike the association. The fog refused to climb in after him, as if Wyden were holding off all natural elements. He had difficulty pushing through the tunnel as his layers of clothing caught on the rock and his two swords wedged themselves into the mountain. He tugged and pulled, working up a sweat that irritated him all the more because the heat of his exertions was sealed next to his skin by his greatcoat. His patience began to evaporate; after a while he wanted only to breathe, to shed the confining armor he had gathered around himself and feel once again the cool breeze run across his chest. Instead his hand, searching for a hold, fell into emptiness. He discovered a gate.

The entrance was narrow, and would have been hidden by shadows in the crevice even had Wyden not deigned to mask its location further. It was a secret egress for the fortress city's inhabitants. Tralane had used a few such conveniences during some of his earlier escapades. They could be easily defended or closed, if discovered during times of war, but were an invaluable aid to the intrigues at court. They usually served rulers, since it was rulers who had structures built or torn down and burrowings filled in or reopened. If customs on this world ran a course similar to the ones on his homeworld, and he saw no reason for them not to since they both flowed from the same human source, the passage that opened up behind the gate would lead eventually to the complex of throne room and royal quarters. There, he was certain, he would find the Emperor of Many Faces and the answers he so desperately desired.

He shed his coat and some of the layers of clothing he

had hastily donned in the Wilderness Flower. He bundled them together, wrapped his coat around them, and tied the whole affair into a pack which he slung over his shoulder; the two sleeves of his coat tied together served as a strap. He tightened the sword belts around his waist and, somewhat relieved, advanced into the pitch-black passageway.

He crept along a wall, an outstretched hand keeping him in contact with the smooth, cool mountain rock. He was impressed by the power that had eaten its way through stone like a worm through soft soil to make the tunnel and wondered whether some sorcerer king from the city above him or the Emperor himself had been responsible for its construction. He drew one of his swords with his free hand and kept the blade across his stomach and chest, suddenly anxious of being caught off guard by such might. He pulled his hand away from the wall, letting his fingers barely graze the surface, afraid of what might snatch at him from the darkness if he passed too close. Dread settled into his heart as he lost count of the steps he had taken into the mountain. Time stretched itself on a rack of fear. At any moment he expected a door to burst open, flooding light and shadow into the passage, illuminating an inconsistent reality in which ambiguous shapes, growing and shrinking with every flicker, converged on him with grim and silent intent.

But if there were any doors, they remained shut. The silence was as thick as the smell of chill, stale air, and the quiet shuddered only a little when his foot struck stone and he fell forward with a sharp cry. He landed on stairs. He rose and began the long, tortuous climb to the city above.

He rested several times on his journey, muttering to himself for not having brought food and water. He especially regretted the water. He should have returned to the Wilderness Flower after slaying the Beast and taken some provisions, or at least snared some game before so hastily departing the last living world he had seen. He thought of the city's inhabitants and of the delicacies and staples they surely kept in storerooms he might stumble across. Yet the land around the mountain seemed bleak, and he had not seen a town or river in the valleys below to warrant the building of a fortress city on the heights. In the brief glimpse of terrain Tralane had received by moonlight, there was nothing to indicate that this world had any delicacies or staples to offer, or even simple vegetation and water. But then, what sustained the Emperor's court and army? Where were the roads? Where was the evidence of an empire, which the title Emperor implied? Even in Tralane's preoccupied stay on the mountain slope, he should have seen or heard some hint of the vassals at the Emperor's command—a cluster of lights from an outpost on the slopes, the dim sounds of revelry before the fog closed in. It did not make sense that there should be an Emperor and no subjects. Tralane began to wish for the discrete guard sometimes found in such passages, for at least then he would have proof of some kind of life.

After his third rest, with his mouth parched and his back frozen by the creeping cold of the steps, Tralane bumped against a barrier. His hand swept across the impediment for several moments before he realized it was a door. He pushed with his hand with no result, then shoved with his shoulder and heard the creaking of hinges. The door gave way, and Tralane found himself in a large, circular room, barely distinguishable in the dim glow from a stairwell at the opposite end of the room. A series of doors lined the walls to either side, and at the center of the room a stone pedestal stood raised to waist height. Something lay flat across its top.

Tralane crossed the distance between the pedestal and the doorway, wary of any dozing guards hidden in shadowy corners. The purpose of the place came to him—it was a dungeon, perhaps a private one for the exclusive pleasure of the city's rulers. With a secret entrance and exit, enemies could be spirited in and endangered friends allowed to escape, all under the guise of a mysterious death. Tralane knew the system well, having seen it first hand at the more civilized courts of his homeworld.

The victim, human in shape but no longer in appearance, who lay spread-eagled on the pedestal, with coagulated blood pooled beneath him, had all the markings of the most civilized mutilation Tralane's old masters might have practiced. Under the bard's palm, the chest was still, and the ears were deaf to his urgent whispers. The hands and feet were free of bindings, as if the will to move them had long since drained out of the body along with the blood. If the victim was not dead, he might as well have been.

Tralane turned away to examine the doors and found they were cast from the same heavy, black metal as the door separating the dungeon from the passage through the mountain. Each had a small hatch near the bottom through which food could be thrust. He opened them one by one and peered into the dark recesses of each cell. He had gone nearly halfway around the room when he found one inhabited. A body, stinking and unkempt, lay on the floor near the hatch. Tralane released the latch and opened the door, pulled out the body. To his surprise, he found a woman in his arms.

She shivered, opened her eyes slightly, and struggled weakly against him. Her mouth opened and closed around soundless, inarticulate words. Her chest heaved with unnatural strength as a shriek of terror struggled to be set free. Tralane held on to the woman firmly, caressing her filthy, matted hair. Her skin was cold, though she had stopped shivering after his initial embrace. Her eyes opened wide, showing the invulnerability of her fear. She refused to be comforted by his efforts to soothe her.

"Who are you?" Tralane asked in a whisper, still waiting for the cry of alarm from a hidden warden. "Why are you being held here?"

The woman's persistent silence led him to believe that they did not share a common language. Then he caught a glimpse of her tongue and felt her throat; he saw that language was not the only barrier. He frowned at the cruelty of her mutilation. Careful surgery, the rudiments of which he had learned as a boy in Mathi's tower, had turned her into a mute. The words of any language could not cross her lips, and her loudest cry would amount to nothing more than a hoarse, choked whimper. Her suffering made him forget his own physical discomforts.

Tralane inspected her clothing for some symbol of her identity—a jewel, bracelet, an embroidered sign, or the patterns of her dress and its material. But he could not detect the markings of either nobility or servitude which, he had assumed, would be common in an emperor's fortress, where rank should descend in proper order from the royalty of the head to the baseness of the feet.

She wore a simple frock that had once been a dark blue or gray but was now black with grime. It could have been a princess's casual gown as easily as a maid's dress.

Not knowing when a guard might pass by, Tralane glanced anxiously back at the stairwell leading up into the fortress city, then slowly helped the woman get up. When they were both standing, she recoiled from physically touching him and staggered to a wall. He motioned towards the door, but her face twisted into a mask of disgust at the escape he offered her. He casually noted that when her face settled back into its natural contours, there was a chance that her high cheeks and dark eyes might make her a beautiful woman. But there was too much darkness and filth between them for Tralane to be certain, and other matters demanded his attention. After she refused his offer of clothing from his pack, he left her to do as she wished. If he survived what was to come, he would return and force her to safety.

He started toward the stairwell, stopped before he reached the first step, and listened to the barely audible sounds coming from behind him. Then a pounding sound echoed in the dungeon, as if something soft and desperate were trying to beat down a hard and implacable barrier. With a backward glance over his shoulder, Tralane saw the woman hunched over the spread-eagled man on the pedestal. Her face was hidden against the stones, and she heaved as if she were weeping. Yet when she rose, even in the bad light he could see that her eyes and cheeks were dry. He went back to the pedestal and listened for the man's heart beat, checked for a pulse, and put his ear to the other's nose and mouth to try to catch the sound of breathing. There were still no signs of life, despite the fact that the corpse was not yet decomposing. He appeared to be on the verge of death, frozen in that waiting moment when life was still calling to a soul with every heart beat while death hovered in plain view, hands outstretched.

The woman collapsed to her knees, and Tralane knelt beside her, holding out his hands helplessly. She stared at them blankly, with only the recognition of the death of someone she had loved lighting her eyes. He waited a while, searching for a way to comfort her, to communicate a sharing of grief. He started to rearrange the position of the body, so that it would at least appear to rest easier, but the woman started to her feet and dragged him away from the pedestal. Finally, with a disconsolate shrug of his shoulders, he set out again towards the stairs.

To his surprise, after he had climbed a few steps, he heard her following him. He proceeded cautiously, seeming to take for granted that she should follow him, but listening carefully to her movements. He was afraid she might take him for an agent of the man's murderer and revenge herself on him. However, they progressed steadily up the stairs without incident, and soon his suspicions were assuaged.

They rested several times on their way, the stairwell being longer and steeper than the tunnel Tralane had already passed through. This time, however, some light was provided by patches of phosphorescent moss set at regular intervals on the walls. By this glow, he saw that she kept to a constant distance of twelve steps from him. When they rested and he saw her sitting forlornly in the gloom, her eyes twin vortexes of darkness glistening with restrained tears, he could not fight back the urge to try to comfort her. The rebuffs he received first angered him, then filled him with sorrow for having been irritated by her grief and the suffering of her imprisonment. He wanted to take her to her kinsmen, where she might feel free to

relieve herself of her pent-up emotions, but his ignorance
of the world they were in prevented him from granting
even this small favor. Perhaps when they reached the
more frequented halls of the city, she would see herself
to safety. Tralane did not wish to entangle her in the dangers of his own life and hoped she would conveniently
disappear before his inevitable confrontation with the
Emperor.

They climbed for what seemed in that timeless place
an infinite age. At last, they found the stair's end. Tralane
held up his hand to the woman, then crept ahead. The
door blocking their path was like the previous portals he
had encountered, and he tested its firmness with a few
shoves. The door gave way, and he pushed until there
was enough space for him to squeeze through.

He came out at the end of another tunnel, but in this
passage the walls had been constructed from blocks of
stone, not carved through the mountain. At the other end
of the passage stood an ornate door, larger than any so
far encountered and made from wood. The moss light
revealed its gilt and circular, cosmographic carvings of
stars and strange creatures. It was an imperial symbol,
for on each corner of the door a crown and scepter stood
out in bas relief. The secret entrance and dungeons did
indeed lead to the royal quarters.

He reached this latest door and put his ear against the
crack of space at the lintel. He heard nothing except for
a faint whistling as air pushed through from the other side.
With a tug at the handle he found at the center of the
door, Tralane opened the way into the fortress city.

He found himself looking out across a darkened ballroom, through a frame of tattered curtains drawn to con-
ceal the doorway. Stepping through the door, he found it
had been camouflaged to look like a continuation of the
ballroom's walls. Cautiously, he drew aside the curtains
and studied the corners, balconies, canopied stages and
high-arched exits for signs of the guards he expected to
find. The ballroom floor, a spiral pattern of white and
black chips of polished stone, was covered with an undis-

turbed coat of dust. Awnings, tapestries depicting battle
scenes, and pieces of furniture were all in dilapidated
condition. The ceiling, a dome of frescoed deities caught
in the act of exercising their particular powers, was punctured at several points. Moonbeams stabbed through the
breaches to land in spots on the floor. Again, there was
an absence of guards.

Tralane was puzzled by the silence, and the abandonment of such regal confines to the exigencies of disuse.
The fallen grandeur of the room was contradicted by its
size and decoration; if indeed the Emperor made the fortress city his sanctuary, such a hall would be an appro-
priate throne room or gathering place for the court. The
spiraling path betokened a ritual procession, even a dance,
if the kingdom and its people had retained enough of their
spiritual gaiety, though a glance at the grim-visaged,
impossibly endowed heroes and gods depicted throughout
the room showed the marked inclination towards self-
aggrandizement of its makers. The people the Emperor
had come to rule were solemn and serious, burdened, like
the woman he had released from the dungeons, with emotions that were expressed in settings of grand formality
rather than wild intimacy. Yet, if this were so, what had
happened to the city's inhabitants to make them neglect
their own dwelling place?

Certainly, the area should never have been left
unguarded. But perhaps the complex of chambers was
banned to the citizens of the city. The crime committed
must have been great to have resulted in the wasting of
such an opulent setting for rule. There was also the possibility that the area was the domain of some spirit, either
mistakenly summoned by a court wizard or never properly put to rest. Tralane had known of entire towns and
their protecting castles that were laid to waste by such
rampant demons, who overcame their earthly masters and
practiced their hatred of death by destroying all living
things within their reach. Plague was an equally unpleasant explanation, though a simple one might be the retreat
from fashion of large, open spaces for the practice of

power. However, Tralane did not detect the skeletons that would have been neglected in a general outbreak of disease; and he could not conceive of any power, once gained and acknowledged, refusing to take advantage of all its privileges.

With the numerous possibilities of danger dancing in his mind, and with the knowledge that, whatever the reasons for the ballroom's lack of use, the dungeon that led to it was still an active part of the city, Tralane crept across the room. His eyes sought to penetrate every darkened recess that could possibly hide an enemy. His feet sank soundlessly into the carpet of dust. He was startled by a motion, only to discover that the woman was following him across the room. He motioned for her to go back to the hidden entrance, but she ignored his warning and stopped at roughly the same distance from him that she had kept on the stairs.

"It's your skin as well as mine, then," Tralane whispered in resignation.

He set out again in a half-crouch, the sword which had never left his hand since his entry into the mountain cutting the air ahead of him. Only when he reached the opposite end of the room and was flattened against a shadowed wall did it occur to Tralane that, if the woman was from the fortress, she would know the location of his goal. He could not trust her untroubled behavior in the hall, since she might have forgotten, or simply not cared about the dangers in the area. But perhaps the shock of her term in the dungeon and her sudden release had not touched the most basic memories of her heritage, such as the location of the Emperor's throne room.

"The Emperor," he whispered to her as she swung behind him to stand passively by a frayed, partially fallen tapestry. Apparently, his precautions had infected her disinterested attitude. "Can you take me to him?" he continued. "You can escape, and I'll help you if I can, but can you show me where the Emperor stays?"

Tralane continued scanning the ballroom, wishing for a guard, a stray noble, a worker, anyone other than a mute to question. He repeated the word Emperor several times until he was beginning to despair of receiving any help from her. He took a step forward, setting out in a random direction, when she cut in front of him and proceeded boldly, if to his mind foolishly, into the next room.

The chamber they entered was much smaller and completely bare. The exit opened into an arched hallway, and there the sacred precincts of royalty ended. The walls had once been covered with sheets of milky stone, most of which lay shattered on the ground, emitting a feeble glow. The bold depiction of gods and heroes, all manifestations of earthly pretentiousness by mortal rulers, dwindled into detailed carvings of wooden arch frames fashioned to resemble the branches of trees from which seemed to peer strange, shadowy faces. In a change of style—either an old traditional view that had not yet been completely replaced or a new artistic perspective that was beginning to spread—there were clusters of decorations, stands, pieces of broken doors and molding done in a curious mixture of stone and wood. The two elements seemed to merge and were carved with delicate, repetitive patterns of geometric shapes. Another fashion, far less frequent but much more fascinating to Tralane, depicted voluptuous women with faces a shade too square, with six fingers instead of five, and with what appeared to be a third eye on their foreheads, done as statues of black stone. The figures varied in size but were consistent in their smooth, curving lines, as if a lost being from a distant world had spent his time feeding the jaded tastes of the inhabitants of the fortress with new, exotic fantasies.

Tralane found the variety at first entertaining; but after a while, it became more wearisome than if the citizens of the city had settled comfortably into one motif. There was a sense of desperation in the jumble of rooms and clash of styles. A chamber whose floor was covered with rotting pillows, and whose walls were etched with lewd drawings, stood directly opposite a long room with a low ceiling that opened up into distant galleries of books. The confusion was unsettling in that it revealed a hysterical search for something by shaping and manipulating space and elements. As they passed the workshops of artisans, banquet halls, and private wardrobes and baths of nobles, it became apparent that the forms were empty of life, the elements used ruined by meaninglessness.

Finally, they came to a series of rooms given over to the collection of idiosyncratic objects of desire—daggers, unidentifiable beasts' heads, swatches of materials in all textures and colors, and spherical objects in a gradation of size and color, from small and dark to huge and light. Suddenly, the woman stopped, and Tralane almost ran into her trembling figure.

The bard stepped forward and examined the room she had stopped beside. He tried to follow her eyes to see what the source of her fear was, but all he saw was a forest of masks hanging down from the ceiling on threads of various lengths. The masks stared emptily out at him. He entered the room, brushing the false faces away with the point of his sword. An eerie sensation came over him as he probed deeper into the room. The blank, pale outer faces yielded to deeper layers of comedic, tragic, elemental, and spiritual disguises. All of them were finely crafted, with the proper shades of natural or symbolic coloring each mask required to achieve its expression. He reached out and touched one of them, and recoiled as the warm substance from which they were made felt uncannily like living flesh. He laughed nervously, sending ripples through the veils of faces that surrounded him, falling from the ceiling all the way down to his feet. Dismissing the masks as yet another aberration of the elite fortress-city dwellers, Tralane turned to leave, when a pair of living eyes, where only blackness should have glowered back at him, arrested his attention.

Tralane froze in mid-motion, his mind drawn to the eyes which stared at him from behind a blank, crystal mask. The crystal was green, and resembled the Jade Warrior's facial construction. For a moment the Warrior was resurrected in Tralane's imagination. But the eyes were sunken, showing corners of flesh behind the eyelets.

They were human eyes, but Tralane failed to find comfort in them.

"Welcome, Tralane," a deceivingly gentle and soothing voice said, drifting to Tralane from the direction of the eyes. "I had not expected to find you slinking about in my own refuge, but it is a pleasant surprise to have you. I see you've met the Lady Akyeetha. A fine woman, even if she is the last of her degenerate race. She will return to confinement shortly, after I have dealt with you."

"Are you the Emperor?" Tralane asked boldly, taking in the information the Emperor offered but not acknowledging it.

"The Emperor of Many Faces is my title."

"What is your name?"

"I've forgotten." There was a moment's hesitation. "It's been so long since I've had a use for one."

"You seem to remember mine."

"Ah, but you are different." There was a malevolent languor in the Emperor's words. "You are the quarry."

"I was."

"No longer?"

"I stand before you in contempt of your wishes."

"Contempt is a strong word. You have inconvenienced me, as far as my servant is concerned."

"Your son, the Jade Warrior?"

There was a flicker in the eyes, and the rhythms of the Emperor's speech stumbled slightly. "Yes . . . You won more than I thought you could. Still, you have graciously returned the Eye and Fangs of Wyden to my care. For that, I am grateful."

"Don't talk as if you were about to get them back."

"Oh?" The masks around the crystal face started. "So the pup snarls? You've come some way since Agathom surprised you in his tent."

Thoughts coalesced in Tralane's mind, and lightning illuminations from their merging gave him flashes of insight.

"Though I'll wager you haven't learned to match your tongue and spirit with your nature," the Emperor continued. "No, you are still a coward at heart, Tralane, hiding behind a display of ignorance and cowardice."

"How would you know that?"

"I would know, better than any." The Emperor's tone lent his words an air of omniscient condescension.

Tralane replied gruffly, "And would a brave emperor rule over a phantom empire?"

"What? Can—do you dare question my power?"

"I haven't seen your power, Emperor. All I've seen are two wretched prisoners, one tortured to death, the other mutilated into silence. Where are the warriors, servants, nobles? Where is the city that should be clinging to the walls of your fortress, its people basking in the glow of your strength? Where is your empire?"

The masks quaked as the emperor, his face still hidden, moved brusquely forward. Tralane retreated, wondering if he had provoked too sharply. Yet he had to maintain his bravado in the face of the Emperor's advance in order to gain mastery of the game he was trying to set in motion. Containing the fear that would, in earlier times, have been reason enough for him to part with the Emperor's company, Tralane leveled the point of his sword and stood his ground at the doorway. A grim sense of purpose steadied his hand, and his courage rallied around the key to his quest. The guile that was his life's trade and the strength newly discovered in his love for Cumulain fell into harmony, allowing his mind to think clearly even while death was a mere sword's length away.

Flight or rash action, the staples of Tralane's life, failed to satisfy his hunger. He was baiting a line and patiently waiting for the most dangerous sustenance he could desire—knowledge. The Emperor seemed intimate with his history, a natural conclusion even without the Emperor's testimony; through contact with the Eye and the Jade Warrior, the ruler had been able to follow Tralane's moods and movements. Yet how would he know, better than any, as he claimed, that Tralane had marked himself with the brand of cowardice and lived his life accordingly? Why should a ruler of a world distant from Tralane's bother to discover that an insignificant bard's love of tales was founded on an inability to pursue the objects and engage in the actions of his heroes? Of what matter was it to the Emperor that Tralane would indeed rather slink—and had done so on many occasions—and bandy assuaging words instead of testing truth in a confrontation? In short, how did Tralane come to be so important in the schemes of a far-off sorcerer?

The amulet had found its way to him, drawn as Gibron had informed him, by the forces focused on Tralane. But why was a youthful bard and archer a fulcrum of power, fated to become a Keeper, and not a sorcerer like Agathom or the magic woman who had brought the plainspeople to their Nushu Land? Only one thing could have made Tralane so crucial to whatever plan the Emperor was formulating. A relation existed between himself and the Emperor, one which was enough of a threat to upset those plans, and close enough to warrant care and discretion in the elimination of that threat.

Tralane was sure of his hold on the truth. He knew himself to be a son, and the man hidden behind the mask to be a father. And he decided that the Emperor of Many Faces was no one else but his father.

He withheld speaking questions pertaining to his abandonment in the care of Mathi, to the identity of his mother—for he was no spawn of Wyden, judging by the Jade Warrior—and to the reasons why the Emperor had sought to hide behind the Warrior's cryptic remarks and had not simply acknowledged their relationship. Tralane struggled with the pain of his father's rejection and the fact that his own sire had doomed him.

The Emperor stopped short of Tralane's sword point. The youth could hear heavy, tremulous breathing through the mask, as if violent emotions were being stifled by the false visage. The Emperor's jade-and-turquoise gown, partially visible through the screen of masks, rustled with an impatient movement. Tralane's hope that the rage would be converted into speech rather than action bloomed as the Emperor began to speak in a low, guttural tone. His

eyes glowed with fierce intensity. Madness seemed to
burst out from them in long, sinewy strands, enveloping
Tralane and nurturing the seed of that same madness within
the bard.

"My empire," the Emperor said, arched over Tralane's
sword but carefully avoiding its touch, "is all around you.
It is the air we breathe, the land we stand on, the walls,
the sky, the stars, and the moon you call Wanderer blocking out the emptiness and filling the night with light. I am
ruler of all that is in this existence, just as I am lord of
all these faces here in my chamber. What do I need with
people? Warriors? Craftsmen? Farmers? I live by my own
hand, for my own amusement, untroubled by petty chal-
lenges to my power. After you are gone, there will be no
one in all the worlds that ever were who could even attempt
to strike me down."

The Emperor took a step back and turned his head
aside. He gazed at one of the blank masks near him,
touched it with a finger and set it into a slow spin. He
looked again on Tralane.

"I was once an adventurer, Tralane," he began, his
voice calm but not as soothing as it had once been, "as
you are now, young and foolish in the realities of the world
and of magic. In my studies, I undertook to probe the
realms of sorcery, seeking for some key, some secret with
which to better my master and prove to him and myself
how worthy I was of power. One night, as I lay drunk
with vapors, leaving my mind open to those realms I
wished to explore, I touched upon a creature who called
itself Wyden, and claimed to be a god. I heard its call,
but in my ignorance I took it to be a minor demon crying
for a worshiper. I laughed at its tale of surviving all the
gods in a world beyond the ending of all worlds, with no
one but a few weak members of a dying race to give its
existence meaning. This Wyden promised me power, and
again I laughed, saying, "What do I need with an empire
of death?" Again it called, its voice fading as it made a
last attempt to win a convert, and promised me the freedom of travel across the broad width of time as it rolled

implacably forward like a massive wave, filling each
moment with a flash of existence. Still I disbelieved, but
the words, distant as they were, entertained me with their
inventiveness. I decided to save what I thought was a
mere demon and use it for a familiar. I answered its call,
binding my mind to the creature's so I could drag it to
me through my paltry powers. But as soon as we were
linked, I felt myself being stretched out and drawn across
space. My eyes were blinded by the blinking of many
images. I was in a thousand places at once, each segment
of my body occupying a different point in time and space.
I tried to anchor myself in my own world, but I had already
left it. There was a floating time in an endless expanse
that surged about me. There were wars, plagues, and
patches of idyllic splendor. Gods and sorcerers of many
worlds caught a glimpse of my passage, were puzzled,
and chased me briefly. But I was pulled along with great
speed and easily escaped their scrutiny.

"Then I saw this city, and the image did not fade from
my mind. So I flew to it as a harak dives after fish in a
stream. I fell somewhat roughly on the ground before the
gates. A pale, sorry band of lords and ladies waited for
me within and a great, sickly worm, its head reared up,
watched me from a little further down the slope with its
single eye. My head was filled with laughter that was not
my own.

"I was comforted by the other humans. Some of them
were survivors of the race that had built the city, others
were dabblers in magic from different worlds, duped by
their own greed, naïveté or stupidity into the service of
Wyden. The two groups bickered briefly over me; but,
as soon as I had gathered my wits, I joined the gathering
of fools like myself, since I had nothing in common with
the natives of this world. I was not about to accept my
fate, as these others were content to do. I was a teller of
tales in my own world, and I knew the tricks gods and
mortals played on one another. I explored the fortress
even as I helped to maintain it as a temple to Wyden. I
read the manuscripts, after learning something of the native

written language, and I used what I learned to befriend
the ancestors of the city-builders. They were eager for
one of the off-worlders to join them, and to mediate
for them among the more numerous aliens to their land,
for they feared our frustrated desire for revenge against
Wyden would fall on them. They feared rightly. Daily, we
cursed the ancient people who had built the fortress city
and sustained the god Wyden beyond the proper ending
of all life. And our hatred and fear was the sustenance of
the god, who had chosen his followers for those traits.
So there was little I could do for them, except listen to
their complaints and learn their ways.

"As I consoled them, they showed me the secret passages, the mechanisms of defense that had lain dormant
for millennia, the libraries of sorcerers, and the pleasure
chambers they had once enjoyed freely. One night they
brought me here. When I saw all these masks, I knew I
had found my weapon against the god.

"The next morning I neglected my duties and went
down the mountainside to speak with Wyden. The god
watched me, but did not yet dare destroy so potent a
source of nourishment as I had become for disobeying its
will. I stood before this monster, though I will admit I
quaked within myself with fear, and pointed at its enormous eye.

"'You have lied to me, O great worm,' I said with all
the wind I could muster. 'You told me you had no worshipers, and would grant me power if I came to you.'

"Wyden laughed as it had done the first day of my
capture. 'I have not lied to you, O master of my fate,'
was its reply, spoken into my thoughts. 'You are one of
a very select few who nourish me and keep my temple
from tumbling down on me. What greater power can you
ask for than to hold a god to your services?'

"'None, my lord worm. But you have hidden the greater
part of your followers from us, in a chamber in the fortress
city above us. Why should we few labor for you, while
they sit quietly and enjoy the fruits of your blessing? They
rob us of our purpose, and our rewards in serving you.'

"Now Wyden was curious, and the creature raised its head slightly to take in the city walls. 'There are no more people in this world—I have searched with care.'

"'Then you have also been fooled, my great lord, for by my soul there are more eyes staring down on us than you know how to count.'

"There was wrath in Wyden's voice when it cried out, 'Where, where are the hidden ones?'

"'In a room in the upper reaches of the fortress. A thousand of them, many thousands, smiling for fear their laughter would guide you to them.'

"There was a scream of rage that shook the rocks loose from the slopes and burned a wound in my mind. Slowly, yet with all the speed I'd wager the god could muster, Wyden reared its head and bared its fangs. It began to climb the mountain, winding up the sides and sending its worshipers into hiding. I raced ahead. Since I climbed straight up, I reached the fortress ahead of Wyden. I set the defensive machines in motion, and those still functioning offered the god enough resistance to fuel his anger and make him believe there were indeed a thousand people raining boulders and fire on him.

"I went to the uppermost ramparts and yelled like a madman, taunting Wyden on. I gestured to the wall, behind which lay the room of masks, and when the god had almost reached it, I left my post and hastened to the room and hid myself among the faces.

"An angered god makes short work of a mortal edifice, and it was not long before part of the wall tumbled and Wyden poked its head into what it believed to be a cache of humanity. Ah, then, Tralane, was the test of my desire, for while I had the worm believing what was not, I had power over a god. I sprang forward, and before Wyden could brush me aside I sank my arms into the tissue surrounding the eye. With all my strength I heaved, then fell backwards as the god shook me off. But I came away with my prize—the eye, freshly plucked, was in my hands. The organ dissolved even before I regained my feet, and I was left with the jewel that is the heart of the amulet you carry. The god bellowed with agony, blinded and lost. I ran out and renewed the rain of boulders, then took a sword from an armory and returned to the chamber of masks.

"Again I sprang forward, and this time my sword sliced into the mouth of Wyden so that its fangs were loosened. These I pulled out with my bare hands before the god realized what new source of pain was torturing its mind. When Wyden knew it had lost its sight and fangs to a mortal, it sank to the floor and allowed the rocks to pile on its neck and seal its head into the room. Yes, I conquered a god—and more. I promised the god I would give it new life if it told me the secret of its eye and fangs.

"'Yes, please, give me life,' the old god pleaded.

"'Then tell me, what is the nature of your eye?'

"'My Eye is the power that brought you across the cresting wave of time.'

"'And your fangs?'

"'They have given me victory over my brother gods and poisoned these worlds that are behind and before us, separated by mere moments of existence.'

"I understood then what I had done, and the magnitude of my deed dizzied me so much that I saw darkness closing in. But I recovered and gave dear Wyden the life I had promised, with my seed. From that union came the Jade Warrior, my ally and instrument. And from that joining I became immortal, never to know the darkness again.

"But this was only the beginning of my legend, Tralane. I became the ruler of a world; there was not a living thing capable of defying me. I captured and imprisoned my fellow priests of Wyden and separated them into the two rival camps. I fed their hatred of one another, condemning one as the degenerate native race that had supported Wyden while railing against the other group, calling them usurpers and invaders. Then I set them all free to hunt each other down, and there was much sport to be had in watching that deadly little contest. The old race, though far outnumbered, slew the others using their knowledge of the city to trap and kill their enemies. I had to capture them all, so that justice could be practiced on them. In the years that followed, when I was not otherwise preoccupied in implementing my plans, I went down to the dungeons and extracted from one or another of those degenerates a part of their life and soul. The last stands behind you, shocked into immobility by my presence, no doubt. I am the terror of these subhumans, Tralane. I do not know what I shall do for justice when she is gone...

"I took my title, the Emperor of Many Faces, from my victory over Wyden. And what do I rule? This world, for now. But after you have been destroyed, Tralane, after that last portion of my nature has been scourged from all existences, I shall open a door through all the worlds and bid Wyden go through. The worm will be stretched across all the possible worlds of the moment, and will link the entire, ever-breaking, ever-expanding crest of Time. I will control all that is to come, on every plane of existence. There will be one Wyden and one Emperor throughout the variations of Earths. The gods will not stop me, for in that action I will have overthrown fate and destiny, transcended the gods and become Time. Is that power enough for you, Tralane? Will you call me Emperor now?"

It was indeed power, though not of the genre in which Tralane had been taught by Mathi. The Emperor's power was founded in the material world; it did not seek to escape the limitations of physical reality, but rather to turn the limitations into a tool, serving the purpose of a single will. The Emperor's sorcery was founded on greed, fueled by wealth, and vulnerable.

Tralane was speechless before the depths of the Emperor's nightmarish vision. There was no doubt of the Emperor's insanity. Even his eyes, framed by the green mask, bulged with tormented emotions. Was this man his father?

The Emperor had not mentioned a wife, or leaving sons and daughters behind. Was he, after all, only a brother, left with some wizard to study the arts, like Tralane? This Emperor also loved tales, as well as adventure. There was blood between them, but what kind? Was Tralane an

heir or a brother to madness? How could he slay his
kinsman, knowing he might eventually succumb to the
weakness that had flawed the Emperor.

Wrestling with the issue left him short of breath, so he
grasped at words to fling into the air between them.

"How did you lose Wyden's Eye, then? Can an Emperor
be so strong and allow an act of common thievery, or
perhaps even an act of personal carelessness, to threaten
him with dethronement?"

"Fool! You still don't understand? It is not your possession of an amulet, or even the swords, that is a danger
to me. I did indeed throw the Eye into a pool of worlds,
as your would-be benefactor Gibron once told you. It was
my purpose to let you come into its possession. I had
hoped, with the aid of the Warrior, that you would destroy
yourself as so many of my enemies have done. That was
the easiest way. But now I must destroy you myself, for
it is your being that contains me. No act, no words you
could utter would disrupt my plan. It is merely your life
that is the threat. And that is about to be remedied."

"And will you deal with me as you did with Wyden,
or the Lady Akyeetha's people? Or can you face me,
without deceit, as I hold the symbols of your power? No,
my Emperor, the same blood runs through us both. I am
also adept at subterfuge, and I am not so easily fooled.
The Fangs of Wyden, I'll wager, are as deadly to you as
they were to this god's rivals and to your own son."

"Really, Tralane? And do you think you are the only
one who has ever penetrated this far? Do you know what
happened to the others, the wise, brave, all-conquering
heroes who followed the bait of the Eye and thought they
could humble the Emperor of Many Faces?"

The ruler leaned forward. With a slow, graceful gesture, he set one of the faceless masks near Tralane's head
into a spin. He stepped back to where the mask he had
previously set into motion was still revolving and examined his handiwork.

Tralane said nothing, nor did he move in response to
the Emperor's gesture. He watched the twirling blank face

and heard his strong words wilt in the quiet heat of the
Emperor's madness. His eyes began to feel heavy, his
thoughts lumbered into one another, and his awareness
lulled itself into stupefaction. Dimly, through the rolling
fog that was creeping into his mind, the implications of
the Emperor's words reached Tralane. There had been
others, others like himself, other brothers and sisters from
the alternate worlds, and perhaps surviving mothers and
fathers—all slain by this renegade. The deed's infamy
nauseated Tralane and stoked his hatred. Yet he could
not express his revolt against the crime. He saw the blankness closing in on him and recognized too late the Emper-
or's subtle spell of entrapment. He fought against the
listlessness that was burying him, but found he could not
lift the great burden of the Emperor's sorcery.

"A peculiar punishment these people devised for their
criminals," the Emperor commented, his eyes now fixed
on Tralane. "They would destroy their enemies by strip-
ping layers of the mind, selecting some aspect for preservation while eliminating others. They could preserve
the faces of the people they thus destroyed, empty of
personality yet frozen in some expression of emotion or
mood, forever imprisoned by the limitations of some petty
feeling. During the height of their civilization, they were
masters of the art. These blanks are my crude imitations
of their work. They lack the essence of the heroes I've
reduced to this state, something I've been unable to capture. But that is just as well, for it is the essence that I
first set out to annihilate. You will be the last, Tralane.
Gaze into the emptiness, hero, and lose yourself in that
void. I hold a mirror which absorbs your being. How can
you resist, when all these others have failed before you?"

Tralane clenched his teeth and pinched the palm of his
free hand with his nails in an effort to retain a hold on
himself. Then he relaxed. Cumulain's aroma, her touch,
her concerns welled up within him to beat back the emptiness. The black sword, Wyden's Fang, was solid in his
hand again, a tool to carve meaning in the mask that was
the focus of the Emperor's sorcery. Yet Tralane could still

not bring himself to strike his enemy. Even with his own survival at stake, Tralane had the knowledge of relationship with his foe, and that frail link to his own identity was too precious for him to slay. The recollection, which he had long been struggling against, of Detrexan's fate sealed him in paralysis.

The Emperor set another mask into motion, then stopped the retreat of his hand. His eyes were gazing over Tralane's shoulder, and their bulging concentration changed to amazement, then fear. Tralane felt a prickling sensation at the base of his neck, then nearly whirled about when a hand grasped the hilt of his second sword and pulled the blade out of the scabbard. Tralane fell sideways against the door frame, crouching low and holding his weapon over his shoulder, ready to sweep down and brush aside any attack. Without letting the Emperor out of his sight, Tralane watched the figure behind him advance into the chamber. He smiled grimly as the Lady Akyeetha walked stiffly by him, the sword she held dragging next to her leg.

The Emperor cried out and backed away. Tralane followed her, then took her flank against the Emperor. A quick glance revealed, beneath the layer of accumulated dirt, a paler skin. Her eyes were not focused on the Emperor, or on anything that was a part of the flesh and blood world. The sword in her hand trembled, just as her limbs shook with the effort of will she was performing at the command of some inner voice.

Tralane sensed the souls of the dead moving in her. He had seen possession before, and Mathi had taught him some rudiments in how to call and turn back possessing demons, so he knew the nature of Akyeetha's action, which no doubt she would never have undertaken on her own. Once, while serving some middle kingdom's court with songs and arrows, he had seen a band of wild hillmen break their diplomatic containment and burst into a raging mob of murderers. Their appearance of illness and dishevelment prior to the break with their mission of peace matched perfectly Lady Akyeetha's presentation at the moment. He heard the same faint cries, a warning for those whose souls had ears, signaling the approach of spirits. The hillmen had been difficult to subdue, even by the full complement of court guards. The spirit their sensitive minds had absorbed had corrupted them beyond sanity, and they had fought maniacally to the last man. Tralane hoped Akyeetha was not taken by the ghosts, which he saw as those of her friends and family, to the point where she could never regain possession of herself.

Lady Akyeetha circled to the left of the Emperor, Tralane to the right. The Emperor of Many Faces withdrew from the blank masks to stand among the finished ones, his legs wide apart as if to brace him, his arms extended in front of him. His eyes went from man to woman and back again. Neither Tralane nor Akyeetha stopped their encircling movement.

The fog that had closed in on Tralane's mind was breaking slightly, as the Emperor's control slipped. Akyeetha's intervention, prompted by her dead ancestors and relatives, was straining the Emperor's concentration, as he now had to face the spirit of the people he had destroyed along with whatever threat Tralane represented, both armed with the Fangs of Wyden. For Tralane, the balance of control was at last shifting to him, just as the weight of power was drifting away from the Emperor towards Akyeetha and the bard.

A high-pitched keening rose from among the masks, as if their hollow mouths had suddenly won tongues and were mourning the passing of their own souls. At first, Tralane suspected the piercing shriek to be the Emperor's doing, since under its assault he was hard pressed to maintain a hold on his dearly won control over his motions. Then he saw Lady Akyeetha's lips shaped around a howl, the muscles of her throat tensed with exertion. Distinctive voices emerged to lead the chorale of agony emanating from Akyeetha. Her chest heaved, and the bones of the fingers holding the sword were white against her skin. The masks trembled violently as the keening became louder. A haze formed around the woman, obscuring the details of her features and shielding her from the Emperor's defenses. Tralane, when he saw what was happening, laughed at the irony in his deeds.

Once again Tralane played the heroic savior, but this time his people were the restless, betrayed, unavenged spirits of the dead race the Emperor of Many Faces had conquered. They had fallen to the Emperor, but their struggle against him followed them into death. Hovering on the edges of life and death, waiting while countless other heroes—brothers and sisters to Tralane—fell before the Emperor, seeking one who would rescue them from the borderlands of existence, they had rallied around Tralane's staunch resistance. By rescuing the last of their race and providing the spirits with a vehicle for their revenge, he had won himself an ally. Alone, neither could have defeated the Emperor. Together, they forced the Emperor to retreat.

But the death struggle had yet to be fought, and neither party was anxious to initiate the final engagement. Tralane swung the point of his sword back and forth, more to ward the Emperor off than to threaten him. Lady Akyeetha was hesitant and awkward, first dashing forward with a vicious thrust of her blade, then collapsing into a stumbling retreat. The haze that had attached itself to her like a second skin also fluctuated in density, as Akyeetha fought to save her identity while still serving her ancestors.

The Emperor fared little better, as his power was divided between the two, trying to break down their resistance to his will while parrying their swords with invisible shields. Beads of sweat trickled down his neck.

"Where are you from?" the Emperor asked hoarsely, directing his question to Tralane.

"You should know—you led me here," was Tralane's shaky response.

"You are not the one who stole the Eye from Agathom; that was a kind of courage I could easily conquer, one I understood only too well. By Wyden's life, why don't you succumb to my spells? How can you be so strong?"

"I'm not so wise and mighty in the art, perhaps, but

I've lived in these last few weeks as I've never lived before. Your seductions are meaningless."

The Emperor recoiled as some root of his being was touched. "What? But I offer peace—"

"When there are people who need me?"

"Need you? You are worthless, your life is pointless, except as an extension of my will. No one wants you."

"The Lady Akyeetha?"

"Yes, of course, for the moment. But later, will she even turn her head to look at you? She is of royal blood, and we—you, no, we cannot be of such blood. But I offer the eternity of the masks."

"They are not warm to consider; an eternity of lonely oblivion is all they hide."

"So? And what will you do in your welcoming crowds? Will you teach Akyeetha to speak and convert her from my plaything to yours? Do you plan to save those who are weaker than you, so they can turn against you when your task is finished? Join me, Tralane. I'll give you Akyeetha. You may keep the swords, the Eye, this world. I will make you an immortal, and we'll rule all the paths the world has taken through time. We'll be gods together; you shall be the warrior, and I the sorcerer. None will stand against us, Tralane."

"Now you offer me power, Emperor? You are generous with the trophies won from the blood of others."

The Emperor shook his head in a mixture of disbelief and disgust. "You've gained noble sentiments, where most lose such weaknesses with experience. Don't be a fool; follow your nature. I, better than anyone, know what you truly desire."

Tralane stood his ground, but the Emperor's words shook him. How could the bard know which of his many contradictory desires was his core nature? Or were they all a part of him, pulling him first in one and then another direction? He was aware of the choice he had for so long abstained from making. He could follow the moment's strongest desire and change with the moment, becoming a satiated slave of his impulses. Or he could select a road, forego the tainted, isolating pleasures offered by the Emperor, and assume the burden of his freedom. The past and future beckoned with equal insistence, just as the forces of magic flowed among the three in the room, never resting, creating more tension the longer a decision was withheld. The point of the fulcrum shrank, and the balance of power became even more unsteady. Both the Lady Akyeetha and the Emperor waited on his decision. The masks in the chamber ceased to tremble as the keening fell to a hum.

The lessons of the past propelled him forward. His own ghosts—the spirits of the dead he had abandoned—rose up, called from memory, and surrounded his form. Protected by his own flickering aura, Tralane resolved the conflict in his blood. He turned away from the unlimited expanse of possibilities that had threatened to consume him and chose instead to stay and fight the madman before him, even if it meant the death of the father he had sought and the unbounded future he had wished for

The Emperor, even before Tralane spoke, sensed his decision and faltered before the strength of spiritual walls he had never before encountered. The tide of uncertainty fell back on the Emperor. His shields faltered; the sorcerous transformation of reality into the dreams he harbored broke down. Tralane knew that now, while the Emperor's will failed at the sight of his victim taking a path he could have chosen himself, was the time to strike. If the evil was allowed to recoup, if the Emperor were allowed time to grab hold of his crumbling delusions and summon the mad strength to impose them on reality, Tralane, Akyeetha, and all of existence would be swept away and drowned in the bursting flood that would issue from the Emperor's mind.

It was the Lady Akyeetha who struck first. Her sword penetrated the Emperor's shield, and she stumbled stiffly toward the startled ruler. The haze blazed about her, then was stripped away as the Emperor faced her with all his power. But before the sorcery could touch her, the point of Wyden's Fang was pricking his flesh.

Tralane followed an instant after Akyeetha. He broke through the Emperor's shield immediately after her and was singed by the spells the Emperor had directed against her. But his own aura was enough to protect him from their backlash. He drew blood, and the air sighed with the evaporation of magic.

Their swords pierced the Emperor at the same time, sliding through the ribs on both sides. Instantly, the Emperor stiffened and his arms fell, bouncing off of the broad sides of the swords to hang limply at his sides. Tralane withdrew his sword just as Akyeetha finally gave in to exhaustion, releasing her hold on her sword and sinking to the floor. The Emperor took a few steps backward, cutting a swath through the hanging masks as his sharp movements knocked them into each other and onto the floor. Amidst the clattering, he groaned and finally came to rest against a large, blackened mound protruding from the back wall of the chamber.

Tralane went first to Lady Akyeetha. The voice of her people was still, the fire of revenge having burned itself out. She breathed, and her face was once again that of a forgotten prisoner just recently released. He covered her with his cloak, then went over to where the Emperor lay and knelt beside the body, which still stirred with the dying embers of life.

The mound on which the Emperor rested shone with splinters of green and blue, as if jewels were buried beneath the thick, stringy growth that darkened the heap. The colors named the mound as Wyden, or what was left of Wyden's head. A thickly bunched cluster of finger-width strings, spilling out from an incrusted pit, showed where the serpent's Eye had been. The god was no farther from death than the Emperor, and did not even stir from its stupor when at last it had the opportunity to avenge itself on its conqueror by swallowing him whole, or lifting its head and crushing the Emperor beneath it.

Tralane's hand hovered over the Emperor's mask before removing it. When he finally removed the false visage and saw the Emperor's face, he was numbed. He barely felt

the frigid breeze that whipped through the room, now that
the Emperor's containment of the elements was lapsing
and the elements were resuming their seige of the fortress
city. Tralane's throat was choked with sounds, his mouth
formed inarticulate words. Then he laughed, and tears
carried out the pent-up emotions and released him from
the fears of madness and murder.

"You are not my father," Tralane exclaimed, still heaving from the unleashing of so many frustrated feelings.

The Emperor, his eyes clouded and his limbs lax, turned
in the direction of Tralane's voice.

"Father?" he asked weakly. He coughed, and his lips
turned black. The swords' infection was spreading, corrupting immortality with base death.

"Fool, fool," he continued, shaking his head. "We have
none. All the brothers I've sought and slain, singly and
in bands, all lured by Wyden's Eye, all slain by their
selfishness or granted oblivion by my hand, and not one
of them knew. Whose seed are we? Whose blood nurtured
us? In all possible worlds, all who carried our face and
our form were ignorant of their origin. How can this be?
No matter, I would have conquered all. The void would
have been filled. Do you understand? Do you see what
you've thrown away? What meaning is there for you with
no past or future? You cannot conquer as I would have
conquered. Artless as you are—powerful, perhaps, like
all of us, stained with the unknown, but ignorant, fool...
everything is beyond your reach... except death... yes
...that..."

The Emperor convulsed, and his eyes widened with
the enormity of a final vision. Then he died, and his body
shriveled into an unrecognizable skeleton covered with
ash.

Tralane stood and returned to Akyeetha. He gathered
her in his arms, lifted her, and walked out of the chamber.
The Emperor's final taunting questions were left with his
corpse, along with the necessity of mourning a father or
a brother who had shared the same womb. The many

surfaces of the bard's mind and emotions, uncovered for the first time, glittered like a friendly star within him.

He climbed to the parapets of the fortress city and took out Wyden's Eye, in which he searched for and found the familiar moons and star forms of his home world. Holding Akyeetha securely, he stepped onto the wall and looked out across the last, barren earth. The moon glided overhead, appearing ready to pounce on Tralane, but he only smiled at the thought. With the Eye in his fist, Tralane leaped over the precipice and plummeted through the air. His fingers passed over the jeweled center of the Eye, and he continued to fall long after his body should have shattered against the slopes of the mountain. Above him, the overbearing moon began to fade, and with it the reflection in Tralane's eyes of the Emperor's true face, the face he had seen and recognized before, on another world, with the rank of a mere captain, and the name of Detrexan.

Chapter 19

Tralane and Akyeetha were camped by a stream in a grove of jehaffa trees filled with trilling sunu-kon greeting the morning sun and slate-blue sky with their rapid two-note song. Akyeetha was bathing in the stream, oblivious to the two thorts sipping water along the banks and to Tralane, who lay among the twisted, partially surfaced roots of one of the larger trees. She swam up and down stream several times, then rested somberly against the far bank, her eyes closed against the sensual assault of an unfamiliar world.

Tralane's gaze was fixed on a distant tower peeking over the crests of some nearby hills. Memories blew to him on the cool breeze running from the tower, almost making him shiver. The shade of the tree under which he sat seemed deeper, isolating him from the rest of nature, when he recalled his days of childhood spent with these gentle hills and valleys. How many times had he sat in such secluded spots, staring off at the horizon and following the songs of birds with his heart, wishing his own ballads could travel the wind over the horizon and catch the ear of a possible companion? On such days, he had often been late in returning to the dull studies awaiting him under Mathi's tutelage.

Even now, Tralane was reluctant to return to Mathi's

tower, though the keys to many of his questions lay within those cold and lonely walls. Akyeetha and Tralane had traveled together for a month; she had trusted him to guide her through a new world while she sought, without hope, some trace of her own dead people in the faces of strangers they met on the road. He had taken her from the Ousho Plains, on which he had opened a doorway for them to tumble through after using an elementary wind-harnessing spell augmented by the Eye's power to slow their descent, then led her through the decimated remains of the southern kingdoms, and finally into this beautiful but uncolonized corner of the world where hermits and wizards frequently came to escape the constraints of everyday reality. The journey had been deliberate and leisurely, fulfilling its rationale as a scouting mission to survey the damage wrought by the Sorcerer King's campaign of conquest. He could just as easily have brought them to the tower first, allowed each to recover from the trials they had experienced, and then ventured out. But he had picked the site where Agathom had lost his amulet to a wandering, scheming bard and archer instead. He had decided to show Akyeetha as much of her new home as possible, so she could absorb and be absorbed by her new environment. He had wanted to retrace the Sorcerer King's steps and work out a strategy to undo the evil Tralane was, in part, responsible for unleashing. And most of all, he wished to delay the confrontation with his past as long as possible.

From the scene of his last, and most grandiose, flight from the demands of his world to the first place and person to suffer from his abandonment, Tralane's thoughts had dwelt almost solely on Mathi, the only parent he could claim. He had tried to console Akyeetha as she mourned the passing of her world, but since he was not even sure his words of solace could be understood by her, their communication was limited to soothing sounds and physical comforting. Despite these limitations and their individual preoccupations which distracted them from one another, a friendship had struggled into existence which

Tralane hoped would be nurtured into strong bonds. But since she could not speak, Tralane's thoughts had rarely been interrupted.

He wandered the labyrinths of his past, dreading the dead, quiet corners he so often found himself in—walls looming in the shadows, dwarfing the image he had constructed of himself. He could not rise above the walls, like his mythic heroes who, with a twist of their magic rings or the hasty summoning of a familiar, could relieve themselves of any task. He knew the walls were built by him, stone by stone, deed by thoughtless deed, and still he was unable to break through these barriers. Driven to the point of despair, Tralane had frequently wept in the night while Akyeetha slept. Her gentle caresses and questioning eyes, when she awoke to find him thus, could not stem the flow of tears. But the thought of Mathi, outrunning the relentless hounds of death, waiting for Tralane's return, kept him anchored to life. No matter what frustration or pain he had to endure, Tralane was determined not to fail again. The return to Mathi's tower was inevitable, for only through that return could Tralane beat down the walls which closed him in, trapping him in a world of darkness and confinement.

He knew the passions that had sparked the souls of Akyeetha's people to continue existing on the borderlands of life and death. He was a ghost himself, waiting for the act of redemption that would free him to escape into life, as they had escaped into death. In Cumulain's Wilderness Flower, a part of him had died, been buried, mourned over, and finally forgotten in the rushing of new life. Beneath this sloughed-off shell, a new form was waiting to emerge, pushing and kicking to be born. Akyeetha was also a ghost, since her people had used her to free themselves from the lust of vengeance, and thus released her from the same tyranny that had destroyed them, leaving her to carry on the memory of their race, to grieve for the fall of a world and bear the light of a new life. Together, their souls fought to overcome the shackles of the past and start again the journey through life. Compelled by the dead, Akyeetha was struggling for a place among the living; compelled by the past, Tralane was battering against the insulating armor that had protected him for so many years, and which now threatened to stifle him at the moment of his rebirth.

The song of the sunu-kon and the padding of Akyeetha's feet on the ground as she walked by, leaving beads of water on the bowed blades of grass, momentarily raised Tralane from the depths of his revery. But the nearness of the tower and the prominence of Mathi in his mind quickly cast his brief surge of happiness into gloom. As he watched Akyeetha dress, donning the leggings, skirt, shirt, and jerkin received from a Tribe Nation along with the thorts in exchange for Tralane's help in healing and entertaining the nomads, he thought back to his younger days. A friend such as Akyeetha would perhaps have changed the frigid innocence of his childhood. Reared in the backlands of the world under a brief-worded, unaffectionate guardian, Tralane had moved on into the vast world without any expectations other than meeting people. Their cruelties, blatant as they were, he accepted. Their kindnesses, subtle and equally unexpected, he did not know how to meet and was thus unable to receive.

The old ache in his shoulder awakened, as it always did when the winds changed and the air became heavy with impending storm. He peered into his shirt and traced the scar, sensing the roots of his past and the fissure that would break open his detached manner. Tralane scowled, knowing from the clouds that the weather was not really changing for the worse. Mathi's hand, reaching out from the tower, had touched the wound as a warning. Death was waiting for him outside of the prescribed path. Tralane had wandered, long ago, and received punishment by a demon's hand. Then he had broken away, wandered, and once again faced death. But this time he was returning, blazing his own trail through the wilderness, to show Mathi that his was not the only way through life, to power, to wisdom, to the strong, firm step that could lead where the eyes and senses and even the mind were clouded and dulled. He would return Mathi's cold touch with a warm one, proving that death had not taken him, and showing there were other things in life besides the pursuit of the obscure and inhuman.

Tralane's anxiety was somewhat relieved by this realization of his mission in returning to Mathi's tower. By mastering such a small aspect of Mathi's nature, at least some measure of his own freedom would be gained.

Tralane climbed out from among the roots and helped Akyeetha to dress. He smiled and kissed her as he touched her, and she looked at him with amusement and slight puzzlement. Her dark eyes regarded him somberly. Her hair was bound up tightly in a spiral pony tail at the back of her head, leaving the sharp, angular planes of her slim face fully exposed. She had gained weight to cover the sharpness of her bones, as well as strength and endurance over the course of their traveling. But she would need a great deal of rest and attention to return to the self that had been destroyed by the Emperor, and he knew better than to press his needs and attentions on her at the moment. He smiled back at her. Then he went off to fetch the thorts while Akyeetha gathered their satchels of provisions and blankets. When they were mounted, they rode slowly and in silence towards the tower.

Chapter 20

The land had not changed since Tralane's departure, protected as it was for seven times the span of Mathi's living years against the advances and erosions of nature. In this way, Mathi's spirit had time to transform itself into whatever form had been the wizard's goal, and not be hampered by sundry slave-demons released from their bindings to his tower as his prisoners or guards. The tower was also unchanged, standing on a wide clearing at the crest of a hill. The single doorway was closed, the windows dark. The stonework, competent but not spectacular, was still covered with vines which hugged the curving walls and crept into the windows—a sorcerous skeleton reinforcing the physical walls and protecting Mathi's stronghold from being breached by magical forces. To the north, a carpet of forest covered the last of the dwindling hills.

Tralane and Akyeetha dismounted when they came into the range of the tower's shadow, and led their thorts to the rickety shack leaning against the tower, which was used to house the mounts of occasional visitors. As they walked, Akyeetha was absorbed in studying the tower's every detail, as if she could feel the emptiness around which the delicate walls of sorcery had been constructed.

At last, the emptiness made itself felt to the bard, and he could no longer deny the sense of his guardian's absence.

They left their thorts in the stable hut and stood outside, each hesitating before choosing a direction. Tralane could not accustom himself to the wizard's death, and so waited for some sign of his approach. He had wanted everything to be the same as when he had left, so that his departure would not have seemed so drastic. His mind knew better, but his feelings did not.

Tralane finally left Akyeetha and headed for the tower's door. She took the opposite direction and began to wander over the grounds. She was weary of traveling, and the gentle stillness, brought on by the spells of preservation, visibly relaxed her. She was in a haven where, at last, she could contemplate the currents that had swept her to this time and place. Tralane hoped the setting would help her heal and that a time would come when they could see each other without awakening memories of fear, pain, and distrust. If not, the land would protect them from the world and each other for the rest of their lives.

Upon opening the door to the tower, Tralane found the antechamber in a shambles, as if a brawl had occurred. Dust blown in through the slit windows had settled into an undisturbed carpet of gray covering the overturned tables, benches, and torch-holders. Looters had broken in after noting that the tower was unoccupied. But what could they have stolen? Wizards who left the commercial paths of the world did not have any wealth to surrender in death, and the spellbooks they used could be more easily bought, or stolen, in the cities to the north. And since Mathi's explorations in the realms of sorcery had been motivated by private desires, any discoveries he would have made had died with him.

Tralane entered, his foot breaking the seal of dust.

As he passed through the ground level chamber, heading towards the central, spiral stairs that wound through the heart of the building, the manner of Mathi's death haunted Tralane. Had the wizard known his time was over and sequestered himself in the uppermost chamber, which

would serve as his tomb for as long as the spells of preservation persisted? Or would the bard find his tutor
sprawled out and mutilated, victim to one of his own
conjurings? Had he been interred by a servant or another
adopted child, taken on after Tralane's departure? The
jumble of furniture and tapestries stoked Tralane's discomfort. He looked into the rooms at every level and
found the same disorder, signs of someone's indiscriminate pillaging of the wizard's possessions. Yet, as far as
he could tell, nothing had been taken. The same tomes,
instruments, charts, and vials that were familiar from
childhood studies were still in the tower. Some containers
were broken, their contents blown away by the wind whistling through the windows, but there was no other sign
of a thief's hand.

Tralane continued his climb to the top of the tower,
pursued by guilt. His examination of Mathi's belongings
in the present harkened to childhood pryings among these
same possessions. Now, as then, Tralane could not find
any evidence revealing a profound understanding of the
forces of magic on Mathi's part. All the mechanics of the
art were available: spell books, filled with collections of
words in known and barely known tongues, which could
only harness the power of sorcery through the proper
spoken sequence, rhythm and intonation; containers of
powders and liquids, easily obtainable if one knew the
secrets of picking roots and herbs, grinding them, and
giving them the substance or phrase activating their power;
and tapestries, statuettes, and seemingly haphazardly put
together forms constructed of sticks, whose mazes of lines
led to hidden energies. Yet in none of them was there
even a hint that Mathi had unveiled a mystery or probed
a previously secure meaning to reveal a new and subtler
mystery in an effort to penetrate the core of some aspect
of existence. And now, with Mathi's sparse words silenced
forever, the disillusionment with Mathi's wisdom and abil-
ities, as well as with Tralane's own failures in the art,
would never be relieved by the solace of understanding.
For a moment, Tralane stopped his advance and consid-

ered withdrawing from the tower. To see Mathi dead would be to lock Tralane's emerging self within the walls of his childhood. But he had to see and make certain of Mathi's demise, for only then could he consider that path closed and begin to search for a new direction.

At last, Tralane stood before the door to the tower's uppermost chamber. He drew a long breath, setting aside his suppositions and preparing to receive reality. When he opened the door, he let the breath go in a long sigh.

Mathi was laid out on an elevated bed, his eyes and mouth closed, his ears and nostrils sealed with wax. His right hand had not had time to cross his chest after he had sealed shut the last orifice, and the limb rested on his side. The body and the room's contents were in order.

Tralane walked to the body and crossed the right arm over the left, shaking his head over the fact that his tutor had overlooked the proper placement of his arms in weaving the spell that had closed his eyes and mouth after his death. Perhaps his soul had flown off an instant sooner than expected.

Mathi was the same as the day Tralane had left him— thick brows, wide nose, thin white hairs falling over his ears and from his chin. The face was slightly emaciated, but not overly angular from the emergence of the bone structure. There was even color in the wizard's cheeks and hands, though the flesh was cold to the touch. The spells of preservation were, in Tralane's uneasy mood, far too efficiently woven. Even the dust had failed to settle on Mathi's white funeral robe.

With the physical certainty of Mathi's death before him, Tralane was at a loss over what to do next. The emotions he should have felt were still locked away, tangible in his heart and stomach as well as in his trembling hands, but otherwise inexpressible. The things he had wanted to say, explain, and ask were caged within him. It was not so easy to choose another road, when all his energies and hopes had been committed to a final confrontation with Mathi.

Tralane left the chamber suddenly and descended into

the lower rooms. He rummaged among their contents, looking through the volumes on the shelves and strewn over the floors for a particular manual, used by him only once. He searched methodically and energetically, quelling the occasional surge of hysterical terror that threatened to send him fleeing from the tower with cold, savage denials. His shoulder burned with the urgency of his task.

The manual, a small, black leather volume with pages made from thin foils of metal, was in his hand before he recognized it. He smiled humorlessly, recalling the panic accompanying the theft of Wyden's Eye. He clutched the book in both hands and returned to Mathi's chamber, where he opened the volume and turned the pages until he found the passage he had uttered once before, long ago. The words came to him easily, though his throat was dry and the book shook in his hands. The knowledge of the language in which the passage was written was a product of tedious study, but the manner in which the spell had to be recited was garnered from surreptitious listening through the cracks in locked doors. He repeated his lessons without error, and not even the cold, sharp pain that raked his skin along the length of the throbbing shoulder wound distracted him from the completion of the summoning. And when he was finished, he was not surprised to find Mathi's eyes open and resting on him.

"My son," the dead man whispered. The familiar, if inappropriate, greeting was barely recognizable in the harsh crackling of a long unused voice.

"Mathi," Tralane replied simply, not believing what he had done. The manual fell from his hands.

"Why . . ." The question remained unfinished as Mathi struggled to become familiar once again with a carcass he had long abandoned.

Tralane assumed that his tutor wanted a justification for disturbing him from the process of transforming his soul into another form.

"I have been away, Mathi," Tralane began, repeating a speech formulated since his return to his home world. "I have traveled to the ends of this world's probable exis-

tences. I've met myself, as I could have been. I will be
remembered where I have passed, for my deeds have been
worthy of tale-telling. Yet I have been groping, Mathi. I
searched without knowing the object of my quest, and
only by surviving my trials did I become aware of things
I needed. I've killed with a sword, slain my own flesh,
and seen death's shadow cross my journey's road more
than once. And all for the question you never answered.
Mathi, who bore me? Whose seed am I?"

Mathi's eyes locked with Tralane's. The life flickering
in them was weak, a sign that much of what the wizard
had once been was committed to another form. Tralane
hoped there was enough left of Mathi's personality, enough
of his memory, to recall what he wanted to know.

"Please give me an answer, Mathi. I'm sorry I left you,
but I could not stay with someone who was not of my
blood and who hid the nature of my birth from me. I
would not be the son you never had, Mathi. You must
understand and forgive me, if you can. But most of all,
you must tell me who were my parents."

At first, only the wind, carrying the scent of the ever-
blooming flowers and dew-speckled leaves preserved by
spells, answered Tralane. Then the wind changed, and
stale, cold air from some cul-de-sac was carried out by
the new current. The chamber was suddenly transformed
into the tomb it had served as, draped in clouds rather
than buried in the soil. But the sense of closed portals,
of sealed exits, and eternal silence, was the same.

Mathi answered at last.

"I waited . . . for you, Tralane . . ."

The bard nodded, prepared to receive condemnation.
The possibility of Mathi's anger having fired itself into
revenge occurred to him at that moment, though he had
never seen his tutor lash out against a living being. Tralane
had become accustomed to a harsh, authoritarian hand
in his travels, and it was only with great difficulty that he
separated the memory of the sometimes brutal and ever-
guarded rulers and courtiers in his experience from the

gentler, if stoic, image of his guardian. Tralane relaxed, trusting Mathi to be fair.

"I waited, beyond my death, Tralane. I knew some day you would return. If you lived, if you followed the course you embarked on and survived, there was little else for you to do. You touched my misplaced hand, waking me from my last work in the deepest parts of dreams. I waited for you to summon the courage to call me, and you did. I am here ... now ..."

There was laughter from a distant place which chilled Tralane. He had never heard Mathi laugh before.

"I chased them away. People came and tried to settle. Wizards pried at my spells, seeking to master them and take this place away from me. They came for the peace and stillness of my tower, which belongs only to my child."

Tralane, startled, asked in a broken voice, "Who is your child? You never told me. Does this child still live?" Unreasonably, he was jealous of this unknown other person in Mathi's life, who perhaps had taken so much from their common guardian that there had been little left for Tralane.

"Yes," Mathi continued, unperturbed, "I have a son, and he still lives. A goddess bore him and was slain by her father. The gods are vengeful when mortals interfere with their destinies. There are so few gods now. They keep away from the paths of men and from each other. They prefer the quiet contemplation of mysteries to the turmoils of unbound souls, mortal or immortal. But I won a goddess. I sensed her presence when I was a youth. She was warm, and innocent. A young goddess, protected behind impenetrable walls of magic by her elders. She was to be the bearer of a new generation of immortals. She was one of the last they had conceived, and they were careful to shield her from curious sorcerers and godlings for fear she would be led away from the mission they wished to impose on her."

"The tale of Gen-jima," Tralane offered.

"Yes."

"But the sorcerer's name was not Mathi, nor was he described to be like you."

"Do you think a sorcerer hated by the gods would keep his true name and form?"

"No," Tralane replied sheepishly. He was curious to hear what Mathi's unaccustomed frankness would reveal, but impatient that he had allowed himself to be led away from the answer to his question.

"I won the goddess Gen-jima," Mathi began again. "I was called Suthra then. I was the outcast son of a Wizard King, hiding in the caves below the ice palaces, studying the art by stealing into my father's fortress and taking what I could from their library. When I finished with the books, I would return them and borrow others. With so many novices and apprentices studying the art under court tutelage, my thefts were assumed to be caused by a student's diligence in study and were quietly ignored."

"Why were you banished?" Tralane's version of the story did not give Suthra's background, other than that he was a wizard.

"For not paying proper homage to the gods. The Wizard Kings owed their ascendance to the gods. At one time they were a poor people, small in number and power, until the gods, also dwindling as the aeons passed and the carnage wreaked by CuChani's theft went without healing, broke from their uneasy withdrawal and struck a pact with the north people. In return for power, the Wizard Kings would subjugate the world and bring it once more under the sway of sorcery. The stronger flow of magic was to feed the gods and make the human feats of strength and logic pointless. With the Wizard Kings as their instruments, the gods could rule unchallenged over the destiny of mankind.

"I was not so eager to sell myself into bondage. The cold wastes seemed a more comfortable haven for my spirit than the stifling ceremonies of obeisance that were performed at my father's court. I should have been killed for blasphemy, but, to save my life, my father gave me the choice of banishment. Yet he feared I would return to cause his downfall by disrupting his court and angering the gods. So he gave me no food or clothing, and threw me naked into the snow. I had seen only seven summers.

"It was then I discovered Gen-jima. My hands were frozen, yet I dug into the snow, seeking the rocky ground so I could touch it and work a simple warming spell I had by then learned. In my fear, my mind reached farther than it had ever done before and brushed against a wall. Something moved behind the wall, felt my coldness, my pain, and my fear, and answered my call. I was enveloped in heat. My feet melted the snow. I ran from my family's ice palace, knowing I could expect a spear through the heart in place of their mercy. My aunts and uncles, along with my mother, I recall, had petitioned for my death.

"I wandered for days, going down the mountainside, avoiding the roads, the outposts, and the patrols. I found a cave used by a pair of maulkens as their lair. I killed them, blinding them first with a flare spell, then crashing a rock onto their heads. Their fur hides warmed me as the heat surrounding my body faded. I fed on their meat and slept in the cave.

"Then I searched for my benefactor, but my mind was not strong nor disciplined enough to retrace the route it had taken. So I returned secretly to my father's palace and learned what would have been my birthright. I watched the court sorcerers perform secret rites, listened as the gods spoke through a seer and instructed the wizards on new avenues to the tapping of elemental power. I read and followed behind the minds of the sorcerers as they journeyed into dimensions only the spirit could enter. I saw where the gods allowed them to go and where they were forbidden to wander. I was crafty and I was small. I hid myself in my smallness. When the gods and wizards looked behind them, they saw only the fluttering of a bird-soul or the dim sparkle of a tree-spirit. Thus I escaped notice and learned. I knew the path I had taken as a child was a forbidden one, so I could only find my benefactor by exploring what the gods feared to be known. This was to take time and power.

"Hidden in my cave, fed by kitchen-looted delicacies and the yield of my hunts, I practiced my art. I was not encumbered by the restraints and supervision of my elders, nor was I limited in the paths I could explore, as were the southern sorcerer-rivals of the Wizard Kings, who lacked immortal guidance. For ten years I labored. As my body grew, my spirit strengthened and expanded to powerful proportions. At last, I found what I had been seeking. The wall, a resilient blankness immune to probing, brushed against me one night. A voice whispered, and heat embraced me. I whispered my gratitude in return, and promised the gift of freedom. Then I waited and thought, but I did not have too long to wait.

"The fires of battle came. The Karthasian Empire turned to the north, to strike at the corrupting machinations of the Wizard Kings. The armies of the warm countries, backed by sorcerers wielding the primitive energies of the earth, faced the encroaching coldness of the north and the distant, frigid powers of the sky and stars. The war shook loose the stones buried beneath the ice, and warm blood dissipated the snow into a perpetual crimson fog. I was for neither side; their conceits did not concern me. I watched, biding my time until the gods were too distracted to guard the realms of sorcery. When I sensed the moment had come, I hurled myself against the wall, calling for the creature on the other side to join me.

"Even the gods cannot fight two death struggles at the same time, and I had chosen my time well. Fearing they would lose all on earth, they had weakened their defenses around the prisoner. I attacked again and again, raking and clawing, setting a fire behind the gods as they tried to hold back the Karthasian sorcerers. At last the wall fell, and I found before me a goddess. She gave me her name—Gen-jima—and I gave her mine, and then I led her away from the dimension of the spirit and abstraction and into the world of the physical. She took on a form that made my heart beat wildly, and I too seemed to please her. While mortals slew each other and immortal powers vied for supremacy, we held each other in a lover's embrace and let our races follow their desires, as we followed ours.

"We taught each other many things, in both the realms of feeling and of the mind. We were slow and langorous at first, but our fear grew as the war reached a climax. Whoever won would not let a goddess and a mortal stay together in peace. So we planned an escape together. We were to slay our mortal bodies and release our spirits. The ties to corporeal life would not bind me to the limits of time, and without the captivity of immortality, Gen-jima would be similarly free. The strength of our beings, our essences, would transform us into entities beyond the reach of time and space. We were to merge with the fabric of existence, retaining our individuality, yet surrendering our capacity to act for the opportunity of becoming a part of the whole. This was to be no mere transformation into spirit, or into another mortal form. We were to escape completely the barriers to our love. We would join, min-gle, serve, and be served by being.

"Such was our plan, but it was not allowed to pass. Pichen-ma-thele, lord of all gods and father to this god-dess, found her on the eve of the last battle in the north. He must have known what was to come, for he did not even allow his daughter to plead her case. Rather than leave behind one of his kind, Pichen-ma-thele slew his daughter before she could even speak. I saw. I became small. I wept. I was helpless.

"The god did not see me, nor did he have time to search. The call to battle drew him away, since he was bound to support my family and the other Wizard Kings against the Karthasian Empire. But I heard his pledge to destroy the mortal who had won from him the hope of the gods, Gen-jima, before he sealed the cave to make it his daughter's tomb. The ice and rock fell, but I did not grow large again. I wanted to remain small, forever, in the airless darkness, in the silence, in the netherworld of unfeelingness.

"But my senses would not be denied. I could hear the battle rage above, and when the din subsided, there was

nothing left but the frail cry of a child. I made light shine
from my hand and saw the unblemished body of Gen-jima
give birth to an infant. I drew the child out from the
corpse. I grew, filling myself with some spark of power,
and nurtured the young one as best I could. The luxury
of death had been taken away from me. The responsibility
of life, the child's and my own, was forced upon me.

"I kissed Gen-jima one last time and stroked the hand
that had given me comfort and wisdom. I did not weep,
for I knew the mere taking of her life was not the signal
for the end of our happiness. I had risen from the ashes
of my sorrow. Gen-jima had merely taken a path we were
to have taken together. I had found her before, I would
find her again.

"So I found myself cursed by my people and by the
gods, expelled from the comforts of the ordinary by my
knowledge of the art and the magic of the gods. I had
nothing that I could call a home, nor would I be welcomed
in the dwellings of men or gods, were my origin and identity revealed. Remaining small, I worked only minor won-
ders and led the unassuming life of a humble sorcerer
quietly seeking the way to spiritual transcendence. I
emerged from the tomb carrying a child I had to renounce
as my own, for to claim it would mean calling a god's
vengeance on us both. Yet the child survived, born from
the dead, raised in obscurity and cast onto the fates without sail or rudder. And I also survived, living in constraint,
working in secret and within narrow borders, searching
for the path Gen-jima had taken.

"But we both won, Tralane. Though the measures were
harsh, and perhaps unjust, I found my path, as did my
offspring. The same blood runs through both of us, as
you must know by now."

Tralane's mind spun, caught in the whirling vortex of
Mathi's words and being drawn into a point he did not
wish to see.

"I've heard...I've even told the tale of Suthra and
Gen-jima," Tralane said in an unsteady, accusing voice.
"It is a bawd's tale of a god cuckolded, a goddess raped,

and a presumptuous mortal buried with his mistress. There was no mention of a child in the story."

"Then consider how fortunate you are to have heard the truth behind a tale told by bards and courtiers."

Tralane was startled by the wizard's pointed comment. The firmness of the dead man's voice shattered Tralane's predilection to deny the story, yet the acceptance of Mathi's origins sparked an entirely new set of conflicts in the bard. It seemed incredible that he was the son of a goddess and that all his alternate-world brothers and sisters were similarly descendants from immortality. But then, the Emperor had taken on the mantle of godhood far too easily for a full-blooded mortal, and both he and Tralane had survived trials that would have severely tested the most experienced champions. Both Gibron and Cumulain had hinted that there was more to him than the mere identity of an orphan bard and archer could explain.

Tralane pursued the complexities of alternate realities, trying to find in them some flaw that would unravel Mathi's assertion. Time had been shortened in some worlds, while in others it had been lengthened. The Emperor's words had implied that he had been searching through the possible worlds for more than one lifetime, and the mysterious woman who had given the tribespeople their Nushu Land had passed there at least a generation or two before Tralane. Yet the Emperor was an unquestionable double, as had been some of his victims. They were all bound by common blood, and by the mystery of an unknown heritage, across time and physical realities. But there was something else that linked them all, a common mission above and beyond the fulfillment of a quest for identity. Were they all born from the carnage of a war between mortals and immortals, to seal forever the links between the two? Was Tralane conceived, as were his alternates, by some remote, time-encompassing awareness, to serve as the restorer of balance between human and godly existences? Gibron's talk of fulcrums and balances made more sense to Tralane now and also cut him off from using the inconsistencies in the alternate worlds to deny Mathi's claims. Perhaps Mathi had been born sooner in some of the other worlds, or perhaps even Mathi's father had taken his role, with his seed blooming into the tribespeople's witch woman. The specifics did not matter so much as the intention that Tralane and his alternates be driven not only by their own individual pasts, but by the momentum of the histories of their various worlds.

Mathi broke into Tralane's revery, taking the bard's silence and confusion as the need for further explanation.

"We were your parents, Tralane. Born from the dead, I was the only guardian you could claim. Your father and mother did die—Suthra and Gen-jima were slain in that cave. Only I emerged from that tomb, a humble wizard who traveled south as one of the civil war's sorcerous veterans with a child he had picked up from a devastated village. You were an orphan in fact, but not in spirit or blood."

Tralane's mind withdrew from the cosmological mystery he had touched upon, finding greater comfort and more digestable meat in Mathi's words than in the thought that he was the instrument of a destiny he could barely envisage.

He found he was not reacting as he always thought he would when faced with his ancestry. The names, he had always known, would be strange, though they had not turned out to be totally unknown. The nature of their deaths, if that was the fate they had suffered, he considered might be painful to know. This was brought home to him after Oram's self-revelations, but the knowledge was important to him nonetheless. He had considered searching for a relative, a family member, someone to link him with his past by going back to the place of his birth and speaking to those who might have known his family. Now, these dreams broke on the sheer cliffs of what was and what could never be.

"Why did you hold this from me?" Tralane asked defiantly.

"To have told you in candor would have destroyed the

few bare shreds of childhood I could give you with a secret that would mean our deaths if it were known to the world."

"It was a lie."

"Childhood usually is. But that does not take away its joy and freedom."

"But when I was older," Tralane protested, "when I summoned—"

"Yes, when you summoned a goddess, thinking only to bring back a mortal's spirit. Had you succeeded, my pains for secrecy would have been wasted, as well as my efforts to regain Gen-jima. I wanted to follow her into the safety of the resting place of souls, to trace the exact path she had taken, to not to drag her back along it. Pichen-mathele would have discovered the presence of his daughter and destroyed us all. It is a testament to your power that, as a mere youth, you managed to achieve the summoning at all. It was fortunate for all of us that Gen-jima's warning drew blood and broke your spell, though you must forgive a goddess who perhaps has forgotten the frailty of mortal flesh. And you must forgive me, Tralane. I allowed you to leave me, so you could find your own way with the tools and clues I gave you. Suthra's sin has always been to be headstrong, to think of the paths ahead, and not of the road on which his feet stand. If my attention was drawn away from you, then it was so only to bring me back to Gen-jima. I was selfish in that way, and I beg the forgiveness of my son."

Tralane shook his head in dismay. "I came in part to ask for your forgiveness and now I find I must grant it myself. We are not far removed in some aspects of our natures, Ma—Suthra. We follow the call within us, and are not so eager to hear the voices around us."

"There is good and evil in every voice. One can only ask for the greatest good and the least evil."

There was silence between them for a long while. Tralane absorbed the knowledge he had struggled to obtain, amused by the irony of his origins and the circumstances leading to his ignorance and subsequent discoveries. But the amusement was only the surface swell in a deep ocean of thought and feeling. The identity of his parents, and the discovery that he was speaking with one of them, did not open any hidden reserves of emotion. The years spent with Mathi were not made any pleasanter by the truth of their relationship, nor did the knowledge bring him closer to the spirit inhabiting his tutor's corpse. The completion of the quest left him empty, as if the one hope he had to deny his own nature was banished with the acknowledgement of Mathi as a parent and a slain goddess as a mother. The search had ended with himself at the court of the Emperor of Many Faces. There was nowhere else to run. The last weak hold on the delusion of freedom from all restraint was annihilated.

He sighed and turned his head to look out a window and was surprised by the figure of Akyeetha standing in the periphery of his vision. She was staring at Mathi's body, morbidly fascinated by its animation. He took her hand and brought her to his side, anxiously studying her face.

"I must leave you," Suthra interrupted, oblivious to the woman's entry. "My task is finished here, as yours is also. We must both leave, having done and said what was owed. This tower has nothing more to offer. I will release the spells of preservation and set my servants free. You had best be far from here when that happens. Time will rush in to fill the vacuum left with the departure of magic, and the land will be in turmoil."

"Wait," Tralane cried out, thinking ahead of his inevitable confrontation with Agathom. "I need your help."

"I cannot stay long. The gods have sensed your summoning, and they will eventually unmask my disguise of smallness. I must leave to join Gen-jima, whose path I discovered before I died. You would not deny me that, after all that has happened?"

"No, no, I would not. But this world is in danger. The gods will destroy the land for the sake of envy and jealousy."

"And what is that to me? I am gone, I am almost beyond any call or power."

"But what of me? What of the world that helped to feed and protect you when you were almost helpless, in your cave in the north. What of Akyeetha, who escaped one deathworld only to be brought to another? I ran, but I returned. I will fight to save the world I was born in. Can you do less than what your own son will do? Or will you be like your father, and banish me to my death as he exiled you?"

In the silence that followed, Akyeetha straightened herself and took a step forward. Tralane followed, noting that her eyes were bright, free from the clouds of remembrance. The sword that had been Wyden's Fang was in her hand. She glanced once at Tralane, but then kept her eyes on the corpse laid out before them. The almost tangible presence of death was rousing her from the protective shell of isolation into which she had withdrawn. The internment chamber was like a small theater in which Akyeetha's death-laden soul could siphon off its infection, making way for life-giving emotions. If she did not regain her identity after the ritual play between father and son had run its course, Tralane was certain she would be lost to him.

Tralane drew his own sword and pointed it at his father.

"Will you lend your power to this sword?" Tralane asked in a steady voice. He would fight, with or without the allegiance of his father.

"Yes," Suthra answered, and the body that was dead rose to join the son.

Chapter 21

They did not have much time to plan.

Suthra took them down to Tralane's old room in the tower's cellar. Akyeetha trembled as they went down, and Tralane studied her for any sign of panic. But she did not waver at the door to his room; she settled there free from the shadow of the Emperor's imprisonment. They ate from their provisions while Suthra went to his library. At night they met in the tower's high chamber, the conjuring room, where Mathi had always worked and taught Tralane.

Suthra had brought out two chairs, and the living sat in them while the Wizard stood by one of the windows. His white hair lifted with the breeze.

"What do we do?" Tralane asked.

"First we see what you've learned."

Tralane took out Wyden's Eye, held it up to the light from the candle in the middle of the room. Suthra looked at it, but did not move towards Tralane or reach for the Eye.

"So?"

"This is what started it all. I took it from the Sorcerer King."

"Who comes for us now."

"He knows?"

"Only that what you hold has returned. He felt its presence as soon as you entered this world and has been following its progress, as any competent sorcerer would, to gauge the power and purpose of its bearer. Now that you have come here, this Sorcerer King must act. He fears the power locked in this tower, which he has thus far avoided. Evidently, he has been well advised by Karthasian sorcerers. But now he must come, thinking to stop the amulet's bearer before the power can be used against him. All this is evident, the spells are in the air, and there are great disturbances in the sources of magical force.

"So, Tralane, you have not learned so much, after all."

Tralane shrugged his shoulders. "I am not so wise as you in the ways of wizards . . . Father." The last word was difficult for him to use in the course of conversation, but did not frighten him as much as he had thought it would. "But I remembered your lessons. I can control the power of this amulet now. I've used it to travel between worlds and to heal myself."

"Yourself? Then why haven't you healed her?" Suthra nodded in Lady Akyeetha's direction. "Show me."

Tralane did. He gazed into the gem's facets and caught the flickering lights within it in the grip of his will. He saw, as he had seen before in the Wilderness Flower, the streaks of color, the darkness, and the moving shadows. He saw two bright lights, his and Akyeetha's, and he saw one dim light that did not flicker so boldly. There was nothing he could do for that one—already, the strength of his father rested mostly between the worlds of the living and the dead. Instead, he concentrated on Akyeetha's flame.

A shudder passed through her body.

Suthra did not help him. Tralane focused all of his being on Akyeetha's flame, until he saw the black spot that was her mutilated speech. On this spot he set loose the power of the amulet, shaped by his mind in the form of a healing spell.

He was not aware of the passage of time, nor did he

see until the end the sheath of night that had come over Akyeetha—a sheath that throbbed and constricted and was without stars. By the time he saw his work, it was almost over. As soon as he turned away from the amulet, the darkness dissipated from around Akyeetha. Her eyes were wide and filled with tears, but she did not release them. She touched her lips with slim fingers, caressed her cheeks, looked first at Suthra and then at Tralane.

"I . . . can speak," she said at last, in a low, hoarse grumble.

"Not badly done," Suthra said, "though it would have been easier had you done this—" Suthra made a sign in the air that was close to the one Tralane had been taught to use for the passage between worlds. "You don't yet see the pattern in these powers or the way to summon them. And I presume you knew the sign to go between worlds, too. But still, not badly done."

"For a novice."

"For a wizard, son. You have not yet earned my head of hair, nor my poor teeth, but you're on your way."

Tralane smiled sheepishly and glanced at Akyeetha, who was fingering her tongue, then the skin of her throat.

"But I'm still no match for Agathom, the Sorcerer King."

"Indeed. And now you must tell me about this Sorcerer King. I have felt his attention for some time, though he, like the gods, has not yet uncovered me. He has sent us callers and he follows in their wake. We must be prepared."

Tralane, precipitously reduced to feeling like the misbehaving child reporting to his master by Suthra's brusqueness, described the Sorcerer King's arrival, the theft of Wyden's Eye, and his journey through alternate worlds to the ultimate confrontation with the Emperor of Many Faces, where he also found Lady Akyeetha. Through his storytelling, he relived his adventures and saw once again the lessons he had learned. After a while, he did not feel so much like the lowly pupil, but like the man who had committed wrongs and tried to atone for them. Shame left him, and he was able to look steadily into his father's eyes and into the stern, compassionless face. As he finished, he did not expect or need his father's approbation. Nor was he belittled when Suthra took the initiative in planning, for was he not the child of the Wizard Kings? Had his father not won a goddess's love? Had he not floated between the worlds of life and death, waiting for his son to return to him?

And Tralane did not hesitate to speak his own mind, to help shape the plan. He did not fear his father's ridicule or his anger, as he had feared Mathi's. He understood what he could expect from Mathi-Suthra and from himself. There were no questions of confidence or supremacy, no jealousy of Suthra's wisdom, or vanity in his own strengths.

It was when Lady Akyeetha raised her voice and added her thoughts to their talk that the full meaning of his stand with Suthra came to him. And though Suthra made clear the dangers they faced and the death waiting for them all at every turn, Tralane could not help smiling at all he had discovered on his journey, in himself and in the world.

They went on into the night, as Star Speaker and the Wanderer shed their light through the windows and cast double shadows on the floor. Lady Akyeetha would not be deterred from playing her part in gratitude for Tralane's rescue, and Tralane held her hand in thanks. He was not sure which of their hands would have trembled more, when Suthra brought an end to their conference by shaking his head from side to side and, with a sigh, left to prepare the grounds of his domain for the battle.

Tralane put Wyden's Eye away and led Akyeetha down to his room. They slept there for the rest of the night, she on his old cot, and he on the floor in the company of mice. He dreamed of a father. When he woke, he saw in her sweat-stained garments the terror dreams that had come to visit her. When he went upstairs to prepare a morning meal and saw his father still walking across the mist-shrouded grounds of his tower, Tralane recalled that the dead sleep but do not dream. He would have to add to that saying by including that they may, however, sometimes walk.

Tralane prepared a meal for two, ate, and spent the day gazing into the crystalline visions of worlds in Wyden's Eye, while Lady Akyeetha stayed in Suthra's library, reading the history of gods and men aloud to practice the art of speaking.

Evening came quietly, with an overcast sky. The stars were blinded, and the two moons, Wanderer and Star Speaker, were like pale eyes gazing out from the veiled face of night. There was a stillness deeper than that caused by the spells woven around Suthra's tower. The weight of power, heavier than the gathering storm clouds on the horizon, had settled on the land, patiently waiting for its prey.

With the first stab of lightning in the distance, wrapped in a rolling cacophony of thunder, came the first demon. The trees and grass that were touched by its shadow withered and died, leaving a scar across the earth reaching back to the point of its summoning. It bellowed with the effort of its unsteady flight, as a thousand wings struggled against the currents of wind. Tendrils snapped at the air, and long strands of white hair—twice the length of a full-grown man—flowed backwards from its gray, wormlike head, to be lost among the fluttering wings. A thick yellow fluid oozed from orifices all along the body of the demon, like human sweat, only to be devoured by tiny, skittering parasitical creatures. Two longer tendrils, emerging from its head, swayed back and forth in a rhythm free from the influence of the winds. Small, blinking circles of blackness dotted the length of the twin appendages.

The demon was approaching Suthra's tower from the northwest, where Agathom was said to be waging war against the crumbling Karthasian Empire. Around its neck was a collar of black and gold, the colors of Agathom's tent. When it reached the tower, it spoke only its name— Waithrae—in a soft, seductive whisper which mingled with the sonorous rustlings of its wings. It circled the tower, dipping up and down, a sickly sweet odor spreading in its wake. The two thorts in the shack whinnied with terror, and the flailing of their pounding hoofs against the doors was like the distant sound of war drums calling legions to battle. But the pounding ceased as the demon's scent settled over the shack, and only the thunder claps were left to echo the animals' fearful rappings. Still Waithrae circled, tightening the circumference of its flight, until Akyeetha emerged from a trap door on the tower's roof. She held Wyden's Fang in her hand and she was draped in a gown and cape of black silk. At the sight of her, the demon shuddered and widened its path around the tower.

"Who?" whispered Waithrae, whose voice was heard as if the listener were in a dream.

"Akyeetha," the woman answered, shouting defiantly. The accent was strange to this part of the world. Her tongue was uncertain, dragging the name out as if it were a novelty to her. "Why are you here?"

"I answer a call."

"I have not summoned you."

"Yet you have, by your power. Across the world, your awakening was felt by my master. You have returned from the dead. He has sent me to give you back to the dead."

"I am from the dead, but I have never died. Your sending was an error. Who is your master?"

The soft rustling of unseen creatures scurrying in the brush signified the demon's laughter.

"Why should I name him, when you have not named yours?"

Waithrae then circled closer, and its scent thickened into a yellow fog. With every pass the demon came nearer, until it was within a spear cast. Akyeetha's hair and robe waved in the wind.

"Why do you not sleep, as every living mortal must when my scent hangs in the air? Are you a demon, or are you rotting flesh?"

"Neither, as I have told you."

"Your words are empty. Master or servant, it does not matter. I shall give you the peace of your ancestors."

Waithrae climbed into the air, fighting the alien environment to gain altitude. Then it wheeled about and dove, its limbs stretching to snatch Akyeetha.

"I have only just given my ancestors peace. It is too soon for me to join them."

The sword came up in her hands. The trap door behind her opened a crack. Waithrae did not take notice and closed in on her. The demon's limbs reached for her as Waithrae came upon the tower. Tralane sprang from the trap door and took the sword from Akyeetha, as she withdrew back into the tower.

As each tentacle whipped around him, he drew her sword's edge across the demon's flesh and opened a gaping wound. He never stabbed or sank his sword so deeply into the demon that he could not pull it out. His movements were precise and unhurried, following a prescribed pattern of swordsmanship that created a sphere of flashing edges. When Waithrae had finished his first pass. Tralane turned to meet the demon's return.

The creature stopped and hovered above him, the wind from its wings almost knocking him off balance. The demon came closer as Tralane's sword found the wounds he had already inflicted and completed the work by severing the loosened limbs. Waithrae screamed, in a high-pitched whine that could be heard above the thunderclaps breaking overhead.

Tralane's arms ached from the strain of maintaining a defensive perimeter while not losing the sword in a hasty thrust or having it knocked out of his hands. Then, at last, the poison that was the death of immortals reached the demon's main body. The wings faltered in their rhythm. The demon's hovering became erratic.

The door behind him opened once again, and Tralane's name was called out. He turned and scrambled into the tower, even as Waithrae fell. The trap door slammed shut just as the demon crashed onto the roof. The walls of the tower shook, the beams groaned, and dust was shaken loose from joints. Yet the structure held, supported by Suthra's spells. As the demon gave its last death throes above them, three figures climbed down the tower's winding stairs.

"Tralane the Demon Slayer," Tralane said, breathless but laughing.

"Tralane the Healer," Akyeetha chimed in.

"Suthra is bored with the praises of unseasoned years," Suthra commented, as he led them down to the tower's main gate. "True, my son healed your voice, but it was I who taught him the rudiments of magic many years ago, which he barely remembers now that he has need of them. I would have done the task myself if my death-shadowed touch would not have cursed the words you sought to speak."

"And it was I," Tralane said, mocking and challenging his old teacher good naturedly, "who made the old wizard stay long enough for him kindly to offer his help."

A silent moment followed. Then Tralane spoke again, lightly but with respect, "The weight of years always seeks to make itself felt."

A bolt of lightning struck a nearby hill, flashing through a window and illuminating the three figures with garish, electric light. Suthra's face was lax and expressionless, while Akyeetha's was frozen with a fear she refused to feel. Tralane's face was also a mask, which he knew mirrored Akyeetha's visage.

"Another demon will come," Suthra asserted as they reached the base of the tower. "We will wait here, and Tralane will face it when it comes. But the poison sword cannot work to our advantage; it will be expected. I will help deal with the demon in my own way."

Tralane nodded, agreeing once more to the plan they had fashioned the night before. The three then sat at the entrance to the tower, while the storm broke outside, lashing the building with rain.

"There should not be a storm," Suthra whispered as they waited. "My spells weaken before the onslaught."

The statement died in the air.

The living slept briefly, ate, wandered among the ground floor rooms, and explored without interest. The dead merely sat, unmoved by the relentless rain and steady gloom that was broken only by lurid flashes of lightning. Dawn and dusk were mere gradations of gray.

Then the sound of trees snapping at the base brought Suthra to his feet. Akyeetha and Tralane came to his side.

"You know what must be done," Suthra said to his son before opening the door. Tralane nodded, then left, while Suthra and Akyeetha climbed the tower back to its highest chamber. They watched through Waithrae's mangled limbs, dangling in front of the window, as Tralane walked out into the open.

Outside, the wind drove the rain like a many-handed demon hurling daggers. The ground was soft and muddy, the air filled with a senses-dampening curtain. But Tralane could see the form of his foe breaking from the cover of the trees, and he froze the creature in motion in a spear of light issuing from his hand, a spell Mathi had taught him and Suthra had refreshed for him. A demon was revealed; a thousand spindly, triple-jointed legs of black bone jutted from its hard-shelled body. Four diaphanous wings protruded from its back, vibrating with insistent fury yet impotent to raise the massive body of the demon into the air. A short, pale-gray tube squeezed through an opening at the front of the shell, displaying a black and gold band around its middle. Two stalks grew from the tube and wavered like serpents studying victims before striking. They watched an illusion, as Suthra cast his own image on Tralane from the tower.

"Stay, demon," Tralane commanded. "You trespass on guarded lands. What is your business?"

The sound of clicking stones fought with the wind for command of the air. In the battle, a series of sounds became distinguishable as words.

"I shall stay, light-wielder, to challenge the guardian of this land and avenge my brother."

"Is that your brother?" Tralane asked, swinging the beam to the top of the tower upon which Waithrae lay transfixed.

The clicking stones momentarily won the battle with the wind, and the earth shook with the clamor.

"Is that all you have come to do?" Tralane asked when the din subsided, swinging the beam back to the demon. "To see your brother and join him?"

"Kalkilyn has questions."

"Yours, or your master's?"

"I would answer such a question from *your* master."

"I am the one you seek, the one who was dead and now lives."

"My brother sought you, to know who brought you back and why. The woman commands you?"

"No one has brought me back. I was waiting."

"For what?"

Tralane laughed, though he was not amused by the game of deceit being played.

"For what has come. And now I must wait again, for what is yet to be."

"Then you wait for another death."

Kalkilyn charged from the line of trees, trailing branches and shattered wood caught between its pounding appendages. Tralane did not retreat, though the distance between them diminished with alarming rapidity. Instead, the intensity of the spear of light issuing from his hand increased as Suthra added his power to Tralane's. A cloud of steam formed along its length as the rain hissed into vapor at its touch. The spear's point was focused on the demon's shell; where the point rested, a fiery red eye burned in response.

Tralane fell before the demon's charge, and was lost in the trampling of clawed hoofs.

Akyeetha screamed, and Suthra cursed. The wizard raised his arms and cried out with agony as he wove and cast spells of protection to accompany the power of the burning light he was sending to Tralane. He staggered forward to the window, then leaned out and dangled precipitously over the sill. Tralane, amid the flailing limbs and flying earth, gasped with the effort of focusing the burning light as its power coursed through his body.

Akyeetha rushed forward, grabbing the wizard's shoulders. The clouds lowered, booming around them, while arcs of lightning rushed through vents and cracks in the clouds and wracked the demon's back. The wizard looked over his shoulder to Akyeetha. She cried out, but her words were lost in the torrents of rain and sounds. But Suthra understood, as did Tralane when he felt the strength of a third spirit, a third will, scream through his veins and his mind.

The light did not waver, springing from his hand like an indomitable pillar of fire, opening a seam in the demon's shell that ran from the shoulder to the belly. Kalkilyn's furious assault made the earth beneath it splash away, forming a deepening crater. Suthra's tower, its walls sagging from the burden on its roof, swayed.

At last, the spear of light pierced the demon's core. Kalkilyn froze in mid-motion, as if its case had suddenly come to contain something far larger than its fleshy aspect. The wind blew away the sound of clicking stones. In a last desperate fit of motion, the demon clambered out of the crater it had dug and staggered toward Suthra's tower, as if it sensed that the source of its demise lay behind the stone walls.

But before the demon could reach the tower, its legs began to collapse. Kalkilyn stumbled, then slowly settled to the ground as the strength drained from its legs. The earth beneath the demon became black with a spreading pool of thick liquid. The cracking of bones was dimly heard as the mass of the demon's torso crushed the legs that had supported it. With a final sigh and rush of clicks, Kalkilyn followed Waithrae into annihilation.

When the battle was over, the storm subsided to a gentle rain and a rumbling of clouds. The crater dug by Kalkilyn's attack was still.

The door to Suthra's tower opened and Akyeetha came out. She walked to the lip of the crater, avoiding Kalkilyn's corpse and blood, and waited. She carried two black swords, one in each hand, and her face was barred by soaked strands of hair clinging to her skin. The vigor that had filled out her face and body since her arrival in Tralane's world had faded, and she resembled her former emaciated self in the Emperor's dungeons.

Her vigil ended with the stirring of the earth at the bottom of the crater. A hand pushed through the mud, followed by an arm. A leg flailed out, flinging more mud into the air. Finally a figure stood, dripping earth and water. It climbed the crater's walls, slipped, fell back, but regained the ground tenaciously, until it was at Akyeetha's feet. She pulled the figure onto level ground.

"Now, I am also a demon slayer," Suthra said without amusement behind her. Tralane wiped the dirt from his eyes, then looked. He saw Akyeetha and was shocked. Fear hit him, however, only when he first glanced and then fixed on his father's frail, near-skeletal form.

"So much power, for only his demons?" Tralane asked, bringing himself up to his knees.

"He is curious," Suthra said, "and more than ever, he is cautious. Your Sorcerer King will come, but now he is less sure than ever what waits for him. The plan is going well."

"I'm glad. Though, if this is success, I'd hate to see failure."

Akyeetha helped Tralane to stand, and they helped each other walk to the top of a hill overlooking the tower and its grounds. Suthra, following them, touched Tralane's arm.

"It is time to go back," the wizard said. "He is near, and you must finish what has been started."

Tralane let go of Akyeetha. He considered the two swords she still carried slung over her shoulders, but decided against bringing them. His best—his only—weapons he carried already in his mind and in the pouch hanging from his neck.

"Remember, he must not suspect," Suthra said to him in parting.

Tralane spread his arms, displaying the tattered remnants of his clothing, the bruises and welts covering his arms and chest, and the gash along his thigh where a talon had pushed mightily against the protective shields raised by Suthra and strengthened by Akyeetha's life force.

"Would you be threatened by this?" he asked, and smiled as he left for the tower.

Tralane entered the tower and sat on a stool in the antechamber. He listened to the rain. After a while it stopped, and a cold wind blew through the room. The chill air kept him from becoming drowsy, but added an edge to the hunger in his belly. He ate a few fruits with detached, mechanical interest, and allowed his mind to become absorbed by the counting of volumes on Suthra's shelves. Occasionally his thoughts would touch upon his solitude, or on his disarmament. The doom under which he moved would peer at him from lofty, shadowed corners. A stranger's eye was glimpsed in a mirror. At such times, Tralane was careful not to allow his thoughts to elaborate on his fears. He dwelt only in the moment, content to be aimless. His courage was an armed ring around his consciousness, giving him the space for patience while shutting out extraneous emotions.

Then, in the utter silence that had befallen the land around Suthra's tower since the storm's abatement, Tralane heard a dim rushing of wind, like a breeze ruffling the uppermost branches of a dense forest. He tilted his head up slightly, giving up the peacefulness of his contemplation, and closed his eyes. He shivered in the frigid air, and recalled the Emperor's dead world. Another Emperor was coming. Tralane was not afraid.

He went to a window facing the direction from which the two demons had arrived. There were two exits from the forest, marking the parallel paths the demons had taken to arrive at Suthra's tower. As Tralane watched, a third exit appeared, revealing a path that pointed towards the northwest.

The trees yielded their space without a sound, bending to the side as if of their own will, without snapping or breaking. The branches trembled, and leaves were torn from their stems by the invisible hands of the wind. A dark point appeared where the path met the horizon on the crests of distant hills, and rapidly grew into a gray-skinned flying demon. Its flesh was wrinkled over its wide wings and long, bony torso. The eyes on the sides of its triangular head, set above its short beak, strained to see what lay behind instead of what was before it. The demon flew low. Around its neck was a band of black and gold. On its back, wearing the same scarlet, rune-covered robe Tralane had seen him in at the camp, sat Agathom, the Sorcerer King. The wind raised from the speed of his slave-demon hardly ruffled his white hair.

Within moments of his appearance on the horizon, Agathom had cleared the forest. The demon circled the tower, then slowed until it finally settled to the ground by the exit of the road it had beaten. Agathom descended and walked towards the tower, oblivious to the demon's cold, severe scrutiny. The Sorcerer King stopped for a moment and stared up at the top of the tower, where Waithrae was blackening against the misty sky. He went further, until he was next to Kalkilyn's corpse, and he surveyed the remains of his servant without any betraying expression. He then continued until he stood not far from the tower's entrance. Tralane kept the door closed, and watched his enemy through a slit window. Agathom spoke, in the quiet, intense manner that had once made Tralane's will crumble, but which now only caused him mild uneasiness.

"Who has dared to challenge the Sorcerer King?" Agathom asked, looking halfway up the tower, as if his eyes could pierce the walls in their search for the identity of his enemy. "Who has slain my demons, those whose might alone has crushed the mortal armies of many kingdoms?"

"I have returned," replied Tralane.

Agathom started slightly and fixed his gaze on the slit through which Tralane was looking. He could not penetrate the spells with which Suthra had enveloped the tower.

"What are you playing at? I felt the presence of the Eye in this world, though I never expected to see it again. But who brings it, and from where?"

"From the dead, though I have never quite died."

"Always death, yet never in the same form. A woman, an old man, and now a stranger hiding in shadow. Are you all one?"

Tralane laughed. "Do you expect me to reveal my power to you?"

"Your power and that of your allies cannot stop me. Surrender."

"I will not surrender."

"Your will is of no concern to me."

"But my presence is. I have destroyed two demons. One more is surely not too much of a burden on my strength."

Agathom spoke softly, in an ominous tone. "Perhaps if I were another demon, that would be true. But I am the Demon Master, the Sorcerer King. They were but my slaves. Now you face their master."

"Have you come to master me?" Tralane asked ingenuously.

"If you are a demon, yes. If you are a god or some sorcerer of this world I have already vanquished, you shall be destroyed."

"And if I am neither?"

Agathom rose a hand's length off the ground and floated towards the tower without taking steps. The runes on his robe glowed fiercely.

"I am aware of your strengths and I am protected. I do not walk the earth, nor touch the sky. I will find your weakness, whoever or whatever you are, and then your nature will not matter."

Tralane retreated from his post, slid back into the tower, and hid in the furthest corner of the ground floor rooms. He was not certain Agathom would come through the door, and watched the walls, ceiling and ground for any attempts to catch him by surprise. But the sorcerer was bold and confident. He blasted the front door into flaming fragments; before the fire had subsided, he entered. Tralane greeted him.

"Welcome to my home, Agathom. I've decided to return

the courtesy of shelter which you so kindly granted to me."

"You!" Agathom exclaimed, shock contorting his face into a complex rune of hatred. Then the Sorcerer King's face relaxed into a mask of contempt. "Is it only you . . . ."

"Didn't you bring a few of your knights along, or have you grown so powerful that such toys are meaningless?"

Agathom advanced carefully into the tower, until he stood by the winding stairs. "I am not distracted as when we last saw one another," he said with a pretence of condescension. He turned slowly, examining the walls for signs of a trap, probing the rooms for the origin of Tralane's voice. He found the bard's hiding place and spoke directly to him. "No matter what powers you've gained in your travels, they will not be enough to stand against me." He stopped, considering Tralane's shadowed form. He smiled and seemed at ease. "I know you now, wanderer. You should have stayed in some safe little world beyond my reach and played your little game of power with strangers and those even weaker than you. I haven't made the same mistakes as I did on my home world. This time, I flaunt my power against the gods. I mean to draw them out, to have them face me in their anger. And then I'll destroy them and take their power. With that, no other family of immortals, on this world or any other, will ever drive me away again. Do you understand? I have the power to crush the gods."

"And what if they decide to hurl a moon or two at you again?" Tralane taunted.

"I will go to them and fight them on their own ground. They may destroy this world, but what do I care? I'll have their power, as I will take back what you stole from me. There are other worlds, and with the amulet and the strength of mortal and immortal sorcery, the need for these feints and strategies will have vanished. If first the gods are conquered, how can the people defeat me?"

"By never allowing you to bring doom to their gods."

Agathom began to advance, holding out a hand.

"Give me Wyden's Eye and your death will be quick."

Tralane smiled and melted into a shadowy recess.

"Cause me the pain of effort, and I will punish you for the destruction of my servants," Agathom warned.

Tralane slid into the space separating the tower's inner and outer walls through a natural crack hidden in the recess. He crept between the walls, not as easily as he had when he was a boy, but quickly enough to give him some distance between himself and the hidden entrance.

"You are in my house, Agathom," Tralane shouted. "Are you afraid the dust will soil your robes? Will your demon lovers turn away when you come to them stinking of sweat?"

Agathom laughed and sent a flurry of stinging lights after Tralane.

"You are a foolish boy. You cannot goad me into a trap, when I seek to lure the gods out with the same ploy. The spells of preservation will give way. Then, when you've been stripped of protection, I shall make your skin, your muscles, your veins, and your bones each burn with a different, agonizing fire. And do not think your torment will end soon. Death will be a star lost in the blinding light of day."

"Poor Agathom," Tralane replied mockingly as he reached the loose stone in the outer wall, through which he had escaped from his studies so many times as a boy. His tutor Mathi had sat by the tower's entrance, preparing the evening meal or reading by the afternoon sun, preventing Tralane the normal means of taking his walk through the dusk. It was only when Tralane had suggested the plan they had followed thus far that Mathi, now Suthra, told him he had been aware of the boy's escape route. "A soul constrained consumes itself," was Suthra's only comment to Tralane's expressed surprise at the discovery of his childhood deceit. It was then that Tralane knew his father had given him as much as he had been capable of giving.

Tralane pushed the stone out, then crawled through the opening. Breathing heavily from his effort in squeezing through the passages of his youth, Tralane circled the tower, then burst into a long-strided run toward the hill to which Suthra and Akyeetha were to have retreated. As he ran, he waved an arm to signal his father to take the next step in the plan.

At the first rumblings of the earth and the creaking of walls, Tralane glanced back over his shoulder. Around Suthra's tower swirled wisps of radiant white mist, which rapidly came together into strands of blinding whiteness. The tower was caught in the eye of a vortex that linked the earth with the sky. For a moment, Tralane was not certain whose magic was being worked. But then the vortex disappeared with a sudden rush of wind into the clouds, and the tower's walls began to bulge, crumble, and disintegrate.

As Tralane returned his attention to running, the tower collapsed with a resounding crash, weak with age and unable to support Waithrae's weight without Suthra's spells.

"Is that all you can do?" Agathom cried out after him, his voice filling the air as the thunder had done. "Is that all you learned, all you hoped you would need to overcome me? If your allies could protect themselves with spells against my demons, what made you think that I could not do the same? Did you think the sight of you would make me throw off caution?" The Sorcerer King laughed, then burst from the rubble of the tower to float above the ruins.

"Is that you running? How pathetic you look. You were dressed better when you stole the amulet from me. How ever could you get women to do your bidding now?" Once again, Agathom sent the stinging lights after Tralane. They scorched his skin and singed his hair, until finally he tripped and fell.

The Sorcerer King approached him, gliding along the rising wind.

"Where is your fast thort now, Tralane? Where is your laughter? Noble intentions have slowed your wits, young man. You were much cleverer when you were not trying to save your world."

The wind battered Tralane and beat him back to the ground when he first tried to get up. He struggled, gained his feet, and started running again. Agathom swooped in behind him.

"Faster, Tralane. You must be quicker. Doom is standing on your shadow, reaching for you. Do you feel its fingers in your hair, Tralane? Is its touch as soothing as Crecia's? Don't you want to lie down, rest, and join that Crecia of yours?" Agathom's laughter would not stop.

Tralane continued to stumble forward, using his arms to keep his balance. And as his arms waved about, he snatched at the pouch hanging from his neck. He drew out Wyden's Eye, keeping it away from Agathom's line of sight. Then, when the Sorcerer King's laughter seemed to resound in his skull, Tralane deftly made the signs over the face of the amulet that opened the way between worlds.

They went to the world of the Emperor of Many Faces.

Tralane fell on the dusty, exhausted earth and rolled forward. Agathom, floating above him, stopped his pursuit and looked around at the barren world, the huge, terrible moon, and the putrefying corpse of the serpent god stretching from one horizon to the other. Agathom raised his hand as if to shield himself, and his laughter died among its own echoes in some nearby mountains.

Then Tralane scrambled to his feet and started to run once again, repeating the signs over the amulet.

"Wait!" Agathom cried out, but Tralane did not.

The way between worlds opened, and Tralane went back to the world he had just left. And once Tralane's feet touched familiar earth, he continued to run, not with joy over having escaped Agathom again, but with eagerness to rejoin the world of the living.

He was back on the tower grounds. All around him, the earth was losing its solidity as demons and spirits, mastered and buried by Suthra so he could use their power, awakened from their sleep and discovered themselves unbound. Caskets opened, bottles shattered, and unearthly hands broke through clinging soil to reach for light. In the distance, to Tralane's left and right, trees and rocks sundered as beings imprisoned within them escaped the merely physical aspects of their prisons. Baleful eyes stared up at him from murky pools of rainwater.

Without breaking stride, Tralane continued his run. He could see Akyeetha perched atop a boulder, anxiously watching his progress. Next to her, the dark, broken shadow of his father stood, his glowing eyes watching the awakening of his enemies. He strained to run harder, knowing Suthra was keeping the earth he ran on safe for him. Every moment Suthra waited for his son was a moment his enemies could use against him, to prevent his transformation.

The air was full of violent crackling and explosions, and Tralane glanced up at the sky, expecting another downpour. The clouds were struggling with one another, and once again thunder, this time directly overhead, shook the earth while lightning lashed the ground. Shadows raced up the lances of bright light, like insects scrambling up ladders to reach the safety of a farmer's loft.

Wind came to beat against his advance and threatened to carry him up into the sky. Branches on trees were like spears of a marching army, the leafy blades challenging the clouds above.

Some rain fell, but not as much as might have been expected. He was about to glance up at the sky again when an explosion behind him almost caused him to lose his balance and fall. Instead of water, clods of earth and small stones fell on him. A quick look revealed a huge shape lifting itself upward from behind the ruins of the tower. The magical beings were beginning their journey back to the nether-universe of their origins. The winged creature on which the Sorcerer King had arrived, the collar around its neck gone, was among the first to be lost in the sky.

Tralane reached the hill just as several other bursts of sound ripped the air. The storm above was being met by a host of unleashed powers released from below, and for once the earth was not allowing the sky to have its way without a challenge. A battle was taking place in the air above Tralane, as rain and lightning fell on, and were absorbed by, a torrent of fleeing spirits. Earth, trees, and rocks followed in the wake of the demons, thrown starward by the wind caused by the departure of sorcery. Wearily, Tralane climbed the hill until he felt strong hands around his arms and shoulders. When he sensed rock beneath his feet, he collapsed to his knees. He looked over his shoulder and watched the frenetic spectacle of elements and sorcery caught in conflicting purposes; while the elements fought, the sorcery fled.

Suthra came up behind Akyeetha and Tralane. The energies that had kept him among the living were at last exhausted, and he could hardly stand. Tralane listened carefully so he could hear his father's words over the din.

"I must leave now, Tralane," Suthra said at last. "The gods are watching, and soon they will know me. Pichenma-thele would still try to keep me from Gen-jima."

"Is it over?" Tralane asked, reluctant to let him go. "What of the demons bound to avenge the Sorcerer King's death? What of his armies?"

"The demons will not rise, for he is not dead. And he cannot return to raise any more monsters or trouble this world with his sorcery. As for his armies—I remember the Karthasian Empire was quite capable of handling itself when it came to war. And without Agathom's sorcery, his forces will crumble in pitched battle. It is over, my son."

Tralane thought he heard, for the first time, a plea in his father's words. Was it only a trick of the fury of sound coming from the tower grounds? Or was it a sign of Suthra's physical weakness?

"You have my thanks, Father." Tralane thought he saw Suthra shrug, but was not certain whether the motion was really a sign of indifference.

"It was my duty, as you made me aware. And perhaps this has somehow made amends for what I was never able to give you."

Tralane framed a reply, but the child within him would not let the words come out. Akyeetha came up beside him, rescuing him from the verbal paralysis resulting from the clash of adult understanding with childhood feelings.

"You have ended your time by serving the gods you hate so much," she said, her voice surprising Tralane with its mixture of pity and anger. She had regained complete mastery of her voice, and he envied the range and depth of emotions she felt for his father.

"Only to do in human fashion what they, in their arrogance, would have done through a god's means." Suthra pointed to the grounds of his old domain, saying, "There, at least, no one was harmed."

Suthra took a few steps down the hill, away from them, then stopped, facing the scene he had painted across reality with deft strokes of his magic.

Tralane stepped forward.

"Father, I will make you proud," he said quickly. He felt the release of pent-up emotions within him, and he reached out. "I didn't know—"

"Yes."

"—if it had been different—"

"It would have been the same. But I am happy the tale of Gen-jima you know is false, and the Wizard King and the goddess did indeed love each other and have a child. Add that to the tale, Tralane, and make the Wizard King glad at what his son became."

And Tralane shook his head from side to side, smiling at his father's reticence even to the end, while sadness burdened his spirit over the loss of a father so recently gained. Then, with the suddeness of a breeze blowing out a candle's flame, the body of Mathi that was also Suthra crumbled into an unrecognizable heap of matter which was absorbed into the ground. Akyeetha and Tralane were left alone on the hill's slope.

They left before the storm had subsided. At the crest of a hill, where the wind blew towards the sky, Tralane drew out the pouch containing Wyden's Eye and threw it into the air. The pouch vanished into the clouds, to be sucked into the demon dimensions in the wake of the last of the escaping spirits, where he wished the amulet to remain, out of the reach of men and gods. They then walked downhill and followed the road they had taken to reach the tower, until the wind was just a caressing breeze and the roar of the storm resounded only in their memories.

They slept beneath a clear sky filled with stars that night, comforting each other in the cold breath of immortal loneliness. And when they awoke the next morning, the mystery of what they had done seemed as remote and inconsequential as the night's sleep and dreams from which they had just emerged.

About the Author

———

Gerard Daniel Houarner was born and raised in New York City. He is a Breton/French/American whose family came from in and around Pont-des-Lutins—the Bridge of Elves— in Brittany. He has accumulated a B.A. in writing from CCNY and master's degrees in counseling and psychology from Teachers College, Columbia University. He has worked as a delivery person, secretary, office manager, and counselor. He is currently a Certified Rehabilitation Counselor, with past experience in working with a psychiatric population. He now holds a position in a drug clinic in a section of the city charmingly known as Alphabet Land.

His first exposure to fantasy was Tolkien, at the age of thirteen, and *The Lord of the Rings* settled nicely into the ground prepared by mythology and science fiction. The Ballantine Adult Fantasy reprinting of classics in the field fastened his interest to the field of fantasy.

He resides in the Bronx with his wife, Clara, and writes from an office in an otherwise spotless house, surrounded by his collection of books and dust.